WAITING FOR LOVE

The Taverstons of Iversley
Book 3

By Carol Coventry

ARE YOU SIGNED UP FOR DRAGONBLADE'S BLOG?

You'll get the latest news and information on exclusive giveaways, exclusive excerpts, coming releases, sales, free books, cover reveals and more.

Check out our complete list of authors, too!

No spam, no junk. That's a promise!

Sign Up Here

www.dragonbladepublishing.com

Dearest Reader;

Thank you for your support of a small press. At Dragonblade Publishing, we strive to bring you the highest quality Historical Romance from some of the best authors in the business. Without your support, there is no 'us', so we sincerely hope you adore these stories and find some new favorite authors along the way.

Happy Reading!

CEO, Dragonblade Publishing

CHAPTER ONE

October 1813
Village of Iversley

F ORTUNATELY, THOUGHT LADY Olivia Taverston, everyone knew she loved weddings, so no one found her giddiness excessive.

As she had only been to two in her almost-nineteen years, Olivia admitted her enthusiasm was based on limited experience. Limited but varied. A distant cousin's grand event in London's magnificent St. James's Church had fired her imagination when she was young. And then, nine months ago, after her stodgy brother Reginald had captured the heart of the most beautiful girl in London, he'd married her in a simple ceremony here in Iversley Village. In keeping with expectations, she'd gushed the whole time.

Olivia adored her sister-in-law Georgiana, who was everything a lady should be. But she was even more captivated by Mrs. Vanessa Wardrip. In a few hours, Olivia's eldest brother Jasper, the duty-before-all-else, newly ascended Earl of Iversley, would be married to a widowed *commoner*. And that wasn't even what shocked the most. Vanessa had been Jasper's *mistress!* It was positively scandalous!

Olivia couldn't wait to get to know her better.

Arranging her itchy wool skirt with care, Olivia settled in the family coach for the short ride from Chaumbers, the family's country estate, into the village along with the rest of the Taverston ladies. The church awaiting them was ancient and looked it—in a quaint way, not a decrepit one. Its medieval stained glass windows had survived the outrages of the past and were now the pride of Iversley Village. Olivia had long since changed her mind about preferring St. James's splendiferous church. London, a day's ride away, was a sooty, foggy, crowded place. *This* was where she would marry someday.

While her carriage mates—Mama, Vanessa, Georgiana, and Georgiana's cousin Alice, an honorary Taverston—were almost annoyingly self-composed, Olivia could hardly contain her excitement. Thankfully, her reputation for innocent exuberance stood her in good stead. Because as pleased as she was to be attending another wedding, she had a private reason for wanting to race to the church. *He* would be there. At least, Jasper had offhandedly mentioned that he had invited his new steward and old friend to the ceremony: Mr. Benjamin Carroll.

It had been almost five years since Olivia had seen Benjamin. For a long time after he'd left the Taverstons' home, *hustled* out, she had hoped never to see him again. But she could face him now. She was no longer a silly child infatuated with her brother's handsome friend. And she wanted him to know that.

Olivia pushed the curtain open a crack as the bouncing of the carriage eased. They had left the rutted country lane for the packed dirt of the village's main road. The few shops and homes appeared shut tightly, but the woodsmoke of their hearth fires wafted to her nose.

"Almost there!" she cried.

Georgiana and Vanessa exchanged indulgent smiles. Georgiana was a strawberry blond with perfect, perfect features who never looked anything less than stunning. Vanessa had a plainer face, a little careworn, but oh, how it lit up when she smiled! Given how different they were and especially given their individual histories with Jasper, Olivia found it entertaining how quickly the two women had become friends.

"You'll be next, Olivia," said Alice in an encouraging tone. Since her first Season had not been a success, Alice's words were especially generous.

Olivia's London debut had been twice postponed, first due to her father's illness and then because of his death and the necessary year of mourning. Everyone assumed she was chafing at the bit. Which was absurd and a little insulting. She would gladly give up going to London altogether if she could have Papa healthy and whole again.

Naturally, two years ago, when she'd *thought* she would be going to London to enter Society, she'd been impatient. She'd dreamed of meeting someone new, someone to love. But that was before Papa had fallen ill. Before she'd experienced true grief. Before she'd discovered the ubiquitousness of marital infidelity. She was warier now.

Nevertheless, she grinned broadly for her audience. "Not necessarily. It could be Crispin."

They all laughed, even Mama, although the joke was sad as well as funny. Crispin, Olivia's middle brother, was wedded to the army.

His antipathy to marriage also had something to do with an illness he'd suffered as a child and had apparently never quite recovered from. Alluding to it angered Crispin as nothing else ever did. He wouldn't marry but he did have an eye for women. Olivia had overheard him snickering with Jasper: *So long as I have a few shillings in my purse I can find love on any street corner.* It had taken her a while to decipher that, but she did. Most things that Olivia knew that she wasn't supposed to know she had learned from eavesdropping on her brothers. Sadly, they were home so seldom anymore it was putting a true crimp in her education.

The carriage rolled to a stop. A moment later, a footman threw open the door. Mama disembarked first, then Georgiana, then Olivia, all wearing shades of gray, Mama's so dark it was black. Alice was not in mourning, she wasn't quite family, but she dressed somberly, nevertheless. Georgiana's gown was cut very full, a failed attempt to hide the fact that she was increasing. They made an unusual bridal party.

The footman handed Vanessa down last. An unusual bride. Olivia still had a hard time believing Jasper was carrying this off.

Vanessa was beautiful in high-waisted dark-green silk, Taverston-heirloom diamonds sparkling at her ears, but she looked nervous, blinking in the weak October sunlight. Olivia rushed over and squeezed her hand.

"I'm so glad we're going to be sisters!"

Vanessa smiled faintly. "I am too."

A score or more curious, excited villagers, all in their Sunday best, gathered in the churchyard. They would stand in the cold as long as necessary to cheer their earl and glimpse his new countess.

Mama swept the bridal party up the stone steps to meet the curate at the church door. They entered, except for Vanessa, who waited to be summoned. Jasper's closest friend, the endearingly amusing Viscount Haslet, known to all as *Hazard*, approached and gave one arm to Georgiana and one to Alice, to usher them to the family pew before joining Jasper at the front of the church. Olivia started when Reg stepped forward to escort Mama. Hadn't he volunteered to walk Vanessa down the aisle?

A good-looking stranger about Olivia's own age stood in the back. His clothing was fine. His bearing was confident. Olivia could not put her finger on why he looked familiar. Then she did. He had Vanessa's eyes. Vanessa was estranged from her family, but someone had come, and, given the limited attendance, he stood out.

The ceremony was small by choice. Not only were the Taverstons still in mourning, but the exclusive guest list was also strategic. They didn't invite anyone who might be tempted to snub them with a "no." Olivia felt confident that Jasper's popularity and influence would soon have the ton clamoring for invitations to his parties, but best not to test this on his wedding day.

Music began, the deep sonorous strains of Handel's *Alla Hornpipe*—Olivia's cue to begin processing down the aisle. Vanessa had asked her to stand up with her. The fact that Mama permitted it, despite the potential for scandalizing the ton even further, made all the difference.

Olivia matched her stride to the organ's refrain, then cast her gaze side-to-side, taking it all in. *Oh! There! Crispin!* Crispin was here! Her giddiness erupted into sheer joy.

She hadn't expected him. A captain in the king's army, he was always coming and going to and from the peninsula. Apparently, he was one of General Wellington's couriers, and when the great man called, Crispin jumped. Because of this, he'd missed Reg's wedding. She was relieved he was not going to miss Jasper's.

Crispin leaned forward a hair, allowing Olivia a glimpse of the man standing beside him. For a moment, her feet felt like deadweight, and she nearly stumbled. *Benjamin.* Unmistakably Benjamin. But he wasn't alone. He held a pretty, dark-haired child in his arms.

Olivia continued her march to the altar, a huge smile on her face that was now decidedly false. When she reached the front of the church, she nodded to Jasper, who looked calm and lordly, then gave Hazard a quick punch on the arm before taking her place. She turned to watch Vanessa enter the church, heard Jasper's breath catch, and watched sister-in-law-number-two walk down the aisle.

She didn't look at Benjamin. She couldn't. Not when she felt so ridiculously betrayed. Why hadn't anyone told her? It didn't matter. Of course, it didn't. It made sense he would be married with children by now. It made no difference. She was no longer in love with him. She never had been. She'd been a child!

So why did it feel as though her whole world had just been emptied of joy?

MR. BENJAMIN CARROLL knew he should not have come to the wedding. He was steward to the Earl of Iversley, not Jasper Taverston's friend. Those boundaries were not porous. The fact that Jasper was marrying a commoner changed nothing. Or, if it did, it meant Jasper should enforce the boundaries in his other dealings more rigidly, not less so.

And yet, once Crispin had slipped into the pew beside him, laughing at the world and poking fun at Jasper behind his back, Benjamin forgot himself. He joked in return. It was as if they had parted ways yesterday not years ago. He relaxed and allowed himself to admire, once again, the beautiful old church with its shadowed niches, dark mahogany pews, candle-wax scent, and startlingly colorful windows. He had always enjoyed accompanying the family here for services. For nearly an hour, he fell back into the role of an old Oxford chum.

Until the processional music began. And he glanced toward the door. And there she stood.

Olivia. It knocked the wind from him. She was, of course, no longer the skinny, braids-in-her-hair hoyden who had relentlessly tagged after them, all over the Taverston estate, when he'd accompanied Jasper and Crispin home on break from university. Nor was she the earnest, embarrassed, blossoming young girl who'd horrified him with her ill-suited pink ruffled dress, wide eyes, and utterly inappropriate declaration in the billiard room. With no one else present.

She was…a blow to the chest.

In that billiard room, he'd been as gentle as he could under the circumstances, but she'd still burst out sobbing. This girl who could bark her shins on a wooden boat or tumble down a rocky slope and skin her elbow raw without shedding a tear, had cried because of him. *Lud.* He'd thrust a handkerchief into her hand, fled the room, fled the Taverstons' estate. He'd fled to godforsaken *Canada.*

He should have stayed there.

Benjamin shifted his attention to Hannah, the little Canadian squirming in his arms. He had intended to leave the girl with Miss Jamison, her nanny, but the combination of the long coach ride from London and the strangeness of the Danforths' cottage had the poor child terrified and he couldn't abandon her. She was well-behaved, generally, so long as he was near. He was probably spoiling her, as Miss Jamison warned, but Hannah had suffered far too much in her two-and-a-half years. He wouldn't allow her to suffer anything he could prevent.

Upon joining them, Crispin had assessed the situation correctly, which somehow didn't surprise. After greeting Benjamin, he offered his hand to Hannah with a winning smile. When Hannah turned away to bury her face in Benjamin's shoulder, Crispin didn't tease her for shyness or insist upon being acknowledged or, worst of all, pat her head and exclaim about her curls. Instead, he withdrew his hand and ignored her. Tantrum averted.

A change in the sounds around him from fidgeting and coughing to delighted *"ahs"* alerted Benjamin to the fact that the bride had appeared. He turned with the rest of the congregation to face the back of the church. So this was the woman who had won Jasper's heart. She was very pretty, with thick chestnut hair and a pleasing figure, though not the stunning beauty one might have expected. No simpering debutante, she possessed an air of maturity that made sense, given her history. A war widow as he understood it, from Jasper's telling. And she'd been making her own way these past several months, imagining marriage between an earl and a mill owner's daughter turned courtesan to be an impossibility. Leave it to the Taverstons to make the impossible possible.

Along with the rest of the congregation, Benjamin pivoted as Vanessa walked past on the arm of a proud young fellow who could be a cousin or brother. Benjamin followed her with his eyes until she reached the altar. To stand beside Olivia. It was wrong to think it, but the bride paled in comparison. Olivia's smile captivated. Her golden hair, piled atop her head, shone like sunlight. The gray gown she wore set off the cream of her skin, skimming the curves of her slender frame. Benjamin dropped his gaze, his face warm. He had no business noticing her curves.

Age was not the issue. No doubt the now-marriageable young woman would soon be betrothed to a gentleman older than Benjamin's twenty-seven years. But she was a *lady*. And he was her brother's steward.

His throat tightened. This train of thought was absurd. He had never considered Olivia in these terms. She'd been a child. And he didn't know the young woman she had become. It would be disastrous to start thinking of her with *any* sort of familiarity now.

Thankfully, she could not still be carrying a torch for him. Nevertheless, he would continue to reject Jasper's suggestion that, for everyone's convenience, he should move into a wing of their home. Not until after she married and moved away. Just in case. An infatuated Olivia was one complication too many.

The music ended and the rector exhorted them to bow their heads. Benjamin scarcely listened to the rote words but "Amened" after *And now abide faith, hope, love, these three; but the greatest of these is love.* He started at the emphatic *amen* echoed by Crispin. Then smiled at Hannah's "menmen" and her tentative patting of Crispin's arm. Crispin goggled-eyed her, and Hannah laughed her sweet baby laugh.

The ceremony began. When the rector asked, "Who gives this woman…" the young stranger answered, "I do," in such a forceful tone that no one questioned his right to do so, not that anyone would have questioned the Earl of Iversley's right to claim her.

It warmed Benjamin to the core to see Jasper's expression as he made his heartfelt responses. Vanessa too. Their happiness had been hard-earned.

He only hoped it would last. There was no greater recipe for marital disaster than the clashing of the classes.

CHAPTER TWO

THE WEDDING BREAKFAST was a lovely tradition, one that allowed the newly married couple to finally eat after the nerve-wracking preparations of the morning. The guests too.

Olivia clutched her sausage-and-bread-roll-laden plate while surveying the dining hall. Instead of their long, formal dining table, tea tables were scattered around the room. It made for a comfortable, casual arrangement that would permit the family and guests to circulate as they sampled the fare—cakes of every sort, brandied pears, dried berries and cream, sausages, kippers, sliced ham—all arrayed temptingly on the buffet. The tall windows along the east wall were closed against the October chill, but the silver velvet drapes were pulled back to let the sun warm the blue-and-white tiled floor. Olivia and her brothers made fun of Chaumbers' architectural irregularities, but none of them had ever complained about the dining hall.

She was looking for Alice. They had become fast friends a year earlier when Alice accompanied Georgiana to Chaumbers.

There. Alice sat at a corner table with Hazard. Olivia hesitated to join them because they were engaged in a serious-appearing tête-à-tête. Which was odd for Hazard, who was the least serious man Olivia knew. It was odd, too, that Hazard was not sharing Jasper and Vanessa's table along with Reg and Georgiana. He'd been Jasper's dearest friend forever, and, from what Olivia had heard, he'd also established a close bond with Vanessa.

But Hazard and Alice? Olivia *had* noticed that the two were friendly, but she'd immediately dismissed the thought of any romance between them. Alice had been a debutante just last Season. She was twenty years old to Hazard's…forty? He was going a bit gray at the temples. Though that alone needn't be a deterrent to a courtship. True, Hazard required an heir and Alice needed a husband. But Hazard was a confirmed bachelor. Only recently had Olivia come to understand what that meant. It had dawned on her while watching Hazard's face at unguarded moments—while he watched Jasper. It had seemed bizarre to her at first. But then, she'd thought: *well, why not?*

Poor Hazard. Unrequited love was unrequited love. At least he did a better job of hiding it than she had.

At any rate, she wouldn't interrupt their conversation.

Mama was at another table with older folks, her friends and Papa's. Olivia didn't want to intrude on their reunion either. It was good to see her in company again after so long. One younger man sat with them, the marquess of someplace or other—she'd been introduced to him briefly the previous evening. He was so somber faced he might have been at a funeral rather than a wedding. Although, even without a smile, he was decent looking, fair haired with angular features and a…dainty nose. He wore a fashionably cut but understated morning coat. It was intriguing. She didn't know why he was here, but since Mama didn't wave her over, she suspected she wasn't destined to find out.

She chose an empty table, empty but for glasses of champagne awaiting consumption. The moment she laid down her plate, Jeremy and Jeffery, Squire Willowsett's sons from the nearby town of Crofton, attached themselves to her sides. She welcomed their company with a grin. The twins, brown-haired, brown-eyed, gangly lads, were a bit younger than she was. They had all grown up together and had successfully passed through the silly phase where the boys imagined themselves in love with her, so now they were all friends again.

"Who was that fellow who gave away Lady Iversley?" Jeremy asked, before forking a kipper into his mouth.

Lady Iversley. Vanessa. Mama was no longer Lady Iversley, but merely the dowager. Vanessa was the countess. Jasper was the earl. Olivia knew this, but it hit her hard with a new depth of understanding—it carved a hollow in the pit of her belly. Father was gone.

Everything was changing. Even she was different. Sister, not daughter, of the Earl of Iversley. How very *old* she was becoming.

Crispin arrived at the chair beside Jeremy, carrying a plate of the strange dry-as-dust oatmeal biscuits he favored. She was glad he took his seat quickly. Standing, he always seemed to loom. He was an inch shorter than Jasper but because he was so thin, he looked taller unless the two stood side-by-side.

"I think it was Lady Iversley's brother," Crispin said. He was an even better eavesdropper than Olivia. He heard *everything*. And if he said "I think" it meant he knew. Or else, he knew otherwise but wanted to misdirect the listener. She loved Crispin with her whole being but still took everything he said with a pinch of salt.

Another quick sweep of the room showed Vanessa's brother was not there. And neither was Benjamin, although it looked as though everyone else from the church had arrived. Olivia didn't know if the twinge she felt was disappointment or relief.

"Where'd he go?" Jeremy asked.

Crispin shrugged, stirring his tea. He had that look about him though. He knew. Well, if it was Vanessa's brother, it meant he was a Culpepper. A commoner. Although it was crass to talk of such things, the older Mr. Culpepper was said to be one of the richest men in England. Olivia had overheard that Vanessa's family cut her off when she ran off with her soldier, but it appeared at least one of the Culpeppers cleaved to her enough to attend her wedding—her wedding, but not a breakfast hosted by an earl. She supposed he'd feel out of place. Maybe that was Benjamin's excuse too.

The mounting volume of chatter in the hall suddenly silenced when a clinking of cutlery on crystal turned everyone's heads. Reginald rose to make the first toast.

Reg, Olivia's quiet brother, was the only Taverston to have inherited their mother's dark coloring. He was also average in height and build rather than towering over everyone else the way Jasper and Crispin did, and Olivia was grateful she did not. Although not as arresting as his older brothers, Reg was handsome in his own understated way and recognizable as a Taverston by his bright-blue eyes and square chin. Five years older than she was and four years younger than Crispin, Reg had always occupied a space of his own, one populated by books and ancient peoples. He never seemed to mind the fact that, for as long as she could remember, *she* had played the part of pesky little sibling to their older brothers, the role that he should have played.

"A toast!" he said, raising his glass. "To my brother and new sister: Fortune and love favor the brave!"

"Hear! Hear!" Crispin called, teacup in the air.

A warm blanket of comfort wrapped around Olivia as her brothers behaved true to form: Crispin, abstemious as always, and Reg with an apt quote from Ovid.

Other voices echoed, then they all drank. Footmen scurried about to refill their glasses. Olivia returned quickly to her sausages before the next toast. She didn't want to be tipsy before teatime. From the corner of her eye, she saw Crispin gesturing a "come closer" wave. She lifted her gaze and found Benjamin, who looked pained rather than pleased to be there.

The sausages and champagne sat heavily in her stomach as he approached. The last time they had spoken, she'd put him in a terrible position and mortified herself. She'd sworn inwardly—the moment she'd learned that Jasper had hired Benjamin—that when they met again, she would be lively, cheerful, and mature, and act as if she'd forgotten everything. As if it had never happened. Instead, her face felt as though it had caught fire, and her hands began to sweat.

Benjamin reached them. Up close, he looked older. More serious. Harder of face and of body. His clothes fit well though they were not finely tailored, and they revealed he was muscled like a laborer where he used to be wiry. His intriguing iron-gray eyes were no longer laughing but cautious. Thick, dark-brown hair framed his face. *Lud.* He was handsomer than ever. She felt a tightening deep in her belly that was almost like fear, but wasn't.

"Lady Olivia. Captain Taverston." He made an appropriate bow, then tilted his head to Jeremy and Jeffrey.

"Mr. Willowsett and Mr. Willowsett," Crispin said, introducing them archly. No one called them that. "This is Mr. Carroll. Mr. Carroll, will you join us?"

Benjamin hesitated before nodding and pulling out a chair.

"Where is Hannah?" Crispin asked, spreading a thin layer of jam on his biscuit. "We were just starting to be friends."

"With her nanny." Benjamin sounded wooden. "She was overtired."

Olivia's tongue felt paralyzed by the weight of questions she could not ask.

Then Crispin stated to the table at large, "Benjamin adopted the little mite. Too soft-hearted to leave an orphan in Rupert's Land."

And this was why Olivia adored Crispin! He might have made the announcement for her sake, or he might not have. He rarely let on how much he knew. Nevertheless, she now found it perfectly natural to face Benjamin, raise an eyebrow, and say, "Oh?"

"I knew her parents," Benjamin said, a rough edge to his voice. "They died of fevers within a week of each other."

She didn't know the appropriate response, so only said, "I'm so sorry."

He nodded, apparently wordless as well. But he gathered himself and, turning to Crispin, said, "I am indebted to Iversley for the opportunity he's given me. It will allow me to bring Hannah up in safety."

"In *safety?*" Crispin squinched his brow.

"Meaning not in poverty."

Benjamin's answer was so blunt that Crispin's head drew back, and he blinked three times. It was rare to see him caught unprepared. But the reaction was only momentary. Crispin put a hand on Benjamin's arm, squeezed it, then pulled away.

"I understand that, Benjamin. But don't forget you are also our friend. And *don't,*" his eyes narrowed, "make me remind you of what I owe to you."

"You don't owe—"

"Very good." Crispin laughed. "I always say friends don't tally debts. That way, I come out ahead."

Benjamin breathed out a huff. Olivia wondered what Crispin could possibly owe Benjamin. This was the trouble with her having been so young when the three met at Oxford. She didn't know how their friendship started. Only that, naturally, they had drifted apart after Benjamin went to Canada. He wouldn't have said anything to her brothers about…the billiard room, but they hadn't been blind to her adoration. She wondered if his mention of indebtedness and poverty was made for her ears rather than Crispin's.

Well, he needn't warn her off. She'd learned her lesson. And they were different people now than they had been. In fact, it was conceited of him to think she still cared.

Clinking began again. This time, Hazard stood, glass raised. They all got to their feet and lifted their champagne flutes, even Crispin, who normally avoided all spirits as though they were poison.

"A toast to Lady Iversley, whose entrance into the Taverston family saga *still* has me agog. And to Iversley himself. The very best man that I know."

Before anyone could cheer, Jasper protested, grinning, "After Crispin and Reg."

Hazard cocked his head a moment, then said, "The *third* best man that I know." And quaffed his drink.

Olivia laughed along with the others as she sipped, though it seemed to her Hazard and Jasper were exchanging private jokes. Or maybe it didn't matter after scads of champagne on empty stomachs combined with an abundance of joy. Everything and anything would make them laugh.

Hazard sat back down and said something to Alice, whose face brightened as she nodded vigorously.

"What are they talking about?" she wondered.

"Who?" Crispin asked.

"Alice and Hazard."

He chewed his lip a moment, regarding them. Then said in tone so disgruntled it had to be genuine, "Bedeviled if I know."

She giggled. To her delight, Benjamin laughed too.

Jeremy jostled Crispin's arm. "Captain, now that we're old enough, Jeffrey and I want to enlist. Don't you think we should?"

Jeffrey put in eagerly, "Could we join your regiment? Father couldn't say no if—"

"Boys," Crispin said, unsmiling, talking down. "This is a wedding. No war talk."

"Yes, but don't you think it's our duty?" Jeremy pressed. "If you speak with our father—"

"Do not put me between the king and your father." He used a tone of voice that chilled Olivia's blood and left the twins slack-jawed.

To Olivia's relief, the clinking started up once more.

Lord Billings, an old friend of the family, made a dull toast to the happy couple. More champagne followed. And then Squire Willowsett rose and said something jumbled about the beauty of love or the duty of love, and they all drank to whichever.

The sight and smell of sausages was beginning to make Olivia queasy. She nibbled her bread roll instead. Her head felt heavy and her body warm. She was afraid to look in Benjamin's direction, afraid she would say something she didn't mean to say.

This was silly. The tables were set up so that people could move around. She would go join Hazard. He was *her* friend before he'd become Alice's. And if she said anything stupid, it would be of no consequence.

She stood abruptly. Jeremy gave a cheer and started clinking his glass with his spoon. The clattering rose to a crescendo and everyone watched her and waited. Mama looked alarmed. The young marquess at her table seemed to perk up.

Oh, bosh.

She put on her most exuberant smile, hoisted her flute, and said the first thing that popped into her head.

"A toast to Lady Georgiana. For saying no to Jasper."

There was a moment of silence so complete she heard the wind outside blowing. Then Crispin began hooting with laughter. When Crispin laughed like that, it was impossible to resist laughing along. Vanessa raised her glass to Georgiana. The whole room followed suit, crying, "To Lady Georgiana."

When the laughter finally died down, Hazard gestured lazily and drawled, "Well, Captain Taverston. Your turn."

Crispin got to his feet, muttering, "Reg took Ovid. That leaves me with this new fellow, Lord Byron."

They waited. He lifted his teacup. To Olivia's mind, he was savoring the moment. Then he smirked. "To Lord and Lady Iversley! I have great hopes that they shall love each other all their lives as much as if they had never married at all!"

CHAPTER THREE

*T*HAT WAS TORTURE. Benjamin had told Jasper the offer of the steward's job at Chaumbers was a godsend. And it was. Yet during the past few hours, posing as a wedding guest who belonged in such exalted company, he felt as though he was being tempted by a thousand devils. Kindly devils. The most dangerous kind.

The duties of a steward were all-inclusive. In addition to keeping the books for the estate, Benjamin would be overseeing its management: hiring staff and firing them if there was cause; making sure the tenants were producing and paying their rents; managing the managers of the livestock; settling any disputes among the tenants or staff; overseeing the care of the land and any improvements the earl should wish. Benjamin looked forward to the challenge. His education had prepared him and his own innate bent toward organization worked in his favor. The time he had spent at Chaumbers as a guest of the elder Taverston brothers had imbued him with a deep love for the place. Truly, he was made for this job.

But his history also worked against him. Were it any other estate, or any earl other than Jasper, Benjamin would settle comfortably into the role. He'd know his place. And his duties would *not* include sitting at the earl's wedding breakfast with the earl's brother and sister; of that, he was certain.

Thank God the celebration was over. Or close enough that he could leave.

Shortly after Crispin's toast, a toast of dubious taste that had nevertheless elicited raucous laughter, Jasper and Vanessa exited the hall to embark upon their honeymoon. The wedding guests followed them out to the drive to give them a cheering send-off.

Since Napoleon had cancelled grand tours of the continent for Englishmen, the happy couple was heading to a lakeside cottage near Binnings, Crispin's inheritance, a place they called quaint, and Benjamin called palatial. He had spent a month there with the Taverstons nearly a decade ago. He remembered aching with envy and gratitude as they swam, boated, hiked among the trees, went riding, picnicked…while servants of every stripe catered to their whims.

It had not been the wealth and privilege that attracted Benjamin to the Taverstons. It was the family closeness. Their generosity. But he could not deny that he was jealous of their ease.

Jasper had never been one to flaunt his position, heir to the earldom though he had been. He did not spend ostentatiously; yet Benjamin found the very carelessness of Jasper's attitude toward money almost as painful to witness as profligacy would have been. His own situation—son of a laborer, attending Oxford on scholarship—was so damnably different.

Watching the newlyweds ride off in the earl's well-sprung coach, accompanied by liveried outriders, with its trailing carriage stuffed with baggage and servants, made Benjamin feel almost physically ill. It was all so extravagantly fine. The long, straight portion of the avenue leading from the estate was lined by beech trees that had been coaxed and shaped to identical heights, their autumn leaves coppery in the afternoon sun. Earls even tamed nature to their fancy.

Benjamin didn't begrudge his old friend any of it. But the divide between their world and his was unbreachable. No matter how chummily Crispin behaved. No matter how insistent Jasper was in calling up their shared past as if it still mattered. No matter how sweetly amusing Olivia was.

With Jasper and Vanessa's entourage fading from sight, the cheers quieted to chatter and muted laughter, rustling pelisses, and boots clomping on manicured grass. Benjamin supposed the locals would stay through teatime. The few Londoners would spend the night. Family, which apparently included Alice and Viscount Haslet—Hazard, he might as well call him since everyone else did—would likely stay longer.

There was enough bustle that his own absence should not be remarked upon. For excuse, should one be needed, he could say he had to return to Hannah, who would be wide awake by now and looking for him. Not only an excuse, it was the truth.

He edged his way through the twenty-odd guests who were slowly filtering back toward the house, wondering the politest way to take leave. Who was the host? Or was the dowager the hostess? He had learned a good deal of society protocol over the years, but the finer points still escaped him. Four years in the wilds of Canada hadn't helped.

Ah. There was Reg, standing just at the edge of the drive. That would be the most convenient out.

He strode closer. "Mr. Taverston? I should make my good-byes. I—"

Reg turned, a faint grimace on his face that quickly dissolved as he said, with barely perceptible irony, "You're leaving, Mr. Carroll?"

The exchange of "misters" sounded pretentious even to his ears. A long-forgotten memory flashed to the fore and Benjamin had to choke back a laugh. Young Master Reginald, who must have been ten or twelve, called him "Ben" the summer he'd taught the boy how to spit.

They'd been playing a bastardized version of cricket. Reg shouted something and a particularly large and evidently nasty-tasting bug flew right into his mouth. The boy stood there drooling, trying to peel legs and wings and antennae from his tongue while his brothers laughed at his misfortune as only older brothers could. Apparently, Reg had imbibed as gospel the lesson that gentlemen did not spit. He did not know how! Benjamin stood beside him, desperately attempting to keep a straight face, while explaining how to let saliva pool in one's mouth to expectorate.

"Yes, I'm leaving," he managed to say. "I told Miss Jamison, Hannah's nanny, I wouldn't be late. I suppose I should find your mother first?"

Reg pursed his lips thoughtfully, then chuckled. "I don't know who you should find. All I am sure of is that it isn't me. But I will pass your goodbyes along if you'd like."

"Thank you. It was wonderful seeing everyone and I don't wish to be rude…"

"Oh, I don't believe the breakfast will continue much longer. For Georgiana's sake, I hope not. She tires easily." Reg smiled sheepishly. "I'm not supposed to refer to such, but there it is."

He sounded pleased and proud. Benjamin smiled back.

"Will you come around tomorrow?" Reg asked. "Jasper asked me to show you where the old account books are kept. And there are files in Jasper's office that deal with estate matters that I'm sure he looked at, then shoved right back into the cabinets."

It was natural that Jasper expected him to dive into the work. He'd intended to. But now he balked. "Perhaps not tomorrow. I thought I'd wait until your guests left Chaumbers. I don't want to disturb anyone."

"Disturb anyone? *Us?*" His eyes widened, incredulous. "Is that why you're staying at the Danforths? You *are* aware we have entire empty wings in this monstrous place."

"Well, that is only partly the reason. I got to know the Danforths quite well over the years, you see, and I thought Hannah might be more comfortable there. Out of the way."

Reg gave him a narrow look. "You know us better than that. Hannah would not be 'in the way.'"

It must appear he was shirking his duties, since he had avoided coming to Chaumbers for the past three months and shunned the work even now that he was here. But that wasn't the case. He *had* been working, learning what he needed to know.

"I'm ready to take up the reins, but first, I've been going over various affairs with Mr. Wilkerson and Mr. Tate." Jasper's solicitor and his man-of-business, respectively, both in London. "I was surprised to learn of the extent and variety of Iversley's assets. The Mayfair home and Chaumbers are only a small part..." This was not going well. Reg's frown had deepened. "I realize that my duties will be focused mainly on Chaumbers, but as Iversley wants to make improvements to the property, I needed to better understand the finances." Benjamin heard how defensive he sounded, so he switched tack. "I don't mean to put my nose into your business, but the house deeded to you in Bath is a substantial asset in itself."

"The townhouse? An *asset*?" Reg scowled. "It is a *home*. My great-aunts live there. I am not interested in selling it out from under them."

Great-aunts? Tate had called them "the great-aunt and her companion." Well, it wasn't pertinent.

"Of course not. But my understanding is they are both quite elderly and utilize only the ground floor. The first and second floors have a separate entrance and are entirely habitable, though likely in need of a thorough dusting. It is in a fashionable district. Good apartments in Bath are currently difficult to come by. You might consider leasing it out."

Reg looked surprised, then thoughtful. "I suppose I might."

"That was, Mr. Tate gave me to understand, your father's intention."

"My father's? How do you mean?"

"Your father mentioned to Tate that he wanted to ensure you had an income should you decide against entering the church. A lease won't bring in as large an income as the livings your father had to dispose of, had you taken all four, but it isn't an insignificant amount."

Reg just stared. Then he ducked his head, frowning, before looking up again.

"It astonishes me how greatly I underestimated my father," he said in a quiet tone. "He understood me better than I thought. And I never really knew him at all."

In equally serious measure, Benjamin answered, "I believe that is the way it should be. In the natural way of these things."

His own father-son relationship had been the opposite. His father had been a brutal drunkard who'd attempted to beat his son's sensibilities out of him. If not for the local vicar taking him in hand, recognizing his abilities… It was quite likely his father would have succeeded.

Reg cleared his throat. "This is very welcome news. Since you've seen the family balance sheets, you must know Jasper reinstated my allowance. I told him not to. But then, the pay I've been receiving for my translations does not stretch as far as I thought it would. I want to set Georgiana's dowry aside for our children." He trailed off. "I apologize. That's quite an earful."

"Not at all. It's my job."

"Not to look after me, it isn't. Though I appreciate it." His brow furrowed and he looked at his shoes. "How-how much do you think?"

Reg was obviously uncomfortable with the discussion. The quality did not discuss money. But Benjamin's footing was now more secure.

"So long as the furnishings are included, I believe you can ask upwards of eighty guineas per annum."

Reg blinked. Then said, "But I wouldn't want my aunts disturbed."

"If you'd like, I can screen the applicants for you."

"That isn't necessary," Reg started to protest, but then thought better of refusing. "You must take a percentage then."

He chortled. "Your brother already overpays me. Let me do this."

After a pause, Reg gave a curt nod. "Thank you." Then he

added, "Perhaps you might drop a word into Jasper's ear that this was Father's idea. Otherwise, you know Jasper. He'll simply raise my allowance."

Benjamin snorted. Because that was exactly what Jasper *would* suggest. And Reg should let him because it wouldn't put the tiniest dent in Jasper's fortune. He wondered how Crispin and Reg could be so blind to the injustice. So content with their lots.

Probably because they were wealthy enough. Moreover, they were gentlemen. Status was worth more than mere money.

"You'll come around tomorrow then?" Reg said, withdrawing a step. "Most everyone will leave in the morning. No point waiting for the rest of us to depart. Georgiana and I will be here for the next few months. She wants Alice to stay. And Crispin is leaving tonight."

"Tonight! To go where?"

"He says London."

"But he won't get there until dawn!"

Reg shrugged. "I've given up trying to keep track of Crispin. Apparently he believes the war effort would collapse without his unceasing efforts."

"Would it?"

With a laugh, Reg said, "Probably."

Benjamin had no further justification for staying away from Chaumbers. If Reg pressed him again, what on earth could he say? That he was afraid of Olivia?

Oh, good God. Enough was enough. He'd been skulking around London for three months hiding from the memory of her tear-stained face. He should never have let it come to that. He should have absented himself from the Taverston home as soon as he realized her puppy-like devotion had turned to a fourteen-year-old's infatuation. Selfishly, he hadn't wanted to distance himself from the Taverstons. Pathetically, he was probably pretending he was another brother.

But the one thing he was *not* guilty of was trying to weasel his way into the family by way of securing the affections of their underage sister! The fear of being accused of such a thing could still raise a cold sweat. He should never have gotten himself into such a stupid situation.

He was not going to make the same mistake twice. He knew his place. Caretaker of Chaumbers. There were a few adaptations he'd picked up in his travels, workarounds to some of the stultifying traditions of English lords and their tenants…if Jasper allowed him enough latitude…

He wanted this job as much as he needed it.

"Yes, I will be around tomorrow. But I don't want to start off with account books and piles of paper shoved into cabinets. I'd like to ride about the estate. See what, if anything, has changed from what I remember of it. That is, if I might borrow a horse."

Reg grinned. "We'll borrow two."

Chapter Four

OLIVIA WAS CROSS. She woke with a headache whenever she drank a little champagne, and last night, she drank more than a little.

There was only one thing for it.

"Tansy? My riding habit. The dark blue."

Her maid glanced with dismay toward the bed. On it lay a gray frock—enlivened with a few white stripes—that had clearly just been pressed. Olivia had told Tansy she would be wearing it today.

"I'll change into that *after* my ride," she said apologetically. She didn't want to be one of those imperious mistresses who could not make up her mind and kept her maids scurrying. "I need to blow cobwebs from my head."

"Yes, my lady."

She rushed off to the dressing room to fetch Olivia's riding clothes. Newly promoted from chambermaid to lady's maid, Tansy really was a dear. Mama had taken Anna, her own maid, down to the dower house, which made it impossible to borrow her any longer. Olivia had chosen to have Anna train Tansy instead of hiring someone hoity-toity, which would have been Mama's preference. The poor girl had a lazy eye and some of the other servants made fun of her. They wouldn't dare tease her now!

Tansy was handy with a needle and thread, and strangely enough, had a good sense for fashion. Olivia had never needed much fuss, but accepted the fact that she soon would. In a few months, she would throw off mourning and leave Chaumbers for London. To attract a husband, she would have to change clothes a hundred times a day, start perfuming herself with rosewater or lavender, both of which made her sneeze, and wear her hair up in ridiculous ringlets. And everyone imagined she was dying to go!

Fleetingly, she wondered if Benjamin found all the feminine enticements alluring. But what could it possibly matter? Look at the previous steward's wife. Mrs. Bradwell had been a plain woman who dressed starkly. Moreover, the poor woman seemed overawed whenever her path crossed that of one of the Taverstons. Given that she and Mr. Bradwell had lived in a small apartment in the south wing at Chaumbers, that should not have been an infrequent occurrence, but Mrs. Bradwell preferred to use the servants' stairs and back entrance. They rarely ever saw her.

Olivia shook away the image. Mrs. Bradwell died several years ago and Bradwell went into a decline. They'd had no children. She felt a twinge, picturing such a lonely future for Benjamin, should he marry someone like that.

But then, there was Hannah. The thought cheered her. Benjamin would not be alone.

Tansy returned, arms laden. She dressed Olivia with the quick efficiency she must have perfected while undertaking the many onerous duties of a chambermaid. Then she twisted Olivia's hair into a tidy chignon that would tuck easily under her bonnet.

"Very good," Olivia announced after a quick glance in the mirror. "If anyone asks, I've gone down to the stables."

She descended the wide, swooping main staircase and hurried to the entryway, avoiding the breakfast parlor in case any of the guests had risen early, though that was doubtful. Being London men, they would not keep country hours. They were mostly older gentlemen, her father's friends rather than Jasper's. Inviting them had been a courtesy and a political expediency, since Jasper, new to the House of Lords, was courting favor. That one younger man, the Marquess of Ebersom—Alice had reminded her of the name—was an up-and-coming Tory. So, Olivia surmised, he was a potential ally of Jasper's own generation, but not a close friend.

Her brother had not invited any of the young blades in his set, perhaps to keep them from circling about her before her formal coming-out. She had made the leap from schoolgirl to highly eligible young lady seemingly overnight. No doubt he would introduce her to appropriate suitors come spring. Courtship and marriage would proceed apace. With her connections and dowry, she hardly even needed to be there. Jasper could just choose one for her. She wished he would. It would spare her the Marriage Mart in London.

She nodded to the porter who opened the front door for her.

"Going riding," she informed him, although it wasn't necessary. He would have guessed by her clothes.

The morning was brisk and the sky gray. The grass was coated with chilly dew. Her riding boots were well-oiled so her feet would stay dry, but her walking boots would have been more comfortable. And prettier. Vanessa had discovered a small bootmaker's enterprise in the little town where she had been hiding from Jasper after their falling out. Wounded veterans made special decorative Hessians for ladies that were beautiful as well as practical. One good thing about going to London was that Olivia could help set a fashion for them and aid Vanessa with her cause.

Despite the chill, Olivia enjoyed the walk down to the stables. Her head already felt better.

There was more bustle near the stable than she had anticipated. The doors were wide open. Perhaps some of the guests intended to leave early after all. But when she stepped inside, she saw that wasn't the case. The grooms had Reg's favorite mare saddled, as well as Goose, a silly spirited gelding that everyone loved. And standing there in the dust and straw, conferring, were Reg and Benjamin. *Oh, bosh.* Benjamin was going to think she was chasing him.

She waved a greeting. They waved back, but as she drew nearer, she thought they both seemed a bit grim.

"Good morning." She squinted at Reg. His eyelids were heavy and pink. "You look tired. Did Georgiana have a bad night?"

"Not Georgiana." He grimaced. "I had to play host to Lord Billings and Lord Jeffers. We played cards almost until dawn."

"Couldn't Hazard relieve you?" Of course, with Jasper and Crispin gone, the host's duties would fall upon Reg, but Hazard had been Jasper's best man. And he was practically a Taverston.

"He fell asleep on the davenport."

Olivia laughed and saw that Benjamin was smiling as well.

Benjamin said, "I told Mr. Taverston that we could postpone this until later."

"This?" Olivia asked.

"A survey of the property. To refresh Mr. Carroll's memory," Reg said. "But there is no need to put it off. A good ride will wake me." He paused. "You're up early."

She wouldn't mention the embarrassing headache. "I want to spend every minute on horseback that I can. Crispin warned me there is no place to ride in London."

"There are places," Reg said. "But Crispin is correct that they won't likely suit you. You'll have to ride sedately, and you won't be able to go out alone." He laughed at her groan. Then he said, "Join us, won't you?"

Benjamin's smile hitched, but that was no reason for her to reject Reg's company. She didn't see enough of her brothers.

"If you don't mind waiting until Oatmeal is saddled."

She'd named the mare for her ugly mottled gray and tan hide. But the horse's strong legs and perfect gait more than compensated for her appearance.

Olivia called to the nearest groom, who was mucking out one

of the stalls. "Fergus, would you ready Oatmeal for me?"

"Of course, my lady." He leaned his rake against the wall and went to fetch the horse.

Olivia turned her focus to Benjamin. The more they interacted, the easier it would become. "What would you like to see first?"

He shot a questioning look at Reg, who gave him no help. Then he said, "I hadn't planned so far in advance. Where were *you* thinking of riding?"

She feigned a shrug. "I hadn't planned so far in advance."

Benjamin responded with a grin. The success of her jest gave her heart a small squeeze. He looked more like *himself* when he grinned.

Reg said, "Then let's ride out past the lake to Everet's plot. The old man has been setting badger traps. Jasper told him to stop, but he complains the badgers get into his barley."

"Is he trapping things he shouldn't?" Benjamin asked.

"No, but Jasper suspects he is selling the animals to sportsmen for badger drawing. He sold several in the past, and Jasper thinks he is still doing so despite being warned."

Olivia winced. Another thing she was not meant to know about. Some men, not only low-class men but supposed gentlemen, enjoyed wagering on bloodsport. They set up arenas for cock fights, dog fights, or badger drawings where dogs were set upon badgers to the detriment of both.

"I am to ascertain if the traps are still there?" Benjamin asked, setting his jaw.

"First, I'm merely supposed to introduce you to Everet. Give the man a week to get rid of them without confronting him. Then go back and check the grounds. If they are still there…"

Benjamin nodded. Olivia let out a slow breath. What was he supposed to do if Everet did not comply? She'd have to say something, either to Benjamin or to Everet. If he was selling badgers, it was likely to help his daughter and his large brood of grandchildren. The man was crotchety, but not mean.

Fergus brought Oatmeal around, and Reg cupped his hands with his fingers interlaced to give her a footstep into the saddle. Then he and Benjamin mounted their own horses, and they all set off.

It was turning into a beautiful morning. She loved Chaumbers in the autumn. The summer heat was gone but winter did not yet threaten. The grasses were browning, going dormant. Wildflowers along the paths had gone to seed, promising a riot of color in the spring. She loved springtime too. And summer. For that matter, she even loved the winter. Chaumbers was so pretty covered in snow.

She hoped whomever she ended up marrying had a country home and intended to spend a good deal of time there. She would be miserable trapped in London. The city was all soot, and rain, and crowds. Of course, she might also be miserable in any country home that was not Chaumbers. There was something unfair about a system that nurtured girls in one environment, made it the center of their world, and then tossed them out of it. Jasper *preferred* London. He would no doubt spend most of his time there. But he was the earl, and Chaumbers would be his.

For a while, they rode three abreast, trading comments on the scenery. Then the path narrowed, and she and Reg led the way with Benjamin behind. But Reg kept calling to Benjamin over his shoulder, so Olivia slowed to let Benjamin ride beside Reg instead. She thought that with their two dark heads and square shoulders, they appeared more like brothers than Reg and Jasper or Crispin. Of course their faces would dispel that impression at once. While Reg had a toned-down version of Jasper's Adonis-like features, Benjamin's face was more...rugged—chisel chinned, with heavy eyebrows and skin that was a bit sun darkened even in October.

They were discussing some of the tenants. Difficulties of various sorts. A dog in the Davis' henhouse. A dispute over Tilden's borrowed stud bull. An order of hay that hadn't been delivered to the Crofts. Nothing as disturbing as Everet and the badgers, just things that had been brought to Jasper's attention. Reg was passing along direction. And Benjamin was *taking* direction. It made Olivia feel strange. Like hearing them call each other "mister."

From the pitch of their voices, they did not find it strange. They sounded comfortable. It was the way Reg was speaking, she thought. Not with Crispin's joking familiarity or Jasper's fondness. But not with overbearing lordliness either. He seemed to strike just the right tone.

She supposed she might try to copy Reg, though she wasn't sure she could carry it off. Reg had not professed his undying love, then wept a torrent when Benjamin did not react with appropriate delight. Her face grew heated, and she was glad she was behind where they would not see. She'd been such a sapskull!

The path broadened into a soggy patch where a stream couldn't make up its mind as to its course.

Reg slowed, cueing Benjamin to do so also. Olivia dropped a little farther behind so she wouldn't be spattered by clods of mud kicked up by their mounts. They all picked their way until they reached firmer ground. Reg gestured to the meadow before them. "Why don't you two have a race to the lake. Let Oatmeal and Goose stretch their legs. I'll catch up."

Reg had never been much for racing, but of course he knew his sister and must have supposed she was itching to gallop. She turned to Benjamin. They had raced in the past. He rode well for someone who did not ride often. And he loved horses. She knew that about him, just as she had always understood he would never be in a position to own one.

"Well?"

He grinned at her. "Do you want a head start?"

Her jaw dropped. "You can't be serious!"

"No?"

Reg laughed. "I'll give the signal. Are you ready?"

Olivia whirled Oatmeal about. When Reg shouted "Go!" they went.

OLIVIA PULLED AHEAD at the last and, two lengths ahead of Benjamin, crossed the invisible line between two larches that had always marked the end point of Taverston meadow races. Laughing with glee, she slowed as he drew up alongside. He was windblown and red-faced, and she suspected she was the same.

"A head start? Ha!"

"Olivia! You could outride a Blackfoot!"

She blinked and regarded him questioningly. What did that mean? *Oh!* And he'd called her by her given name. As he used to. A moment later, they were both looking anywhere but at each other. Her heart rate slowed by measures as the horses calmed. Her embarrassment faded and since the flush left his face, she assumed Benjamin's did too.

"I beg your pardon, my lady," he murmured. "That was inappropriate."

She knew better than to suggest that he *could* call her Olivia. To ease the tension, she tried the taunt her brothers had begun throwing at one another when one performed unexpectedly well at some challenge or other.

"You've been practicing."

He answered ruefully, "I suppose I have."

He dismounted, patted Goose's withers, then came to her side and offered his hand. She nodded and moved her leg from the pommel so he could more easily lift her down. He was quick. His hands didn't linger on her waist, and he took a step back as soon as he released her. His haste drew attention to itself. Even a stableboy would have waited a moment to be sure her feet were firmly planted.

Before the silence between them grew *too* uncomfortable, he gestured to the nearby stand of trees. "I suppose we might walk over to the lake." The lake was just beyond the trees. "Iversley mentioned the boathouse could be in need of refurbishing."

"Is that your job now? Pulling rotting planks from the boathouse?" The question was rude, but she was feeling peevish.

Benjamin smiled grimly. "I'm not expected to wield the hammer and nails." He was evidently trying to jest. "But I'll hire the carpenter if I think something needs to be done."

"If? But Jasper said it needed fixing."

"He said to use my discretion." He pulled a hand through his hair. "Lady Olivia, my job, if done well, is not to simply carry out Iversley's orders but to anticipate what needs to be done. I am to lift the burdens of the care of Chaumbers from Iversley's shoulders so he can concentrate on weightier matters."

She sniffed. She understood what being a steward meant.

Oh, but this was hard. She still thought of their steward as old Bradwell. Not Benjamin. Who had once skipped rope with her for half a morning when she was feeling blue because Jasper had told her she couldn't accompany them swimming that afternoon. Underneath this new seriousness, was he still *that* Benjamin? The one who had bothered to look beyond her Taverstonian bravado—and understood that sometimes her brothers' teasing did hurt?

"If you're supposed to *anticipate*, why has Reg been telling you what to do all day?"

"He has been familiarizing me with ongoing issues with the tenants." A gentle exasperation sparked his voice. "He could leave me to figure it all out for myself, some lords would, but that would be a terribly inefficient way to go about it."

Funneling information through Reg was hardly the most efficient course. "So *Jasper*, who has hardly spent any time at Chaumbers this past year, told *Reg*, who has spent even less, what to tell *you* to do."

He paused, giving her a sympathetic look before staring hard at his folded hands. "They all care a great deal for...for Chaumbers, even if they could not always be here."

"Yes, of course, they do." He misunderstood. She missed her brothers, certainly, but she was not whining about their absence

or neglect. She was annoyed by their assumption of her useless-
ness. "That isn't the problem. It's that they still see me as a
darling featherbrain to be cossetted or ignored as it suits them.
And you'll follow their lead, I suppose."

His gaze flicked up, wide eyed and startled, then away.

"My lady, Iversley has placed his trust in me."

That sounded plaintive. She noted his lowered eyes, his reddening ears. *Oh, good Lord!* Benjamin still saw her as a child. A
fatuous fourteen-year-old admirer. Which she was *not*! She almost
told him so. But that would not be pretending "it" had never
happened. Instead, she lifted her chin.

"I care a great deal for Chaumbers too. I *am* a Taverston, after
all, Mr. Carroll, and I also appreciate efficiency. So I suggest we
go look at the boathouse rather than waste time standing around
here."

Chapter Five

BENJAMIN KICKED HIMSELF for overreacting. Olivia didn't need him to explain the duties of a steward. Good God! Or to shove a wall between them by mentioning Jasper's *trust*, as if she might tempt him to betray it—when the temptation was only in his awakened imagination. He was a fool to have found a race so affecting. To find *Olivia* so affecting.

"We can let the horses graze by the lake," she said, tossing the words over her shoulder as she turned to lead Oatmeal toward the coppice.

He should never have indulged in a playful race, but finding himself seated upon such a fine specimen of horseflesh had fired his desire for a good strong run. Olivia was right about his horsemanship. He had been "practicing," if one could call riding for one's life practice. Stealing company horses *back* from the Blackfoot natives was a fool's errand. Assignments like that were why he had not signed on for another term. He was willing to die for his king, but not for the governor of the Hudson's Bay Company.

Still, Benjamin knew he was a better-than-decent rider. For a moment, he'd actually believed he would win, until she lengthened the lead he'd thought he was narrowing. He could not have caught her. He could only chase after her. Awed.

Olivia on horseback—throwing caution to the wind. She was

magnificent.

He trudged behind, scuffing through the brittle leaves littering the footpath.

The devil. Things had been going well. Of all the Taverstons, Reg was the best intermediary. As an earl's third son, Reg was marching down the social ladder himself. He could have lived comfortably and respectably as a rector, but chose instead the life of classicist, studying ancient Greek philosophy. A marginally acceptable eccentricity for a gentleman, if he were a hobbyist fading into genteel poverty, but Reg was being *paid* for his work. Which put him, in the ridiculous eyes of the ton, on the outside of polite society. By all rights, Reg's branch of the Taverston family should shuffle off into oblivion. Instead, hilariously, Reg had married a duke's daughter who came with twenty thousand pounds. Her respectability salvaged Reg's. As long as they didn't have too many children and dilute that dowry, they could all remain prominent, if untitled, members of the ton for another generation or two.

Perhaps three. While sorting through Taverston financial affairs, Benjamin had come across Crispin's will. He left everything to Reg. And while his officer's pay would end with his death, his cottage in Binnings was another valuable Taverston asset.

Even so, Reg would understand the fine line Benjamin must walk. A steward was not a servant. He could use the front entrance and be invited to sit in the earl's presence. But he *was* an employee, not a friend. A friend might be forgiven an indiscreet word; an employee would not.

They emerged from the coppice, and the expansive, sun-speckled lake lay before them. Benjamin could just make out the opposite tree-lined shore. His heart tightened, remembering lazy days he'd spent here with the blessed-by-the-gods Taverston brothers—until the divide between them grew starkly evident, because of their sister.

Of course, Benjamin had not fled across the ocean merely to

escape Olivia. The Hudson's Bay Company offered a man of moderate intelligence and good education a steady job with a livable wage. More importantly, Canada promised a chance to leave behind the rigid hierarchy of class. Unfortunately, these promises had proved to be myths, and the New World presented the same temptations as the old one.

The deuce. Jasper should not have hired him without references. He shouldn't have implicitly trusted Benjamin to exercise sound judgment. Not when impatience, greed, and shockingly *poor* judgment had led to his difficulties in Canada. Jasper had never *asked*.

"We can leave them there." Olivia interrupted his thoughts, gesturing to the scrub grass stretching from the shore up a small hill. "They won't stray far."

"All right," he said, keeping a close rein on his tongue.

He had not told Jasper the whole story. He should have, but he needed this position. Now, he would do nothing to betray the man's blind trust. So he trailed Olivia up the hill, training his eyes upon the backside of her horse rather than the gentle sway of her hips, and prayed Reg joined them quickly.

After setting their mounts to graze, Benjamin walked with her back down to the boathouse. She pointed out two boards at water level. "Those have softened."

He nudged them with his boot. Rotting. "You *are* efficient." He made an effort to smile. "Did Iversley mention the boathouse to you, also?"

She rolled her eyes. "I've been living at Chaumbers for the past two years while my brothers have been flitting about London. I told Jasper."

"Ah." If he didn't stop underestimating her, she would probably clock him.

He knelt in the dirt and prodded the boards more thoroughly. Then he took out his pocketknife and pressed it into the soft spots, carving out flakes of wood. Tapping his knife into other boards yielded nothing.

He sighed. "Well, the quickest course would be for me to yank out these boards and replace them. I am, in fact, quite competent handling a hammer and nails."

"Will you then?"

"No." He shook his head. "I'll ask Willy Pyle to have a look."

"Willy?" She sniffed. "He'll say we need a new boathouse."

Benjamin chuckled. "Yes. Yes, he will." Willy Pyle was the preferred carpenter in the village. He did very good work, but he never did anything by half measures. "I'll let him tear this one down and build a new one." He glanced up. Her eyes were not the intense shade of blue that her brothers' were. Hers were ice blue. And they were puzzled. He didn't want to repeat the mistake of patronizing her, but he felt the need to explain himself. So as he rose to his feet, he said, "If I were to mend this, the Taverstons would have a perfectly functional boathouse, but that would be all. Whereas if I call in Willy, he will have a weeks' long project that promises to pay him in actual coin. Maybe his daft nephew too. That coin will likely make its way to a farmer or two, and the butcher and tavernkeep in Iversley Village. Perhaps into some of the other shops as well."

"Oh."

"The people in Iversley are interdependent, as in any small village. But coin inevitably flows upward."

"Rents and tithes. So Jasper needs to send some of that coin back down."

"I don't mean to say that it is *required* of him."

"Oh, but of course it is! *Noblesse oblige* and all that." To Benjamin's surprise, Olivia beamed at him. "Mr. Carroll, you have just spared me at least two miserable months in London."

"What?"

"Mama intends to drag me off to the best shops as soon as Reg and Georgiana's baby is born. Late January or early February. I've been wearing mourning for a year, and before that, I didn't leave Chaumbers for another year because Father was so ill. Mama needed me. So now I must have more than the usual new wardrobe for my coming-out. Mama is determined to engage the ton's favorite modiste before anyone else does…" She stopped rambling abruptly and scowled. "Don't look at me that way. It isn't my idea."

He realized he had been giving her a "look." To his mind, first in line at the modiste's shop was a frivolous concern. He blanked out his frown.

"But there is a perfectly wonderful dressmaker here in Iversley Village!" Olivia continued, excited again. "Mrs. Byrd. She made our mourning clothes. There is no reason she couldn't make my coming-out wardrobe, and every reason she should!"

"Well, yes, but…" The last thing he needed was to be blamed for Olivia's revolt. "The London fashions," he said weakly. "She won't know the latest—"

"Georgiana does. And Vanessa." Olivia pealed with laughter. "Or I can go straight to the source and ask Hazard." She clapped her hands with delight. "No one wants to go to London just when the first new Taverston baby arrives. It's only that they all feel so guilty for neglecting me."

"Neglecting you?" Young Olivia had never acted like a spoiled child. He could not see her as a pouting society miss demanding attention.

"Yes, it's ridiculous. I've tried to tell them I don't need to race off to London for *clothes*, but they all think I am playing the martyr or something. It's no use to say I don't need all this fuss. Mama says it's no fuss at all, and Jasper says it's his duty and his pleasure to spoil me." She huffed with irritation. Then her smile burst forth once again, spraying him with sunshine. "But if I insist upon hiring Mrs. Byrd, with all the aforesaid arguments, I might not have to go to London until March, or even April!"

He stared. Olivia was a beautiful young lady. She would be nineteen now or near so. She couldn't possibly be saying she didn't want to go to London.

"Aren't you eager? For the balls and such?" For all the earls and dukes and baronets who would be laying flowers at her feet?

Her smile dimmed. "Well, yes, of course I am."

"You don't sound eager." Strange. He thought every gentle-woman lived for her coming-out.

"What alternative do I have?"

What alternative *did* she have?

Olivia gave a small, humorless laugh. "I suppose there is always Jeremy or Jeffrey."

That was in no way amusing. The Willowsett twins were mooncalves.

It didn't have to be the London Marriage Mart. Jasper could always hold a house party. Invite his eligible friends. But somehow that sounded even worse. Displaying her for the taking without even the comfort of...of a herd of other marriageable ladies contending for the attention of wife-seeking males. *Good Lord. How awful.*

He managed to say, "I'm sure, once you are in the midst of a Season, you will enjoy it." In fact, he wasn't at all sure of that.

Her eyes flashed at him. "Yes, of course. Everyone says so."

She turned from him and walked away, leaving him to kick the rotting boards one more time before following her back up the hill. Fortunately, Reg appeared at the edge of the coppice just as they reached their grazing horses.

"Hullo!" Reg called. "Who won?"

"Who do you think?" Olivia called back.

Reg laughed. "Sorry, Mr. Carroll. But don't feel bad. Crispin is the only one who can beat Olivia anymore."

"Only on Mercury!" Any trace of bitterness was gone from her voice. Was she play-acting, or had she not been as upset as he'd thought?

Reg dismounted and brought his horse to theirs. After watching the animals nibbling the grasses for a few moments, Reg lifted his head, glanced out at the lake, then said, "I take it Olivia showed you the boathouse."

Benjamin nodded.

"What do you think?" Reg asked.

"A few boards gone bad at the waterline. But I think it better to be cautious. There could be more structural damage than is readily evident."

Olivia put in, "He's going to ask Willy about tearing it down and building a new one."

"That seems the wisest course," Reg said, eyeing Benjamin with something that seemed not quite skepticism, more a reservation of judgment.

"And I'm going to have Mrs. Byrd create my new wardrobe," Olivia said.

Reg's head swung around. "Pardon?"

"To support the village."

Reg cast a glance from one to the other. "And whose idea was this?"

"Mine." Olivia said. Now her lip did jut out in a pout. "You can't deny it's a good one."

"Except I *know* that you are settling for a substandard dressmaker instead of a fashionable modiste, just so that Mother can spend a few extra weeks with her grandchild. Olivia, you needn't sacrifice your debut. You want your coming-out to be special."

Olivia's face fell. She must have been counting on Reg's support. With Crispin gone, he would be her most likely bulwark.

Before he even knew what he was doing, Benjamin said, "*Ask her what she wants.*"

Startled, Reg said, "Ask what?"

"Don't *tell* Lady Olivia what she wants. Ask her."

"All right." His tone quieted. "What is it then, Olivia? What do you want?"

"I want to spend the winter here. At Chaumbers. It could be..." Her voice shook. "Oh, bosh! It probably will be my last winter here. The last winter when I'll belong here."

"You'll always belong—"

"That isn't true. You know it's not. I'll be mistress of some other estate. Wherever my husband drags me off to."

That, Benjamin thought, was overdoing it. No one would

drag her off. But Reg's expression softened.

"We aren't chasing you away."

"I know. But it feels like it sometimes."

"Oh, Livvy." To Benjamin's surprise, Reg walked over and wrapped his arms around his sister. Reg had always seemed the least demonstrative of the brothers. "If you want Mrs. Byrd, you shall have her."

"Mama will be upset," she said, her voice muffled against Reg's chest.

"She'll come round." He gave Olivia's shoulders a little shake. "It doesn't matter who the ton anoints as this year's most sought-after modiste. Jasper would say Taverstons don't follow fashions, they set them." He cleared his throat and spoke over his shoulder. "Mr. Carroll, let us put off visiting Everet until tomorrow."

"Fine by me." He stroked Goose's nose. Then mounted. This was a family affair. "If you'll excuse me, I'll go have a word with Willy Pyle."

CHAPTER SIX

OCTOBER SLID INTO November. The days grew colder and shorter, and the landscape turned from green to orange and yellow to brown in the space of a few short weeks. Olivia rode every morning unless it poured down rain. She enjoyed the freedom she had to go about without an escort at Chaumbers, but that didn't mean she shunned company. Hazard accompanied her three times before hying back to London, claiming he daren't leave his mother alone any longer or she would redecorate his house. Alice or Reg rode with her occasionally. Still, most often she went out alone.

To satisfy Mama, and because she did have *some* common sense, Olivia no longer rode in the wee hours of the morning, but waited until the sun was up. Today, she'd asked Fergus to saddle Bluebell, an old pony that was getting fat from lack of exercise, an animal she could mount without aid. She had a duty to perform, visiting the Fowlers, tenants on the estate. *Noblesse oblige*, Mama would say.

Yesterday, their local physician, Dr. Haraldsen, had come to pass on word that Mrs. Fowler had dropped a heavy pot on her foot. "She'll be laid up a week or two," he'd informed Olivia. Olivia, not Mama. Ever since Papa's first fit of apoplexy, Mama had delegated to Olivia the task of seeing to the welfare of the tenants in little things like this. So now she was knocking on the door of the Fowlers' cottage. She'd brought them a meat pie and a peck of apples.

Sam and Jon, mischievous little scamps whom she adored, let her in. "It's Livia-lady," shouted Sam.

"Ah, bless your heart," Mrs. Fowler called out from her bed, spying the gift. Her foot was propped on what must have been every spare bit of cloth in the house, mounded up. With her uncombed hair and unkempt gown, she looked as though she'd aged ten years. "Tell your mother we're grateful, we are."

On previous visits, the small cottage had always been cluttered but clean; however, now there was mud on the floor and ashes spilled beyond the hearth. The air had a curdled-milk smell.

Olivia set the basket and pie pan on their small trestle table, while the boys jostled her in their attempts to hug her about the waist. "Would you like me to serve out some pie to the boys?" she asked, handing them each an apple. They laughed their delight and retreated a few steps, while continuing to watch her as if waiting for more bounty to fall from her hands.

"Oh, no!" Mrs. Fowler protested. "Mr. Fowler is in the field. He'll be pink to see a real supper. Mabs come over from across the way the last night to boil us some beans—right nice of her— but Mr. Fowler says he don't want to see another bean." She waved her hand to gesture vaguely at the room. "He asked the Widow Tabor to help out, but she can't come until tomorrow."

Good. Gert Tabor was always looking for work. She would tidy the cottage and keep the boys fed and entertained.

Sam bounded suddenly over to his mother and tried to climb up beside her. Mrs. Fowler winced and went pale.

"Sam!" Olivia called. "See what I have?"

He turned and scrunched his face at her, curious. She reached into the basket and fished out four wooden cows, the size of her fingers, that she'd found in the Taverstons' old nursery. She held them out. "These are for you and Jon. But you have to play with them here at the table."

Both boys approached, eyeing the toy cows with awe.

"For us?" Jon asked. Then he looked at his mother. "Can we?"

Mrs. Fowler cleared her throat. "Yes, if you thank Lady Olivia." She sounded teary.

They thanked her effusively in their high-pitched little-boy voices. They were so sweet that it made Olivia's heart hurt a little.

"Can I do anything for *you*, Mrs. Fowler?" she asked, turning to the injured woman. There was a fine line, she was learning, between helping enough and offering too much. "I'd like to bring a pillow or two for your foot. It would be more comfortable." The short tower of cloth looked lumpy.

Mrs. Fowler's brow creased. "Dr. Haraldsen said to use one, but…"

"I'll bring it tomorrow." Olivia tousled Jon's hair, then brought an apple over to Mrs. Fowler. She would also bring fresh milk. And a boiled chicken and some potatoes. "Try to eat a few bites if you can."

She waved her goodbyes, went back out to Bluebell, and hauled herself into the saddle.

She left the Fowlers with a vague sense of unease. The Earl of Iversley's tenants were better off than many, but the last two years had been hard on everyone. The neglect since Bradwell's death was beginning to show around the edges. Benjamin would soon have the place thriving again. He was conscientious and hardworking, and the way he'd hired Willy Pyle when he didn't have to showed he cared about the people of Iversley. But what about the little things, like meat pies and pillows?

When Vanessa returned from Binnings, the duties of the lady of the house would fall to her. But while Mama and Papa had only gone to London for short visits, Vanessa and Jasper were likely to be there for most of the year. Who would see to the *little* cares of the tenants? It would be awkward for Mama to return to the role. That would be stepping on the new countess's toes. And Olivia wouldn't be here.

Her throat tightened. She'd miss them all so much, tenants,

villagers, *everyone.*

Since it was still early, she decided to visit the lake to cheer herself before returning to the house. Willy Pyle had torn down the old boathouse and had begun framing a new one. Benjamin had told him he needn't rush. The boats, two somewhat shabby rowboats, were tucked safely away in the carriage house until spring. Olivia liked to watch the progress.

She wended her way along the path, musing about Georgiana's crankiness that morning and Reg's discomfiture when she'd left the breakfast table weeping. He'd hurried out after her, leaving his eggs to grow cold. It was almost, but not quite, funny.

She emerged from the trees and discovered the lakeside was occupied, but not by Willy. Benjamin stood beside a tipped wagon. Just seeing him gave her spirits a little lift, although he could not be happy. Crates had spilled onto the grass. He had already unhitched the carthorse, Pudge, and was surveying the damage. She couldn't hear him, but assumed he was swearing.

"Hullo!" she called out. He turned, then took off his hat and waved it to her. She went to him. "What happened?"

"Axle snapped."

"Can I do anything to help?"

She expected a no, but his forehead smoothed, and he smiled. It was not a welcoming smile, more something tired. "You can. If you could go to the carriage house, after your ride, of course, and ask Mundy to bring the small cart and a few men to drag this mess back to the yard, I'll figure out what to do from there."

Olivia nodded. "I'll go straightaway. What is in the crates? May I ask?" There were five of them, two in the wagon bed and three on the ground. They were about two or three feet long and one in the dirt appeared cracked, but she couldn't see what was in it.

"Traps."

"Hmm." He was not forthcoming, so she said, "What kind of traps?"

"Badger traps."

That didn't sit well. "Does this have to do with Everet?"

"It does." He sighed, then ran his hand through his hair before redonning his cap. He was not wearing gloves, and his hands were quite filthy. She should have found that off-putting, but she had a hard time keeping her hands tidy as well. "He took up all his traps after I visited him, but he set them out again. So I'm going to offer him an alternative."

"More traps?"

"You won't appreciate this either."

She shifted in her saddle and waited.

"Lady Olivia, you are an intelligent and imaginative young lady, but I doubt you could possibly comprehend the scope of the enterprise behind all the delightful furs and pelts your friends in the ton like to wear. I doubt my ability to explain. All I can say is, although I was not a fur trapper myself, I learned a thing or two about the business."

"No one wears badger fur, Mr. Carroll."

"You would be surprised. Of course, no one *knows* they are wearing badgers."

Olivia couldn't help shuddering.

"You won't be wearing any local pests," he assured her with a short laugh. "You pay for quality and give your custom to reputable clothiers." He glanced at his crates, then his hands. He rubbed his palms on his trousers with a grimace. "To be brief, I have some sympathy for Everet. The beasts have dug up his barley field and it's full of holes. He needs to get rid of them and he saw a way..." He hesitated before going on. "He's an old grouch, but he isn't a brute. He has a daughter who married over Ipswich way and gave him five grandchildren. He passed the coin along to his daughter."

"Bess." She nodded. "I suspected as much."

Benjamin gave her a studying look before dropping his gaze and continuing in a less condescending tone, "He understands Iversley tasked me with putting a stop to his selling live badgers. And I will. I won't abide wanton cruelty. But I am aware of a few shops in London that will buy a few 'beaver' pelts, no questions asked. These traps I'm bringing him,"—he gestured to the crates—"kill quickly."

"And you will sell the pelts for him?" That was going above and beyond.

His expression darkened. "The few shillings they will bring in will be split between Everet and Iversley. I'm not—"

"For pity's sake, Benjamin!" she gasped. "I was thinking how kind you were. Not that you were doing something underhanded."

Benjamin flushed. "I apologize. For my defensiveness. I've had a bad morning."

"As I can see."

He mumbled, "And a worse night." He removed his hat again and rubbed his temple as if his head hurt. "Mrs. Danforth visited the Claybornes yesterday evening and came home to announce their youngest is breaking out in spots. Miss Jamison is trying to keep Hannah away from Mrs. Danforth, who says she is being ridiculous."

She gasped. "She is not being ridiculous! Spots spread. Does the Clayborne child have a fever?"

"I don't know."

"I'll ask Dr. Haraldsen to stop around. Honestly, Mrs. Danforth should know better!"

"Their cottage comprises three rooms and a loft. There is also a chicken coop and a small barn. There is no place to isolate a child."

Olivia bit her lip. She didn't want to worry him any more than he already was.

He went on, "But Hannah was fussier than usual when I left the cottage this morning. I'd hoped to return quickly. And now this."

Three rooms and a barn. Olivia's ire rose.

"Perhaps Mrs. Danforth is not being ridiculous, but I do know who is."

His head shot up.

"Mr. Carroll, there is absolutely no reason for you to crowd into the Danforths' home while Bradwell's old apartment gathers dust. I will tell Mrs. Hardy to have the rooms aired, and you must go to the Danforths' at once and retrieve Hannah."

"If she is about to break out in spots, I cannot bring her near Lady Georgiana."

"And you will not. I can count on one hand the times I saw Mrs. Bradwell at Chaumbers even though she lived there for years. Hannah will be nowhere near Georgiana."

For a moment, Benjamin appeared torn. Olivia wanted to challenge him further. She suspected it was not an aversion to Chaumbers, but rather herself, that kept him living in the village so inconveniently. She was *not* still a besotted schoolgirl! But now was not the time to confront that issue.

Care for the child won out.

"Thank you," Benjamin said, nodding. "I— I will bring her as soon as I sort this—"

"Just leave it. No one will bother a few crates of badger traps. If I weren't riding sidesaddle, I would offer you Bluebell. But if you can ride bareback, just throw your leg over Pudge. He isn't fussy. Or I'll lead him back if you'd rather walk."

He gave her sidelong look. "Why do I feel you've just served me a challenge?"

She raised her eyebrows.

With a snicker, he strode to Pudge.

"Just don't ask me to race," Benjamin said, knotting the reins to shorten them, then mounting and tossing the excess length over his shoulder.

Olivia laughed. "A race between Bluebell and Pudge would be something to see." She turned Bluebell back toward the trees. "But we are going in two different directions. I'll find Mundy, then go talk to Mrs. Hardy. You fetch Hannah and Miss Jamison."

"There is that Taverston efficiency again." Benjamin smiled a true smile this time, one that held gratitude and, perhaps, Olivia hoped, a touch of esteem. He nudged Pudge's sides and rode off.

IT HAD BEEN three days, raining for two of them, and Olivia had not heard a peep from the south wing. Reg reported to her that Hannah remained healthy, but Benjamin insisted upon confining her to their apartment for a full week. Olivia had put together a basket of bread and sweets and taken them down to the Claybornes in between thundershowers. She didn't go inside, but only handed the basket through the door. She had been pleased to return with the news that their little one was recovering.

Olivia and Alice engaged in yet another game of billiards prior to teatime. Alice nearly always won, but Olivia was picking up a few tricks to use the next time she played against one of her brothers. Alice sank the last ball with a thwack and thud, then hung up her cue.

"Teatime!"

"And a good thing too." Olivia rubbed circles on her stomach. She laid her cue across the table. "Mama said we'd take tea in the parlor this evening."

They left the billiard room and walked the long corridor. Olivia thought she saw Alice stifle a yawn. Olivia wondered if she was bored. The thought unsettled her. *How could anyone be bored at Chaumbers?*

"Is there any word from Jasper?" Alice asked, glancing sideways and down.

"Not that I've heard."

"But he does intend to be back by Christmas?"

"So he said. Why?"

Alice shrugged. "Just curious. Did he invite Hazard?"

Olivia peered at her friend a moment longer. Was she longing for more diverting company? She *was* bored.

"Probably," she chirped, to be encouraging. "But even if he didn't, Hazard will invite himself."

Alice smiled, then abruptly changed the subject back to billiards.

Reginald, Georgiana, and Mama were already in the parlor. The teapot, cups, plates, and a platter of buns and dainties sat untouched on the tea table. A glance at the wall clock showed that she and Alice were a few minutes late.

"I'm sorry, Mama. We were in the middle of a game, and I didn't notice the time."

Mama accepted the excuse and apology with a terse nod, then began to pour. The conversation centered on baby names, as had far too many conversations in the past few weeks. A daughter would be Mary, for Georgiana's mother. Unless it was one of ten other names. For a son, they were thinking of Crispin. But Georgiana thought that Crispin might, just might, want to reserve the name for a son of his own. Olivia had suggested asking him, but had been roundly accused of insensitivity. So she kept her mouth shut.

They were nibbling and sipping and talking, when the butler, Peters, entered with a few cards and a letter on a silver plate which he handed to Reg.

Reg flipped through the cards then passed them to Mama. He glanced at the letter.

"From Haz," he said, puzzled, breaking the seal.

Everyone saw a folded slip of paper fall out of the letter and drop to the floor. Reg scooped it up and scowled, his eyes going to Alice. "This is not acceptable."

Now everyone stared at Alice, whose face went pink. "We didn't arrange this between us. Good heavens, Reg. What can you be thinking?"

Mama said, "Reginald is right. Prearranged or not, you may not engage in a clandestine correspondence with Viscount Haslet."

Alice was an unmarried lady currently under the Taverston roof. Of course Mama could not permit any impropriety. It would ruin Alice and harm Olivia's prospects too. Poor Alice looked mortified.

"Oh, bosh!" Despite the growing tension, Olivia laughed. "How secret is it when he sends the letter through Reg?"

"What does he say?" Alice asked, chin tucked down, eyes peering up. "In your letter, I mean, Reg."

He lifted his own page and read aloud.

"'Good day to you, Taverstons. I'll make no comment on the weather in London, though I understand that is how letters usually begin. I hope Georgiana is well. And the rest of you. I am writing to tell you that I am not shirking. A large box of fabrics and ribbons, and etc., will arrive before long, along with several sketches that should show Mrs. Byrd the height of next Season's waistlines, the depth of the necklines, the placement of baubles, and the size of the bows. But I will not be there to deliver these myself. A friend has invited me to the country to sit before a roaring fire, pat his large shaggy hounds, eat biscuits, and drink tea. And I have taken him up on the offer. Normally, I expect you all to be goggling over that news, but I suspect you are more concerned about the missive I included.'"

Reg looked up, still scowling. "What is he up to?"

"Continue, Reginald," Mama commanded. "So that we may find out." She looked even more annoyed than Reg did.

"'There is nothing improper in Miss Fogbotham's letter. I invite you to read it aloud, as you are no doubt'"—Reg barked a laugh—"'as you are no doubt doing with this one. I merely wished to mention a few things I heard at Brooks's that might be of interest to her. If you don't wish to bore everyone else, you may simply pass the letter along.'"

Reg flipped the letter over, noted the seal, then held it out between two fingers for Alice. He returned to his own letter.

"'You need not fear I will ask you to facilitate the exchange of *billet doux* as I will be out of the city and unable to receive any reply from Miss Fogbotham in any case. Your obliged and affectionate friend—Viscount Haslet.'"

This was met with a moment of silence before Alice said,

"Would you like me to read my letter aloud?"

"No," Olivia said, before anyone else spoke. There would be nothing improper in it. And as Hazard did not engage in casual gossip, the content would very likely be political and dull. Alice had a peculiar interest in such things.

Mama lowered her eyes to her folded hands and said, "It isn't necessary. But Alice, dear, don't encourage this sort of behavior. We may all find Hazard very amusing. But not everyone does."

CHAPTER SEVEN

BENJAMIN WATCHED OLIVIA from a third-story window of Chaumbers' south wing. *Where was she going today?*

Since moving from the Danforths' a fortnight prior, he'd developed a routine. He would rise, wash, dress, then retire to the sitting room to drink coffee while waiting for Miss Jamison to bring Hannah in for breakfast—breakfast that someone from kitchen had fetched up along with a bucket of piping hot water, another of the perquisites of living in the Taverston home.

Early on, he'd made the mistake of standing by the window while he planned his day. The first sunny morning, Olivia appeared. And now, every morning when the skies were not actively dripping, he made sure to take his coffee by the window. Were another man to do something so surreptitious and unnerving, Benjamin would treat him to a horsewhipping. Yet he'd formed the habit and could not stop.

She intrigued him. He'd discovered that while the dowager had been grieving her husband, Olivia had taken up the duty of care for the tenants: looking in on the ill, bringing food to the struggling, visiting the lonely. From the affectionate way they all spoke of her, he knew they recognized her goodness of heart. Evidently, she was not the same charmingly silly creature he remembered. And yet, she was. She had the same smile. The same laugh. And, no doubt, the same fierce, absurd desire to compete with her brothers.

This morning, she was wearing her brown riding habit. He favored the blue, but the brown was nice also. He couldn't have helped noticing how both flattered her, even though she was lanky, and his preference had always skewed toward the voluptuous.

Who was she visiting today? She was carrying an enormous basket. Her long, slender arms must be stronger than they appeared. He envisioned equally strong, long, slender legs. *The deuce.* He should not be spying. It put all the wrong thoughts in his head.

She disappeared over the ridge, and Benjamin turned away. This must stop. In a few months, she would be gone to London and that would be that. But he could not spend the next few months watching her from windows.

He moved to the table. He had just chosen a sweet bun when Hannah charged into the room, hair half-combed, followed by a huffing Miss Jamison.

"Cake!" Hannah demanded.

"I am sorry, sir," Miss Jamison said, corralling her. "She is being difficult this morning."

"I would be too if I knew cake was awaiting me." Benjamin held out his arms and Hannah ran to him.

A little guiltily, he ignored Miss Jamison's frown. He wasn't making her job easier. He had chosen the woman for her grandmotherly appearance and list of references as long as his arm. She was stuffy, but he thought that would be a good balance for his tendency to be indulgent. He shouldn't keep overriding her discipline, but he did.

He lifted Hannah onto his lap, and she grabbed his breakfast with both hands.

"Tea, Miss Jamison?" he said, gesturing for her to sit across from him, knowing she would not.

"Thank you, sir, but I will go fill Hannah's bath."

He chuckled, surveying the damage the sticky coating had

already caused. "She'll need one. I may too."

A faint crinkle appeared alongside the nanny's eyes before she nodded and turned. She didn't entirely disapprove of him.

He shared the bun with Hannah, poured the tiniest bit of tea into a saucer, sugared it well, and gave it to her to slurp. She babbled something he could not quite make out. He agreed with her, and she babbled some more. As the weather promised fine, he suspected Miss Jamison's plans for the day would include another visit to the garden alongside the west wall. Being winter, everything was trimmed back and ugly, but it gave Hannah room to run about. And dig. The gardener was completely won over and had even gifted her with a trowel. When the weather turned nasty, Benjamin would have to find someplace within the house where she might roam. Perhaps the conservatory. Or the music room. They were generally empty.

But this was exactly what he had wished to avoid. Hannah was not a child of the house. She would not belong in the nursery with Jasper's children or whatever young Taverstons came to visit. Nor should she run about with any of the servants' children, wee ones who were taught from an early age to keep out of the way of the lords and ladies until they were old enough to perform tasks of their own. Benjamin hated that she would grow up on an estate where she would occupy some lonely in-between sphere, belonging neither with the masters nor with the servants. That was where he was. That lonely space.

Idiot. He was in an enviable position and moping over it was unbecoming.

For now, his daughter was sated and an absolute mess, so he scooped her up to deliver her to Miss Jamison, who had the washtub, soap, and towels at the ready. Rather than witness the battle ahead, he said, "I'll be working in the house today."

"Yes, Mr. Carroll."

He hurried out. He always told the nanny where he intended to be. Thankfully, she had never had cause to bother him, but he wanted her to know that she could. He would return at teatime.

Hannah's supper. Afterward, with the little mite put to bed, he would work in his office and let Miss Jamison have a few hours to herself.

Benjamin trotted down the south stairs and over to the main part of the house. The place was an architectural disaster with a maze of corridors that did not connect with one another on all levels so one was always going up and down stairs, and four wings—north, south, east, and west—that corresponded poorly to the actual points of a compass and were not even at right angles to each other. Jasper, Crispin, and eventually even Reg mocked the "old pile." But Benjamin loved every crooked stone.

His destination was Jasper's study. Jasper had made an effort to sort out his dying father's unattended-to business, as well as the work that the aging Bradwell had let slip. Reg had tackled the account books. Benjamin had learned this when he first put foot back in England and found a box of tidy ledgers awaiting him. He'd had no difficulty picking up the accounting where Reg had left off. The man was meticulous. His hand was so neat, Benjamin would almost call it feminine.

But the accounting was the least of it, as the mass of paper stuffed in Jasper's cabinets proved. A few files were labeled "seen to" and the papers in them were scribbled with notes attesting to what Jasper had done. In addition to estate matters, there were folders containing personal correspondence that Benjamin did not touch. There were also a few boxes of material dealing with Jasper's political interests: pamphlets, newspaper clippings, texts of speeches, notes, and letters. Benjamin thought this likely fascinating, but not within his purview, so he set those aside.

Jasper had told him to open anything that looked urgent. The only thing he'd opened was a letter from the Marquess of Ebersom. He didn't recognize the name, but a marquess might well expect a response in a timely manner. The man sent regrets. He would not be able to come for a visit over Twelfth Night. They would have to discuss their collaboration when they both returned to London. *Working on a bill over the holidays? Jasper?* He stuck the letter in with the personal correspondence, though it might belong in the political file.

And that left the pile that Jasper had left specifically for Benjamin to "please look into."

There were some things that needn't take more than ten or twenty minutes if he didn't first have to hunt down whos, whats, and wheres. There were also daylong and weeklong projects that needed to be checked upon, or started, or cancelled. *God, Jasper.* He couldn't imagine the poor fellow's pain, discovering the disarray of his father's affairs.

Benjamin plodded his way through the pile on days when he did not have set chores on the property or in the village. Today's first task was a simple one. A bill from a London jeweler. *Past due.* Benjamin tucked away his annoyance. No gentleman paid his bills on time, yet they all wondered why their accounts were always in a tangle.

The next...*the deuce.* Benjamin glanced at Jasper's calendar, then flipped over the page. It was November, not October. And halfway through that.

Christmas party for the staff. *Please see to this.*

How long did it take to plan such a thing? Jasper's staff was huge. Was there to be music? Spirits? Gifts for any little ones? Where on earth did one start?

He struggled to decipher Jasper's scribble, then settled back with an irritated sigh. Jasper thought the staff deserved a special revel since the old earl's death had meant there had been no celebration the previous year. A *special* revel? Benjamin had never thrown a damn party in his life.

Chest burning, he set that aside and turned instead to the record of the month's rents, summarizing Wentworth's report in his own account book. Bradwell had wisely hired an assistant to handle collections. It put a bit of distance between the steward and the tenants' disgruntlement—no one liked rent collectors. Wentworth was a good man. His numbers always tallied. Benjamin tapped his pencil against the page. Jack Fowler had missed a payment.

He rubbed his chin, considering. Was it the first time or a pattern? He'd have to look into past reports and then pay Fowler a visit.

He shut the account book and returned to the problem of the Christmas party. He could not put this off. The hardworking staff deserved a decent celebration.

A potential solution occurred to him. No doubt Olivia was as cozy with the household as she was with the tenants. He groaned inwardly, mistrusting his own motives—their paths had not crossed in weeks. He pulled out his pocket watch. It was nearly 11:00. She was likely to be back from her morning ride.

He returned the pile of papers to the cabinet, then left the office to search the house.

Likely she could be found in the billiard room, but he would not approach her there. He hoped the parlor, but it was empty. He moved on to the ladies' sitting room. There they all were: Olivia, Georgiana, and Alice. He squelched his disappointment. Of course, he hadn't wanted to find her alone.

He was interrupting something. The ladies were all laughing the way men only did when foxed. While he hesitated in the doorway, Georgiana threw up her hands, letting knitting needles and some misshapen yarn thing slide from what little lap she had left onto the floor.

"It is a sock, not a cap!" she exclaimed, with exaggerated indignation.

"It can't be!" Alice teased. "You're having a baby, not a cow."

Olivia snorted, then dissolved into giggles. They were, all of them, adorable.

"Mr. Carroll?" Alice said, noticing him first. "Is something amiss?"

"No. Well, yes." Four heads were better than one. "Lord Iversley wishes me to…to plan a Christmas party for the staff." He turned up his hands to communicate his helplessness. Georgiana and Alice regarded him expectantly, as though awaiting an explanation of the problem, but Olivia let out a huff.

"He didn't give you a clue how to go about it, did he?" She pursed her mouth. "He probably has no clue himself."

"Please say you do. I'm at a complete loss where to start."

She rolled her eyes. "Your job is merely to loosen Jasper's purse strings. Peters and Mrs. Hardy do the planning."

The butler and housekeeper. He should have thought of them first, rather than envisioning a tête-à-tête with Olivia. "Good. I will speak with them. Thank you."

She went on, "Bradwell's role was always simply to stand between them and take the battering so they would not injure each other." She gave him a conspiratorial smile. "I imagine you are to throw around the words 'budget' and 'expense' then accede to most of their wishes."

"Most?"

"You'll have to refuse a few things, or they will think you and Jasper are both daft."

"I see." Surprisingly, he did. He didn't mention that it was to be a special revel, not wishing to remind them all of the sorrowful anniversary. He'd use his discretion when it came to granting requests. "Thank you. I'll find them directly."

He tore himself away from the cozy gathering and headed to the stairs. Going down, he met Reg coming up.

"Ah, there you are," Reg said. "I've been looking for you."

"I'm sorry, I—"

Reg cut him off. "No apology needed. I just wanted to ask if you'd heard from Jasper recently."

"Iversley has not communicated with me. No. Why?"

"Then I just wanted to inform you that Jasper"—he put a slight emphasis on the name—"will be home in two days. Apparently, Crispin's cottage is a little too rustic, and as Vanessa has forbidden him to fix anything, he is returning to his creature comforts posthaste."

Benjamin tried to glean from Reg's expression if there was an actual problem. He hoped the honeymooners had not fallen out.

Thankfully, Reg appeared more amused than worried.

"That all sounds rather Taverstonian," Benjamin said.

Reg grinned. "It is. The cottage was shamefully neglected. But Crispin wants to handle any renovations himself."

"From Portugal? While fighting a war?"

Reg nodded. "Exactly. So if Jasper puts anything to you—"

"I'm not getting in the middle of that." He pictured Jasper and Crispin in fighting mettle. Then he laughed out loud. In truth, no bond was ever tighter.

Reg chuckled along. Then, offhandedly, he asked, "Are you busy? Will you join us for luncheon?"

"I'm afraid I do have a rather pressing matter to attend to."

"Tea, then."

"I—" He shook his head. "That is my time to spend with Hannah."

"Bring her."

An ache spread throughout his whole body. He wanted to. That was the danger. How badly he wanted to. The earnestness of Reg's expression made him ache more. He was the brother who should understand.

He set his jaw and ground out, "Mr. Taverston, don't."

Reg flushed and his eyes darkened, wounded. He answered quietly. "All right, Mr. Carroll. I won't. But you can expect Iversley will."

CHAPTER EIGHT

JASPER'S MESSAGE HAD thrown the household into an uproar that increased rather than subsided over the next two days. Olivia was thrilled, naturally, that he and Vanessa would be home that evening. She missed Jasper, and it was high time for her to become better acquainted with her sister-in-law, but she didn't understand why his return was the cause of such fuss. It was only Jasper, even if he was the earl, arriving with his countess, to take up residence at the estate.

Every surface had to be swept and washed. Every bit of silver polished. Chandeliers were taken down and scrubbed till they sparkled. Draperies were brushed and sponged. Rugs were taken outside and beaten. Feasts were planned and bake ovens were kept full day and night. Cards were sent out to the neighbors. It was ridiculous.

The overwhelming scent of lemon oil and silver polish in every room made Olivia's head throb. She had taken an extralong ride that morning, but it hadn't sufficed. Still, she didn't dare go out again lest she miss Jasper and Vanessa's arrival. They said evening, but if the roads were clear and the horses quick, it could be any minute. She decided to go sit in the garden so she could breathe.

Although their garden was spectacularly lovely from early spring through late fall, this was not the time to admire it unless one was enamored of brown stems poking up from the earth among pruned, sad-appearing, hedges. Still, winding paths made it a good place for a brisk walk, since she could stroll a mile without ever being too far from the house.

She had chosen her route, a narrow shrub-lined path leading to a cluster of statuettes. According to Jasper, one of the cherubs looked just like her, though she had never seen the resemblance. She was certain he insisted just to vex her.

She stepped inside the gate and turned to latch it. To her surprise, she heard a child's whispery sing-song voice. It had to be Hannah. How lovely! Miss Jamison was so scrupulous in keeping the poor thing away from the family, it was if she thought they were all harboring spots.

Instead of her intended route, Olivia followed the sound and soon found Hannah sitting in the dirt at the foot of a lilac bush. She was dressed warmly in a red woolen dress and knit cap. The cap was askew, and two fat braids extended down to her shoulders. Miss Jamison reposed on a nearby bench, darning in her lap, eyes closed. Olivia felt a moment's peevishness at the laxity of her attention, but at least her eyes snapped open upon Olivia's approach.

"Good day, Miss Jamison," she said in her sunniest tone.

Miss Jamison bobbed to her feet to make a curtsy. "My lady."

"It is a lovely day, is it not?"

"Yes, indeed. I hope you don't mind us here. Mr. Carroll asked permission of Mr. Taverston."

"I don't mind! I'm glad of the company."

Olivia whisked off her cloak, laid it on the ground, and plunked herself beside the little girl, who started and shied.

"Hannah?" Olivia held out her hand. "I am Olivia. I am a friend of..." Good Heavens. What did the child call Benjamin? "...Mr. Carroll."

"Papa," Hannah said, with a toddler's confidence. Then she put a dirty trowel into Olivia's hand.

"Oh, Hannah, no!" Miss Jamison said.

Olivia laughed. "No, don't scold. It's very generous of her to share."

"We are trying to stay out of the way," Miss Jamison offered tentatively, seating herself again. "With all the bustle in the house."

"Yes. So am I." Olivia smiled. "I'm tempted to greet my brother like this." She held out her now-dirty hands and gestured to her cloak. "But I'm afraid it would scandalize Peters and Mrs. Hardy."

Miss Jamison smiled nervously. To spare her, Olivia turned her attention to Hannah, who was unintimidated by the fact that she was playing with one of the ladies of the house.

They took turns digging. Olivia loved the scent of freshly turned soil. She tried entering Hannah's imaginary world, where they were searching for fairies, who liked to hide with bunnies. All went well for quite some time, until Hannah suddenly became furious that the fairies remained hidden. She threw the trowel across the path with some force.

"Hannah!" Miss Jamison said, reddening. "I am so sorry, my lady. She is at the difficult stage where she will not nap even though she needs to."

Olivia stretched across the path to grab the trowel, then returned it to Hannah.

"I think it is fairy naptime," she said. "That is why we are having so much trouble finding them. Shall we hunt for buried treasure instead?"

Hannah cast her a scowl, her skepticism enhanced by dark, peaked eyebrows that contrasted sharply with her pale-ivory skin. She could be a fairy herself.

"Try here." Olivia pointed to a shallow hole they had begun and then discarded. "We will look for gold. I'm sure pirates have left some."

"No," Hannah said firmly. Nevertheless, she began to dig. "Fairies." She began singing again to herself, a muddle of words Olivia could not distinguish, except for "king" and "Papa" and "bunny."

Olivia helped by scooping out dirt and pebbles with her hands, accomplishing more than Hannah did with her trowel. She enjoyed the game immensely. She was too old to play but had been an imaginative child and regretted, at times, that make-believe was frowned upon in the adult world. Maybe it was selfish, but she wished Benjamin wouldn't be so strict. It wasn't any of her business, of course, but Benjamin was busy all day and Miss Jamison was not exactly lively.

As these thoughts spun through her head, she noticed Hannah again growing petulant. So she sneaked a pin from her hair and, after distracting the girl with a gesture, dropped the pin into the hole and sprinkled dirt over it.

"No fairies yet, but maybe fairy gold," she suggested. "Keep looking."

Hannah plunged the trowel into the hole.

"Oh, Hannah! Look! You found it!"

While the child laughed and squirmed, Olivia brushed the dirt from the pin.

"Treasure!" she exclaimed. "You found gold!"

The game was not a new one. Crispin used to bury pirate treasure all over the estate for Olivia and Reg to "discover." She imagined it to have universal appeal, but Hannah appeared confused. Treasure and gold were apparently not in her vocabulary. Trying to hold Hannah's interest, she threaded the pin in and out of one of the girl's braids until it held firm.

"Very pretty," Olivia said, letting the braid rest on Hannah's shoulder.

Hannah reached out a grubby hand and patted Olivia's hair. "Pretty."

Olivia smiled. "Thank you."

At that moment, she heard the sound of the gate banging and pattering footsteps. In a few moments, Tansy appeared, breathing heavily.

"Oh, Lady Olivia. Here you are! Your mother sent me to find

you and I've been looking all over!"

"I've been here. What is it?

"A rider has come. The earl will be here within the hour."

"Oh!" Olivia scrambled to her feet, suddenly embarrassed by her soiled gown and dirt-encrusted hands. "Oh, good heavens." She bent over to address Hannah. "I'm sorry, love. I have to run." Then straightened. "Excuse me, Miss Jamison."

Hurrying along with Tansy, Olivia scolded herself for foolishness. It did no good to complain her brothers still treated her like a child if she continued to act like one.

As PER TRADITION, the entire household lined up in the drive to meet their new countess, even though several of them had already glimpsed her in the days before the wedding when she was merely Mrs. Wardrip. And several more had waited upon her at the wedding breakfast. But now, she was undeniably the countess, and tradition must be maintained.

Olivia stood between Mama and Georgiana. Mama only nodded, but Olivia and Georgiana dropped curtsies along with everyone else. The display was not silly. It was necessary. Given Vanessa's history, it was important to accord her their utmost respect to indicate that everyone else must also.

Head held high, Vanessa walked the long gauntlet of servants, finding a word for each of them. It took a long time.

It surprised Olivia to note that Fergus, a fine groom but young, stood beside George, who ruled the stables. George was gruff and growing old, but there was nothing he did not know about horses. Henley, who was second after George, should have been next to him. Henley was good with horses, but he was a nasty fellow who believed women did not belong anywhere near the stables. He had always tried to bring out spiritless mounts for Olivia and once, to her face, said it didn't matter to him if she cracked open her head, so long as he was not blamed for it. Olivia preferred to fight her own battles, generally, but this she reported to Jasper. Who apparently had words with Henley because he ceased being openly disrespectful. It was strange that he would let Fergus stand in his place.

But that was not her concern. Not today.

She nudged Alice's arm. She seemed a bit overawed by the ceremony and Olivia wanted to include her as family. She *was* family.

"Doesn't Vanessa look marvelous?"

Olivia's new sister wore traveling clothes that were plain but of obvious quality. And, when she'd stepped down from the coach, Olivia had caught sight of her boots, a yellowish leather tooled with what she suspected were roses.

Alice nodded. "Jasper looks fine too."

They snickered together. He always did.

When the couple reached the end of the line of servants, Jasper dismissed them all then strode over to Benjamin, who had been standing apart. Olivia couldn't hear what they said, but Jasper clapped him on the shoulder and laughed, so it must have been more than just cordial. Benjamin bowed and took a step back but did not otherwise move until Jasper took Vanessa by the elbow and walked toward the family. Then Benjamin melted away, following the retreating servants. Olivia felt a twinge of disappointment. She'd hoped Jasper would draw him into their circle. Reg had tried already and failed.

"Let us clean up a bit," Jasper said, gesturing to himself as he reached them. Olivia snorted. His clothes were immaculate, he smelled of sandalwood, and he had not a shining blond hair out of place. "Then I think tea? If we are not too late?"

Mama laughed. "You may order tea at midnight, if you like, Jasper. But no, you are not late. Go. Change your clothes. I'll speak to Mrs. Hardy, and we can meet in the parlor in an hour." She looked buoyant. "It is so good to have everyone together again." Her smile faltered. "If only Crispin were here."

And Papa, Olivia thought. But she didn't want to be the one to inject grief into celebration.

An hour was good. She could soak her hands in hot water first. Her gloves hid the dirt under her nails that had not completely come out with simple scrubbing. If she wore gloves while eating tea cakes with her brothers, Mama would want to know why. And "I was playing in the dirt, Mama," was not an acceptable answer.

⋙⋘

SOAKED CLEAN AND gloveless, running late, Olivia dashed toward the main stairway, but halted when Benjamin emerged from around the staircase and stepped in front of her.

"Benjamin!" she gasped, almost skidding.

"Lady Olivia," he said harshly, "may I have a word?"

"Well, yes, of course—"

"This is yours." He pulled her hairpin from inside his jacket and thrust it forward, nearly jabbing it into the hand she stretched out to receive it. She pulled back without taking it.

"Oh! But it is merely a hairpin." Why on earth was he so angry? "Hannah may keep it."

"She may not. She is far too young for frivolous vanities—"

"For pity's sake." She glared. What did it mean to him that she had at least a half dozen of these "frivolous vanities" stuck around in various parts of her head? "It is a toy to her. Not an adornment."

"Nor do I wish her exposed to greed and gold lust when she is not even three!" He was not shouting, but his voice was so hard that its quiet was worse. "You should be grateful she is young enough that tragic memories have not stayed with her. Or your foolish game could have reroused night terrors that took months to quell!"

"Night terrors?" she whispered.

He turned his head. She could see a muscle twitching in his jaw. His whole body was tense. Even his fists were clenched.

"I'm sorry, Mr. Carroll. I would never intentionally have frightened her."

"The harm you do is never intentional."

Heat spread up from her neck to her hairline. What harm? Hannah had not appeared frightened while they were playing. And Benjamin said himself that her memories had not stayed with her.

She set her own jaw. "I have apologized for whatever thoughtless crime you think I have committed by entertaining your charge. But I will not continue to beg your pardon for unspecified harms when I believe I am guiltless."

He faced her again, his muscle still ticking. "I will thank you to leave Hannah to Miss Jamison's care and to mine."

It felt so much like a slap that her head snapped back. His eyes widened, then his gaze dropped.

"Please don't give her any more gifts," he murmured. He placed the hairpin against her palm and, with surprising gentleness, closed her fingers around it. The warmth of his hand rippled through her. She wanted to speak but couldn't think of the right words to say.

He let go and walked away, taking the warmth away with him.

CHAPTER NINE

H E WAS NOT wrong. Benjamin knew he was not wrong. Hannah's mother was dead because of his gold lust. They had nearly all died. It was not a game.

But Olivia didn't know that. There was no excuse for snapping at her.

However, remorse—even if he could make amends, which he doubted—was not a priority. Jasper was back, and he was a conscientious lord who meant to stay abreast of his estate's affairs. That meant Benjamin's time was fully occupied.

For three or four hours each morning, Benjamin joined him in his study. Even though it was December, the spacious room was warm and full of morning light. Jasper sat behind a formidable desk of an unusual honey-colored maple. Nothing was changed from the old earl's time, not that Benjamin could discern, except for Jasper's square-armed chair, whose lack of wear and faint scent of leather spoke of newness. Benjamin's old chair was a lightweight thing he could pull up to the desk, making it easy for them to put their heads together.

After Jasper did his part, he dismissed Benjamin, leaving him to follow up on what they had begun. Jasper either remained in the study to read his political papers, or left to attend to other matters.

In addition to paperwork, every few days they rode about the property. Jasper pointed out what needed attention, or, more often now, Benjamin pointed out things to him. They got on comfortably even if Jasper persisted in calling him Benjamin and he consistently responded with "Iversley," or worse, "my lord."

There had been only two bothersome exchanges. Bothersome to Benjamin, who felt put in his place. True to form, Jasper seemed to consider each incident settled and done.

The first was when Jasper asked what had happened with Everet.

"Taken care of," Benjamin replied.

To his discomfiture, Jasper regarded him with a flat stare until he explained. Unlike Olivia's quick understanding, Jasper was angered.

"Why," he asked, "would you think I would wish to be a party to your selling of counterfeit pelts to some crook in London?"

When he put it like that... "Technically, Iversley, the animals are yours. It would be criminal for Everet to sell your property and pocket all the proceeds."

"*You* would not take a percentage."

"Of course not!"

"But you imagine I would sell my good name for a few shillings?"

"No one will know—"

"Oh, for God's sake, Benjamin. If I had thought you would engage in 'no one will know,' I would not have—" He halted before finishing the thought. Then said, jaw tight, "Is there anything else *I* should know?"

Benjamin made a quick accounting of his conscience, then said, "No, my lord."

"All right." Jasper pulled on his earlobe, a habit that meant he was thinking. His scowl slowly faded. "If you feel you must sell the pelts, give all the ill-gotten gains to Everet. I suppose it is better than his dealing in live badgers. But Benjamin, don't do anything like this again."

And then, another morning, they had an even more uncomfortable discussion.

Before settling in to the day's work, Jasper looked up from the coffee cup poised at his lips. "I understand you fired Henley?"

"Yes, my lord." He hesitated. "I'm afraid it was necessary."

"Was he bothering Olivia again?"

Bloody hell! "What in the blazes do you mean by *again?*"

Jasper's eyes narrowed. He set down his cup. "He made disparaging remarks about ladies riding. Olivia took offense. It wasn't anything…depraved. I told him to stop and assumed he did." His mouth pursed. "If Olivia didn't complain about him, what was the trouble? You know George has come to rely upon him, and he was in line to take over."

Benjamin ground his teeth. He had walked into the stable the day before Jasper's return to hear Henley shooting his mouth off. He called Vanessa "the countess-whore." Thankfully, none of the other grooms laughed or he would have fired the lot of them. Fergus told Henley to shove it. Henley said something even ruder. Benjamin stepped into the fray and fired Henley on the spot. Then told George to promote Fergus. That last might have been overstepping.

Jasper awaited an answer and appeared peeved that it was slow in coming.

Carefully, Benjamin said, "Henley insulted the countess. I will not repeat what he said, so don't ask."

Jasper's face changed. Worried. Then angry. "The devil! I should have anticipated something like this. Were any others involved?"

"Not that I could tell. The young man, Fergus, took issue. But I stepped in before it went further."

"Henley left without incident?"

"I paid his back wages, but gave him no reference. George said he left for London in the morning."

Jasper nodded. "Good." Then: "Don't say anything to anyone else. It will only upset them."

Jasper should not have felt the need to say that. A steward's job required discretion.

"And Benjamin?"

"Yes, my lord?"

Jasper gave him a more direct look. "If Olivia had needed protection, I would have seen to it."

Jasper definitely should not have felt the need to say that.

"Of course, my lord."

Thankfully, Jasper had a gift for making a point without dwelling on it. Aside from those two incidents, those caveats, they worked together very well. At least, they were learning how to work well together.

⫸⫷

WHENEVER ONE TASK on the estate was completed, two more sprang up, which made it easy for Benjamin to justify avoiding Olivia. He was busy. He knew he owed her an apology. If he could apologize without explaining himself, he would, but she deserved both, and might not accept one without the other.

A delegation of villagers and tenants came to ask Iversley to allow them to cut firewood for the winter. Another tradition. The earl granted permission as a matter of course. But it was evidently Benjamin's job to pick the coppice and mark which trees they might take. That had busied him for three days that he had intended to spend doing other things. Now he felt he'd fallen behind.

Finally, he found a spare afternoon to ride over to Jack Fowler's, after crawling through three years of Wentworth's receipt books and finding only one long-ago incidence of late payment.

Nothing appeared amiss in the vicinity of the cottage. However, when Jack opened the door and saw Benjamin standing there, his eyes darted away as though guilty of something. He chewed his lip, then mumbled, "Come in, Mr. Carroll."

Benjamin glanced around the room looking for evidence of trouble, but lit instead upon Olivia, seated at the table with the Fowlers' two little boys. They had a board and pegs between them, playing Fox and Geese. Mrs. Fowler was at the sink. When she turned around, he saw that she limped. That was new.

He swept the cap from his head. "Excuse me for interrupting." Mrs. Fowler was regarding him with the same unease as her husband. Olivia's expression was distant. Reserved.

"You'll be wanting the rent, I'spect," Jack said, gesturing for Benjamin to move with him over to the wall. He glanced quickly at his boys, then back at Benjamin with a pleading look.

"Well, no, I—" Benjamin halted. He hadn't come to collect. That was Wentworth's job. He'd come only to see what was the matter, and if he could assist. He certainly had no intention of shaming the man in front of his children. *God.* He had enough bitter memories of his own father being dunned. "I'm only paying calls."

Olivia tapped the board, laughing, "Here now, look at that, Sam!" drawing the boys' attention back to the game.

Grateful to her for distracting them, he gathered his scattered thoughts and took a stab at salvaging the situation. "I'd heard…I thought I'd heard that Mrs. Fowler was injured." She *was* limping; that he could see.

Mrs. Fowler nodded. "I dropped a pot. Cracked my foot. But it's getting better."

Jack hurried over to her, then grabbed a lidded bowl from behind the sink. "I got half of it here," he said, pouring out a handful of coins. He spoke very quietly. "The rest next week, Mr. Carroll. I'm good for my word." He held out the money.

Benjamin's neck grew hot. Equally soft-voiced, he said, "I didn't come to harass you. Only to see if you and Mrs. Fowler needed anything." He would have come sooner, *if he had known.* He pocketed the coin. He would offer to forgive the rest, but could not do so without consulting Jasper. He was going about this whole thing ass-backwards.

Mrs. Fowler smiled, relieved. "We're all right, Mr. Carroll. Lady Olivia brought us apples and pillows. And the Widow Tabor has been helping."

So they'd hired Gert. That was why they were behind.

"Well," he said, clearing his throat, "Mrs. Fowler, I'm glad you're on the mend. I won't take any more of your time." Then, because it was the right thing to do, he said, "Lady Olivia, if you are returning home, I'd be honored to escort you." *Honored?* He should have said "pleased."

She gave him a cool look. "No, thank you. We are not yet finished with our game."

She was angry with him. Of course she was. He was angry with himself. If he hadn't been hiding from her, surely she would have said something to him about all this. It would have saved him hours of combing through old receipts, and spared them all this embarrassing encounter. And he could have arranged for a postponement of the rent.

He would have to find a way to apologize. Soon. But obviously, not now.

He stepped to the door, made her a short bow, and nodded to the Fowlers. "Good day to you."

THE STAFF'S CHRISTMAS party had taken place yesterday evening. The day before Christmas Eve. By tradition.

Thankfully, Mrs. Hardy and Peters had things well in hand. Benjamin's only difficulty had been deciding what to refuse since their requests were so reasonable. Use of the ballroom. Food. They wanted two fiddlers for a couple of hours of country dancing. And drink. Arbitrarily, Benjamin had made them accept ale instead of rum punch. Sweets and whistles for the little ones. He said no to a large number of candles, which he suspected they requested just to give him something to reject. There were lamps enough in the ballroom at one tenth the cost.

By the noise, they had all enjoyed themselves. He did not attend. He didn't want them to think he was spying.

The Taverstons had cleared out to dine with the rector and his wife. This, too, was something he'd learned they had always done. Benjamin had only spent one winter's fortnight at Chaumbers in his younger days, one which did not include Christmas. His mother wished him home for that and he dutifully went. He'd resented it at the time, but now was glad he had set no precedent. The rector had not thought to invite him, so he did not have to decline.

Today, Christmas Eve, Jasper had informed him he was not to work. So he bundled Hannah up in her warmest dress, wrapped her in a cloak, and took her out riding, setting her in the saddle before him on Bluebell. They went out to the folly, a pretend remnant of a medieval abbey. Of course, Hannah was too little to appreciate its whimsy. But there were heaped stones to climb upon and a scattering of snow to push into piles. And she loved being on the pony.

It was too cold to stay out long. Moreover, the sky darkened early. So he reluctantly returned to the stables. He left the pony to Fergus's care and carried Hannah back to the house, soundly sleeping in his arms. The minute he stepped through the door, a footman approached.

"Mr. Carroll, Lord Iversley requires you in his study."

"Of course."

Bother. He had told Miss Jamison she was free for the day. Well, it was Christmas Eve. Jasper wouldn't fault him for carting Hannah along. He climbed the stairs, careful not to wake her. Then knocked lightly upon the study door.

"Come," Jasper said.

When Benjamin entered the room, Jasper's face softened.

"Sleeping?" he whispered.

Benjamin nodded.

"Well, I won't keep you. Supper is at eight o'clock. Followed by games in the parlor. You are to bring Hannah and Miss Jamison."

"I—"

"That is not a question. Are we understood?"

"Yes." He felt oddly grateful to be given no option.

"Good." Jasper smiled. "Then you may go."

HE WAS ASSIGNED a seat between Hannah and Alice. Miss Jamison had Hannah's other side. A clever arrangement to corral her. However, the mite was so well rested after a long nap, that her behavior was exceptional. Or perhaps it merely seemed so to him, fond father that he was.

Olivia was a long diagonal away, between Georgiana and the dowager. They all still wore mourning, but Olivia had a red ribbon in her hair and a festive glint in her eyes. He liked to see her happy.

One could not be reserved at a Taverston supper table. Not when surrounded by so much laughter and love. For a while, they tried to guess who was Hazard's Christmas host. The clues—country house, warm fire, shaggy hounds, biscuits, and tea—were no help. His presence was clearly missed. And more so Crispin's. After a few "just like Crispin" reminiscences, the Taverstons referred to his most recent letter. He had groused that because of Jasper's wedding, he'd missed Wellington's crossing the border into France. He could not believe "the Peer" had not waited for him! But he would not hold the inconvenient timing of the wedding against Jasper since there was still work ahead for the army.

"How the devil is Boney still holding on?" Reg mused. "After such a sound thrashing in Russia? And Leipzig?"

"The man has the devil's own luck," Jasper said. Then he

waved his hand to end the discussion. It was not for Christmas Eve.

The food was exceptional. A large joint of beef. Fresh bread. Mashed turnips. Dried berries and cream. Pickled asparaguses. Blood pudding. He could go on. An overly attentive footman topped off his wine glass practically every time he picked it up and set it down. He'd lost track of how much he had imbibed until his ears started to thrum.

After the final course, which included a towering cake, a bite of which made Hannah squeal with delight, and a round of claret, the dowager suggested they retire to the drawing room. Miss Jamison offered to take Hannah back to the south wing, but Vanessa said, "Oh, no. Miss Jamison, we want you with us." Benjamin could not allow her to withdraw after that. Especially not when she flushed with evident pleasure.

They all rose from the table. Benjamin took Hannah's hand, but before they reached the door, Reg swooped down upon them and scooped her up.

"Practice," he said, carting her off, calling, "Georgiana, look what I've got!"

Benjamin found himself walking beside Olivia. He wasn't sure how. He thought she might have waited for him, but his head was foggy enough that he might have hurried to catch up to her. High time he got this over with.

"Olivia." God damn him. He was foxed. "*Lady* Olivia."

She inclined her head. "Mr. Carroll?"

"I should apologize."

Her brow furrowed. "For?"

"For scolding you for being kind to Hannah." That sounded right. Right enough.

"Seeing as it is Christmas, I will accept your apology." She sounded more curious than angry.

"I should also explain."

"Yes? Well, I am listening."

"Oh, God." Why had he said that? "I should, but I won't.

Damn. I mean—" Horrified, he realized he had just sworn at her. "Pardon me."

"Mr. Carroll, I believe you may be bosky." Her eyes were wide with amusement. And her lips curled. God, those lips.

"Your footman was overgenerous."

She laughed. "Fie, sir! Blaming the footman?"

"Yes. No." He smiled awkwardly, aware he was making an idiot of himself. "I should have paid more attention."

"Benjamin!" Jasper called over his shoulder. "Come help me haul the card table into the drawing room. I had the parlor arranged, but Mother says drawing room."

"The parlor is too drafty," the dowager said. "I don't want Georgiana catching a chill."

"That is unlikely." Georgiana half-laughed, half-groaned. "I feel as though I'm being cooked like tomorrow's goose."

"Mother says drawing room," Jasper insisted. Then, laughing, "Benjamin, come along."

Benjamin hurried forward, a smile stretched across his face. Were they all a bit bosky? Or had Jasper just ordered him away from Olivia?

CHAPTER TEN

OLIVIA SIMPLY WANTED to relax and enjoy her last Taverston family Christmas. She had tried to be lively, cheerful, and mature when Benjamin approached her to apologize, but she didn't know what to think when he said he *should* explain himself but *wouldn't*. That made it worse. However, watching Benjamin with Jasper as they tried to wrestle the card table across the threshold gave her to conclude that the men were all just drunk. Even Reg was speaking more loudly and slower than usual, as he and Georgiana set up a chessboard in a corner. Chess. That must be Georgiana's influence. Reg had never been fond of chess.

"Oh!" Alice cried out in exasperation, making Olivia jump. "Turn it on its side and lead with the legs. For heaven's sake!"

After a burst of laughter, Jasper and Benjamin managed to tilt the table and thread two legs through the door, then turn it to maneuver the rest. Benjamin was in front, walking backwards. The close fit of his jacket, cut tight to form, emphasized his muscular shoulders. Olivia felt shy, watching, but could not look away.

At last, they were through the door and situated the table close to the fire.

"Piquet?" Jasper said. Benjamin nodded. They sat down to play.

The ladies, aside from Georgiana, seated themselves near the window. Vanessa ignored the empty chair beside Olivia to sit next to Mama. Olivia could swear her sister-in-law was avoiding her. Vanessa never sought her out. They hadn't had one private conversation. She refused any invitations to ride—not even to meet the tenants. It was puzzling.

But for now, they all fussed together over Hannah, who curled in Miss Jamison's lap on the davenport, thumb in her mouth, eyelids heavy.

"I suppose I'll have to break her of that after Christmas. She will be three in May and that is too old to be sucking her thumb," Miss Jamison said.

"I suspect she will abandon it on her own before then," Mama said. "Most children do. I must say, I've never seen the harm in it."

Miss Jamison smiled. "That is my sentiment exactly. But I've worked for some who have been insistent to the point of, well, of cruelty to the little ones."

Then Mama began to gently draw Miss Jamison out. She had a sister, married to a curate in a small town south of London. She had helped raise their five, then began her career nannying for others. She adored her little charges, but they grew up too fast, so she was always moving on. Alice went very still and her eyes dulled. *Was she comparing her situation to Miss Jamison's?*

Vanessa changed the slightly melancholy subject by saying, "It will soon be too cold for playing in the garden. You must make use of more of this home. Too much of it lies empty."

Miss Jamison flushed. "That is very kind of you, my lady. But it is Mr. Carroll's decision, and he feels it is better if Hannah is not underfoot."

And he felt it was better if people did not play games with her or give her gifts.

Mama said, "Well, he cannot object to you bringing her down to the dower house. You and I can have tea. I would appreciate the company."

"Oh! You rogue!" Jasper cried out, slapping his cards on the table. "You have been practicing."

Benjamin smiled a bit wolfishly. Evidently, he hadn't heard Mama, though she had spoken loudly enough that he might have. Olivia wondered if Mama would repeat herself, but whatever might have followed was interrupted by thudding footsteps in the hall, followed by Peters's appearance in the doorway. Alice gave a small gasp, and for a moment, her face seemed to brighten.

"My lord—" Peters began.

The next instant, Crispin slid past him. "Peters, my man, you will have to learn to walk faster."

"Captain Taverston is here, my lord," Peters finished, eyes glowing with pleasure.

The room erupted in a chorus of "Crispin!" with Jasper adding wryly, "And *that* is 'just like Crispin'" while Crispin brushed the light dusting of snow from the shoulders of his greatcoat then stripped off his wet gloves.

Olivia's heart fairly burst. She didn't have a favorite brother, of course, but if she did, he had just come home.

Mama, all smiles, said, "It would be lovely if you were to give us some warning for once. Why didn't you let us know you would be here? Peters, please make sure Captain Taverston's room is made ready."

"It is being attended to, my lady."

Crispin peeled off his aged coat and a battered tricorn hat that Olivia had never seen before, and handed them to Peters along with his gloves. A messy tangle of blond hair, half falling out the leather thong he'd used to tie it back, drooped against his shoulders. Beneath the outerwear, he wore his redcoat with its gold braid and shiny brass buttons, black pantaloons, and boots that were coated with mud. He looked every inch the returning hero and Olivia was thrilled.

"I didn't know I would be here until about seven hours ago. If I had waited to send a letter, you would have *it* but not *me*!" He crossed the room to Mama, then bent down to give her a quick kiss on the cheek. "I'm supposed to be in London, but so are a lot of other men who are not there, so I thought I may as well not be either."

"Meaning?" Jasper asked, raising one eyebrow.

"Meaning I came to London with two saddlebags full of letters, at least half from Wellington and so probably more than just Christmas greetings, and I was supposed to wander about London playing postman. Moreover, I had reports to make. But no one was at home to hear them." His smirk turned into a scowl of irritation. "It is as though no one in England remembers there is a war being fought."

"We remember," Vanessa said in a low tone.

"Yes, well," Crispin gave her a grateful look. "I should not complain. It gave me a day or two to come here."

"A day or two?" Jasper said. "Surely—"

"Surely by then you will be sick of me."

Olivia burst out, "Crispin, please say you will stay through the New Year. It is only a week!"

"Ah, Livvy-pet." He sighed. "Perhaps we will be lucky and be blizzarded in." Then he turned and focused his full attention on Georgiana. "You are the real reason I am here."

Georgiana colored, her hand going to her swollen belly. "Well, as you can see, you are too early. You must return to us in February."

"Oh, I am not here to see little Arthur."

"We are *not* naming our child after Wellington," Reg said gruffly, but his eyes were laughing.

"We will see," Crispin said, moving toward their corner. "Although I am glad to note you are in health, Georgiana, I came for a different reason entirely." He pulled a piece of paper from inside his jacket, unfolded it, and held it out. "One of the men I was to see in London, who was not there, was supposed to have a look at this. Rather than chase him down God-knows-where, I thought I might better show it to you."

"What is it?" Reg asked, leaning in as Georgiana took it.

"A page full of numbers." She raised her eyes to Crispin in a question. Olivia and everyone else held silent, waiting for the odd scene to make sense.

"Wellington took it off a captured frog. It is a cipher. We all have taken a crack at it, but no one made any headway."

Reg scowled so darkly, Olivia thought for a moment he might rise and take a swing at their brother, but Georgiana bent her head over the page almost eagerly.

Jasper said, "What are you playing at, Crispin?"

"Georgiana is good at puzzles," he said mildly.

"But not war games," Reg erupted. "On Christmas Eve, no less. To pressure her with *spying*, in her condition—"

Crispin waved a dismissive hand. "I'm not pressuring her. The scrap is more than a month old. If it were urgent, it is not anymore. But it is a new cipher. Or possibly a resurrected old cipher, now equally opaque." A weary, frustrated note crept into his voice. "And Wellington has tasked me with *deciphering* before we run up against it again."

"An old cipher?" Georgiana asked.

"Numbers substituting for letters. We are generally more sophisticated now. Code books. Grills. Fences."

Georgiana looked bewildered. "Fences?"

"You run your letters up and down the rails. Then write out the letters along the top, middle, bottom…like this." He took the scrap back and flipped it over. "Pencil?" Reg fished one from his jacket and put it in his hand. Crispin bent over the table and scribbled something.

"Yes, I see," Georgiana said, a bit impatiently. "But these are numbers, not letters."

"Which is why I brought it to you." He straightened. "Our best fellow in the field was injured and is now stupid with laudanum. Our man in London is not in London." He shook his head. "I just thought…"

"Well, then, hush," Georgiana said, peering at the page again. "And don't watch me. I will be flustered."

Almost as one, they all jerked their heads away.

"Come, Livvy," Crispin said, crossing the room again. "Make a fourth with us. We'll play whist." As she stood, he added, "You must be thrilled. London, finally, in February?"

She shook her head. "I'm having some dresses made here. I don't have to go until April."

His gaze sharpened, and she felt herself redden. "Have to" was the wrong choice of words.

"Ah." He gave a short nod. "A grand entrance. Heightening the ton's anticipation. Excellent plan of attack." His eyes went to Vanessa. "Fearless and unapologetic."

Vanessa started. Her face went slack. Vague. Olivia felt a bit vague as well. It wasn't a *plan*. They didn't have a plan. But Crispin evidently believed that they needed one.

She beckoned to Vanessa with a tilt of her head. "You must join us too. We can play loo instead of whist."

Vanessa bit her lip. "I have no head for cards tonight, but thank you."

Another "no." This was becoming…uncomfortable. It wasn't as if Vanessa avoided everyone. She *had* gone with Mama and Georgiana into the village to visit the shops when Olivia was otherwise occupied. She swallowed a sharp lump in her throat.

Well, fine. She had no experience of the world. Vanessa probably found her uninteresting and unbearably young. But the gossips would eat that up when they got to London. *The Countess cutting Iversley's sister? It should be the other way around.*

Crispin caught her arm and led her to the card table where she was obliged to sit next to Benjamin, who nodded to acknowledge her but didn't smile. If anything, he looked wary. Everyone was avoiding her!

Jasper dealt out their hands. They didn't bother bidding since they were not paying much attention to the game. Rather they all kept stealing looks at Georgiana. She whispered to Reg, who fetched her more paper; then she made marks, frowned ferociously, and occasionally *tsked* her tongue.

"*Eeesht*, Olivia," Crispin winced. "Why would you play a

knave when I just played a queen?"

"Sorry." Her cheeks warmed.

"You can take it back," Benjamin offered.

"Watch out." Jasper laughed. "She gets angry if you condescend."

To prove Jasper wrong, she snatched back her card and laid down a three.

"Oh!" Georgiana gasped. They turned to see her flip over her paper and begin scratching away upon it, a strange look in her eyes. Then she said, "no," several times. Then "yes!" Then she blurted, "Oh, but it is in French."

Crispin laughed. "One would hope so. What does it say?"

She pushed back a loosened lock of hair with the end of the pen. "In English it would read 'The leopard is at Vera watch the Nivelle.'" She glanced up. "Does that mean anything?"

Crispin dropped his cards and beamed so hard it gave Olivia a chill.

"The French call Wellington the leopard. We were at Vera. We took it. And then, Nivelle. I imagine this missive was supposed to have made it to Soult before we did."

Benjamin set his cards, then his arms, on the table. His left arm rested so close to her right arm that she could feel his heat.

Crispin rose and went to Georgiana. "Show me." He bent over her to see what she'd done.

"It is simple, really," she said. "There are far too many numbers here for an alphabetical substitution. So I had to get rid of some. If you look," she pointed to something with her pen, "there are various strings of numbers that add up to eight. Cross those out," she flipped over the paper, "and you are left with these numbers and these stops. Then you run the numbers up and down the fence."

Olivia had no idea what Georgiana was saying, but Crispin must have understood some of it because his frown was intent. "*L* is the twelfth number in the alphabet. That is a seventeen."

"Yes, but three *Q*'s? No message would have three *Q*'s. And there are not three *U*'s. So you have to subtract five. Or add two or three, but it didn't work with three *S*'s or three *T*'s, which I also considered."

Crispin laughed, a peeved sort of laugh. "Of course. Eliminate strings of eight. Subtract five. How on earth did you come up with this?"

Olivia glanced at Benjamin to see if he, too, was awed, but found him looking at *her*. He blinked and shifted his attention to Georgiana, but did not move his arm away and neither did she.

Georgiana was flushed. "It is just seeing the patterns. And a little trial and error."

Crispin gaped a moment, then he dropped into a nearby chair, stretched his legs in front of him, and said, "You are a marvel. Reg, may I take her back with me?"

"No. And because I suspect you are serious, I will say again, no."

"Wellington will be pleased. He might even deign to say so." Crispin's smile was so broad, Olivia could see a mouthful of teeth. Then it faltered. "But the next string could be different. Adding to six instead of eight. Or there will not be three *Q*'s." He frowned, rubbing his chin. "I suppose now that we know what type of cipher we are trying to decode...but I don't know anyone who would see the patterns as quickly as you do."

Georgiana shook her head. "It was actually quite simple. Whoever constructed it must have been in a hurry."

Crispin laughed. He stood again, took up Georgiana's hand, and planted a kiss on the back of it. With an earnestness that was unlike him, he said, "Your country thanks you."

"Don't be silly."

"I am not." He turned around, letting his gaze pass over them all. "None of this is to leave this room. If it turns up in the *London Times*, as these things are wont to do, all Georgiana's efforts are for naught." He paused a moment, as if suddenly noticing Miss Jamison, whom he did not know. "Please," he said, eyes darkening. "Not a word to anyone."

Despite the "please," Olivia thought he sounded threatening. Everyone else must have thought so also because they all murmured assurances, either staring at him wide-eyed or looking down at their feet.

Crispin nodded briskly, then said, "Now I must go down to the kitchen and forage. I haven't eaten since daybreak."

"Sit," Mama said. "We will send for a plate."

He grimaced. "No. My way is better." He took a few steps for the door. "And then I am off to find my bed."

Jasper rose and stepped into his path. "Will you be kind enough to assure us you will still be here in the morning?"

Crispin drew in a breath, then made a mocking bow. "As you wish, Iversley. My intention is to attend church services in the morning. Then eat Christmas supper with my loving family. After that, my plans depend upon the weather. May I take my leave now?"

Jasper stood aside. "I only half trust you are telling the truth."

Crispin left, laughing. All the energy went out of the room with him.

Georgiana got up, pushing a fist to her back. "I'm afraid I must retire also."

Reg jumped to his feet, ready to assist.

Miss Jamison said, "Hannah is fair worn out. Thank you, for including us—"

"Is she sleeping? I'll carry her," Benjamin said, rising quickly. His arm brushed Olivia's. Had he done it on purpose? Or might he think she had?

They all shuffled about, saying their goodnights. Olivia walked down the corridor of the family's wing alongside Alice until they reached Alice's door. She seemed as pensive as Olivia felt, though surely, they had different reasons.

As Alice put a hand to her door, she murmured, "Merry Christmas," in a tone that was anything but merry.

Olivia couldn't bear to see her downcast on Christmas Eve. Since they were now alone, she asked, "Alice, did Miss Jamison's story disturb you?"

She looked confused for a moment, then shook her head. "Oh, that. Momentarily."

"But *you* won't be a nanny—"

Alice drew back and laughed a bit indignantly. "Well, I might, but I wasn't disturbed for myself. It's that this is the plight of so many women." Then she tossed her head. "It's not something *you* could ever fathom. If the impossible were to happen and you don't marry, your brothers will fight over who *gets to* take you in, not who *must* support you." Her expression turned abashed. "I'm sorry to speechify. If I seem deficient in holiday spirit, it has nothing to do with Miss Jamison."

"Then—"

"It's just that when Crispin arrived, I thought for a moment it might be Hazard." Stunned, Olivia gaped, and Alice laughed. "I know, I know! It's *Crispin*! I'm not *disappointed* to see him. But I've been wanting to talk to Hazard." She sniffed. "I can't write to him, obviously, which is ridiculous." Glancing away, she drew in a deep breath, then sighed. "Well. Crispin will do. Merry Christmas, Olivia." She opened her door and went into her chamber.

"Merry Christmas." Olivia stood another moment, regarding the closing door. Then she snorted. Crispin would *do*?

CHAPTER ELEVEN

W*HAT A BIZARRE* *Christmas Eve*, Benjamin thought, still ruminating on the events of the previous night. The Taverstons never failed to amaze. How on earth had Crispin known of Georgiana's unusual talent? *Good at puzzles?* An absurd understatement. Yet the only one who had not been surprised had been Reg.

At least the drama had kept the attention off *him*, seeing as he could not keep his where it belonged. He felt he'd spent the entire evening staring at Olivia, leaning close, captivated by the festive perfume of seasonal greenery and cinnamon that seemed to cling to her.

The weather on Christmas morning was abysmal, with sleet rather than snow. Benjamin wondered if Crispin could be stranded at Chaumbers after all. Wellington might be peeved, but it would make a nice Christmas present for Olivia. For all of the Taverstons.

Because of the cold and wet, they were taking carriages to church instead of walking the two miles into the village. The earl's coach carried the family while Benjamin, Hannah, and Miss Jamison followed in a slightly humbler conveyance. Crispin joined them since the earl's coach could only fit so many. Just before they started off, Alice rapped on the carriage door. A footman opened it and handed her up, bringing in the scent of lavender. She slid onto the bench beside Crispin, a determined expression on her face.

For a moment, Benjamin wondered if she was pursuing the captain. Crispin, for all his married-to-the-army status, was a well-to-do brother of an earl—and currently Jasper's heir. Alice's launch into Society had thus far been disappointing, from what Benjamin understood. He wasn't sure why. True, her dowry was whispered to be minuscule, but there were enough men who might overlook that if the girl was well-connected and attractive, which Alice was. Her brown hair had a soft, touchable appearance and she had lively green eyes. Moreover, if she were to dress to better enhance her assets, she could easily find beaux.

As she leaned toward Crispin, he appeared to pull back nervously. Which was interesting.

"Captain Taverston," she said, her eyes rather piercingly fixed upon him, "I have some questions for you."

"I do not wish to be interrogated, Miss Fogbotham. It is Christmas. No questions."

"Oh, for pity's sake." She crossed her arms over her chest. "I suppose you believe ladies are only ever allowed to make silly pleasant conversation."

"That would be welcome," Crispin said. His body remained rigid.

Alice harumphed. The next moment, a transformation came over her face. The intelligence of her usual expression dissolved, replaced by an insipid softness. Her eyes widened. He wasn't sure, but he thought she even pushed back her shoulders to draw eyes to her bosom.

"Captain Taverston," she simpered, "I have been informed that you waltz exquisitely. Do you know, my dance card for this evening is not *entirely* full?"

It was a very apt imitation of a ton flirt.

Crispin smiled with something like relief and relaxed. "How very pleasant!" He flirted back with equal irony. "I was unaware that such were the plans for tonight, but if we are pushing aside the chairs in the music room, I would be delighted to satisfy you as to the trustworthiness of your informants."

"Oh," she breathed a sigh. "I am sure that with just a *bit* of your...attention, I would be *more* than...*satisfied.*"

Crispin gaped. Miss Jamison gasped. And Benjamin nearly choked with laughter. Crispin was actually blushing.

"Now, Crispin," Alice said briskly, "pleasantries aside, I want to ask you a few things. I assure you, this won't hurt."

"Blast." Crispin rubbed a hand across his eyes. "You win. Jasper warned me you are trying to light a fire under Haz. And you were likely to probe for something to work into some Whiggish speech to tempt him to speak out again." He frowned. "You may ask whatever you wish. That doesn't mean you will receive an answer."

"Good. I often find it more instructive which questions are not answered."

"Ruthless," he muttered.

She proceeded to ask him a series of pointed political questions about Castlereigh and Liverpool. Had he heard that Granville Sharp had died, and didn't he agree a monument ought to be put up? Then she touched on the Irish question, and even on what he thought of the government providing subsidies to the families of infantrymen fighting on the peninsula instead of those in the militia. Crispin responded with short factual answers, never venturing opinions. Any question that included Wellington's name, he refused to answer at all. Benjamin watched the exchange as fascinated as if he were at the theater, not only the topics, but the way Alice probed, and Crispin parried.

When the carriage rolled up in front of the church, she settled back with a contented expression. "Thank you, Crispin."

"I will not say it was my pleasure. And I intend to claim the dance tonight as recompense."

Alice smiled a genuine smile. "Good. Olivia will be pleased that you're not disappearing right after church."

"I said I would not!" He put on an air of indignation. "I said I will stay at least through Christmas supper."

An early supper, to replace both luncheon and tea. Jasper had again insisted Benjamin and "his ladies" attend. After the family celebration, Jasper would have to be the earl. Villagers and tenants would come wassailing, and he would receive them and distribute warm punch, chestnuts, and cakes. It was the sort of thing Jasper excelled at, though it had fallen to Benjamin, Mrs. Hardy, and Peters to lay in the supplies.

"Yes, Crispin," Alice said. "But Olivia only believes half of what you say." Then with a bit of reproach, she added, "It hurts her when you go away like you do without even a goodbye."

Crispin muttered something no one could hear. The carriage stopped. They all clambered out into the wind and the cold, and hurried into the church.

Benjamin, Hannah, and her nanny took their now-accustomed places near the back. The Taverstons filed into the family pew in the front. With Alice, they filled it.

The rector was an uninspiring preacher. One would think a clergyman could come up with something more rousing in honor of the day. Bored with the message, which he knew by heart, and rather than concentrating on prayer as he ought, Benjamin observed Olivia, which he ought not. Whether it was merriment or simple contentment, even when wearing half-mourning at Christmastime, she glowed. He swore her light never dimmed.

When Hannah grew fussy midway through the long morning, Miss Jamison took her out. They had arranged, in case of such, for the carriage to take them back to Chaumbers and then return. For the rest of the service, Benjamin was alone. He should not have minded, but his solitude made watching the Taverstons, packed together on their bench, all the more painful. He envied them, and envy was a dangerous emotion.

The service ended and they returned to their carriages. This time, it was Vanessa who joined them rather than Alice. She and Crispin conversed much more amiably, exchanging news about old army friends. Tension slowly lifted from Benjamin's shoulders. It was not until they arrived at Chaumbers and exited the carriage that the tension returned. Crispin touched his arm and said, "If you have a moment, there is something Jasper and I would like to discuss. Will you join us in his study?"

What could be so important on Christmas Day? Nothing good.

"I can come right away if you wish."

"It isn't that urgent." Crispin gave one of his unreadable smiles. "But why don't we meet there in an hour. Before supper. Just in case the weather clears, and I disappear."

⤞⤜

BENJAMIN COULD NOT hold onto his melancholy when he entered his apartments and found Hannah, prettily dressed in a new yellow frock that Miss Jamison had stitched for her, singing Christmas carols at the top of her lungs. Miss Jamison coaxed her along, laughing, as Hannah sang "When Shepherds Watched Their Flocks by Night." Most of the words were intelligible. Hannah truly was a bright little lass. He gave her a kiss, then turned to the nanny.

"I have to meet with the earl before supper. If I am not back on time, please come with Hannah to the dining hall."

"Yes, Mr. Carroll."

While they continued singing, Benjamin went to his dressing room-cum-office and exchanged his neck cloth for a fresh one. He settled down to review notes he had taken on the farmers' opinions of which crops had done well the past few years, and which hadn't. He didn't expect to debate estate matters on Christmas Day, but it wouldn't hurt to be prepared.

He hoped it was something to do with the estate. He couldn't think of anything else that they might wish to discuss. Not unless it was Olivia. He'd managed to convince himself he'd imagined Jasper's suspicions, but then, he might have raised Crispin's.

Seated at that card table, he'd practically fawned over her.

With a quarter hour to spare, he made his way over to Jasper's study. The door was open. He wasn't sure whether he felt reassured or even more concerned when he heard all three brothers inside, laughing. He knocked on the door frame and entered. The laughter abated slowly, then they all turned to him. He felt he was walking into an Inquisition.

"Sit, Benjamin," Jasper said, indicating a chair that had been dragged in from elsewhere. Benjamin sat. "Firstly, there is this." Jasper leaned across his desk and passed a slip of paper to Crispin who handed it to Benjamin. Benjamin lifted the seal and unfolded the paper to find a bank draft for twenty-five pounds.

Why? "What is this?"

The three brothers exchanged glances and chuckled softly.

"You may call it what you wish," Jasper said. "Either a Christmas present or an addition to your salary in gratitude for your work."

"Thank you." He let out a breath. Not severance. "I had not anticipated any such thing, but I am grateful." In truth, he was somewhat embarrassed. He was already very well paid and accepting a monetary gift struck him as lowering. As if they were reminding him of his place. But at least it seemed he was not in danger of losing it.

"There is something else," Crispin said. "Jasp said you were reluctant to move into the south wing."

"Not reluctant. Not exactly."

"Well, it is certainly understandable if you were. The situation worked well for the Bradwells, but they were a strange pair." Crispin's brow furrowed. "The arrangement began well before our time. It is not something that needs to be continued."

"I don't understand."

Reg spoke up. "Crispin reminded us that prior to Bradwell's tenure, the steward had a cottage similar to the dower house, out beyond the folly."

"It is still there," Crispin said. "Quite run down, I'm afraid.

But it would not take much to set it to rights. Hannah could run about at will and Miss Jamison might feel less nervous about disturbing the family. Not that we are at all disturbed, mind you."

"Moreover, your situation is nothing like Bradwell's." Jasper cleared his throat. "Serving as our steward should not prevent you from having a life. If you wish to court, you must do so. Most wives would prefer a home to live in rather than being confined to a few rooms."

"A wife?" Benjamin said, incredulous. This was why they had summoned him? "You are suggesting I take a wife?"

"You have a child," Reg said. "A nanny is all well and good, but a mother would be better."

Heat flooded Benjamin's face. He wasn't sure if it was embarrassment or anger. They had all been discussing his private business behind his back. And had concluded his arrangements for his daughter were wanting. With Reg pretending to dole out expert advice.

"I believe that is my own affair."

"Well, exactly." Jasper harumphed. "You don't need nosy Taverstons looking over your shoulder. Moreover, the third thing is—you work too hard."

"Too hard?" Benjamin laughed, disbelieving. This was worse than an Inquisition. He would rather face Torquemada than the three Taverston brothers. "Surely no one complains of a steward who works too hard."

"I'm not complaining. But just as you said you did not want to take advantage of my friendship, I don't want to take advantage of your eagerness to be of service. Benjamin…we should not make this difficult. If you want to remain in the house, then stay. We only thought to offer you an option. We don't want you to feel uncomfortable."

No? What could make him more uncomfortable than suggesting he find himself a wife? No doubt one suitable to his station. If this whole thing was, in fact, about Olivia, they may as well accuse him now. Openly.

"And what makes you think I am uncomfortable?"

"Because you refuse every invitation to be sociable unless I frame it as an order." Jasper's voice rose.

"In Benjamin's defense, Jasp, you can be overbearing," Crispin said, studying his nails. He glanced up, laughter in his eyes. "Not everyone needs as much society as you do. Is that not so, Reg?"

"Well, Jasper wears *me* out," he agreed.

Jasper pursed his lips. It was evidently a familiar taunt.

"Just have a look at the old steward's cottage," Crispin said. "If it does not appeal to you, forget I suggested it."

So it was Crispin's idea. Benjamin didn't know whether that was better or worse. Well, he hadn't thought it wise to move here. A little distance would be a good thing.

"I will ride out and have a look at it, certainly. Thank you."

"Let me know what renovations are needed," Jasper said. "And what the cost may be. Whether or not you choose to live there, it is a worthwhile improvement to the estate. There is no point letting a cottage go to ruin."

Benjamin nodded. The Earl of Iversley would have his way, regardless.

Reg stood up. "We had better move to the dining hall. Mother will not be pleased if we are late for Christmas supper."

CHAPTER TWELVE

THE TABLE SEATING had been rearranged again. Olivia thought it must have been Mama's doing because Vanessa would not have placed her mother-in-law at the foot of the table with Miss Jamison and Hannah. Olivia scanned the remaining chairs. Jasper sat at the head, of course, with Vanessa beside him on his right. Then Georgiana, Benjamin, and finally, Alice. Crispin had the place to Jasper's left. Olivia was next to Crispin. And then Reg. The Taverston siblings reunited!

She took her seat and tried not to let sorrow intrude upon her gladness. She wanted to hold onto this. They were never all together anymore except for special occasions: funerals, weddings, births. The next wedding *would* likely be hers. And then Chaumbers would no longer be home, and she would no longer be a Taverston.

She caught Benjamin's eye across the table. He looked wistful too. He quickly averted his gaze.

Circulating footmen began setting bowls of orange soup in front of them.

"So, tell me, Jasp. How was Binnings?" Crispin asked, in a tone that was far too innocuous. He was starting something.

Jasper groaned. Vanessa bit her lip to keep back a smile. Olivia knew Crispin's cottage was in a sad state of repair, but he wanted to restore it himself. Without Jasper's interference.

"Mother said you came home early from your honeymoon?" Crispin pressed. Then he glanced down at his bowl. "What is this?"

"Pumpkin," Olivia said. "Pumpkin and cream. The Crofts have started growing it. It's very good."

He dipped his spoon and tasted. Then grimaced and set it aside. The footman behind him replaced it at once with a bowl of broth. Olivia ignored this. As did everyone else.

Jasper said, "Yes, we came home early." He sounded defensive and annoyed. "Vanessa refused to let me touch anything."

Crispin sniggered. Olivia was slow to catch why, but saw Reg and Benjamin repressing laughter and even Georgiana smiled. *Oh!* She got it. Jasper's face reddened as he realized what he'd said.

Vanessa smiled wickedly. "I told him to restrain himself. But he insists on having his way."

Now everyone laughed, everyone at their end of the table. Mama and Mrs. Jamison were engaged in a conversation of their own.

When the laughter subsided, Crispin said, "Confess. What did you fix?"

After a grudging moment, Jasper said, "I had the chimneys swept. They were dense with soot, and I thought it better than letting the place burn to the ground. Maybe I was mistaken."

Crispin tapped his spoon lightly on the table. "What else?"

"Nothing of note."

Vanessa cleared her throat.

Crispin said, "You brought six servants with you. Where did they sleep?" The spoon tap-tap-tapped. A little louder.

Jasper let out a huff. "I had to have the roof patched. It was leaking and the attic stank of must."

"So you had the servants' quarters cleaned as well."

"Yes. Lud, stop with that drumming, Crispin. If you must know, I also had a Rumford stove installed in the kitchen. Mrs. Badge cannot cook in an open hearth."

"Mrs. Badge cannot cook," Crispin said, resting his spoon. "A stove will not help."

Olivia couldn't tell if Crispin was amused or angry. It made a little knot form in her chest.

Then Crispin laughed and everything was right again. "Vanessa said you came home because you found a mouse in your boot."

Jasper's expression turned wry. "That was not the only reason, but it was the most compelling."

"Well," Crispin said, "I thank you for your restraint. I'll look into hiring someone. I know it's too much for the Badges."

"I will—"

"No, Jasper. *I* will." Then he grinned. "Or I'll ask Benjamin. He doesn't seem to have enough to do."

Her brothers all laughed. Benjamin did too, though not as easily. She wondered what that was about.

The conversation settled along more familiar lines as the second course was served.

Olivia enjoyed nothing more in the world than listening to her brothers' banter. Their light-hearted insults. Mostly Jasper and Crispin played off one another, their voices rising to crescendos then dissolving into laughter. When they brought in Reg, he held his own. Olivia was never mocked, though she was teased, and when she tossed in rejoinders they roared, including her equally. She felt warm and happy and wished dinner would never end.

Cook outdid herself. There was haddock and ham, pudding, potatoes, beans, pickles, three types of black butter, two breads, and Crispin's crumbly oatmeal biscuits. Their custom was to drink mead rather than wine on Christmas. She was not fond of mead, it had an off-putting earthy scent, but curiously, Crispin partook. She noticed Benjamin drank sparingly, and when the footman came around to refill his cup, he placed his hand over the rim to indicate no. Evidently, he was determined not to repeat the overindulgence of the previous night.

All too soon, footmen served out gingerbread and syllabub.

Ignoring the desserts, Crispin turned to Reg. "How are your translations progressing?"

Reg gave a modest, "Fairly well."

"Reginald!" Georgiana cried, laughing. "He has been extended an invitation to speak at Oxford come the new year. And Frederick, Mr. Bastion, has offered to front the costs of publishing the first three manuscripts in a small volume. Better than 'fairly well'!"

Everyone congratulated him and teased him. A book and a babe in the New Year! His brothers were comparative sloths!

After this, talk swirled in quieter eddies until they came to the end of the meal.

"We will retire to the music room," Mama said. "Crispin has agreed to play for us, and we can sing carols until the villagers come."

"And dance?" Alice asked.

For some reason, that made Crispin laugh.

Mama touched the brooch at her neck, a plain piece she had worn since Father's death. Then she nodded. "I suppose we might."

The music room was a long way from the dining hall, almost all the way to the library. Olivia tried to walk slowly, to give Benjamin opportunity to fall behind as well. But Alice looped an arm through hers and propelled her along.

"Oh, this corridor is chilly," Alice complained.

Fortunately, the music room had been prepared with a woodfire at one end and a coal brazier at the other. Servants had already lit the lamps. Crispin sat at the pianoforte and let his fingers roam over the keys. He started to sing, and Georgiana added her beautiful soprano. It was such a lovely duet, everyone else simply listened. Then he began to play "While Shepherds Watched Their Flocks by Night." Precious Hannah jumped up and down, singing at the top of her lungs. The family joined in, laughing as much as they sang.

After a few more carols, Georgiana, growing breathless, was

obliged to sit. Crispin struck up a country dance.

"Push back the chairs, Taverstons!" he cried.

Olivia clapped her hands, delighted. She hadn't danced in so long! She helped drag the chairs against the wall. Everyone but Georgiana formed lines and swirled from partner to partner. Reg swung Hannah up into his arms and they passed her around. Soon they were *all* breathless. Crispin drew the tune to a close.

"All right," he said, rising from the bench. "Mother, will you entertain us with a waltz?" He gestured for Mama to sit. "Come, Alice. Dance with me."

"Crispin, really!" Mama scolded.

"Pardon me." He bowed with a flourish. "Miss Fogbotham, will you do me the great honor?"

Jasper wrapped his arm around Vanessa's waist. Reg glanced at Georgiana, who shook her head. He offered his hand to Miss Jamison. She blushed bright red, but stood, nodding. That left Benjamin, standing near the brazier, and Olivia, on the opposite side of the carpet. He had little choice but to walk across.

"Will you favor me with a dance, Lady Olivia?"

"Yes, of course, Mr. Carroll."

Mama began to play. Olivia found Benjamin to be a competent partner, although they might move more gracefully if he did not leave quite so much distance between them and if his hand on her waist was less tentative. Reg looked more comfortable holding Miss Jamison.

Reg danced well, but he tended to heavy-footedness. Jasper and Vanessa, of course, waltzed to perfection. And Crispin spun Alice around the room as if they were in flight. He had a way of keeping to the balls of his feet and steering his partner into extra whirls while still keeping time with the music.

After several minutes, Hannah wriggled away from Georgiana and darted onto the floor toward her father. Reg quickly caught her. Even so, Benjamin drew Olivia closer, as if to shield her from a collision, flattening his palm against her waist and tightening his hold upon her hand. And then they were truly waltzing. Olivia found herself gazing into Benjamin's dark-gray eyes. Her heart seemed to liquify in her chest. She held her breath, unwilling to break her gaze until he broke his. He pulled her a hair's breadth closer.

"Whoops!" Alice cried, laughing, as she and Crispin came a little too near.

"Ah! Switch with me, Benjamin," Crispin said, taking Olivia's hand in trade for Alice's and whirling her away. Olivia blinked, then tried to keep the reproach from her expression as she quickened her steps to match his.

"That was not kind to Alice," she said, hiding the true source of her annoyance.

Crispin snorted. "It was not unkind. We aren't at a ball. And I wanted to tell you something." His voice dropped low. "In confidence."

"What is it?"

"I'm leaving before daybreak." He squeezed her hand. "I don't want everyone fussing, but I wanted to tell you goodbye."

"Oh, Crispin." At once, the world seemed a little darker.

"Chin up!" he commanded. "Don't pout or everyone will guess something is wrong. And I hate long drawn-out farewells." He gave her a long sympathetic look, then a scolding *tsk*. "You have a tendency, Olivia, to wear your heart on your sleeve. Step lively!"

He waltzed her gaily around the room.

AFTER THE DANCE, Vanessa asked Jasper to retrieve a large box from behind the drapery. The men gathered the chairs and circled them in front of her, and the ladies sat. Olivia was still warm from exertion and now felt a silly thrill of excitement. She loved presents. Vanessa opened the box and began passing out beautiful boots to the women, including Miss Jamison, who blushed and thanked her over and over. Lastly, Vanessa pulled out a tiny pair for Hannah.

"Oh, how sweet!" Georgiana cried, then they all exclaimed over the cheerful little daisies engraved in the leather.

"That is very kind," Benjamin said, his hand on Hannah's dark hair. He looked touched. "Thank you."

Olivia frowned, peeved not that he graciously thanked Vanessa, but that he had excoriated *her* for letting Hannah have a hairpin. To her embarrassment, Benjamin caught her frowning. His chin dropped and a light flush rose in his cheeks. Guilt, she imagined. He was thinking the same thing.

When Vanessa finished her gift giving, Jasper passed out boxes to the men. Reg received a dusty old book that made his eyes light up. Crispin's box held a new greatcoat. Sorely needed. Olivia suspected it had been Vanessa's gift for Jasper, quickly repurposed. For Benjamin, there was a bottle of whiskey.

"Irish," Jasper said. "I could not locate a bottle from America."

Benjamin gripped it by the neck and held it up like a prize. "I expect you will want me to share."

Jasper laughed. "If you can bear my society."

Crispin and Reg laughed too. Olivia wished they would explain their little jokes. She understood she was female and a good deal younger, but she hated when they left her out.

Peters appeared just then to announce, "The villagers, my lord. They are in the drive."

"Ah, excellent," Jasper said, turning to Vanessa. His voice changed. From laughing to solicitous. "Are you ready, love?"

Olivia felt a catch in her throat. She'd heard that commoners could be brutal when one of their own defied conventions. Just like the ton.

Vanessa rose. Her features were resolute. "Yes, I am."

And then, all the Taverstons stood.

Chapter Thirteen

S UCH A BRAVE woman, Benjamin thought, as Vanessa prepared to face the masses in her new role as the Countess of Iversley. Half the celebrants, more than half, would be less interested in the festivities than in setting eyes upon the scandalous commoner who had snared herself a lord.

Naturally, the Taverstons showed their mettle. They rose and closed ranks. The dowager, who could easily have used mourning to excuse herself, hovered at Vanessa's elbow. Georgiana, who must be dragging after the long day, walked arm-in-arm with Reg, even though her appearance in public, in her obvious condition, smacked of impropriety all by itself. And Olivia and Alice, unmarried gentlewomen who should have shied away from any scandal lest they harm their own prospects, followed close upon Vanessa's heels. Benjamin started to wonder if even Crispin's unexpected presence was a sign of solidarity.

Miss Jamison slipped away with Hannah, but Benjamin was expected to attend the wassailing. He entered the reception hall several steps behind the united Taverstons.

Painted wooden screens were grouped near the back wall. These were generally set in a line near the hearth in order to trap warmth and make the vast hall feel more intimate. But with the anticipated size of the gathering, they would be in the way if left in their usual spot. Benjamin went to the screens and stood discreetly in the shadows.

Everything was in place. A fire crackled in the hearth. The buffet table offered cakes, roasted nuts, medlars, and oranges. There were three bowls of pungent rum punch, one at each end of the table and one in the middle. Footmen and housemaids passed cups into the crowd as quickly as they could fill them, while guests swarmed into the room. The villagers were dressed in their warmest and finest, red-faced from the cold, and boisterous with holiday cheer.

By now, Benjamin knew the inhabitants of Iversley, having interacted with many of them frequently, others less so. He would have to make a point to speak with the Danforths before the night's end. But he had no desire to circulate. He noted, with a flicker of unease, that there were several young misses the right age for courting. It brought to mind Jasper's suggestion he look for a wife and Reg's admonishment to find a mother for Hannah. He hoped none of the girls were thinking along the same lines.

Not yet, at any rate. Reg was probably right. But not yet.

He forced himself not to let his eyes seek Olivia. Holding her in his arms had nearly been his undoing. She moved with the grace of a swan. If they'd been alone…a stolen kiss…The devil! Of course not! He would never insult Olivia like that.

Giles, the tavernkeeper, clapped his hands and began singing. It was more of a shout. The carol was a horrible jumble of offkey voices and mixed-up verses. The singing trailed off, then cheering began. Jasper raised a mug and called, "Merry Christmas!" Which set off a chorus of Merry Christmases and a few cries of "to the lord and lady!"

It was all quite jolly. Gradually, the rest of the Taverstons separated from Jasper and Vanessa to move through the crowd. A word here. A question there. They were all so very gracious. The villagers would be hard-pressed to find fault, though there would no doubt be backbiting gossip behind closed doors. They were only human, after all.

Still, country gossip was one thing. The viciousness of the

haute ton was another. He didn't envy Jasper and Vanessa. Or maybe he did. Because Jasper could get away with breaking the rules. At least, that was what everyone was counting upon.

Benjamin leaned against the wall, shut his eyes, and let the noise wash over him.

Jasper made no bones about wanting to relax the stringent separation between lord of the manor and employee. He wanted his old drinking friend back. But there was a very definite boundary. The Taverston brothers had made this plain. Jasper *did* drag him away from Olivia the other night. Benjamin *had* been offered rooms in the south wing, but now they were to be taken away. And Crispin could not have reprimanded him any more clearly for the too ardent waltz than by snatching away his sister's hand and depositing Alice in her stead.

Evidently, Benjamin had done a poor job of hiding his attraction. And even so. *Even so*, Jasper seemed determined to keep him. Jasper defined the boundaries and trusted him to respect them.

A body thudded against the wall and a shoulder brushed his. Benjamin's eyes snapped open.

Crispin. Crispin unguarded, with dark hollows beneath his eyes and a weary slump to his shoulders. He held a cinnamon cake and regarded it so intently Benjamin wondered what was wrong with it.

"Captain?"

Crispin gave him a sour look. "Eat this, will you?" He tried handing him the cake. "Or I will."

"That is not much of a threat."

"The threat?" Crispin twisted a smile at him. "Regret. A terrible thing, regret."

For a long, knee-weakened moment, Benjamin couldn't reply. What was Crispin saying?

Then the man let out a sigh and let his head fall back to *thwunk* the plaster.

"Give it here," Benjamin said. Crispin was not a man who sighed. But he was a man with bizarre table habits and a history of unexplainable recurring illness. This was about the cake. Not some metaphorical warning. He popped the thing into his own mouth and chewed.

"*Hmmph*," Crispin said. "Good." He brushed his hands together to rid them of crumbs. Then stiffened his spine. "Tell me about Hannah." He spoke in a conversational tone. "She is a charming little thing. How did you come to rescue her? Jasper says her parents both died?"

He swallowed. "Of fevers. One after the other."

"And you were not at the fort? The Company Fort? Jasper said you were somewhere in the interior."

He nodded.

"Why?"

The deuce. When had conversation for Crispin come to mean interrogation? "What do you mean?"

"I mean," Crispin shifted to focus his gaze on Benjamin and pronounced his words very clearly, "what were you doing in the interior? With these 'business partners' who died of fevers?"

"It's a long story."

"Give me the short version."

The hell. "We were looking for gold."

Crispin stared. Then he looked away with a quick shake of his head.

"Look," Benjamin said, "I know it was idiotic."

The Company had sent out several expeditions based on tales of "yellow metal" to be found in the interior. Gold or copper. Either would have made men fortunes. None had ever been found. This was common knowledge. British investors had not been pleased.

"What made you think you would find it?"

He *didn't* think. He'd been bored, desperate, frustrated with his life, and he'd allowed his better sense to be overcome by fantasies of wealth. Wealth and what it could buy. Not a gentleman's status, of course, but the trappings of it. It was humiliating.

"It is none of your business, is it?"

Crispin started. Then he rubbed his eyes and said, "No. I don't suppose it is." He peeled himself from the wall. "We all have our weaknesses. Don't mention the cake. I won't mention the gold. Fair enough?"

Benjamin snorted. "Fair enough."

Crispin walked away. Benjamin watched, then swept his gaze about the room, just once, but didn't see Olivia. With a quiet groan, he stepped away from the wall. He would go exchange pleasantries with the Danforths. And then find his bed.

⟫⟫⟫✳⟪⟪⟪

OLIVIA WAITED FOR Crispin and Benjamin to lose themselves in the gathering before slipping out from behind the screen. She hadn't intended to eavesdrop. Well, maybe just a little. The men often said more to each other when they didn't think she was nearby. She'd hoped Crispin might confide more of his plans. Of course he didn't.

However, now she knew why games of digging for gold hairpins upset Benjamin. Hannah's parents had died on a treasure hunt. A hunt he was embarrassed to have joined.

Unfortunately, just as Mama had threatened, there was a downside to listening to conversations she was not meant to hear. She couldn't tell Benjamin she no longer needed his explanation. He would continue avoiding her so as not to spill the secret he was doing a poor job of keeping.

He couldn't have avoided their waltz though, without outright snubbing her. And there had been something in his eyes, hadn't there? When they danced and he'd pulled her tight?

Olivia sniffed. She was doing it again. As if she were fourteen and smitten, she was imagining things that were simply not there. It was a waltz. Partners were supposed to look into one another's eyes. And Benjamin's arm had probably brushed Jasper's too, and Crispin's, while they were crowded at the table, playing cards.

Benjamin was not interested in her. He never had been. She'd been so certain he loved her because she had counted up clues and misinterpreted every little gesture. Just as she was doing now.

She felt a warm flush rise, remembering his horror when she'd accosted him all those years ago. He'd tried to be kind. He reminded her that she was a Taverston and a very young one. Starry-eyed and determined, she said he could wait for her. She wouldn't always be young.

His face had darkened. "No, but you will always be a Taverston."

She'd wept. All the stupid, stupid things she'd said, even accusing him of pretending to love her. She began listing things he'd said or done that she'd imagined signified something. Until he pushed a handkerchief into her hand and said, with finality, "This is inappropriate." He left her there in the billiard room. Heartbroken and mortified.

She certainly would not do anything like that again. When she made her debut, she would be cool and aloof to her suitors. They would have to profess *their* love to *her*. There must be some gentleman of the ton whom she could learn to love. Truly love. Like Reg and Georgiana. Or Jasper and Vanessa. Not like the silly infatuation she'd once felt, but didn't any longer.

Still, she peered through the reception hall until she saw Benjamin. He was speaking with the Danforths. While she watched, Mrs. Byrd approached them. Mrs. Byrd the dressmaker. She had her niece in tow. Jilly. Jilly was learning to be a dressmaker also. She wore very nice clothes but tended to overdo the ribbons. She was pretty, with her wheat-colored hair, sunny smile, and the type of figure she'd once heard Crispin refer to as "pleasingly plump." She was lively, too. Olivia liked her.

Benjamin bowed courteously in greeting. Olivia watched the interaction. Watched Jilly smile and press his arm. Watched Benjamin smile back. *Oh, that smile.*

An ache spread through her chest. Her imagination was her worst enemy. But the ache she felt was definitely real.

CHAPTER FOURTEEN

THE MONTHS BETWEEN harvest and planting were said to be quiet times in the countryside, but not so far as Benjamin could see.

As the old year passed into the new, he had to balance the books for 1813, pay overdue bills to clean the slate, and begin planning purchases for the spring.

In addition, the rector of the parishes of Fremont and Bellwether passed on, and the livings, Jasper's to dispose of, had been promised to the curate over in Ipswich. On a blustery January day, Benjamin was tasked with delivering the mixed-blessing tidings. To his surprise, the curate, Mr. Tibury, was no older than Reg. More surprising still, he bore an unsettling resemblance to...well, to Jasper. He had the Taverston bright-blue eyes and strong chin. That would explain why so plum a living, two livings, would be given to so young a clergyman. But Benjamin could not, for his life, figure out where to place him on the family tree. Which meant it was none of his business.

He spent a good deal of time at the steward's cottage. His cottage. Out beyond the folly, it was located a good mile and a half from the house. Constructed solidly of old yellow stone, it had a boxy, compact appearance, having been built upward rather than outward. Three stories and a cellar. The windows had all been shattered. Too tempting a target for any local boys,

Benjamin suspected. The woodwork had rotted, but the stonework was as sturdy as a castle keep. With Jasper's permission, he hired several of the tenants to work on the place, who appreciated the opportunity to earn a few pence over the winter. Cleaning out the cobwebs and vermin nests made a world of difference. He was bringing in a glazier from Barring Downs to replace the windows. Willy Pyle would handle the carpentry. Benjamin thought he might hire Everet to paint the interior when it was time. And maybe ask Jack Fowler to start a garden near the well.

Very likely, he and Hannah and Miss Jamison could move to the cottage come spring. Then he would have to hire a cook and a housemaid or two. That expense would be his responsibility. He would no longer be able to hoard the greater portion of his salary to build a nest egg for Hannah, which worried him. He didn't know what life held for her. Marriage, he hoped. A dowry would help. Possibly she would have to learn a trade. He understood this. Yet he wished he could give her the moon and the stars.

Tomorrow, he would bring her to see the cottage. They could stop at the folly on the way, and she could play among the ruins. But now, he should return to the house. Jasper had received a packet of reports from his man-of-business, and he wanted Benjamin to look them over.

He rode Goose, who was quickly becoming his favorite mount. She was spirited and sometimes had a mind of her own, but she was not difficult. With Hannah though, he would only ride the more placid Bluebell.

His mind skittered from thought to thought as he rode. He knew Hannah enjoyed spending time with "Olly." They met down at the Dower house—Benjamin was not such an unreasonable grouch that he would forbid Miss Jamison from occasionally taking tea with the dowager and her daughter. Moreover, whatever games Olivia played with her tired her out and she slept more soundly at night on those days. There was no more mention of gold or pirates, so he had no reason to complain.

Since Christmas, he'd seen very little of Olivia. He supposed she was keeping Georgiana company, spending time with the other ladies, paying her calls on the tenants. Mostly she seemed to be locked away for hours on end with Mrs. Byrd and Miss Jilly Byrd. What a ridiculous name: Jilly Byrd. And a sillier girl he'd never met. All the girl talked about was ribbons and buttons.

Of course, Olivia was preparing for her London debut. And everyone else was preparing to welcome Reg and Georgiana's little one into the world. The Duchess of Hovington had arrived a week ago to be with her daughter. With all the activity, it was easy for a steward to fade from sight.

Upon reaching the stables, he left Goose with one of the hands, then walked up the soggy path to the house. From a distance, he noticed a figure huddled on the steps in the cold. *Olivia.*

Forgoing the path, he made fast straight across the lawn. Olivia was wrapped in a blanket. Not her pelisse. And she was weeping.

"Olivia, what is it?" He ran up the steps.

"Oh, Benjamin." She choked a great gulping sob. "She lost the baby."

His legs went soft, and he collapsed beside her.

"How?" he asked. "There was no indication...how?" *Why?* "My God. Poor Georgiana."

"Not Georgiana." Olivia shook her head rapidly. "Vanessa."

"Vanessa? But—"

Olivia was crying too hard to make any sense. Benjamin put an arm around her and drew her against his shoulder. She was shivering, too, without seeming to realize it, so he pulled the blanket tighter and Olivia closer. For several minutes, she continued to cry. Eventually her tears subsided into hiccupping bursts as she caught her breath.

"We didn't know. No one knew," Olivia managed. "Until Jasper came running down the stairs, white as a ghost, yelling for a doctor."

Benjamin didn't know what to say. What to ask. "The doctor came?"

"Yes, but it was too late." Olivia rubbed a hand across her swollen eyes. "Jasper is with her. Mama went to talk with her, but not for long. She doesn't want to see anyone." She sniffled and pressed a corner of the blanket against her nose.

"Here." Benjamin drew back to pull a handkerchief from his waistcoat pocket and put it in her hand. For a moment, she just stared at it. Then the awful memory of the last time he'd given her his handkerchief flashed into his brain, and it was as though they were reliving the moment.

Olivia made a sound. Not quite an "oh." He thought she would cry again, but instead, she snorted, then wiped her eyes and blew her nose, then tucked the handkerchief into her sleeve.

"It is all just so awful. I know having babies can be risky but..." She trailed off.

Benjamin was thunderstruck. "Is Vanessa all right?" he demanded. "Physically, I mean?" Jasper couldn't lose her. He *couldn't*. It would destroy him.

"The doctor says she will be. She didn't..." Olivia drew a breath. "She didn't lose too much blood, and the baby was very small. Mama said..." Her face reddened. "Other things. I don't know."

Female things. Benjamin didn't want to know.

"Was it a boy or a girl?" he asked, because it seemed the thing people always asked.

Olivia frowned. "They didn't say. Which must mean it was a girl."

"Why?"

"Because." Her voice broke. "Girls are useless, except for *having* boys."

"*What?*"

"Jasper wants a child, but he *needs* an heir. People will try to console them with 'at least it wasn't a son.' People always say the stupidest things."

Benjamin chewed on this. And found himself even more worried he'd say a stupid thing. Still… "Girls are not useless. How can you say that?"

"Not all girls. I don't mean Hannah. But for an earl, a daughter is useless."

"Your father doted on you!"

She sighed raggedly. "Papa could afford to dote on me. His line was well secured." Her lips pressed tight. Then she murmured, "Peers' lines must be secured."

He regarded her steadily for a long moment. She wasn't looking for pity. She was stating a fact. If she had been the firstborn, the earl would have been…disappointed.

Oh, Olivia. His heart pulsed as he heard what else she was saying. *She* would have to give some peer a son. Or die trying. What possible reassurances could he give in the face of *that*?

Finally, he asked, "Has this frightened…Georgiana?"

"I don't think frightened. Reg says she's sad. I haven't talked to her. Alice and the duchess are with her. But I—I didn't feel right barging in too."

Ah, poor Olivia. He knew how that felt, being the odd man out, unsure of one's welcome. He gave her shoulder a sympathetic squeeze and felt her shivering.

"You should go back inside. It's cold out here." He helped her to stand and fussily tucked the blanket more tightly under her chin. "Is there anything I can do?"

She tossed her head. "I wish I knew."

"I mean, for you."

There was a long silence before she murmured, "You have."

ONLY BACK IN the south wing did Benjamin realize how familiar he'd been, calling her Olivia, calling everyone by their given names. It had been unthinking. But doing otherwise would have been unfeeling, which was worse.

Benjamin explained to Miss Jamison what had happened and asked her to keep Hannah confined to their apartments for the next day or two. She had been exploring the music room and the conservatory, but Benjamin didn't know if the sight of a rambunctious toddler was what any of the Taverstons needed.

Not that it seemed likely they would stumble across her. As Benjamin made his way to Jasper's study to read over the reports he'd been asked to look at, he found the whole of Chaumbers to be tomblike. Only servants were stirring, and they tiptoed and spoke in whispers. As best he could tell, no tea or dinner had been served. Everyone must be eating in their chambers. He hoped Olivia wasn't still alone.

The reports were lengthier than he expected. Jasper's man-of-business, Mr. Tate, recommended selling his interest in a few things and investing in others. Benjamin yawned, flipping the pages. There was something surreal about so much money floating about in such nebulous piles. Benjamin preferred working with tangible things. Estates. Property. Things he could see and touch. Fortunately for Jasper, Tate seemed to have a handle on investments. There was nothing wrong with the figures and the strategies seemed sound. He didn't know what kind of advice Jasper wanted from him.

He tidied the sheaf of paper and slipped it all back into its case. Then heard the door swing open behind him. As he turned to look, Jasper walked in.

"I'm so sorry," Benjamin said, rising. "So very sorry."

Jasper nodded. His hair was oddly matted, and his eyes were puffy. He was in shirtsleeves and wrinkled trousers with no waistcoat or jacket. Benjamin had never seen him looking so bad. He took plodding steps forward, then slumped into his chair.

Benjamin cleared his throat. "How is Vanessa?"

Jasper mumbled, "Sleeping. The doctor gave her something."

"And how are you?"

Jasper took a long time considering. Then he said, "Awful."

"I know this is a stupid question, but can I do anything?"

Again, Jasper was quiet for several moments before saying, "Did you read Tate's reports?"

"Yes. It all seems sound."

Jasper nodded. He stared straight ahead. Then, abruptly, he threw his elbows onto the desk and lowered his head into his hands. His shoulders trembled. Benjamin felt he should not be there. Not watching Jasper weep. But he couldn't get up and leave. So he just sat dumbly, wishing he could think what to say.

The door opened again. Reg walked in. He tossed a nod at Benjamin but made straight for Jasper, who had raised his head at the sound. Reg sank to his haunches and wrapped his arms around his brother's shoulders, murmuring. Jasper responded only with nods or short shakes of his head.

After a minute or so, Reg let go and stood. He went to the liquor cabinet to fetch a bottle—a near-full bottle of brandy. He poured three hefty drinks. He waited for Jasper to throw his back, then Reg downed his. Benjamin followed suit. Reg poured three more and picked up his glass.

And Jasper laughed. He actually laughed.

"Reg, I appreciate it, but you can't. You really can't. I'll have to carry you down the hall." He rubbed his face. "God, I need a handkerchief. I left mine in my jacket.

Reg pulled one from his pocket. Jasper wiped his face. Then sipped from his brandy. Then ran a hand through his hair.

"I've only known for a fortnight. I suspected, but she wasn't sure until two weeks ago."

"I don't know if that's better or worse," Reg said. "You barely had time to be joyful."

"She's been so frightened."

"Frightened?"

"She lost one before. Henry's. At Corunna."

She'd been a war widow, Benjamin recalled. Henry must have been the husband.

Reg gasped. "Oh, God, Jasp. God. I'm so sorry. She must be devastated."

"I don't know how to tell her it's all right. She feels so much pressure." Jasper slammed his hand on the desk. "I hate this!"

Reg looked sick. And clearly, he didn't know what to say to that either.

Vanessa was not only mourning the loss of a babe, but worried she could not give Jasper the heir he needed. And how was Jasper to give vent to his own sorrow without making Vanessa feel worse?

Stil, Benjamin couldn't stop his thoughts from returning to Olivia. For all Jasper "needed" an heir, he had two perfectly capable brothers. The Taverston line was well secured. And even if it weren't, Jasper would always love and cherish Vanessa, son or no son. Not every lady was so fortunate.

They sat in a very brooding silence. Then Jasper asked, "How is Georgiana?"

"She feels terrible. I mean, she's fine, but she feels terrible."

"Vanessa says she doesn't want to…she doesn't want Georgiana, or you, to feel you have to…to hide your joy. She's happy for you. She is."

Reg nodded. Then Benjamin asked, because the question kept gnawing at him after having seen her so lost and alone, "Where is Olivia? Is anyone with her?"

Jasper looked startled. "I don't know."

"She's with Georgiana," Reg said. He threw up his hands. "They are all in there with Georgiana. It's a veritable clucking henhouse. And they all want to descend upon Vanessa."

"Tomorrow."

"All right. I'll let them know. Not yet."

Jasper nodded, then turned to Benjamin. "I do have a request for you. Would you ride into the village and find Mr. Leighton? Reverend Brindle is away, but Vanessa likes the curate better anyway. We'll need a burial. Private. Tell him very private. Here. Not tomorrow, I don't think. The next day."

"I'll go right away."

"Tomorrow morning is soon enough."

Reg put a hand on Jasper's shoulder. "I'd best go back to Georgiana if you are all right."

"Yes. Go. And please tell Georgiana…you know."

"I will." He looked to Benjamin. "Good night. I suppose I will see you in the morning."

Benjamin started to rise, but Jasper said, "Wait a moment, Benjamin. I had some questions about the reports, if you will."

He sat back down. Jasper waited with one eye on the door until it closed behind Reg.

Benjamin said, "Mr. Tate's recommendations are reasonable. I—"

"The hell with Tate. I intend to drink that bottle dry. Will you stay?"

Benjamin nodded. "I'll help." Here at last was one thing he could do.

Chapter Fifteen

Olivia woke early. Although she could see drizzle through her windows, she asked Tansy for her brown riding habit.

"It is either go riding or go mad," she said, in the face of her maid's disapproval.

The house was eerily silent. When Olivia entered the dimly lit breakfast parlor, warm pelisse slung over her arm and hat in hand, she saw only one corner lamp burning. But the room wasn't empty. Jasper stood beside the buffet. He held himself stiffly and sipped from a teacup. Tea, not his usual coffee. And the food on the buffet was untouched.

"How are you?" she asked in a whisper.

He made a sour face. His temples had a pinched look. She supposed he hadn't slept.

"Will Vanessa be ready for visitors this morning?"

"I don't think so." He looked her up and down. "It is raining out."

"Not hard."

"Olivia." Then he shook his head. "Just be careful."

He set his cup down and walked from the room.

There was no reason to sit alone in a half-darkened room, so she took a piece of toast for her walk to the stables. When she stepped outside, into air that was misty and cold but without actual precipitation, she was surprised to see Benjamin on the path. He was trudging as if pulling a heavy sledge. Rather than follow twenty-paces behind, she called out, "Benjamin! Wait a moment." She walked quickly to catch up.

"Lady Olivia." He tipped his hat but didn't remove it. "You shouldn't be riding in this."

"I thought Jasper was silly for reminding me to be careful, but at least he didn't tell me not to ride."

He set his jaw but didn't respond. She saw the same head-achey pinched appearance on his face that had been on Jasper's. The same ashen pallor.

"Ah," she said, with a bit of a smile. "You had a chance to speak with him last night?"

He nodded.

"Good. I'm glad. He must have needed a friend."

He didn't respond to that either. But when she started to walk, he fell into step alongside.

"Where are you off to?" she asked. "The cottage?"

"The village. The earl asked me to speak with Mr. Leighton."

Olivia put her hand on his arm and halted. "Please stop that. I am still Olivia, and the earl is still Jasper. You are being ridiculous."

"It's only proper—"

She flung out her arm. "There is no one for miles around!"

He stiffened. "Which makes propriety even more necessary." Then his face flushed, and he closed his mouth tight as though he regretted the words. If she were counting clues, that would be one. He didn't trust himself alone with her. But there were a hundred alternative explanations.

She resumed walking. "Are you to arrange a funeral? Is that why you are going to see Mr. Leighton?"

"A private burial. On Chaumbers' grounds. The earl says Lady Iversley does not want this to become publicly known. She wishes no callers or cards."

"I can understand that. She hasn't had time to become acquainted with anyone beyond family. She shouldn't have to share her pain with strangers."

His head cocked to the side as he regarded her. "That is…perceptive. I wonder… Who she could share with? Besides the earl, I mean." He hesitated. "He is carrying his own grief."

Oh, poor Jasper. "Fortunately, he had you. He must have needed to talk."

Benjamin grimaced. "We drank a vat."

"I thought you might have. What did you talk about?"

"The countess. How they met. How difficult it was when they…when they fell out."

"You now know more than I do."

He smiled a little ruefully. "I don't imagine your brother's love life was ever an appropriate topic for you."

"No." She thought for a moment. She was seeing Vanessa's behavior in a different light now. Of course she hadn't wanted to go riding. Or to fret together over how best to face the ton. "Who can Vanessa confide in? Georgiana might not be the best person just now. Vanessa's brother came to the wedding, but I don't think they are close." She frowned when Benjamin just shook his head. He didn't know either. "She has friends in Cartmel."

"The folks in Cartmel are not…moneyed. And Cartmel is days away. They could not be sent for. They would have to be fetched. The countess would likely see it as too great an imposition."

He was right. She sighed.

"I think she is close to Crispin. But that is no help." She kicked a small stone in her path. "I don't know who she can really talk to, besides Jasper."

He made a sympathetic sound, but said nothing.

Olivia sighed again. "She and I haven't had time to grow close. It all just happened so fast. And ladies can't simply drink vats to become bosom friends."

Benjamin's lips bunched and a little laughter entered his eyes. "No. I don't suppose you can."

As they approached the stables, the mist changed to a light

rain. Benjamin rubbed his arms, then frowned as he swung the door wide.

"You are certain you want to ride in this?"

"I'd rather ride in sunshine if you have any."

He sniffed. "Just be careful," he echoed Jasper.

They entered the stable. It held all of its typical winter gloom with an added helping of damp. But Olivia breathed in the scent of horse, sawdust, and straw and comfort seeped into her bones. She loved this. And she would hate London. But what a bother she would be to everyone if she were to say so.

George came hurrying to them, though he hustled slowly as though his knees hurt. "Ah! I wasn't expecting company this day. I'll fetch one of the lads."

"May I have Oatmeal?" Olivia asked.

He stopped. His bushy eyebrows rose. "Oatmeal? No, miss, m'fraid not. Fergus took her."

"Took her?" Benjamin demanded.

"Aye, he did. Mr. Taverston's orders, see. An errand to London. I told him Fergus was our fastest and Oatmeal best for such a long ride. So."

Benjamin shook his head with what seemed to be annoyance.

George went on, "Dandy could use a good run, miss. And Goose for you, sir?"

"Dandy will be just fine," Olivia said. "And Goose."

George bustled off to fetch one of the stable hands. Benjamin still frowned.

"What is wrong?" Olivia murmured.

"Jasper was adamant that Mr. Leighton be told not to let word get out. Not to even tell Reverend Brindle. I suppose I am concerned why Reg sent Fergus on an errand to London. Jasper didn't mention it. Did Reg say anything to you?"

She shook her head. How odd. Unless…unless Georgiana's pains had started.

"Maybe that is it," she accidentally said aloud.

"What?"

"Well, it would be particularly unfortunate timing if Georgiana's confinement is due, but Reg might have sent a message to her father."

Benjamin's eyes widened with surprise. "Is the duke supposed to come for that?"

"I don't know." She shrugged, feeling an unexpected pang of grief. "My father would have."

"*Hmm.*" He looked as though he wanted to say something sympathetic. Instead, he said, "The timing may not be unfortunate. Maybe everyone could use a joyous event. Besides, Jasper and Vanessa won't begrudge—"

"No, of course not."

She decided not to point out that, when he was not being conscientious, Benjamin reverted to everyone's Christian names.

A clip-clop of hooves sounded on the cobblestones, and she glanced over toward the stalls to see George and a new young groom leading Dandy and Goose.

"Here you go," George said. "Give'er a leg up there, Jim."

"I'll do it," Benjamin said, stepping in.

He didn't simply make a cradle of his hands, but lifted her by the waist the way a gentleman would. She found she had to steady herself with a heavy hand on his shoulder until she was firmly seated.

"Ha!" she laughed, embarrassed by her lack of grace. "We'll have to practice."

He turned to mount Goose without replying. His refusal to flirt, even the tiniest bit, was either endearing or insulting. She rode out the door, Goose close behind. She had made no decision where to go, though she had been thinking she'd head to the orchard rather than the lake. She waited to see if Benjamin might suggest they ride part of the way together.

As they emerged into the open ground before the stable, he tipped his hat once more and said, "Perhaps I will see you this evening."

The orchard it would be.

JASPER CIRCULATED WORD that tea would take place in the parlor at four o'clock. Olivia, who had been sharing a Radcliffe novel with Alice, side-by-side on the davenport in the ladies' sitting room, closed the book abruptly at quarter to four.

"Let's be early for once." This was not the time to test Mama's patience.

Alice looked rather peaked. She wore the somber blue frock she'd worn to the wedding, which was not very flattering, but it was not only that. She seemed uncharacteristically listless. Olivia had asked her if she was feeling well, and Alice replied only that the duchess was smothering poor Georgiana. But when Olivia asked if Georgiana's pains had begun, she'd said, "No. Why?"

Olivia didn't mention Reg sending Fergus on an errand. Everything felt upside down and inside out.

They were the first to arrive in the parlor and took seats as solemnly as if they were in church. Hands folded in their laps, they sat in silence as maids brought in a large teapot and plates of biscuits and sandwiches. They set them on the serving table, then made brief curtsies and tiptoed from the room.

A moment later, Benjamin entered. He seemed amused to see them sitting there like statuettes. He bowed. "Ladies." He went to the fireplace and stood with his back to the fire, hands behind his back.

He looked terribly handsome, Olivia thought. He had changed clothes since his early morning ride. His hair had a glossy sheen to it. He'd shaved. And his dark, plain jacket and trousers were almost comically correct. His neckcloth was tied very simply, more simply than even Reg's would be, and Reg had once argued that having valets spend hours learning elaborate methods of tying cravats was an affront to good sense.

Reg, Georgiana, and the duchess were next to show. It was funny to see Georgiana lumbering, but of course, Georgiana could look graceful lumbering and was beautiful even though she appeared ready to give birth at any moment. The duchess looked dyspeptic. Poor Reg simply seemed tired. He escorted Georgiana to a chair, fussed with pillows behind her back, then retreated to stand beside Benjamin.

Jasper also arrived early. He glanced around the room and his lips curled into a smile.

"This is…rather fun." He strode to the clock on the wall and advanced the hands by ten minutes. He turned around and faced them. "When Mother arrives, we must all look at the clock and then frown at her sternly."

Olivia giggled. They quieted quickly and listened for footsteps. Mama entered the room and stopped abruptly, startled. Everyone obeyed Jasper's request with the precision of trained actors. Olivia thought she'd never seen her mother so nonplussed. Jasper burst out laughing, and of course, they all did. Even the duchess. Even Mama.

Olivia's heart swelled. She loved her family so much.

As the laughter subsided, she sneaked a glance at Benjamin, who might not quite understand the joke they'd played, turning the tables on Mama. He was smiling, but the smile looked brittle, as if a tap might shatter it to pieces.

They settled in. Mama poured. They sipped tea and ate cakes, saying meaningless things until Jasper cleared his throat. Silence fell.

"Mr. Leighton will be here tomorrow morning. We will bury my daughter in the grove on the far side of the lake."

A daughter. *Only* a daughter. Benjamin returned the glance Olivia gave him, his eyes brimming with sympathy. There were nods and a few hums. Olivia recalled that the grove had been a favorite place of Jasper's long ago. She hadn't known he still visited it. It was a lovely, peaceful spot.

"Vanessa will not go. She isn't…it is too painful for her. And for that reason, I think it is better that we not…that it not be something we all do that she will later regret missing." Jasper coughed. Or perhaps choked. He clenched and unclenched his hands. His composure deserted him for a moment. Then he straightened his shoulders and continued. "I would appreciate it if Reginald, Olivia, and Mother would attend with me. I hope the rest of you understand..." He trailed off.

The room fell silent.

Until the duchess said, "That sounds eminently sensible."

A jumble of agreement followed. Jasper looked relieved. No, more than relieved. He looked as though a weight had been lifted from his shoulders. *Oh, Jasper.* On top of everything else, he hadn't wanted to hurt anyone's feelings.

Conversation was subdued. Jasper asked Olivia where she had ridden and Alice what she was reading. Mama said she'd had a lovely visit with Miss Jamison and asked Benjamin what he and Hannah had done. Voices were low. It seemed no one listened very carefully to anyone else's answers. The only question that mattered, no one asked. *Was Vanessa all right?*

Tea dragged on. Nevertheless, they drew strength from being together and no one wanted to be the one to break the gathering apart. Twice, Benjamin threw more wood onto the fire. The teapot went cold, but there were still sandwiches to finish.

Sleet pattered against the window and the sky darkened. Footmen came in to light the lamps. Jasper cast a slow look around the room, then got to his feet.

Mama said, "Stay, Jasper. I'll go."

He shook his head.

And then, there was a clattering sound from outside. Swaying lights appeared in the window, then disappeared.

"Is that a carriage?" Jasper asked. "Who the devil?"

Olivia looked to Benjamin who was looking quizzically at Reg.

Jasper went to the window and peered out, but by the way he bent and turned his head, it was apparent he could see nothing. So they all simply waited.

Several minutes later, Peters came into the room.

"My lord, Viscount Haslet is here. May I bring him up?"

"Haz? Is here?"

The strangest look passed over Jasper's face. The best Olivia could make out, it was gratefulness.

"Yes, yes. Bring him up," Jasper said. When Peters left, Jasper turned immediately to Reg. He didn't say anything, but Reg gave a small nod and Jasper just sighed. It was wonderful.

Hazard walked into the room. With none of his usual insouciance. Olivia was so glad to see him she jumped to her feet and started toward him. But he strode straight to Jasper, ignoring everyone else, and clasped both of his arms.

"You are all right?"

"Yes."

"And Vanessa is safe? Not in any danger?"

"No. I mean, no danger. She'll recover, the doctor says."

Hazard let go of Jasper and wiped a forearm across his brow. He must have been seven straight hours in a carriage and looked it. "Thank God." He took a step back and started to turn. "Where is she? I take it she shares your bedchamber?"

"Yes, but..." Jasper caught his shoulder. "She doesn't want visitors. She doesn't...she isn't speaking much."

Hazard's face crumpled. "Not speaking?"

Olivia's throat felt tight. She could not picture Vanessa, strong Vanessa, lying in bed too sorrowful to even give voice to her hurt. *Dear God.* How were women supposed to bear this?

Jasper shook his head. "Haz, I—" His voice broke.

"You," Hazard said sternly, poking a finger into Jasper's chest. "Stay here."

"Don't—"

"If she throws me out, she throws me out."

He turned about and left the room.

Hazard hadn't appeared aware of anyone's presence but Jasper's. Olivia had been so focused on their exchange, she didn't even notice that Benjamin had crept up beside her.

"Hazard," he said, his lips too close to her ear for propriety. "That is who we forgot."

Chapter Sixteen

THE PREVIOUS NIGHT'S tea was one of the most moving gatherings Benjamin had ever attended. And one of the most interminable.

Familial bonds drew the Taverstons and their relations together in a tightly woven web. When Hazard had arrived, slotting himself into the group like a missing key into a lock, Benjamin experienced again a sense of his own disconnection.

Hazard's sudden appearance had rejuvenated the gathering, but his swift departure left them stunned. Naturally they'd felt they must await his return. The dowager rang for more tea and sandwiches, stating that they might as well eat for there would be no formal supper. Benjamin threw yet another log on the fire. They had waited over an hour and a half, finally finding themselves entirely out of conversation before Jasper dismissed them.

"We have a difficult morning ahead of us. I will check with Peters to be sure Hazard's room has been prepared." He gave a false, weak smile, plainly hesitant to interrupt whatever conversation his best friend was having with his wife.

"Is there anything you need me for?" Benjamin had asked. Jasper merely shook his head no.

Throughout the morning, Benjamin had remained in his own apartments. Miss Jamison entertained Hannah making drawings. Benjamin sat in his study going over various estimates he had obtained for brickwork out at the folly. It seemed ridiculous to repair something that had been deliberately constructed to look like a ruin. It just showed that some lords possessed more money than they knew how to spend.

He concentrated poorly on his work. Time and again, he rose to look out the window. Finally, he saw Mr. Leighton drive up in a battered gig pulled by an aged sorrel. He entered the house. After a while, Reg exited and headed for the stables. Nothing happened for a good twenty minutes. Benjamin wandered back and forth between his desk and the window, unable to settle. Then Reg returned in one of the smaller, more maneuverable carriages. He left the vehicle and went inside.

Benjamin lurked in front of the window and watched.

Before long, Reg, Olivia, and the dowager emerged from the house and entered the carriage. A few minutes later, the curate appeared carrying a box that was heartbreakingly small. He set the little coffin in his gig and climbed to his seat. Three more people shuffled down the steps, swathed in heavy coats. Benjamin gaped, though perhaps he should not have been surprised. Jasper held one of Vanessa's elbows and Hazard held the other. When they reached the carriage, Jasper picked Vanessa up. Reg's hands appeared at the door to help gather her in. Then Jasper hoisted himself up and in. Hazard shut the door and climbed into the box seat beside the driver. The carriage set off. The curate's gig followed.

Thank God for Hazard.

Benjamin went back to work. Still, it was impossible to concentrate. His mind kept returning to yesterday's walk to the stables with Olivia. Riding in the rain—so very Olivia. He wanted to see her as flighty, immature. She was anything but. It had felt dangerously comfortable being with her, talking with her. Of course, the topic was serious. The focus, outward-directed. Which made it easier. All except for his slip. His reference to propriety, which she could not have misunderstood. Yet she let it pass.

And then, like a fool, he'd practically pushed that stable hand aside. He couldn't bear the thought of her resting her hands on another man's shoulder. He'd embarrassed her with his clumsiness; he knew that. Yet in typical Taverston fashion, she turned it into a joke.

Damn it. This was not simply an inappropriate physical attraction. That, he would be able to control. He was falling in love. He couldn't control his heart. So, what was he to do?

He crumpled the piece of paper where he had been listing costs of bricks and labor. A list that had turned into doodling. He tossed it into the bin. For a long moment, he regarded the blank page before him. Then he started a new list. Things in London that required his immediate attention.

HE HEARD THE carriages return but restrained his impulse to spy any more on his employers. Miss Jamison was bustling about in their little kitchen with Hannah when a knock came upon the door. Benjamin opened it to find Reg, hand poised to knock again.

"Mr. Taverston. Is something wrong?"

Reg shook his head. "Jasper asked me to fetch you. To fetch you all. For luncheon." He sniffed the air, which had a faint beef broth scent. "I hope I'm not too late."

"I'm not sure. Miss Jamison—"

"That's all right," she called from the kitchen. Then poked her head into the room. "I can take this off the stove."

She wore such a pleased expression it unsettled him. In her previous situations, did the families include her more often? Was she used to more companionship? Benjamin felt a tightening in his gut at the thought that she could leave them. Stability was important for a child. Reg was right; Hannah needed a mother, but the thought of marrying for such mercenary purposes rubbed him wrong.

"We will be over shortly. Thank you."

He went into the kitchen, where he found Hannah sitting on the floor, her hands deep in a bowl of dough of some sort that had a fair amount of dirt mixed in.

"What are you making, sweetheart?"

"Bread. Good bread."

He laughed. "You will have to finish later. We are going to eat luncheon with the Taverstons."

"No."

"Come along, deary. Let's get you tidied," Miss Jamison said.

Hannah wailed a string of petulant nos.

"Olly is waiting for you," she said calmly. "Don't you want to see Olly?"

"No" turned to an equally petulant "yes."

"Then you must let me wipe your hands and face. You are a mess." Ms. Jamison tried taking hold of her grubby hands.

"Olly likes mess!" Hannah insisted.

"Yes, but not at the table."

Benjamin marveled at Ms. Jamison's reasonable tone. Hannah quieted and held out her hands. She squirmed but allowed the nanny to wipe flour from her face. Then Miss Jamison hoisted her to her feet.

"Oh no." Her face fell. "I think we had better change that dress, deary."

Clumps of dough mottled her frock. But Benjamin remembered young "Olly" coming to the table at the Binnings cottage with muddy hems and reeking of horse. "She'll do." He brushed off the clumps.

He straightened his neckcloth and smoothed his jacket taut. Miss Jamison took off her apron and hung it by the stove. Then she took Hannah by the hand. They went to join the Taverstons.

Everyone was in the dining hall but for Vanessa and Georgiana.

Standing somewhat apart from the others, before taking their seats, Jasper told Benjamin the two were having lunch in Georgiana's sitting room. He smirked. "It's rather sickeningly heartwarming, isn't it?"

"Did everything go well then this morning?" Benjamin asked awkwardly.

"Yes. I think it did." He sounded relieved. Tired and relieved.

Looking at the table, Benjamin saw he was assigned a seat between Olivia and Alice. Olivia wore a lavender day dress he hadn't seen before. It had long form-fitting sleeves and a dip in the neckline showing just a hint of bosom. Just a gaze-entrapping hint. Olivia gave him a bright smile as he lowered himself into his chair. His heart thumped ridiculously. He tried to smile back. There was no doubt. No doubt at all. If he didn't leave Chaumbers soon, he would jeopardize everything.

SHE *HADN'T* BEEN imagining things. Olivia didn't want to make too much of Vanessa explicitly asking Georgiana if they might have lunch in her sitting room. *Alone.* She understood there were confidences that married women could share that unmarried girls could not be privy to. But there had been a chill in Vanessa's manner that truly had seemed directed only at *her.* Olivia could not imagine what she had done to offend her.

After luncheon, a difficult meal where Benjamin, too, had acted oddly, Olivia wanted solitude. Being the cheerful one, all the time, even when being shunned by her sisters-in-law, was wearing.

There was one place at Chaumbers where no one would look for her: the third floor reading room. It wasn't a library. It had only a few shelves and a very few old books. As she understood from family lore, it was where her grandmother used to hide when she wanted peace and quiet. On the rare instances when she felt the need to shut out the world, Olivia would come sit in her grandmother's musty old armchair. It wasn't exactly comforting. Truth be told, her clearest memory of the setting was one of terror.

The room was located just above Papa's—*Jasper's*—study. The study was where Papa used to bring the boys if they'd earned a reprimand. One day, playing, she'd serendipitously discovered that words spoken in the study floated up through the chimney. Since she was always interested in what they had done wrong, whenever she suspected Jasper or Crispin—it was never Reg— might be taken to task, she would hurry to the reading room, to lie down beside the cold fireplace and put her ear to the floor.

Peters had caught her. He said if she *ever* eavesdropped on the earl again, he would report her. Lud, how that had frightened her! She knew, from listening, that Papa sometimes used his belt. It didn't cure her of the vice entirely, but she never again spied on her father.

She curled up in her grandmother's chair, turning pages in an illustrated Bible, without paying attention to anything but the fragility of the pages. Until noise wafted up through the grate. Jasper's voice. But he was never in his study this time of day! A moment later, she heard Vanessa. No actual words, just their affectionate tones. Then silence. Then strange sounds that might possibly be kissing.

Olivia laid the Bible quietly on the floor and stood to leave. There was more talking that was too low to hear. But Jasper's voice suddenly rose. "We don't have to go."

"Of course, we do." They were arguing. That, she could hear. "How will it look—"

"I don't care."

"You *have* to care. For Olivia's sake, if not for mine. How can you ignore—"

"I ignore nothing! But you've just miscarried!"

Olivia gasped. This was about London. And *her*. Wrong or not, she sank to her knees and crawled to the fireplace.

"Jasper, if I could march, half-starved, to Corunna, I can ride in your luxurious coach to London. We have one chance to do this right."

"Then tell me. You say you have a plan, but you won't *tell* me."

Silence fell. Olivia held her breath, blinking to clear tears from her eyes. What were they saying? Their voices were very low. *This was so wrong!*

"No!" Jasper practically shouted. "Vanessa, no. That is not how we do things."

"Oh, spare me your 'we are Taverstons,' Jasper. We can all be Taverstons *after* Olivia's future is secure."

"Olivia won't stand for it."

"She doesn't have to know."

"Well, then, it is cruel! She'll think you don't like her."

"For pity's sake. She isn't a baby! She must know not every-one is going to like her."

"But *you* must."

The pulse in Olivia's ears was so loud, she missed what they said next. And she wouldn't put her ear to the floor. She would *not*.

Vanessa's next audible words were, "If I tell her, she will refuse to play along. Let me do it my way, Jasper. Please. If her chances are ruined because of me, because of us, I won't ever forgive myself. The ton will accept her more readily if they think she has shunned me."

"But love—"

"Please stop arguing with me. *Please*."

Then murmuring. Only murmuring. But Olivia had heard enough. Vanessa was planning to ensure Olivia's success at the expense of her own.

She hated this. She didn't want a "secure" future with a man who would expect her to reject her sister-in-law. Moreover, *Vanessa* was the one who absolutely must succeed. Jasper needed to be in London. Not only had he always preferred the city to the country, but his political aspirations demanded his presence there.

Vanessa's self-sacrifice wouldn't work. If Jasper's actions had tarnished the Taverston name, *he* would never forgive *himself.*

Well, Vanessa was right about one thing. There was *no way* she would play along.

Olivia cupped her mouth and yelled down the chimney. "Fearless and unapologetic, Vanessa!" She heard them both yelp. Jasper swore. She yelled, "You and I *both* are going to succeed or neither of us will!"

⟫⟫⟫≪≪≪

"WHAT DO YOU mean you are going to London?" Jasper shut the book he'd been reading, *Historical Speeches*, with some force. Benjamin had finally cornered him in the parlor, in the early evening the day after the burial.

"Hazard said I may accompany him when he goes back next week."

"I didn't ask how you were going. I asked why. Why now?"

Benjamin tried to keep his voice level. "There are things better handled there than here, and this is the best time to go. Before we get caught up in spring planting and fair-weather restorations about the estate. I'd like to speak directly with Tate. Moreover, the stove and the fixtures for the cottage's new water closet can be ordered in London far more easily." He chuckled. "And I have that box of badger pelts to sell."

Jasper scowled. He looked as though he would argue more, but then his scowl faded, and he nodded. "I suppose it makes sense. Only I hate to lose you and Hazard both. Are you taking Hannah and her nanny?"

"Yes, of course I am."

"You needn't. They are welcome to stay here. Olivia and Mother will be sorry to see them go."

"They will have Mr. and Mrs. Taverston's baby to dote upon before long." Perhaps that was the wrong thing to say. "I appreciate the offer. But I don't wish to frighten Hannah by leaving her behind."

"Well, yes. I suppose I understand that." He tugged his earlobe. "The devil. I guess that as long as you are going, I have something for you to do."

Good. He raised his eyebrows. "Such as?"

"Hire me a social secretary."

Benjamin laughed.

"No, I am not joking."

"Iversley, I know your calendar will be overfull, but the one thing you are good at is juggling your social engagements."

Jasper wrung a smile at him. "The one thing?" Then he said, "This Season is different. Mother told me I must needs be more strategic. We are…we are ensuring Vanessa's success. Which will be difficult. And launching Olivia. Which shouldn't be, but we have made it so. There are events we apparently *must* attend." He grimaced. "And parties we must throw. Including Olivia's ball. And I have to make sure that our events don't conflict with…with events that will give people excuse to send us their regrets. We can't offend the Hobnarths or the Laytons or the Grenevilles by throwing a competing party. We can't…God, Benjamin. It is all musts and can'ts."

"Yes, I can see why you need help." Jasper would never have bothered with such things before. He was welcomed everywhere. Peers would arrange their events around his.

"It's absurd. Whomever you find will have to coordinate with Mother. I cannot keep it straight and it's too important to get wrong."

"I will ask around. We'll find the right person."

"Hazard will have some suggestions." Jasper frowned, then said, "The deuce. I was so concerned about Vanessa, I didn't give due consideration to Olivia's debut. I thought my name carried enough weight…"

"It will."

"At tea this afternoon, after Vanessa had gone to rest, Olivia volunteered to wait another year. Can you imagine?"

"What! No." His pulse raced. "No, I can't. Why?"

"To give the ton time to absorb the fact of Vanessa. Mother pointed out that if Olivia waited, she would turn twenty in the midst of her debut season."

"Twenty is not old."

"No. And it was rude of Mother to make a point of that in front of Alice. It raised a fracas."

Benjamin winced. "I am glad I missed tea."

He'd gone out to the cottage directly after luncheon on purpose to evade that invitation. Luncheon had been difficult enough. There had been a washed-clean lightness in the air, like the aftermath of a violent thunderstorm. Add in Hazard, and the conversation sizzled. Olivia's animation seared a hole through Benjamin's center. To his horror, he found himself picturing her that keyed up and playful in his bed. He had truly lost his mind.

And now they were discussing Olivia's entrance into the Marriage Mart. It was unbearable.

"Alice is astounding," Jasper said, continuing his train of thought without noticing Benjamin's had drifted. "She was amused, not offended. I suppose it helped rather than hurt that Hazard teased her for being ancient. The two of them…" He shook his head. "At any rate, Georgiana explained very nicely that being twenty was no handicap. But that postponing one's debut three times could well be. There were very good reasons the first two times and the ton would be sympathetic. But if Olivia demurred again, people would talk, and gossip would circle back around again to Vanessa."

"So really, the only choice is for the countess and Lady Olivia to throw themselves headlong into the breach."

Jasper hesitated, then sounding strangled, he said, "Yes."

"Well, with the family behind you—"

"I would have no qualms. But it is unlikely Reg and Georgiana will be in London this spring. Arthur will be only a few months old—"

"Arthur?"

"Oh." Jasper sniffed. "You missed that too. Apparently Haz was under the impression the babe will be named Arthur if it's a boy. Crispin led him to believe the decision was made."

Benjamin couldn't help laughing.

"Yes, so now we are all needling Reg." Jasper snorted. "Even Georgiana."

For a moment, they grinned stupidly at one another. Then Jasper grew serious again. He drummed his fingers on his book.

"Georgiana would have been our ace in the sleeve. The Hovingtons have clout. They will still support us, of course, but Georgiana drips respectability."

Benjamin admired how Jasper could so flatly praise the woman who had rejected his suit.

"And Crispin's absence will be felt," Jasper continued.

"I don't see the captain's involvement mattering one way or the other," Benjamin protested. "The objectives are matrimonial, not military."

"You'd be surprised." Jasper rolled back his shoulders. "Olivia deserves better. She has been so patient. She ought by rights to be the diamond of the Season. I want her to enjoy this, Benjamin. This is her time to bask in the glow of all the ton has to offer. It shouldn't be a trial by combat. And I fear I have made it so."

Benjamin could well be wrong, but it seemed to him Olivia would not be overmuch impressed by the glow of the ton's offerings. All she wanted was a strong horse and an open field.

He groaned inwardly. Maybe that was what she wanted, but what she needed was a husband. The right husband. A handsome, young, titled lord. And she would have one.

"Iversley, you worry too much. Lady Olivia will have the ton eating out of her hand."

CHAPTER SEVENTEEN

Benjamin was making himself scarce again, Olivia mused. Naturally, he was doing it to be noble. Since he was burning with ardent desire, simply seeing her might drive him to take her into his arms and cover her with kisses. He was so passionately in love that he must escape to London.

Ha! She could only wish.

Hazard had arrived four days ago and would be leaving in another four days. He was taking Benjamin with him. They both had business in the city. There was nothing noble or romantic about it.

Jasper had tried to convince them to stay longer. He might have succeeded, but yesterday Georgiana began experiencing "discomfort." Mrs. Cooper, the midwife, was summoned. She dismissed the discomfort as false pains, then promised Georgiana's time was near.

Hazard was positively aghast and threatened to leave at first light. He said he adored children and dogs, but babies and cats made his skin crawl. Although it was a rude thing to say, he was so droll saying it that the duchess spit her tea and laughed. The *duchess* did!

Rather than bemoaning the impending loss of Hazard's company, Olivia determined to make the most of it while she could. She convinced Hazard and Alice to join her for a midday ride.

The sun had finally come out and the day promised warm. Warm for January. The folly beckoned.

Had she wanted a race, Hazard alone would have been a better companion than the two of them. They dawdled. And for company, either one of them alone would have suited Olivia better than both. No matter how carefully they tried to keep to neutral topics for her sake, they kept falling back into an argument about the American War. As best Olivia could tell, they agreed more than they disagreed, but they kept finding fine points to sharpen even finer. They were making her head hurt. But Alice seemed so…alive, and Hazard…so much less droll. It was strange.

By the time they neared their destination, she was riding a few lengths ahead, having given up on the conversation. Sunlight filtered through the barren trees. The cold-muted scent of slowly rotting leaves sweetened the air. Olivia was first to see the folly was already occupied. She slowed Oatmeal and signaled to the laggards to slow and to quiet down as well.

The scene made her smile.

Benjamin helped Hannah clamber up onto one of the broken walls until she was chest-high to him. Then she spread her arms and shouted, "Look, Papa!" before leaping into his outstretched hands. He set her down gently. Then he helped her climb up again. They repeated this at least ten times. Benjamin was laughing as though he hadn't a care in the world.

He *was* the same man he'd always been. More serious, perhaps. More mature. More conscientious. But still caring and kind. Protective. And he could still enjoy life. She'd been right to adore him when she was a child. Helplessly. And she was right to love him now. Hopelessly.

Hannah's coat flapped open, and her hat had evidently fallen into the trampled, melting snow. Benjamin had taken off his coat and gloves. They were draped across another of the walls. It was the type of play that would cause palpitations in any nanny, but Miss Jamison was nowhere in sight. Alice and Hazard murmured and chuckled quietly, watching.

And then, perched on the wall, rather than fling out her arms, Hannah pointed and yelled, "Olly!"

Benjamin stretched out his hand to hold her in place before looking over his shoulder. Then he wrapped an arm around Hannah and swooped her safely to the ground. He turned.

"Hullo!"

"Sorry to disturb you," Hazard called out, dismounting.

"You rescued me. My arms are about to give out."

Hannah darted toward them, but Benjamin was quicker. He caught her by the shoulders, then took her hand and said sternly, "No. Hannah, what did I say about horses?"

"Wait."

"Yes. You don't approach horses unless you are holding my hand."

"Horsies now?"

He nodded and began walking very slowly, letting her lead. It was the most precious thing. Olivia felt an almost painful glee building inside of her. When Benjamin and Hannah stopped three feet in front of Oatmeal, Olivia could contain herself no longer. She stepped high in her stirrup, threw out her arms, and cried, "Look, Benjamin!" And then jumped.

He caught her. She knew he would. His chest was rock hard and his arms steady as he set her feet down. He was laughing, very softly.

Then Alice called out, "Haz! Look!"

Olivia whirled around. Hazard had gone to Alice's side to help her dismount. Instead, he caught her flying.

"*Oooff!*" He pretended to stumble, swinging one arm beneath her knees as he straightened. "Lady, you forget my age."

Alice smacked his arm. "You can put me down now."

"Not until I find a deep enough puddle." He started carrying her to the ruins.

"Hazard!" she shrieked. "Don't you dare!"

Olivia could only stare.

"Papa, look! Papa, catch me!"

"Not from Oatmeal, sweetheart. I'll look from the wall."

Olivia followed them to the wall, one eye on them and the other on Hazard and Alice. Hazard wandered through the snow-spattered grass, stepping over stones and fallen bricks. Alice flailed in his arms, laughing.

"Go on, Hannah. Climb." Benjamin's hand rested lightly on his daughter's back as he encouraged her to continue their game.

"No. Catch Olly." Hannah waved her closer.

Olivia gave Benjamin a sidelong look, expecting to see him frown. Instead, he had a smirk on his face.

"You started it," he said, gesturing for her to climb the wall.

"I think you know better than to dare *me*, Benjamin Carroll." She grinned back. Then she scrambled up the wall. Stood on top. Spread her arms. And jumped.

He didn't react quickly enough, and she slammed into him. She started to fall before his arms enfolded her, gripping tight but too high around her shoulders. She slid down his front until her feet hit dirt.

"Olivia!" He buckled over laughing. "You are supposed to yell 'look.'"

"I didn't know there were rules," she gasped out. And then they were both laughing hard enough to cry.

When she caught her breath, she cast a look about for Alice and Hazard. They had gone behind the wall and were now returning, Alice on her own two feet and unmuddied.

"I think we need a new game," Hazard said, coming forward. "Didn't you all used to play one where everyone hid until someone found you? Go on. I will count to ten."

"Fifty," Benjamin said. "We can't hide anywhere in ten."

"Twenty-five. I suggest you run."

"I'll count," Alice said. "You both run."

Crispin used to bring her and Reg here for this very game. Olivia knew all the best hiding places. Maybe it was childish, but it felt so wonderful to play. Olivia found it particularly amusing to see Hazard run. He looked young and free and not at all dignified.

There was something different about Hazard lately that Olivia could not quite put her finger on. He was not an old man, for all he'd started referring to himself as such. He was not that much older than Jasper. But during this visit, he had seemed somehow even less old. As if he had fewer lines across his brow.

They each took a turn hiding with Hannah. And once, Alice stood with the child and counted to ten so that Hannah could find them. Of course, they were within five feet and poorly hidden. Hannah squealed with delight and tagged them all.

Breathless and overly warm, they peeled off their coats and hats and left them beside Benjamin's. Hannah wanted to play *Look, Papa* again, so Hannah, Olivia, and Alice took turns jumping off the wall. It was improper, beyond a doubt, but if Hazard and Alice were doing it… But of course, that was different. Because each time Benjamin caught Olivia, he held her a little longer before setting her down. Or so she imagined. Wishful thinking.

"Alice must catch me this time," Hazard said, puffing with exaggerated breaths.

Hannah patted his knees and said, "Hide me!"

"Ah. Someone takes pity on the old man. Yes. We will hide."

Alice turned her face to the wall and began counting slowly. Olivia took off. She ran to an old stone bench behind the wall, but had second thoughts about crawling under it when she saw the mud. She heard Alice: *seventeen…eighteen…*

She darted to a separate part of the ruins where there was a niche with high walls that they used to call the garderobe because it looked like a medieval water closet. When she and Reg were little, they hid there all the time.

Benjamin was tucked in the niche.

"Twenty-five!" Alice shouted.

Olivia stared wide-eyed at Benjamin, feeling ridiculously panicked. He grabbed her arm and pulled her in beside him. The space was not large enough for two adults. They were squashed chin-to-nose. Olivia was panting a bit from her run, and Benjamin's breathing sounded fast and shallow. She tried to read his thoughts. If he could read hers, he would know she was fighting a wild impulse to kiss him. Her whole body trembled with tension.

She lifted her chin and found him peering down at her. They both began breathing more rapidly. More unevenly. She raised up on tiptoes. He dipped his head lower. Her eyelids fluttered closed, and his lips brushed hers.

She had no basis for comparison, but didn't think it counted as a kiss. She opened her eyes and mouthed, "Kiss me."

This time it was a very definite kiss. A thrill swept through her. This was not her imagination.

Benjamin lifted his head, his breathing even more ragged. Olivia lowered herself to a flat-footed stance, so her view was back on his chin. She was afraid to look up. She knew what she would see in his eyes. Remorse. Guilt.

If they were caught together here, like this, even by Hazard, even by Alice, she would be compromised. Benjamin would truly be wracked by regret. Jasper would be furious. With reason.

In another moment, he would run away from her again. She knew he would, and she couldn't bear it. So she slid sideways, slipped out of the niche, and she ran.

OLIVIA THOUGHT THAT Benjamin should have run after her. Or he should have come to her later and told her he loved her. Or he should have gone to Jasper to ask permission to court her. He had done none of those things.

She had seen him only once more before he left for London. She saw him, but he did not see her. She had been at the top of the main stairs, and he was in the hall at the bottom, speaking with the Byrds. Speaking with *Jilly*, while Mrs. Byrd imperiously directed footmen what to do with several boxes that heralded another morning of bodice pinching and hem marking. Jilly and Benjamin had made an incongruous pair, with Benjamin in his plain dark jacket and Jilly in a bright jonquil frothy construction, trailing ribbons. Even so. They had certainly seemed to have a lot to talk about. She'd backed away from the stairs.

A week had now passed since Hazard and Benjamin's departure. They'd left early in the morning in order to make the most of the daylight hours. Olivia had not gone down to see them off. Rethinking the day at the folly had made her realize the indiscretion had been entirely her fault. She had, quite literally, thrown herself at him. Again. When he'd tentatively touched his lips to hers, she encouraged him to take a greater liberty. Her behavior was inexcusable.

Oh, but that kiss. It proved...something.

Once more, as she had done at least a hundred times, Olivia put her fingertips on her lips to touch where his had been. Such a curious experience. He'd kept his hands at his sides. He didn't put them anywhere on her. Even so, her entire body had grown warm.

Was this something that happened whenever two people kissed? Or would it only ever happen with Benjamin?

"My lady?" Tansy interrupted Olivia's reverie with a note of impatience. "Please stop moving your chin. It loosens the pins."

Olivia's cheeks heated. To hide her embarrassment, she scolded, "I can't walk around wooden faced. If the pins won't stay in with my hair this way, arrange it another way."

How uncomfortable it was, being a lady. She had to walk in flimsy shoes, keeping her head perfectly straight, while long stays pressed into her ribs and lifted her bosoms into a position where they did not belong. All to attract a husband who was surely more interested in her fortune and her family name than in her bosoms.

A husband who might, but who probably would not, warm her with his kisses.

Tansy huffed and took down the side-of-the-head bun she had been attempting and resorted to the usual chignon.

"Better," Olivia said, patting it firmly. She grinned an apology for her ill temper. "The other looked like I'd grown a third ear."

"Miss Byrd says it's the latest fashion!" Tansy protested.

"No!" Olivia exclaimed, widening her eyes. "Three ears?"

Tansy giggled. Olivia picked up her bonnet and pulled it onto her head. She and Alice and Mama were riding to Ipswich to visit the milliner. Two new hats. Just to get her started. Mama insisted the rest must be purchased in London. *Once the baby came.* Although she claimed to be pleasantly surprised by Mrs. Byrd's work, Mama said it was still important to sport some London-made clothes to prove her sophistication.

"You must mean to fake my sophistication," Olivia had replied, making Mama purse her lips. Mama said Olivia's coming-out would be a trial. But she was only teasing. Olivia had heard her telling Jasper that it would be a triumph.

What did that even mean?

Alice burst into the chamber without so much as a rap on the door.

"I'm coming! I'm coming," Olivia said. "My hair didn't work."

"No! It isn't—we aren't going. Reg just sent for the doctor and Mrs. Cooper. Georgiana is having the baby!"

THE DOCTOR, THE midwife, the midwife's assistant, the duchess, Mama, and Georgiana's maid all crowded into Georgiana's bedchamber. Even if Olivia and Alice had been permitted to attend her, there would not have been space enough. They waited in the ladies' sitting room. Aware that it could be a very long wait, they busied themselves with sewing baby napkins. Jasper and Reg were in the study down the hall. Olivia wondered what they did to pass the hours.

Teatime came and went. Olivia was too excited to feel hungry. Excited but not worried. Despite knowing that things *could* go wrong, bad things didn't happen to Georgiana.

Dusk had deepened into night when Mama came to them.

"Oh, my dears," she said, sounding teary but smiling. "They have a beautiful—"

Whooping from down the hall drowned out Mama's words. Then Olivia heard the pounding of footsteps: Reg sprinting. A moment later, Jasper and the duchess came to join them in the sitting room.

"Georgiana was splendid," Mama said.

The duchess nodded. "I must say, she made it look easy."

"Boy or girl?" Olivia asked. "We couldn't hear."

"A boy," Jasper answered for them. He smiled but it looked as though he were trying too hard to do so.

"Reginald must be so pleased," Alice said, then quickly amended, "so *relieved.*"

"Ah, yes," Jasper said. "I'll have to replace my rug. He wore a rut in it."

"Haz will be sorry he missed this," Olivia said. Jasper laughed.

They continued with more nonsense. Then Mama and the duchess compared their own most difficult births. Mama said Crispin. He had come out backwards. Jasper snickered, "Of course." The duchess said Randolph. Her firstborn weighed nine pounds. She got a bit misty eyed. Mama squeezed her arm. A long moment of silence followed. Olivia knew that Georgiana's older brother had died in an accident at school. She couldn't think of anything worse than losing one of her brothers. Bad things did happen to Georgiana.

"Did Reginald send for Hovington?" the duchess asked.

Jasper answered, "A messenger left for Marbury just after the doctor arrived."

Marbury was one of the duke's country homes. Reg once said that it was a good deal prettier than Chaumbers, but Olivia couldn't believe that.

"Good," the duchess said. "Then he will likely be here tomorrow."

"Here he is! Here he is!" Reg announced, shouldering open the door. He carried a large bundle of blankets with a tiny, pink face peeking out. The baby's eyes were closed, and he made adorable mewling sounds. Olivia had never seen Reg grin so wide. She and Alice both jumped to their feet to rush him.

Olivia wept happy tears as she hugged Reg and bundle both.

"He's so tiny. So sweet!" She gushed and gushed. "What will you name him?" She turned her face up to Reg's.

He reddened. Sheepish. "Arthur."

CHAPTER EIGHTEEN

COMING TO LONDON had been the right thing to do. *Of course, it was.* He had *kissed* her! If Olivia hadn't fled from him, terrified or appalled, he would have kissed her again.

And if they had been caught? Benjamin's blood turned to ice. The consequences would have been devastating.

It had been three weeks since he'd begged a ride with Hazard. The viscount was a very pleasant man, but their conversation during the lengthy journey had been superficial given the presence of Miss Jamison and Hannah. During a short rest at a posting station to change horses, Benjamin waited for Miss Jamison to take Hannah to the privy before broaching the topic of a social secretary. Hazard grasped the situation at once.

"But I cannot think of anyone at the moment," he said, scratching his chin. "Come around in a couple of weeks and I may have a few names." Then he smiled in the amused way he had. "Don't come before noon."

So now, the requisite time having passed, Benjamin trudged through the brown-and-yellow snow, nodding to the few equally miserable-appearing city dwellers who had ventured forth on this day of weak sunshine and cold wind after five days of continuous sleet.

Coming to London may have been the right thing to do, but perhaps bringing Hannah had not been. He should not have subjected her to London in February.

Hazard's stonework townhouse was old and stately. Although not as enormous as the Taverston home at 8 Grosvenor Square, it had a substantial heft to it that was partly due to the weight of its history. The Viscounts of Haslet had a storied past, including an ancestor who had gone a-pirating with Sir Walter Raleigh. Hazard's fortune had deep roots.

Benjamin lifted the brass knocker and let it fall. After a few moments, a surprisingly youthful butler opened the door. Benjamin gave him his card.

"Just a moment, sir. I will see if he is in."

Benjamin stood on the freezing stoop, waiting for admittance. It was early afternoon. He had a sudden shiver of worry that he would not be welcome. But before he had time to suffer a true bout of insecurity, the door opened again.

"Come in, if you will, Mr. Carroll. His lordship is in the parlor. I'll take you to him."

Benjamin had never been inside Hazard's home. The entrance hall was striking. Dark, carved-wood paneling covered the walls. Iron candlestands with the longest, fattest candles he'd even seen stood in the corners and in niches beside doorways that were framed by wide moldings. At least a dozen candles burned bright, odorless, and clear. Benjamin tried to guess whether the hallway was kept lit or whether it was the butler's job to quickly light a few when callers arrived. The expense of such massive spermaceti wax candles, if routinely utilized for light and not simply for show, was one of those inconceivable extravagances that made Benjamin's head hurt.

At the end of the entrance hall was a carpeted stairway. Halfway up the stairs, a landing led to a balconied walkway before the stairs continued upward. The butler led him onto the walkway and then through an alcove into an extraordinarily cozy room. The walls were papered in a light-brown design over which had been hung several medieval appearing battlescapes of exceptional quality. A single large window was almost completely blocked by plants. A massive fireplace took up one entire wall. Only a small fire burned in it, but it kept the room warm.

Benjamin was so charmed by the setting that it took him a moment to locate Hazard in it. He sat near the fire in one of two oversized leather chairs. His stockinged feet were propped on a hassock. He waved Benjamin in, dropped his feet to the carpet, and stood.

"James, would you bring another pot of coffee? Come in, Mr. Carroll. Let me introduce you to my good friend, Lord Chesterfield."

Chesterfield occupied the other chair. He stood and nodded. He was a strong-featured man with a barrel chest, graying light-brown hair, and a thin, out-of-fashion mustache. He wore a loose morning jacket and pantaloons. Despite his stature, his expression was retiring. Shy, not aloof.

Benjamin bowed. "Lord Chesterfield."

"Have a seat, Mr. Carroll." Hazard gestured to a cushioned chair upholstered in scarlet. Then he gave his own chair a bit of a shove to widen the circle before sitting down again. Chesterfield sat as well. "Chester and I were just finishing our coffee and debating whether to ring for more. You have decided us."

"Thank you, my lord." There was no point refusing refreshment that had already been sent for. Besides, he could use a warm drink.

"How are you finding London?" Hazard asked. "You are staying at Iversley's?"

"Yes. My previous landlady let out the apartment I had been using. She offered to turn out the current tenant, but that seemed rather cruel."

Hazard said, "Especially since Iversley would have been annoyed to hear you stayed elsewhere. How is little Hannah doing?"

"Better." Then he quickly corrected himself seeing Hazard's brow wrinkle with concern. "Well. She is well."

"Was she not?" Hazard asked. Then he turned to Chesterfield. "Hannah is Mr. Carroll's daughter."

"Her health is robust." He tried to smile. "It is only that London is a far cry from Chaumbers. She misses the fresh air."

"And the company, I imagine."

Benjamin's chest tightened. For the first week or more, Hannah had cried herself to sleep, asking "Where is Olly? Where is Lady?" *Lady*, he learned from Miss Jamison, was the dowager. The crying finally ceased, but Hannah now drifted about with a lost expression that tore at his heart. And she stopped mentioning either Olly or Lady. He didn't know what that signified but thought it sad rather than encouraging.

"Yes, she misses the Taverstons." Benjamin hoped he sounded matter-of-fact.

"As do we all," Hazard said with a chuckle. *God. That was the truth.* "You heard about Arthur, naturally?"

Benjamin grinned. "Iversley sent word. Mr. Taverston did, too. The babe is a blessing, I'm sure."

Hazard turned to Chesterfield. "I told you about that."

Chesterfield smiled. "Captain Taverston had his way yet again."

Then Hazard rubbed his knees and sat straighter as if to say the small talk was finished.

"I have been thinking about Iversley's request. There are a couple names I might suggest, but Chester provided the best one. I think you should start there. A Mr. Nigel Boring."

Boring? An unfortunate name for a secretary. "That name sounds familiar."

Chesterfield snorted. "Yes, well, it would. But not the Earl of Dunleavey. This is a different Boring."

"Related in some way, no doubt," Hazard said. "He is a gentleman. But you'd have to trace back several generations to find a title in his line."

Which explained why the man needed to support himself in such a fashion.

"And why is he the first choice?" Benjamin asked.

"He is very smart," Chesterfield said. "Knows everyone."

"He is currently clerking in his uncle's firm," Hazard said. "Inheritance law or some such. But he finds it stultifying."

"He thinks social secretary would be less so?"

"I believe he would. He's a young man. About your age, I gather. But more...more inclined to put himself forward. I understand he wants to stand for the Commons."

Chesterfield sniffed again. "His politics are sound. And as I said, he is a smart fellow. But he hasn't paid his dues, as one might say. Too young, yet, and he hasn't the funds or the clout for a successful campaign. Working for Iversley would be beneficial to them both."

Jasper's politics were none of Benjamin's concerns, but apparently, they interested Hazard. He wanted to convert Jasper. But Benjamin was certain he would not try to advance his agenda at the expense of Vanessa's entrance to Society and Olivia's coming-out.

The butler arrived with a tray. He gave Benjamin a steaming cup of coffee, refilled the cups of the two lords, set down the pot, and retreated to the door.

"Will there be anything else, my lord?"

"No, James. I will ring when we are finished."

James left the room.

"Good fellow," Hazard said in a low voice. "Has only been with me for three weeks. My butler took ill. I'll have to find a way to keep him when Harrison comes back."

They sipped their coffee. Hazard and Chesterfield discussed the problem of servants. Chesterfield had the typical complaints of his class: servants were not what they used to be. Hazard disagreed. When treated well, they served well. They argued in polite tones, without the quips and laughter Benjamin was used to hearing when Hazard and Jasper traded barbs. Yet they each conceded points to one another with smiles that Benjamin could only interpret as fond.

Then Hazard said, "Good Lord. We are putting poor Mr.

Carroll to sleep. Tell me, how are you finding things at Iversley's? I'll wager the servants have not all deserted their posts with the family gone?"

"Not at all," Benjamin said. Of course, the bulk of the high servants had made the journey to Chaumbers with the Taverstons. Half-staffed, the London home had been "closed." Most of the furniture was now draped in heavy white linen. Fires were kept only in the kitchen and servants' quarters—and now in Benjamin's apartments and the morning room where Benjamin, Hannah, and Miss Jamison took their meals. "They have been very attentive and very welcoming."

"See?" Hazard said, with a smirk. He changed the subject. "Has there been any word from Crispin? Is he in France with Wellington?"

"No word. None of which I am aware."

Hazard sighed. "This war needs to end."

Hazard and Chesterfield exchanged thoughts on Wellington and Bonaparte that were in far better accord than their thoughts on servants. Benjamin drained his cup. He was likely wearing out his welcome.

"My lords, thank you. I should be taking leave and returning to work."

"Let me give you Mr. Boring's direction," Chesterfield said, standing. He reached into his waistcoat as he came toward Benjamin. He didn't watch where he stepped and tripped over Hazard's outstretched feet.

"Sorry, Rupe," he said, giving a sidestep as he caught himself. "Mashed you, did I?"

Hazard blushed. Noticeably. "My fault. My fault." He tucked his feet under his chair as if suddenly realizing he was shoeless. Or maybe it was the name. Rupe. Rupert? Benjamin had never heard him called anything but Hazard.

Chesterfield handed Benjamin a card. "That is the uncle. The address of the firm. You can find young Boring there."

Benjamin stood as he took the card. "Thank you. This is very helpful."

"Ring for James, would you, Chester?" Hazard asked.

Chesterfield went to the wall and pulled the bell cord. A footman appeared. Not James.

"Would you see Mr. Carroll out?" Hazard asked.

Benjamin followed the footman. In the alcove, he heard the scraping sound of the hassock being dragged. Then a soft *"uuuff."* Then very quietly, "Let's see those toes, Rupe. What did I do?"

Benjamin walked quickly away.

❯❯❯❮❮❮

THE FOLLOWING AFTERNOON, he interviewed Nigel Boring from Jasper's office. The office here was twice the size of the study at Chaumbers and the desk was at least three times larger. Benjamin felt like an imposter sitting in the earl's chair, but it would have looked strange not to use it.

Mr. Boring was his own age, twenty-seven, but he had large round childlike eyes that made him appear younger. This was counterbalanced by a strangely long, narrow jaw that practically came to a point at the chin. His hair was rust colored. Benjamin did not like to cast judgment on people's appearances, but the man was ugly. Moreover, he had narrow shoulders and a paunch. But none of this disqualified him for serving as secretary.

Rather, his qualifications were solid. It took only a short conversation to prove he was as smart as Lord Chesterfield claimed. And he was discreet. He said he was aware of Lady Iversley's past, but made no further comment. He understood that the earl's sister was beyond reproach—and that, naturally, her marriage to the *right* peer would be much to Iversley's advantage. He left unsaid that this would be particularly important now, given things as they were. Then he listed several events that he knew Iversley would have to attend, and suggested a few dates when a ball might be held and a few choices for a musicale, along with suggestions for who to hire to perform. It would be best to choose quickly so as to have first choice.

Benjamin was out of his element.

"Iversley suggested that whoever was hired might do best to coordinate with the dowager—"

"I will write to her directly, if you would be so good as to provide me an introduction." Boring flushed as red as his hair. "If you choose to hire me."

Benjamin grinned, thinking of Hazard's description of the man as inclined to put himself forward. Boring was certainly eager.

"Yes, I will hire you. I will write an introduction for you to include in a letter to the earl. Are you able to travel to Iversley Village? I imagine he will ask you to come, and he will introduce you to the dowager himself."

"Yes! Yes, indeed. As soon as they require me."

"Good. If you would be so good as to return in two days, I will have the letter of introduction ready. While we wait for a response, which I imagine will be quick, you may begin making inquiries about performers. Musicians, I think, rather than singers." He had a vague memory of Reg employing an opera singer as a mistress at one point. He couldn't remember the woman's name, but couldn't think of anything worse than accidentally hiring her to perform at a Taverston entertainment when they were trying to tamp down gossip.

"Very good, Mr. Carroll. Very good! I will."

They shook hands. Mr. Boring left.

And now Benjamin faced a decision. Should he return with Boring? Hannah was unhappy. The tasks he'd set for himself in London were complete. Chaumbers' steward belonged at Chaumbers.

Having discovered his inability to control his impulses, he must simply make sure he was never alone with Olivia. Soon enough, she would be in London. It would be better for everyone if he were not.

CHAPTER NINETEEN

O LIVIA'S DRESSING ROOM was crowded with boxes, gowns on hooks where there were not usually gowns, loose fabrics draped over chairs, shoes littering the floor, and too many people. She regarded herself in the full-length mirror. Rather, she regarded her dress and her companions. Mrs. Byrd stood to her left wearing an anxious expression. Vanessa, just behind Olivia's right shoulder, looked pleased. She couldn't see her mother's face but heard a hum of approval.

The dress was eggshell white and made of silk. There was no discernible waistline, but the fabric gathered in pleats under her bust, then rose upward between her breasts where the pleats twisted into what looked like a small white rose. The stitching was complex and rather ingenious, Olivia thought. But the neckline dipped down into the rose and was lower than anything she had ever worn.

The dress required specially made underthings which seemed to hold her bosoms in place rather than rearranging them. Everything was soft and comfortable. And yet…she frowned.

"What is it?" Vanessa asked, her brow wrinkling. "What don't you like?"

"I don't know. I don't think white is my color. I look sickly."

"You look angelic," Mama said from the back of the room. "It has to be white for your debut ball. And don't forget there will be silver threading and pearls."

"I know." Mrs. Byrd had hired an embroiderer in Ipswich to decorate the gown with silver thread and stud it with pearls to catch the light and make Olivia sparkle. Still, white was not her color. She didn't know how she would keep it clean for an entire evening.

"Olivia, you will be stunning," the duchess said from her seat beside Mama.

The gown for a lady's coming-out ball was supposedly the most important one she would ever wear—more important even than her wedding dress. Although, there was also whatever hideous thing the London modiste was creating for Olivia to don when she was presented to the queen. That was significant too, and there were very strict rules. Mama insisted on an experienced London dressmaker for that. Olivia found the whole thing tiring.

She turned a little to the left, then to the right, and looked herself up and down. The style was flattering. She imagined herself with the side-of-the-head bun that Tansy had mastered. She might well be stunning, but she would not look like herself.

"Yes, well, thank you, Mrs. Byrd. This should do very nicely."

Mrs. Byrd sighed with relief. "I'll get this one off to the embroiderer. Would you like to see the yellow next or the blue?"

Olivia winced. They had done this already with a dozen day dresses and now it was time for the ballgowns. Mama had ordered six. The white was the most important and had been done first. But now there were fittings again. And so many choices to be made. Sleeves and collars and beadwork. A million tiny buttons or a half-million slightly larger?

"Bring out the yellow," Mama said for her. "Yellow is a difficult color with Olivia's hair. We may need some contrast about the neck."

Mrs. Byrd turned to bustle about in her boxes. Vanessa and Tansy helped Olivia out of the white silk.

"This is unbearable," Olivia muttered for Vanessa's ears only.

"Stay strong," Vanessa whispered back. "I told Georgiana to

bring Arthur in if we were more than three hours."

Olivia smiled at that. Mrs. Byrd would pack up her wares in an instant when a baby with a tendency to spit entered the vicinity.

If not for little Arthur, Olivia didn't know how she would have gotten through the month. It wasn't simply that February was dreary. She still managed to ride most days, although she had to keep the rides short and stay close to the house unless she was visiting a tenant. She enjoyed being with her family. Parlor games after tea. Billiards with her brothers or the Duke of Hovington and Alice. A few brief conversations with Vanessa—not strategizing, but becoming more comfortable with one another. Olivia wasn't bored. Rather she was sad. This would all come to an end, and she was already nostalgic for it.

Mrs. Byrd held up the yellow ballgown for scrutiny. A pale slip of a satin dress was covered by a white tissue overdress. The sleeves puffed and the neckline dipped, but not too much. Olivia fought her way into it.

"Those are the wrong undergarments," Mrs. Byrd said, biting her lip. "More substantial stays will help with the fit."

Mama came closer and circled Olivia while scrutinizing her from all angles. Then she sighed.

"I can't help thinking we made a wrong choice with that yellow."

Mrs. Byrd fingered the gauzy overdress. "I could have this dyed blue. Or perhaps green. That would change the look considerably."

"Vanessa," Mama said, "what do you think?"

It was grand that Mama and Vanessa were finding common ground. Olivia only wished that not so much of it involved dressing her.

Vanessa crossed her arms over her chest. "I don't believe it is salvageable. It's a beautiful dress, but wrong for Olivia. Do you know, though, it would be perfect for Alice."

"You're right," Mama said, scowling. "Take it off. Let's see about the blue. And, Mrs. Byrd, we'll have it refitted for Alice."

Oh, bosh. That meant starting over with something else. Unless five gowns were enough. But they wouldn't be. She would be going to more than five balls. Many more. They would have to visit a modiste in London after all. They had already overtaxed poor Mrs. Byrd.

She wiggled into the blue. Better. It had a floral print and fit loosely. Olivia could move in it.

"You'll have to tighten the neck and those sleeves," Mama said.

Mrs. Byrd nodded. "Hold up your arms, please, Lady Olivia."

Olivia dutifully held out her arms while Mrs. Byrd put pins everywhere, making what had been comfortable less so. Then they helped her out of the dress, pricking her here and there with the pins.

"Are we finished?" she asked.

"I have the pink day dress back again," Mrs. Byrd said. "I've lengthened the train as you asked." She nodded to Mama. "Would you like to see?"

"Oh, yes, while you are here. Let's have a look."

Olivia held her breath and counted to ten. Surely they had been at this for over three hours. Tansy and Mrs. Byrd dropped a pink cotton dress over her head, then fussed with the buttons. Olivia had agreed to pink under the condition that there be no ruffles or bows. She had worn a dress she hated that Mama called "very pretty, very feminine" to tell Benjamin that she loved him, and he'd run off to Canada. She would never wear anything resembling it ever again. And this one had too many ribbons. She looked like Jilly Byrd.

Mama said, "Oh, yes, that's much better. It's quite lovely."

"Yes, it is," Vanessa said. "Olivia, you *will* cause a stir."

Olivia made herself smile. This was awful. That pink-clad girl in the mirror did not look like her either.

This was all artifice. The beautiful gowns. The elaborate hairstyles. She was supposed to walk with mincing steps. Keep her voice low. Laugh quietly without growing breathless. She should not talk about horses unless she was prepared to agree with whatever idiotic thing the man she was talking to might say. She was not allowed to make jests at her brothers' expense in company—people might misunderstand.

She could not dance with a gentleman unless they had been introduced. Then, whether she wanted to or not, she must dance with him if he asked, unless her card was full or unless she was finished dancing for the evening. Or unless she had already danced with him twice. Two times per event was the limit. Unless it was a waltz. She must never dance more than one waltz with the same man at the same ball. But, of course, a true gentleman would never ask her to break the rules, and she would only be introduced to true gentlemen, so why did Mama keep reminding her of things she already knew?

There was no opportunity for spontaneity. No chance for fun. And no way for a man to know the real Olivia.

Benjamin knew her. But he was not considered a gentleman. And he'd kissed her, which was not a gentlemanly thing to have done, so that proved it. Still, she had encouraged him. What did that prove? That she was not a true lady?

"We are here!" Georgiana called, entering the dressing room with Arthur draped on her shoulder, fussing. For the first time *ever*, Georgiana looked baggy-eyed. "Arthur wants his Aunt Olly."

Olivia shook away her guilty thoughts and stretched out her arms.

"No!" Mama and Mrs. Byrd cried at once.

"Take off the dress first, Olivia," Mama scolded.

Vanessa hurried to undo the buttons and Tansy helped lift it over her head. They exchanged it for a loose dressing gown. Then Georgiana handed over Arthur. He was sucking on his hand and blinking his bright-blue eyes. Everything he did melted Olivia's heart.

"Alice is waiting for us in the parlor," Georgiana said.

Mama said, "*Hmmm.* Send her here. She can try on the yellow gown."

With a whoosh of relief, and a smidgeon of pity for Alice, Olivia snuggled Arthur close and led the way out of the room.

⇢⟫⟪⟪⟨

OLIVIA SETTLED INTO Mama's rolled-arm chair nearest the fire, dismayed by Arthur's continuing to fuss.

"I think he's hungry."

Georgiana said, "It seems so. Give him here."

Olivia reluctantly rose and took the baby to Georgiana, seated on the davenport beside Vanessa. Georgiana opened the front of her gown and put the babe to her breast. Apparently, her mother, the duchess, had nursed all her own children and Georgiana saw no reason to do otherwise. Although it was sweet to see how quickly Arthur was comforted, it was nevertheless a strange thing for a *lady* to do, and certainly looked uncomfortable.

"Do you want Mama's chair?"

"Oh, no. This is fine."

Olivia paced rather than return to her seat. She had been exhausted in her dressing room, but now had too much energy to sit.

"Alice appeared excited, didn't she?" Alice had raced toward the dressing room with the same alacrity Olivia had shown exiting it.

"Yes," Vanessa said. "She did."

Olivia saw the look the other two ladies exchanged. A bit self-satisfied.

"Oh!" She giggled. "You planned that, Vanessa."

"No, your mother did. I was merely her co-conspirator."

Olivia grinned. "Well, then, I'm glad to have been an unsuspecting pawn, I suppose."

Alice was embarking on her second Season, sponsored once again by the duchess, but her father, the duchess's brother, had insisted Alice did not need new clothes. He said that the duchess spent a fortune last year, and Alice could wear the same gowns again. Olivia could sympathize with the man's pride, to a point, but he didn't understand the ton. Alice would be severely handicapped without a few new dresses. He should think of a new wardrobe as an investment. That was what Jasper, teasing Olivia, had said he did.

Olivia heard her brothers' voices in the hallway. A moment later, they came into the room. Reg went to Georgiana's side and bent to kiss her. Jasper took two steps into the room and froze. His face went red.

Arthur was hidden under a shawl that covered Georgiana from shoulder to waist. Nevertheless, Arthur's snuffling noises made it clear what was going on. Jasper spun on his heel, murmured an incoherent apology, and sped from the room. Reg shook his head, and the ladies laughed.

"I spent my whole life outnumbered by Taverston males," Olivia said. "Now the ladies are in the majority and the tables have turned!"

"Don't crow yet," Reg countered. "We are soon to even the score."

"What do you mean?" Vanessa asked.

"Jasper has evidently hired himself a social secretary. Benjamin is bringing him to meet everyone. They should be here later tonight."

Benjamin was returning. Tonight. Olivia held her breath a moment, then let it out slowly, glad that no one could hear the way her heart rate sped up.

Vanessa's brow wrinkled fleetingly, with surprise or irritation or both. "A *social secretary?*"

Reg said, "I think it was Mother's idea. Just for the Season."

Mama's idea? And Jasper had not conferred with Vanessa first? What an idiot.

Vanessa stood and smoothed the front of her gown, her face unreadable. "I'd best make Cook aware. And Mrs. Hardy.

Benjamin's apartments will need to be aired. And I suppose this…?"

"Mr. Boring."

Vanessa's eyebrow twitched upwards. "Mr. Boring will also need a room. If you will excuse me."

Olivia knew she should be concerned that Mama must be worried, but there was no room in her heart for anything but joy. Benjamin would be back tonight. They would have a little more time together. A little was better than none.

CHAPTER TWENTY

W HEN THE CARRIAGE rattled into the drive at Chaumbers, Benjamin almost shouted hurrah. Mr. Boring, whether from eagerness or nervousness, had not stopped talking for seven hours. He was a pleasant enough fellow, but if he did not learn to restrain himself…the Taverstons would likely have a bit of fun.

A memory slipped into his brain, and he snickered to himself.

Seven or eight years ago, he'd been Jasper's guest at 8 Grosvenor Square. The old earl had a guest, too, a particularly garrulous elderly gentleman. The brothers complained amongst themselves, their jokes veering into mockery. No one wanted to sit beside him at supper and the countess grew frustrated with her sons' ill grace—although, as Jasper pointed out, she didn't assign herself the seat beside him either. And then, Olivia spoke up. "I'll sit by him, Mama."

That pleased the countess. At least *Olivia* had manners.

Olivia must have been ten or eleven. Too old for the nursery but too young to converse with adults. She had been relegated to the foot of the table where she behaved impeccably, meaning silently, so that she would not be banished. The countess must have seen it as the perfect solution, promoting Olivia toward the head of the table to sit by their guest. It was. But not the solution she'd envisioned.

Olivia talked the man's ear off. Every topic he tried to introduce, she stole and ran with.

"Kensington Gardens is everywhere blooming." Benjamin could still hear the man's bombast.

"Yes, my lord. We were there just last week. Six days ago to be precise. The roses are particularly beautiful. I do so like roses. We have them in our garden here in London, but they never seem as brightly colorful as those at Chaumbers. I suppose it is all the soot in the air. Too many chimneys. Of course, the fires are necessary or how would we eat? We'd have to have cold meat for every meal. No, I don't suppose even that. Cold meat does have to be cooked, doesn't it?"

"Well, yes. Ha, ha. I suppose it does. One does like meat fresh from the country. The hams at Brownington are the best in England."

"Oh, hams," Olivia made a face. "I'm not fond of hams. They always taste of salt. Though I suppose that is better than tasting of pig. When one looks at a pig, one never thinks, 'I'll wager that tastes delicious.' Nor cows though. Who could eat something with those gentle eyes." She looked at her plate. Beef. "Well, let us not think of eyes. Isn't it too bad we can't eat flowers. Now they look delicious. Anything that smells so wonderful should be eaten. Except ladies."

Crispin had snorted at that, covering his mouth with his napkin. But Olivia wasn't finished.

"That was a joke, my lord. Cannibalism is a sin, don't you agree? I learned from my governess that there were cannibals here in England back in the days of the Druids, but that doesn't seem right to me. I'm not sure I believe half of what she tells me."

Olivia launched into a series of lessons she had been given that were all just a little bit…off. The old man tried to interrupt more than once, but whatever he said just sent Olivia off on another tangent. It was a miracle the brothers managed to keep straight faces. The countess had looked mortified.

Benjamin wondered if Olivia had been punished for it. He did know that her brothers toasted her later in secret, because he'd been with them, laughing just as heartily.

He had always admired her. Always. But he hadn't been *waiting* for her.

He stepped down from the carriage, Hannah cradled in his arms. His feet crunched the gravel as he carried her across the drive, then up the steps and into the house as carefully as if she were made of china. She had spent the first half of the journey bouncing with happiness and impatience and the second half sound asleep.

Peters met them. Seeing Hannah, his voice dropped to a near whisper. "Mr. Carroll, his lordship is in the study. He requests that you bring Mr. Boring to him. Miss Jamison and the child would be welcome in the ladies' sitting room unless she feels it better to go to the south wing."

Benjamin handed Hannah to Miss Jamison, who mouthed, "I had better put her to bed."

The butler led Benjamin and Boring upstairs, which really wasn't necessary. Benjamin would know the way blindfolded. Peters let them into the study. Jasper got to his feet.

"Welcome."

Mr. Boring bowed, spurring Benjamin to do so. When had he stopped remembering to perform the courtesy? He hurried to do introductions properly.

"My lord, may I present to you Mr. Nigel Boring?"

"Mr. Boring, thank you for your letter. Mr. Carroll explained your qualifications. And I had a letter from Viscount Haslet also. I'm sure we will work well together. Please, have a seat. I have a few questions, minor things. Then I will let you refresh yourself after your journey." He glanced toward Benjamin. "Mr. Carroll, you may go to the parlor. Mr. and Mrs. Taverston are there, quite desperate to introduce you to Arthur. There is tea as well."

Benjamin nodded. He could hardly feel miffed at the dismissal given where he was being sent. He left Boring to his own devices.

As he made his way to the parlor, he realized yet again what a gift his position was. Jasper allowed him free run of Chaumbers.

His first duty upon returning was not to give account of his activities in London, but rather to meet the earl's nephew. Looking at the familiar paintings along the walls, hearing Taverston voices emanating from the parlor growing more distinct as he approached, he felt as though he were returning home. But of course, he was not. His home had been a gritty two-room dwelling in an area one step above the London stews, and his father had barely kept them in that.

He stood in the doorway. This was one of the family's favorite rooms, and it was easy to see why. Gauzy drapes allowed sun through the window but never let anyone sitting in the wrong seat be blinded by glare. The furniture, in dark mahogany and forest-green damasks, all had a well-used appearance without being shabby. In the spring, the room was warm enough without a fire. A faint scent of the dowager's Lily-of-the-Valley perfume always hung in the air.

He took in the scene. Reg and Georgiana on the davenport. Georgiana's parents, the Duke and Duchess of Hovington seated in the corner, sipping tea. Alice in the armchair nearby. Olivia, standing, laughing as she peered down at Arthur in her arms. Who was swaddled in so many layers that Benjamin could not see what amused her. But he could hear Arthur complaining in a high-pitched fussy whine.

"Benjamin! Come in!" Reg cried, rising from his seat. "Olivia, bring Arthur over so Benjamin can see him."

Benjamin couldn't help laughing. Reginald, the quietest of the brothers, was adept at under-his-breath witticisms, but had never been one to draw attention to himself. It seemed being a new father had changed that.

Benjamin's amusement faded as Olivia came close.

She wore a faded chemise dress with spit-up on her shoulder. Her hair was half up and half down, as if pins had fallen out. But with that smile, full of joy and love and good humor, she was the most beautiful woman he'd ever seen. That smile and those blue eyes. That smile with those full lips, forbidden fruit that he'd tasted.

"Would you like to hold him?" she asked.

"I—I would."

He held out his arms, and she settled Arthur into them. Unlike most unmarried men, he had no fear of babies. No fear he would drop them or that they would brand him an imposter with immediate wails. He had held Hannah when she was a baby. Not so small as this one, but every bit as helpless. His heart clenched.

The room grew very still. Arthur quieted.

"Oh!" the duchess breathed. "A miracle!"

And then Arthur burst into a full-throated squall.

Benjamin tried a few half-hearted bounces before delivering the boy to his mother. Georgiana stood. "He eats constantly," she said with something of an apology as she took the baby from the room.

Reg sat down and gestured for him to do so also, but he waited for Olivia to sit first. His manners had not deteriorated to such an extent that he would sit while a lady stood.

"How was London?" Olivia asked, as nonchalant as if he had never behaved with rank impropriety toward her.

"The same. Terrible place in the dead of winter."

"Maybe you shouldn't have gone." There was just a hint of archness to her voice.

She sat beside Reg. Then she pushed back the loose lock of hair and grimaced as if she'd just realized what a mess it was. If it had been an attempt to flirt, she failed miserably. But she didn't need to flirt to capture his heart.

"Maybe I shouldn't have." His quiet earnestness struck the wrong chord. He felt an urge to clear his throat.

"Did you see much of Hazard?" Alice asked.

He turned to her gratefully. "Not much, no. Just the one meeting where he recommended Mr. Boring. Or, I suppose, Lord Chesterfield did."

"Lord Chesterfield?" Reg said, frowning. "I know the name but can't place it."

Benjamin shrugged. He hadn't consulted *Debrett's*. He'd thought Chesterfield was just some minor lord who happened to be a good friend of Hazard's.

Alice said, "Lord Chesterfield is the Earl of Gladnorshire."

"Welsh?" Reg said. "I've never met him."

"You might know his sons. Although they are quite young. The younger might still be at Eton."

Reg *hmmmed*. "Is Chesterfield a friend of your father?"

"Not a friend. Merely an acquaintance." Her brow knitted. She looked at her hands. "I don't know anything about him, really. I don't think he spends much time in London."

"Maybe he is the mysterious hound owner who invited Hazard for Christmas." Reg grinned. Alice did not. She looked nervous and didn't say anything more. Benjamin felt he'd misstepped by bringing up the name. He couldn't quite forget the tenderness of that "Rupe" or Hazard's uncharacteristic blush.

He glanced about for a change of topic. "Iversley promised tea."

"Oh!" Olivia jumped up. "It's gone cold. I'll ring for fresh."

"No. Please don't bother. I came to meet Arthur, but I shouldn't linger. I want to be there if Hannah wakes. In case she is confused." He added, to excuse himself for his return, "I—I couldn't keep her in London. She was miserable."

Olivia nodded. "Poor girl. I can empathize."

AFTER JASPER HAD finished with Boring, and after the man had been shown his guest chamber and tidied himself up, he returned to Benjamin to be introduced to the ladies. How that had become Benjamin's job, he could not fathom. Nevertheless, he escorted Boring to the parlor. Boring carried a small valise and a large, rolled piece of paper. His face glowed with excitement.

"Ladies," Benjamin said, "this is Mr. Boring." He introduced the women. Mr. Boring bowed earnestly to each in turn. "You've met Iversley. And this is Mr. Taverston." He gestured to Reg.

"Now, what do you have for us?" Jasper said, taking a seat on the arm of Vanessa's chair. "You said you had a plan?"

"Indeed." A faint sheen of sweat dampened his brow. "May I?"

Jasper made a sweeping motion with his hand. He looked curious and amused. Vanessa, on the other hand, frowned.

"As I'm sure you're aware, you present formidably," Mr. Boring said, bobbing his head as though he were agreeing with them, rather than asking them to agree with him. "And more formidably *en masse*. You must all arrive in London together."

"That was our intention," Jasper said. Then he glanced toward his brother. "Though with the possible exception of Mr. Taverston. He has an engagement."

Mr. Boring frowned. "Of course. But he should not miss Lady Olivia's ball."

"I will not," Reg said. "If necessary, I will reschedule—"

"Reg!" Olivia protested. "You needn't do that."

Mr. Boring pressed on as if there had been no interruption. "It is clever to skip the preliminaries and make your entrance after the start of the Season. It will create an *impression*. But that should not be carried too far." He glanced about nervously, as though worried he might be giving offense. When no one spoke, he said, "April at the latest. Once you arrive, it would be best to have Lady Olivia presented at Court at the earliest possible date, followed as soon as possible by her coming-out ball. The very same night if we can arrange it."

"The reasoning being?" the dowager asked.

Mr. Boring's attention swiveled to her. "My lady, we wish to stun Society in one blow. I don't presume to tell you…" His face reddened. His gaze dropped. Then he presumed. "There is gossip, naturally. But it is tepid. The ton is easily distracted and while Lord and Lady Iversley are tucked away here, they are somewhat out of mind."

Jasper gave a choked little laugh, but no one else was amused. Benjamin imagined Jasper was astonished at the thought he could be "out of mind."

Boring continued, "Lady Olivia should 'take the stage,' if you will, before any ugly gossip has time to take hold or factions might form."

"And I should keep to the background," Vanessa said.

"Ah, no, my lady, if you please. That would be the worst thing to do. The ton will smell blood. Your success depends upon you're being—"

"Fearless and unapologetic," Olivia said.

"Visible and commanding," Boring said.

"But in different spheres," said the dowager. She stood as though to stare the man down. "The countess is not my daughter's sponsor. I am. While I agree that Lady Iversley must not play shrinking violet, neither should she and Lady Olivia appear to be clinging to one another for support. They have different strengths. They must divide and conquer."

Olivia snickered. "That doesn't mean what you think it does, Mama."

Vanessa's eyes lit with amusement, but she kept her lips pressed tight.

The dowager said, "It means what *I* say it does."

Mr. Boring chose that moment to unroll his paper, revealing a chart the size of a battle map. It showed every date from March through June, covered with notes. "This demonstrates every significant Season event planned thus far and a good number of the insignificant ones." Benjamin was impressed by the way he captured his audience. Then Boring put his finger on a spot. "April the eleventh. This would be the best night for the ball. Assuming Lady Olivia can receive her invitation to Court prior to this."

The dowager nodded. "Leave that to me. You hire the musicians and have the invitations printed. We'll need Johnston and Tabbs to cater."

"I'm afraid that won't be possible, my lady," Boring fretted, indicating his chart. "They will have been reserved for the twelfth by the Wingsinghams, and they won't do balls two nights in succession."

"Nonsense," scoffed the Duchess. "They simply need to be coaxed. I will speak to Tabbs. And to Lady Jersey about an invitation to Almacks. Lady Olivia will need permission to waltz before attending too many balls."

The dowager and duchess exchanged determined nods. Boring rolled up his chart, looking smug. Olivia caught back a sigh.

"Are you all right with this, Olivia?" Georgiana asked.

Attention shifted. Olivia squared her shoulders and smiled, but her face was wan. When she spoke, her voice was too bright. "Yes, of course. Tell me what to do and when, and I'll do it."

"Good," Jasper said, rubbing his hands together.

This seemed to be the signal for everyone to start talking at once. Benjamin used the opportunity to murmur, "Excuse me." And slip out of the room. He couldn't bear to listen to more.

⤜⤜⤜⤛⤛⤛

IN THE MORNING, Benjamin reviewed in his head the list of things he meant to do, then decided he would first ride out to the cottage. He had Fergus saddle Goose. The weather was questionable, so he did not take Hannah. That enabled him to bypass the folly.

The sight of the old stone building lifted his spirits. He liked things that were solid. That endured. And this home would be his for as long as *he* endured.

After dismounting and slogging through mud toward the house, he heard a noise from within.

"Hullo!" he called out. There was no answer. He didn't expect to find trespassers. Not this deep into the Taverstons' estate. An animal, perhaps? "Hullo!" he called again.

A man filled the doorway. It took Benjamin a moment to recognize the wiry, grizzled Willy Pyle.

"Ah, Mr. Carroll, sir. I didn't know ya were back. I had a few hours." He made a vague gesture at the house. "Come to see, have ya?"

"Yes. Yes, I'd like to see how the work is going." He paused. "I thought you were finishing the boathouse before starting here." He'd told Willy that work for the earl took precedence.

"That's done. Timmy's just finishing the caulking and painting. The earl will have his boats in place before the weather warms."

"Oh. Very good." He added a ride to the lake to his list of tasks. That trip to London had put him behind.

"Come in, then." Willy stepped aside. "Let me show you the trouble."

"Trouble?"

"T'ain't nothing much. It'll fix. Come in."

Benjamin stomped his boots on the stoop, then entered the hall. To his left was a good size parlor. To his right was a smaller receiving room. Down the hall further was a stairway and beyond that, a kitchen and pantry and workrooms and storage. He took in the improvements. The place had been scrupulously cleaned. The broken windows had all been replaced. Then he noticed another difference.

"Where are the doors?"

"Ah, see, that's the trouble. I had to take them all out. Nothing hangs square anymore."

"All the doors? Upstairs, too?"

"Every bloomin' one." Willy practically beamed with delight. "But don't be worrying. I can reframe the doorjambs and make new doors. They won't be square, but no one notices so long as they open and close."

"But why…"

"Houses settle, Mr. Carroll. If you look in the cellar, you can see where the foundation is cracked. That can be fixed with some gravel fill and brickwork."

"That sounds serious. Are we in danger of the whole thing coming down on our heads?"

Willy laughed. "No, sir!" He slapped a hand against the wall. "This fine house has had almost a hundred years to do its settling. It's not going anywhere anymore."

Willy knew his business. There wasn't much Benjamin could say. Or wanted to. He hadn't come here for conversation. He wanted time alone. Time to soak in this place, this solid, safe home where he would live, work, and bring up Hannah. To remind himself that that was all he needed.

Yet he also wanted solitude to contemplate Olivia and resign himself to the fact that she would be leaving soon to begin her new life. She'd implied she would be miserable in London. He couldn't let himself dwell on that.

"Do you want to see upstairs?" Willy asked. "I've reframed the window casings in the bedchambers. It looks right nice."

Olivia had everything a debutante could wish for: beauty, lineage, a substantial dowry, and herself. Her delightful, witty, fun-loving self. She was everything any suitor could ever want. How could she possibly be miserable in London in the springtime with the gardens blooming, a social whirl, and a blizzard of eligible men lining up at her door?

"*Hmm?* Windows? No, I will wait. I have other things I need to do today, and I should let you get back to work," he told Willy, pulling back his attention. "How long do you think before finishing can be done? I'm riding out to see Everet and I thought I'd hire him to paint."

He wanted to head off any suggestion he might hire Willy's nephew. Word was that Timmy dawdled and didn't pay attention. Willy ended up redoing whatever the boy had done.

"Aye, Everet can use the work," Willy said, scratching his hip. "Two weeks. Maybe three. Or he can start earlier down here while I work upstairs."

"I'll ask what he wants." Benjamin took a final glance around.

"It's cold in here. You can have a fire if you like."

"Well, thank you, Mr. Carroll. But I'm used to working in the cold. All het up, I might stretch out on the floor and nap the day away."

Benjamin would have laughed but he didn't think Willy was joking. The man worked hard.

"All right, then. Good day."

"Good day to you, sir."

Benjamin returned to Goose. The day was not going as planned, but perhaps that was just as well. Roaming the cottage, telling himself it was all for the best—and it *was*—would not have helped.

CHAPTER TWENTY-ONE

OLIVIA SPENT THE morning writing to an old friend who would also be in London for the Season. She'd been promising Mama she would do so. Their fathers had been close, so they had spent time in one another's schoolrooms and music rooms and long weeks at each other's family estates during house parties. Nevertheless, she hadn't seen Isabel for more than two years and their letters had grown infrequent. They should have debuted in the same cohort, but…Papa had fallen ill.

Isabel had married last year so she was busy doing married things, and there wasn't much for Olivia to write about when isolated in the country. Nothing that would interest Isabel. But Olivia would need friends in London, so she wrote to her old playfellow. About Arthur. About her new clothes. She asked after Isabel's family. Then she sealed her letter with wax and a frown.

Done. Hopefully Isabel would respond.

"Tansy, please give this to Peters to see to."

"Yes, my lady."

"And may I have my bonnet and pelisse?"

While Tansy was in the dressing room looking for her things, a rap came on the door, so Olivia answered it herself, then stepped back.

"Alice!" She was dressed like a frump. Olivia wondered if she was saving her better dresses for London. "Good. You can come riding with me."

"Oh." Alice bit her lip. "I can't. Georgiana wants me. But I—I needed to talk to you first." She moved into the chamber. There was a cloud on her brow that looked ready to break.

Olivia sat down hard on the edge of her bed. "What's wrong?"

"Nothing." She spoke too quickly. Then she slid into Olivia's desk chair, continuing to frown. "It's ridiculous. But Georgiana"—she raised her eyes then dropped them—"she asked if you've said anything to me about Benjamin."

A chill ran through Olivia's core. "What do you mean? What would I say?"

Alice shrugged one shoulder awkwardly. "She mentioned that you favored him when you were young. And that you seem...I don't know, *happier* now that he's back from London."

"What a gossip!" She tried to give a disbelieving huff, but it came out as more of a whine. Of course her brothers talked, and everything Reg knew, Georgiana would know. "She thinks I'm chasing after him?" Was it so inconceivable that Benjamin might be interested in *her*?

"Don't be mad at *me*. I told Georgiana she was being silly. I told her I've seen you together frequently and there is no indication..." With a sigh, she added, "Maybe I should not have said 'frequently.'"

No, she shouldn't have. Especially since Olivia didn't see Benjamin frequently enough!

"Benjamin and I are friends. That's all."

"Yes, that's what I told her. But I wanted to be sure. If you need to talk—"

"We're friends," she said stubbornly, "just as you and Hazard are."

Alice blinked. Then she turned her head and fidgeted. Olivia peered more closely. Alice's cheeks turned faintly pink.

"Oh, Alice." This was not good. "Hazard is..." *What?* "You do know that Hazard..."

"His interests lie elsewhere." Alice twisted her hands in her lap and then stood. "Yes, I know that. I knew it even before Georgiana took it upon herself to explain the same thing. But that has no bearing. We enjoy one another's company. Is that not allowed?"

"Of course it is." She could imagine the whole conversation—Georgiana interrogating Alice about her interest in Hazard and Olivia's interest in Benjamin. It was embarrassing. And worse, Olivia believed she and Alice were now lying to each other. And to Georgiana. "I am not scaring Benjamin back to Canada, so Georgiana can put that worry out of her head."

"Well, it might help"—Alice lowered her voice further, apologetically—"if you were to show a little more enthusiasm for your coming-out."

Tansy reentered the bedroom and stood quietly near the wall, pelisse and bonnet clasped in her hands. Good. Olivia felt even more desperate to escape.

Alice continued, "Reg is worried, you know. Worried you are still grieving your father. Clinging too much to Chaumbers. Worried that you are being pushed out into the world before you are ready. But your mother says—"

"Faith!" Embarrassment flooded her. "Have you all been conferencing about me behind my back?" This was worse than being mortified at fourteen! She was no longer a pitiable child.

Alice fluttered her hand. "Not about Benjamin. Georgiana asked that privately."

She was thankful for that small favor, but still. "So Reg thinks I am too immature to debut?" How unfair. No one accused Crispin of immaturity for being so fond of the old Binnings cottage that no one else was allowed to touch it. And Jasper could have no concept of what it would feel like, being pushed out of his beloved home. "And my mother thinks what?"

Alice's brow furrowed. "Your mother says you'll be fine. But Jasper is worried that you're afraid of facing the ton. Because his marrying Vanessa has disadvantaged you."

"No." Olivia pressed down upon her bed, clutching the coverlet. Georgiana recognized that she was mooning over Benjamin, and Jasper thought she resented him marrying Vanessa. It couldn't possibly be worse. "I *am* looking forward to my debut. Good heavens. How could I not be? What I am unenthusiastic about is spending hours in my dressing room being fitted for clothes. They all know me well enough to know that."

Alice nodded, but not as though she was convinced. Olivia vowed to stop complaining. She would laugh and smile and gush. And lie.

"I can't wait to go to London! I just wrote to a friend telling her so." She couldn't let Jasper think she was afraid of the ton's gossips. She shouldn't have volunteered to wait another year. Especially after exhorting Vanessa to be fearless! But it wasn't that she was afraid of failing. She was afraid of succeeding. "Just drop word to Georgiana that I am thrilled the fittings are almost done so now I can enjoy the preparations for London. She'll tell Reg and he'll tell Jasper, and this silliness will be done."

"Yes, I can do that."

"And now, Tansy, my things." She stood up so quickly her knees wobbled. She needed air. She didn't dare say any more to Alice. "I'm going for my ride."

SHE RODE DANDY out to the lake. Nothing was going right. Oatmeal was off her feed and George wanted to keep her close. The meadow was terribly muddy, and Dandy picked his way.

When she reached the lake, she dismounted at the tree stump they kept cleared for the purpose. She let Dandy graze while she wandered out to the boathouse. It was nearly complete. Willy had made it a little larger than the previous one. Tighter. The paint looked fresh, so she didn't touch the boards.

Come summer, the family would come out to swim and row.

They would have picnics. Georgiana would lay Arthur on a blanket. Perhaps he would start to crawl here at the lake.

She would not be here to see it.

Stop that! She would soon be dancing in the finest ballrooms in London. She would go to the theater. Operas. The museum. Bookstores. Vauxhall Gardens. She would eat ices at Gunthers and ride in Hyde Park. Handsome lords would fill her dance card.

She used to dream of these things before Papa got sick. Like any normal young lady, she *did*. Back then, Benjamin had been in Canada for more than two years. She'd put him out of her mind. She *had been* over him.

While trying to sort her thoughts, she wandered back to the grass where Dandy waited. She stroked his neck, then started at the sound of hoofbeats behind her. She turned.

Goose. And Benjamin. Her stomach fluttered. Then sank. She wasn't over him. She would never be over him.

For a long moment, they regarded one another in silence.

"Good afternoon, Lady Olivia. I'm sorry to disturb you."

"Mr. Carroll. I am not disturbed." She forced a smile and gestured with a tilt of her head. "I came to see how the new boathouse looks."

"That was my errand as well."

Her lip curled. How stuffy he sounded. As though afraid she would accuse him of following her there.

She said, "It looks wonderful. Willy did a fine job."

"He's doing good work at the cottage too."

Silence fell again. And grew.

"I understand Jasper likes your Mr. Boring quite well."

"I think he will suit."

After another awkward few moments, Benjamin dismounted. He folded his hands on Goose's neck and studied his fingers.

"My lady, I really must apologize for what transpired at the folly."

"What *transpired?*" She bit her lip. This was ridiculous.

He faced her. His skin looked ashen. "I behaved abominably.

I should have apologized immediately."

The kiss was her fault, not his. And then, she'd run away. The outing had come to a swift close afterward. Hannah had exhausted herself and Hazard claimed she'd exhausted him, too. On the ride back, Olivia had spoken only with Alice. She could not recall a thing that they'd said. She remembered only feeling a strange, floating sort of joy, but knew Benjamin was cursing himself so she had no business being happy.

She drew a deep breath and blinked her stinging eyes. "Let's not do this. I don't need to hear that it was a mistake. Or that it can never happen again. I know all those things. Just tell me why. Why did you kiss me?"

"It doesn't matter why."

"It does to me." Had it been a silly whim of the moment or something he dreamed about? Something he had resisted until he could no longer resist? Or did he readily kiss women in corners? It mattered. She waited, but he returned to staring at his hands. So she said, "Shall I tell you why I kissed you?"

"You didn't. I took a liberty I shouldn't have. You very rightly pushed me away."

"Oh, bosh. I kissed you because I love you."

Here were those words again issuing from her mouth. At least she was not wearing another pink frilly dress.

"No." He shook his head almost violently. "You can't still be in love with me. Olivia, you haven't yet met the man you will love. You are only holding onto an infatuation—"

"Listen to me. Listen, and don't tell me what I feel! I'm not *still* in love with you. I have *fallen* in love."

He practically glowered. How could she make him understand?

"When I was a child, I thought you were a prince. You were so nice to me. And my brothers thought the world of you, so how could I not? But I grew up, Benjamin. If I thought of you at all, after you were gone, it was as a silly, embarrassing moment from my past. You're right that I can't possibly still be in love with you because what I felt then was not love."

He raked his hand through his hair. "So why should you believe it is love now?"

"We are not the same people. We have both grown up. Everything is changed. I think you kissed me because you..." She faltered. It was easier to think it than to say it. She had made the mistake once before. Accusing him. She framed it as a question. "Do you love me?"

His eyes looked tortured. He didn't speak. But he nodded.

Again, she felt that floating joy. As though her heart was lifting out of her body.

"What are we going to do?"

"Nothing," he rasped. "Olivia, what do you expect? I am a steward. I am *Jasper's* steward."

"You don't think he would accept—"

"No."

"But he married Vanessa."

He shook his head. "He is an earl. The world is different for earls."

"But—"

"Don't you see how this *looks*?" He stomped away from his horse. Away from her. Then spun around. "Think, Olivia. A penniless adventurer wheedles his way into the house of an earl and takes advantage of the foolish tendre the earl's sister once had for him."

"You didn't—"

"They will call it a seduction. A fortune-hunter's seduction."

"Oh!" Bile rose in her throat. Such an ugly word. For an ugly, unfair accusation. "I won't listen to what nasty gossipmongers say."

"I am talking about your *brothers*! Your mother."

Olivia was rendered speechless. Her brothers would not... They *knew* Benjamin... Mama might be disappointed. She thought titles were so important. She'd married Papa so she could be a countess. But surely she thought differently now. Love was more important.

"Mama will come around," she said weakly.

"It will not work." Shaking his head, Benjamin repeated, "It will not work. Olivia, you will marry a peer. It is what you are born to. It is what your children deserve." His voice grew stronger. Angrier. "Do you know what I am? My father was a laborer and a drunkard. My mother, God rest her soul, took in washing so that we could eat."

A knot tightened in her belly. She didn't care who his parents were. Except that it made who he had become even more admirable.

"You love me but not enough to brave the consequences."

"I love you too much."

"No. No, I don't believe in that kind of love. You will condemn me to a life of unhappiness to protect your own image of yourself."

His face fell. Not only his face. His whole body drooped. Shoulders. Knees. He seemed to shrink into himself.

"I hope you will not be so unhappy." Then he murmured, "Olivia, I have to think of Hannah."

Hannah. She could be a mother to Hannah. "Do you imagine me incapable of loving her as my own?"

"Not you. You are infinitely loving. But your society excludes. I cannot subject her to that."

How was she to argue against his devotion to his daughter? It was one of the things she loved about him. She'd run out of arguments. Crushed, she slogged across the waterlogged grass to catch Dandy's bridle.

"You have your obligations. I have mine." She waved a hand toward the boathouse. "Go. Look. Don't touch the boards; the paint is wet. I'm going back to the house. It's best if no one knows that we were here together."

He nodded, jaw tight and hands clenched.

"And, Mr. Carroll, we shouldn't be alone together again. I can't bear it."

She led Dandy to the stump, the makeshift mounting block. Her muddied boot slipped as she tried to step up. The next moment, Benjamin was at her side, gripping her elbow to steady her, then turning her to face him. He put his hands on her waist as if to lift her to the saddle. She saw the longing in his eyes, felt the trembling of his hands. Her knees weakened and she began trembling also. "Olivia," he groaned, slipping his hands around her back. He tightened his arms around her.

"Don't!" She turned her head, fighting the desire to let him kiss her, trying to hold onto what remained of her pride. "Don't. You will hate yourself and I will feel stupid."

"I—" His expression was full of regret, sorrow, a dose of self-loathing. It made her mad.

"I don't want a parting kiss. Some ridiculously melodramatic goodbye. Don't kiss me now unless you intend to kiss me again tomorrow. And the next day and the next."

His hands fell to his sides, and he stepped back.

"That is what I thought." With a firmness of resolve she did not feel, she spun around, stepped onto the stump, and mounted Dandy. She was perfectly capable of doing it herself. Then she clicked her tongue and urged the horse along, without looking back.

CHAPTER TWENTY-TWO

IN LATE MARCH, the Duke and Duchess of Hovington returned to London. They carted Mr. Boring off with them so that he could "engage in ton reconnaissance." It was settled. Olivia was to leave Chaumbers the first week in April.

Until then, Benjamin avoided her as best he could. When their paths did cross, Olivia seemed a different person. She treated him as another bothersome brother, with just the right measure of affection and disdain. Her giddy anticipation of her upcoming Season might have convinced even him that she had nothing on her mind but suitors and balls. It crushed him.

He was devastated, but Chaumbers estate was poised to thrive. He had brought every debt in arrears up to date. Miraculously, the tenants had no current complaints. Now he could start looking forward: finding a hardier strain of wheat seed, purchasing a strong young boar for stud, draining the mucky portion of the meadow near the lake. The cottage should be habitable by April's end. There were two healthy foals in the stable. Buds were beginning to appear on the trees. Of course, Benjamin could not take credit for the foals or the trees, but he believed he had proven himself a capable steward. A blackguard, certainly, but a capable steward.

After a day spent helping the Fowlers patch their chicken coop, he found a summons from Jasper: his presence was required at tea. He changed from his sweaty clothes and dirty riding boots into more appropriate attire. A glance in the mirror showed a touch of sunburn. He'd forgotten his hat when he went about yesterday, something a gentleman would never do.

Miss Jamison and Hannah were at the dower house, so Benjamin had to face today's gathering alone. He walked the long corridors, footsteps echoing, until he reached the main part of the house, and jogged up the stairs to the parlor. Reg and Georgiana were already there. Arthur slept in a bassinet in the corner, so they greeted Benjamin in quiet tones.

Two days earlier, Reg had ridden out to the cottage with him, so they returned to the discussion of the work being done. When Jasper and Vanessa arrived, conversation shifted to the lecture Reg was to give in Oxford in a couple of weeks. Alice wandered in. And finally, Olivia arrived, glowing from exertion, her hair braided unevenly as if she had done it herself. She brought with her the scent of springtime.

"I'm so sorry. Am I late?" she asked, stripping off her gloves. She wore her blue riding habit. The one he particularly liked. He thought it might have grown too small for her. When she took long strides, it conformed to the shape of her legs. "I'm famished. I was down at the Crofts saying goodbye to the pugs."

"To the Crofts, too, I hope," Reg said.

Olivia stuck out her tongue.

Vanessa laughed and pulled the bell cord. They all settled into the chairs, talking of nothing serious, simply pleased to be in one another's company. Tea arrived a few minutes later. Vanessa poured. Jasper sat on the edge of his chair. The moment everyone had tea in their cups, he spoke.

"There is a change in plans. I don't wish to pull rank—"

"But you will." Olivia laughed.

"Yes, I will. I had a letter from Hazard. There are some debates coming to the floor that he says I ought not to miss."

"Debates?" Alice's eyes sparked. "Which issues?"

Jasper gave her a narrow look. "Something about a statue of

Granville Sharp, for one. I take it Hazard will be speaking."

Alice smiled like a cat in cream.

It was very clever of Hazard. A small motion to put forth. It would receive the votes. Likely by a sizable majority. After all, the abolitionist was unobjectionable now that he was dead.

Jasper continued, "The weather promises clear for tomorrow."

"We're leaving *tomorrow?*" Olivia's eyes met Benjamin's before she peeled them away. "But my things are not packed."

"They are mostly," Vanessa said. "And can be by morning. We would only spend the next ten days twiddling our thumbs, waiting to go."

"I suppose." Olivia smiled a little too brightly. "London! It doesn't seem real."

"There is more." Jasper turned his gaze to Benjamin. "I hate to do this."

Benjamin tensed.

At the same moment, Arthur gave an earsplitting screech.

Georgiana sighed. She rose slowly, crossed the room to the bassinet, and hoisted the unhappy infant. She put him on her shoulder, patted his back, said "excuse me," and went out the door. Reg looked pained. The noise faded as Georgiana walked down the hall.

Jasper scowled at his brother. "This ridiculous frugality needs to stop. I'm putting another fifty pounds into your account. That child needs a nursemaid. Hire one. Georgiana is worn to the bone."

Reg inhaled sharply. His jaw hardened and he flushed a deep shade of red. Benjamin winced inwardly. For a man celebrated for his charm, there were times Jasper had no tact at all.

Reg spoke in a voice as tight as a vice. "If you ever, *ever*, disparage my care for my family again, I will lay you out flat."

Jasper reeled back stunned. "I only meant—"

Vanessa put a hand on his sleeve, and he went silent. Then he cleared his throat. "I apologize. It is not my concern."

Reg nodded. The rest of the room let out a collective held breath. That was not the usual jovial Taverston bickering.

Reg said, "If you must know, we have engaged a nursemaid in Cambridge who will begin when we return. Until then, I have asked Milly Hearn to accompany Georgiana to London."

"To London?" Jasper's eyes widened. Again, Vanessa put her hand on his arm.

With a long-suffering sigh, Reg said, "Georgiana is perfectly well. And she wants to go to London to see Olivia launched. I'll only be at Oxford for a few days and then I will join her. Arthur will be fine. Milly has six siblings and knows everything about babies that she needs to."

Milly was the eldest daughter of one of Jasper's tenants. A young thing, but older than her years. Benjamin understood Taverstons were once again closing ranks. Having Georgiana in London would be good for Olivia. Good for Vanessa too.

Jasper had a stoppered look on his face. He wanted to say more. After another moment, Reg took pity on him.

"Jasper, if I should ever find myself financially distressed, I will not hesitate to ask for help. But we can afford a nursemaid. Benjamin found tenants for the upper floors of my house in Bath. A quiet older couple who have already made themselves beloved by our aunts."

"You've leased out part of the house?" Jasper said.

As Reg nodded, Benjamin felt his gut tighten, and then flip over when Jasper turned his scrutiny upon him. Thankfully, he quickly returned to Reg.

"An ingenious solution. I would not have thought of it."

"Benjamin thought of it."

"It was Tate who suggested it," Benjamin said. "He said it was your father's idea. In case Mr. Taverston did not want to go into the Church."

Jasper drummed his fingers on the arm of his chair, then put all that aside in the way that he could. "So Georgiana and Reg will be in London. Good. Benjamin, this brings me back to you." He cleared his throat. "I know you are not eager to return to the city with Hannah, but I could use you there and I hope you will come."

"To London? Now?" Startled, he held his head still to keep his gaze from going to Olivia. "Why?"

"Our underbutler, Finley, sent word to Peters that there is water seeping into the wine cellar. I told Peters to tell Finley to hire someone, but apparently that sort of thing was always handled by Bradwell. Peters said there are other repairs that need to be seen to, too." Jasper pursed his lips. "I knew Chaumbers was being neglected but I didn't realize the townhouse was falling apart."

"I didn't notice any disrepair when I was there." That disturbed him. He should have.

"I doubt it's noticeable unless you are going down into the cellars. Or up and down the back stairs." With a grimace, Jasper said, "I know you were hired to look after Chaumbers. If this is too much—"

"No. It is not. No. Things are in hand here. I can certainly go to London."

This would be a nightmare.

"Good." Jasper's brow cleared and he grinned. "Can you be ready to leave by tomorrow morning?"

Feeling lightheaded, he answered, "Yes, of course."

Then he glanced around the room for excuse to see Olivia's reaction. Her eyes were wild. He couldn't tell whether she was pleased or horrified. How could he? He didn't know if he was pleased or horrified himself.

IT WAS LIKE traveling in a bloody king's train.

The earl's coach did not suffice so the ladies divided themselves between the coach and a lesser carriage. Three more vehicles were required for servants and baggage. Outriders guarded the procession ahead and behind. Jasper and Benjamin rode alongside. Benjamin was lent a very fine horse, one of Jasper's personal mounts. Which was either another one of his unlooked-for and unnecessary gestures of friendship or a reward for Benjamin's pliancy. For the first part of the journey, Jasper permitted Olivia to ride Oatmeal, with the understanding that at the first posting station, she would give over the reins and enter the coach. Debutantes did not enter London on horseback.

Olivia showed the appropriate degree of pleasure and gratitude for this concession. Jasper wore an annoyingly condescending look of approval. And possibly self-congratulation. Along the route, he remarked upon the sights to see in London, even though Olivia had been there before when she was younger and had certainly seen most of them. Olivia made all the correct responses. From time to time, Benjamin put in a word: his favorite museum exhibit, a curiosity shop on Tyburn Road that she might find amusing, a recommendation for the apricot ices at Gunthers. He hoped he didn't sound as patronizing as Jasper.

After they had taken tea at the posting station where the draft horses were exchanged, Olivia volunteered to ride with Milly, Miss Jamison, and the two little ones so that Georgiana could spend a few uninterrupted hours with "grown-up ladies."

The journey took the entire day. Entering the outskirts of the city at dusk, Benjamin noticed Jasper growing invigorated. Of course. He was eager to return to his club, the races, the parties, even the halls of Parliament. The man had more friends than Bacchus. At Oxford, Jasper could not walk across a field without collecting men like cockleburs. But Benjamin shouldn't poke fun. Jasper had also made his own university experience bearable.

He'd come to the school on a scholarship as a servitor, the lowest of the low. He had to work for the privilege of attending. He was assigned to one of the residence houses as a bootblack or boy-of-all-work. His fellow students, many of them, served up unimaginably menial tasks for him to perform. They took perverse pleasure in doing so.

Very early on, Benjamin became aware of Lord Taverston, a student living in the house. Lord Taverston never felt the need to degrade someone else to inflate his own importance. If he needed something done, he ordered it done, but without gratuitous insult. So when Benjamin came upon him one night, slumped in a doorway, incapacitated with drink, rather than leave him there, he hauled him up to his room and made sure he was passed out on his stomach rather than his back. He didn't know how Jasper discovered it had been him, but a few nights later, Jasper invited him out drinking, "just in case it happened again." It didn't. Jasper was more careful after that, though he could still drink vats dry with his fellows. And those fellows learned not to harass Benjamin when Jasper was around.

But that was not how they became *good* friends.

The following year, Crispin entered the college. Crispin was...not at all like Jasper. Jasper had the typical gentleman's disinterest in learning. He came to school to carouse away from parental eyes. But whereas Jasper never lost sight of the essential dignity of his position, Crispin was wild. He lacked all discipline.

One would not recognize the boy seeing the man he had become.

Crispin terrified Jasper. Or rather, Jasper was terrified for him. He did everything in excess. Too fast. Too much.

When they were halfway through the first term that year, he disappeared. Jasper admitted only to irritation. Three days turned to four, then five, and more. The seventh night, Benjamin was sleeping in his dank cellar room when he was awakened by a knock and the groan of the door. Jasper stood in the doorway with a taper.

"Can I trust you to be discreet?"

"What? Yes. Yes, of course."

"Then come with me."

Jasper waited while he pulled on his clothes, then they sneaked out of the cellar, out of the house, and out the gate. It was the middle of the night. Leaving the grounds was against every rule. If they were caught, someone would have rapped Jasper's knuckles severely. Benjamin would have been sent down.

He followed Jasper to the ugly side of Oxford Village, to a brothel the boys all agreed was best avoided. Jasper shoved open the door, scattered coins as though sowing seeds, and said, "Where is he?"

"Now who you be looking for guv'nor?" a nearly toothless sow asked, toeing a few of the coins into a pile. "We don't have boys, but if you want—"

Jasper stepped forward and pressed his boot down on her toes. "Don't. Play. Games."

"Daisy!" she called out, eyes fearful. "Take the guv'nor to Cris."

"*Cris?* Damn him." Jasper spat on the floor, enraged this earl's son now had bawds calling him by a diminutive of his given name. "Benjamin!"

"I'm coming."

The place was squalid. The girl who led them to Crispin was so malnourished she looked forty but was probably half that. Crispin lay on a filthy, thin bed in a dark back room. He was nearly naked, stupid with drink, and stank of gin and worse. Jasper cast about for Crispin's clothes and found them lumped in a corner. Damp with God-knew-what.

Jasper swore a blue streak. Then he took off his own jacket and put it around his brother's shoulders. He wrapped the blanket around Crispin's waist like a skirt.

"Stand up, Crispin."

Crispin could not. Jasper and Benjamin each took an arm around their shoulders and dragged him back to the house.

That was the first time.

Jasper kept a close eye on him the rest of the term. If Crispin went whoring, Jasper went with him, or else he gave Benjamin a few shillings and sent him along to be sure that Crispin returned afterward.

When the term ended, and they went home to London on break, Jasper invited Benjamin. Payment, he assumed. But in the Taverstons' warm, welcoming home, he felt it was more than that. Jasper was not rewarding him with a peek at life in an earl's house. He was rewarding him with the chance to become better friends. An opportunity to better himself.

Back at school, Crispin again abandoned any pretense of studying. He drank and whored at a pace that Jasper could not match. This time, when he disappeared for a fortnight, Jasper pretended rigid indifference.

Benjamin was carrying slop buckets to the alley when he heard a *"Pssst,* sir. Sir! Lord Taverston, sir." He peered through the dark until he spied the girl Daisy.

"I am not Lord Taverston."

"Then you are the friend?"

"Yes."

"Can you help? Cris is in a bad way."

A shock of cold fear ran down his neck. "Drunk?" he said, trying to scoff.

"No, sir. He ain't had a drink in days. Nor nothing. He said not to fetch Lord Taverston, but I don't want him dying in—"

"Dying!"

"Yes, sir."

"I'll come."

Daisy did not take him into the brothel, but to the cowshed behind it.

"T'was the bloody flux got him. I was with him, but we didn't do nuthin' coz he couldn't. I thought it was drink, but in the morning, I knew it warn't. Madame, she was angry he brought the flux into the house. She wanted to throw him into the street. But she was afraid Lord Taverston would come, so she had me drug him out here."

"He's been sick with the flux for *two weeks?*" Benjamin shouted at the girl. "And no one sent for Lord Taverston?"

"He said not to! He said it warn't the flux. And no one else got sick, not even me, and I'm the one cleaning him up coz Madame said I had to. But he said he'd get better, and he isn't."

She threw open the door. Crispin lay shivering in the straw. His skin was the color of thin blue-white milk. The air stank of sickness. Not gin. Not sex. Profound sickness overwhelmed even the smell of cow.

Benjamin carried Crispin back to the house.

"Don't tell Jasper. He'll send me home. Don't tell him."

"Don't be an idiot."

He told Jasper. The physician Jasper summoned advised against trying to travel to London or Chaumbers. Crispin was too weak. He said laudanum might help. Which Crispin fought. He'd been given it before. But he hadn't a choice. For the next month, Benjamin nursed him. Dosed him with laudanum until the danger was passed. And then watched him suffer when the drug was withdrawn. Benjamin learned that Crispin had been a sickly child. He was desperate not to be known as a sickly young man.

Supposedly, he was doing better now. In the army. Benjamin wondered how.

The earl's entourage entered Grosvenor Square. Jasper's townhouse loomed large in the distance. Benjamin felt a shadow of the awe that had engulfed him the first time he saw it and understood that a friend of his actually lived in a four-story palace with a gray-stucco façade, an iron-work balcony across the second floor, and a large-porticoed entrance, all overlooking the manicured acres and acres of the garden square.

The carriages rumbled and the horses clip-clopped along the cobbles.

Benjamin thought of the letter he'd received when Crispin left school and bought his commission: "I will be proud to die for King and Country. I would not have been proud to die in a brothel's cowshed."

Maybe his relations with the Taverstons had always been tinged with servitude on his part and gratitude on theirs. But it had not seemed so to him during those halcyon years when they were no longer boys but not yet men. The friendship they offered had seemed genuine.

He'd known he was not their equal, but he'd learned how to ride, how to dance, how to hold his fork, when to wear gloves and when to remove them. He would never be a gentleman, but he learned how not to embarrass himself in the company of gentlemen. Callow fellow that he'd been, he almost believed he belonged in that company.

Until Olivia waved him into the billiard room. And told him she loved him. And every illusion he'd been harboring came crashing down.

It had been easy to break her young heart when she didn't hold his in her hands. But it meant facing the fact that he was who he was. What he was. It meant leaving the cocoon of the Taverstons' kindness to make his own way in the world.

Only to crawl back to them when he failed.

Now, he would have to bear witness to Olivia's coming-out. Other men would woo her. One would win her. He wanted her to find happiness. He *did*.

But the unfairness of the world sapped his strength. Mocked his equanimity. He did not want to resent the Taverston brothers, his *good friends*, but feared he would. He feared he did.

CHAPTER TWENTY-THREE

OLIVIA DECIDED THAT life was simpler when devoted to pleasing others. That was evidently her strength. When she'd tried seizing the initiative—demanding a kiss at the folly, throwing herself at Benjamin at the lakeside—she made everything worse. So now that they were all back at 8 Grosvenor Square, she would do only what was expected of her.

Thus, during her first ten days in London, she attended small breakfasts and teas held by very correct Society matrons, and she rode once in Hyde Park in the early morning, sedately, accompanied by Jasper. That was all.

Since she was not yet "out," evening activities were not allowed. Except for one. The night after Hazard's speech in the House of Lords—which happened to fall on April the tenth, the day before her presentation to the queen and debutant ball—he held a dinner party for his intimates. There were only eleven guests, of which the Taverston contingent comprised the majority. Reg was still at Oxford, so to even the numbers, Benjamin and Mr. Boring were invited. Lord Chesterfield, Hazard's mother, and Mr. Hollywell, an elderly friend of hers, completed the list.

Visiting in the receiving room beforehand, Olivia made sure to congratulate Hazard. His bill had passed on the first vote.

"Thank you, my dear." Dressed to the teeth in a black jacket, yellow trousers, and a striped waistcoat, he looked relaxed and pleased with himself. The scent of oranges and mint wafted from him. "Now let us talk about you. Are you nervous for tomorrow?"

"A little," she confessed. "Not about making my curtsy to the queen. That is just performance. But I do have nightmares no one will ask me to dance." She hurriedly added, "Not because of Vanessa."

Hazard shook his head. "There will be a veritable stampede of men wishing to put their names on your card." He studied her a moment. "I will not press my advantage tonight by asking you to commit to dancing the opening set with me. But if it will spare you a nightmare, I will rush into the breach should there be one. And you must save a dance for me at any rate."

"The supper dance."

"Olivia!" He laughed. "No. That is for an ardent suitor to claim."

"I don't want to be stuck with some ninny at supper. Please, Hazard? It will give me something to look forward to if I am bored out of my wits. And I should not have ardent suitors the first time I step onto a ballroom floor. I would not trust a one of them."

"*Hmm.* Very wise. Put my name down for the supper dance. But if you should have a better offer, feel free to scratch it out."

Hazard moved away to speak with Alice.

When it was time to go into dinner, Hazard took Alice in on his arm and settled her on his right. Of course, Hazard could do as he wished at his own celebration. Yet clearly, he was unaware of her partiality for him, or he would not be encouraging her hopes.

Mama had a different complaint. As they went to take their places, Olivia heard her whisper with annoyance to Jasper, "Hazard should have given his arm to Vanessa. He knows the countess takes precedence."

Jasper merely laughed. "Alice deserves it. She wrote the

bloody speech."

That dumbfounded Olivia. Maybe she *was* blind. She spent the evening rethinking everything she thought she knew.

At least she didn't have to worry about what to say to Benjamin. He was at the opposite end of the table. She conversed mostly with Lord Chesterfield, a very soft-spoken man. He was sweet. She learned he rarely left his estate in Wales. And yes, he had two sheepdogs. She couldn't wait to tell Reg.

All in all, the quiet evening among family and close friends was just what Olivia needed. She hadn't told Hazard the whole truth. Which was that despite her Taverstonian bravado, she was more than a little worried how the ton would respond. Which would weigh more? The family clout or Vanessa's past?

It might hurt to find herself shunned. But it would kill Jasper.

OLIVIA HAD IMAGINED her presentation to the queen would be the lesser of the two evils, but the day started off so poorly she prayed she was getting the worst over first.

If only Crispin could have seen her in her very special gown. Nothing but his howling laughter could have made it all right.

The monstrosity was made of blinding-white silk. Its hoops—required by Queen Charlotte for debutantes presenting at court, even though *no one* had worn hoops for half a century—were enormous. She could have hidden a horse underneath her skirt. The waistline was so high it swallowed her up, leaving her head perched atop a large white dome. An ostrich plume rose from her tightly coiled hair, all held in place with Mama's diamond tiara. Ridiculously, everyone said she looked beautiful. She looked stupid and felt it.

Nevertheless, with a hundred or so gleaming eyes upon her, she managed the long walk down the carpet of the queen's drawing room. Performed the perfect curtsy. Backed out without tripping over her train. There were eight other trembling debutantes with her. The interminable ceremony must have bored poor Queen Charlotte, who gave each the requisite tiny nod. Back in the coach, Jasper handed Olivia a glass of champagne, which she promptly spilled all down her front.

She arrived home to find Reg had made it back from Oxford as promised. He snickered when she walked in the door.

"Nice dress. I especially like the liquid embellishment."

She grinned. "Thank you!" At least someone in her family was thoughtful enough to mock her so she didn't feel so pitied.

Now there was only the ball.

She went upstairs to her dressing room where Tansy and Mama's lady's maid fed her tidbits, stripped off one gown, helped her bathe, and began dressing her in another. Of course her hair had to be completely restyled and redecorated, this time with pearls to match her ballgown. She thought of Reg's complaint about the tedious hours wasted having one's neckcloth tied. He wouldn't last one day as a debutante.

➤➤➤✦⬅⬅⬅

THE TAVERSTON BALLROOM had been transformed. Elaborate floral arrangements lined the walls and a complementing floral pattern had been chalked on the dance floor. But that was not all. To Olivia's delight, half-hidden statues of horses poked out from the flowers, and horses were also stenciled in on the floor.

As Hazard predicted, Olivia's dance card filled quickly. Jasper's friends jostled each other to scribble their names. And so it began. Her entrée into the Marriage Mart. She had to do this right. For Jasper and Vanessa's sake, she couldn't fail. She had to shine.

Lord Carleton led her out for the first set. He was one of Jasper's more frequent companions and also brother to the Duke of Dorchester. He danced well. Unfortunately, his conversation was polite rather than witty. And his cologne was gin scented.

Viscount Howerton was next. He had a pleasant laugh. But he stepped on her toes twice and the cuffs on his jacket were frayed.

Lord Friarby had an unnerving smile, glanced too often at her decolletage, and smelled of cheap perfume—ladies' perfume.

Her fourth partner was unexpected. His Grace the Duke of Lythe. A solid old Tory. He had been a friend of her father. His duchess had died over the winter. His second. Or perhaps third. Olivia thought it was in poor taste for him to be out at parties so soon, but maybe he meant to honor Papa by accepting his invitation. He had a lively step despite his age, carried himself like a duke should, and made her laugh twice. The type of laugh that was no more than three "ha's" and did not require catching one's breath.

Hazard rescued her afterward when the orchestra took its rest, bringing her a glass of ratafia before the duke felt it necessary to do so. He bowed graciously and drifted away.

"I told you so," Hazard murmured, escorting her to the window for a breath of air. "You, lady, are positively stunning. The most eligible gentlemen of the ton are beating a path to your door."

"A drunkard, a gambler, and a rake," she scoffed.

Hazard appeared taken aback. Then he grinned. "Just so. But also, a duke." He reached for her dance card. "Let me see. Ah. Ebersom is next. Good chap. You will like him." He grimaced. "Lord Bryant is a bit of an arse. Hums all the tunes. And Horstman!" He shook his head with mock horror. "Lady Olivia, my dear, the man is notoriously damp palmed. Sweats through his gloves."

She punched his arm. "Stop. I won't be able to keep a straight face."

"Fortunately, you have me after that. I have no faults." He looked at her drained glass. "You managed that one without dousing yourself. Shall I get you another?"

"No, thank you." She sighed. If she needed to visit the necessary, it would take an hour and two maids to fix her skirt.

"Lady, if it will give you strength, I've kept my ear to the wind. You are succeeding. Mrs. Windermere called you a diamond. Moreover, Vanessa is on the attack, charming the hordes." His eyes lit with admiration. "War stories and pretty boots. The biddies have no idea what has hit them. *Ah.* Here is Ebersom coming. Put your smile back on. Dazzle him."

OLIVIA HAD ALWAYS enjoyed dancing. It was one of the few forms of vigorous exercise permitted to ladies. But her heart wasn't in it. She knew she was supposed to flirt lightly, but it felt false, and the words stuck in her throat. Worse, the men didn't appear to notice. Either they were dancing with her at Jasper's request, or they were dancing with an earl's sister in a pearl-studded dress with the promise of an eye-wateringly large dowry. As a bonus, she was not wall-eyed and did not walk with a limp.

In truth, she could not stop thinking of the brief waltz she'd shared with Benjamin.

From what she'd overheard, the only invitation that had been declined was his. With regrets. Because he did not wish to provoke gossip. He was not a gentleman, and he should not be mixing with gentleladies. *Bollocks.*

She did have fun dancing with Hazard. She went with him into supper with a sense of relief. It was to be a formal, sit-down affair, not a buffet, and eating such a meal with any of her other dancing partners would have been torture.

"I danced with Georgiana earlier," he said, pulling out Olivia's chair. He chuckled softly. "How was Lord Horstman?"

"Damp."

"I warned you." He sat down beside her. "What about Ebersom?"

She shrugged. "He didn't step on my feet."

"You should marry the man."

While waiters served the first course, a white soup, he took a pinch of snuff. She tried not to recoil when he sneezed. Then she thought of something and laughed.

"What is funny?"

"Oh, I remember seeing you take snuff at one of our house parties. Other men were doing it too, but none of my brothers ever did. It seemed quite the thing, so I asked Reg why he did not."

"And?"

"He passed me a caster of pepper and told me to hold a pinch in my nostril and sniff it up."

"Good Lord."

"I know. You would think it of Jasper or Crispin, not Reg. Of course, I did it. My head burst into flames. Water streamed from my eyes. I sneezed for a good ten minutes."

"Did the old earl take a belt to your brother, I hope?"

Olivia scowled. "I am not a tattletale, sir. I simply stole Reg's spectacles. It was his very first pair and he wasn't quite used to them, but he liked how clearly they helped him to see. I ground sand against the lenses, then replaced them before he noticed they were gone. For an entire day, he feared he was going blind."

Hazard laughed. "Taverstons."

"How is Georgiana holding up?" It was two o'clock in the morning. She must be dead on her feet.

"She said she would retire after supper. Perhaps during it. She said this is generally when Arthur wakes to be fed."

"It is good of Georgiana and Reg to come to London. I never even asked Reg how his lecture went."

"Splendidly, I am certain. And you know they would not have missed your coming-out. Not for the world."

"I'm sorry we didn't invite Lord Chesterfield." Jasper said his name had somehow been overlooked. "You know you could have brought him along."

A cloud passed over Hazard's face. "It wasn't necessary. He detests these sorts of things. Always has." Then he blinked. "I don't mean *your* ball, of course."

He changed the subject. They spoke of Chaumbers. Then Hazard's estate in Kent.

Over the next course—beef roast, savory pies, haricot lamb, jellies, and peas in sauce—he mentioned his country home in Cumbria. Olivia picked at her plate. She wasn't at all hungry.

"Lovely place, but I haven't been there in over a year," he said, bunching his lips.

"Is it difficult to get to?"

"No. Not so very." He took a sip of wine. "I banished my cousin's son there, you see. Nasty fellow. But the duns were hounding him, and I told him I'd pay his debts if he rusticated for a while." He gave her a stern look. "That is not to be repeated, naturally."

"Of course not." She knew Hazard had a relative that he was not fond of. And unfortunately, the young man was his heir.

Hazard sallied on to another topic. "Your mother is permitting no waltzes?"

Olivia shook her head. "I cannot dance a waltz until I receive permission at Almacks, and my invitation there is not until the end of the month. She thought it would be safer simply not to have any tonight."

"Lest some villain force you to waltz in public?"

She giggled. "It is silly, isn't it? All these rules?"

"Etiquette is what keeps civilization from collapsing." He stretched out a leg as if he had a cramp. "Who are you dancing with next?"

She showed him her card and his eyes slid down the list.

"Hazard," she said, suddenly suspicious. "Did Jasper put you in charge of assessing my partners?"

His gaze flicked up, then away. "Your mother would not have invited anyone inappropriate for you to dance with."

"Is that what I asked?"

He cleared his throat. "No. And yes, Jasper asked me to stand sentry. He thought it less obtrusive than if he were to do it."

She should have been annoyed. Or maybe she shouldn't. What did it matter? The only man she cared to be with had already been ruled out.

Instead, she sighed. "So what will I be contending with the next few hours? Bores? Fortune hunters? Cacklers? Gropers? Men with two left feet?"

"No." He handed back the card. "Perfectly suitable gentle-men."

They were all titled. Not a mister in the lot.

Dessert was served. A cake constructed to look like their townhouse. It was a shame to eat such a work of art. Especially because it tasted bland.

Then they returned to the ballroom. Olivia's feet hurt and she feared she would begin yawning. It was nearing four o'clock. The ball would last until dawn.

The Duke of Lythe strutted up to claim her for the next set. She curtsied, but on rising, said, "Your Grace, I fear you are mistaken. Lord Crawford asked for this dance."

"He yielded it to me. Unless that is unacceptable to you?"

"Of course not, Your Grace." Not unacceptable but terribly uncomfortable.

They formed their squares. From the corner of her eye, Olivia saw Benjamin enter the room. She watched him pause, scan the company, and then make a beeline for Jasper. He didn't reach him before the music started, so he moved to the wall to wait. Olivia couldn't concentrate. She missed a few steps. Worse, she missed what the duke was saying and had to ask him to repeat himself.

"I said," he said with a wry face, "that you are extraordinarily pretty."

"Oh, good heavens. I'm sorry to ask you to say that twice."

He smiled. "I think the appropriate answer is, 'Thank you, Your Grace.'"

She laughed. "Thank you, Your Grace. I'm afraid my brain is not working right. I am not used to keeping such hours."

"Fresh from the country," he said, his eyes darkening in a way that caused a shudder to run down the back of her neck. Surely she was mistaking that look. He was old enough to be her grandfather.

They parted for the next steps. When they returned to each other, he wore a lighter expression. "Lady Olivia, I hear you are an extraordinary horsewoman. Your brother boasts of you all the time."

"How very kind of him."

"I think you would like a mare of mine. A true goer. Comes from the same lineage as Wellington's Copenhagen. Perhaps you will ride with me one morning."

Copenhagen! She all but shouted, "Yes!"

"You have a stunning smile. Though I am heartbroken to think the smile is meant for Cassiopeia not for me."

She wasn't sure how to respond. He was flirting. And she *was* smiling because of the horse.

The music ended and they changed lines for the next dance in the set. She glanced around for Jasper and Benjamin, and saw them conferring, very excitedly, in the doorway. The musicians started, but at a gesture from Jasper, they wheezed to a stop.

He marched up onto the platform. He didn't need to call for silence because everyone had already quieted, curious to hear what the Earl of Iversley had to say.

"My friends," he began in a clear, carrying voice. "The rumors we have all been hearing are true."

Rumors?

A hum began and then ceased. Everyone strained to catch every word.

"The war is over," Jasper said. "Napoleon has abdicated."

A roar went up. Shouting. Clapping. Stomping. The duke snatched Olivia up and swirled her around. "Excuse me," she shouted, pressing herself away. She abandoned him on the dance floor to make her way toward the orchestra's platform. When she was halfway there, Alice caught up with her and grabbed her hand. Meanwhile, Jasper had the musicians strike up "Rule, Britannia!" The cheering went on and on.

Reg joined them as they made their way to Jasper and Benjamin. Hazard was already there. Vanessa and Mama came rushing toward them. In the midst of their laughing and crying and saying over and over "Crispin! Crispin will be coming home!" they embraced each other and spun about and embraced each other more.

Benjamin caught her in his arms. Held her. Then released her. She turned to hug Hazard again, but saw his arms wrapped around Alice. His eyes were closed and there were tears on his cheeks.

Jasper leaned toward her and yelled in her ear. "I believe your ball is over. But my God, Livvy-pet. What a blessed success!"

CHAPTER TWENTY-FOUR

FROM THE DEPTHS to the pinnacle. It was maddening.

First, Benjamin thought there was no better example of aristocratic idiocy than the sight of Olivia in that birdcage of a dress.

Second, Jasper had spared no expense for his sister's coming-out. Nor should he have. All day long, while the family was at Court, Benjamin stood ready to approve any last-minute expenditures as Peters—who had returned to London along with the bulk of the household staff—supervised the army of caterers, florists, and musicians' assistants, coming and going with their wares, as well as extra servants hired for the occasion. He tried telling himself that every shilling Jasper spent was a shilling earned by someone who needed it. He tried reminding himself that this was all for Olivia.

All well and good until he watched a small cadre of artists chalking the floor. They were meticulous. It took hours. The result was mesmerizing: beauty with a touch of whimsy. Yet Benjamin knew that before the first dance was over, it would be nothing but colorful dust on the shoes and slippers of the guests. What must those artists be thinking?

Third, Benjamin could not be one of the guests. When Jasper handed him one of the engraved invitations, Benjamin had a hard time not throwing it back in his face. What did Jasper imagine he would do at a ball? He couldn't dance. It would be an insult to any lady he might approach. He could slip into the cardroom, but he couldn't afford the stakes the other players would casually win and lose. And, God help him, what did Jasper imagine he would wear? His very best clothes comprised a plain black jacket, grey pantaloons, and a pale blue waistcoat that might rival those of a mildly successful solicitor.

So when the hour approached, Benjamin took himself to the servants' corridors, where he would hear the gossip but not be seen by any of the ton. He allowed himself only one chance to spy—when Olivia made her entrance, descending the main staircase. She shimmered like a goddess. An inaccessible goddess.

His ache of loss was so great he wished he had never met a Taverston. He'd have been better off following in his father's footsteps. Drunkenness. Poverty. Petty thievery.

But no. He had Hannah. The pain abated, little by little, as he thought of his daughter. Every step he'd taken in his life, every misstep, had brought him to her.

Benjamin removed to the kitchens and partook of the general chaos and excitement. It was a testament to Iversley's treatment of his servants that they were as thrilled by Olivia's coming-out as the family was.

And so, the fourth act of the night. Supper had ended. Exhausted scullery maids scrubbed pots. Footmen carefully washed china, crystal, silver…and everyone paused frequently to gorge themselves on the leftover food. Benjamin was made welcome. Very welcome. Perhaps too welcome as two of the kitchen maids flirted with him openly, one so suggestively that Cook rapped her on the arm with a spoon and told her to mind herself. That one had the buxom figure he'd always thought he preferred, and he couldn't deny a roll about in an empty room would relieve some of his frustration, but behavior like that would cause many more problems than it solved.

He contented himself with bites of lamb and pie, averting his eyes from two footmen who were sharing a pilfered bottle of wine. Chastising servants was Peters's job, not his.

A hammering knock came upon the back door. An early morning delivery of some sort. Peters sent a girl to open it.

A young man, hardly older than a boy, dashed into the room. A laborer, by his worn coat and thin trousers, but despite his wild eyes, he didn't appear disreputable. He touched his cap.

"I come from the printers. The editor says this can't wait till morning. The nobs, begging your pardon, need to know. So he sends me out. Says to come here first coz this is where most of the nobs, begging your pardon, the *gentlemen* be."

"What are you talking about, lad?" Peters demanded.

"A message for his lordship! Will you bring it?"

Peters looked thunderstruck. "Interrupt the earl during the ball? Are you mad?"

The youth's face fell. "M'boss said to bring it."

Benjamin intruded, asking gently, "Can you tell us what it is?"

"Why, yes, sir." Now he focused on Benjamin, hopeful and indignant. "How else could you bring it?" Since he saw he had Benjamin's attention, he said, "It's Boney, sir. He quit."

"Quit? You mean abdicated?" There had been hints of this in the newspapers. Hopeful rumors out in the streets. The Alliance had reached Paris. The war *should* be over. But with Bonaparte, the war would not be over until *he* said so. Perhaps not even then.

"That's the word." The youth gave a little hop. "We won, sir. We did!"

The room erupted. Peters led the messenger to the table and bid him help himself. He practically threw cake at the lad in his enthusiasm. Benjamin hied off to find Jasper.

And the next scene. Benjamin invaded the ballroom. Ill-dressed as he was. He tried pulling his naked hands into his sleeves. Heads turned, but no one stopped him. Music began and he had to dodge whirling dancers and retreat to the wall. His eyes sought Olivia. She was dancing with an older man, an obvious peer. She moved gracefully. She smiled. But there was a...a heaviness about her. Her glow was gone. He thought she must be exhausted. Or perhaps it was just his imagination.

And then, her partner said something, and she transformed. Whatever it was, it brought all the life flowing back into her. *Oh, my love!*

He should have been happy for her, but…

The music ended, recalling him to his task. He rushed to Jasper. Who kept saying, "Are you sure? Benjamin, are you sure?"

Iversley could not halt the proceedings for an announcement that might prove another false hope. How disastrous, how humiliating that would be. People would remember. They would sneer. His stature would slip. But if the exhausted cream of the ton stumbled home to their beds to be awakened in the afternoon by the sounds of riff-raff celebrating before them…and discovered Iversley knew but suppressed the news…

"Are you certain, Benjamin?"

"Yes. Yes, I am sure."

The final act: The Earl of Iversley taking charge, the pandemonium following, the Taverstons gathering to experience the moment together in the midst of it all. And Benjamin was pulled tight into their circle. He held Olivia. Held her. For that moment, he belonged.

BENJAMIN GOT AN hour of sleep. Perhaps two. Which was more, probably, than half the citizenry of London. Had he wished, he could have gotten less: Sally, the scullery maid, volunteered to accompany him to his chamber to "celebrate." She was very put out when he refused.

He could not fault her. In some circles, he would be considered a good catch. She saw a slender chance to marry up and tried to seize it. It was not that he found the thought of scullery maids distasteful. It was that tawdry phrase: marrying up.

The Taverstons were all still abed, but Benjamin rose and went to find Peters in case there was anything needing attention.

Before the ball ended, Jasper had ordered all the champagne that could be found in the cellars to be brought up. A dozen bottles were given to the musicians. Another dozen dispensed to the servants. The rest watered the guests, the floral arrangements, the furniture, the floor. Peters would have to hire a crew to clean the place. Assuming he could find anyone willing to work. The whole city would be foxed before teatime.

He wandered into the morning room, hoping for coffee. He was not actually surprised to find the buffet held an assortment of breads, pastries, sliced fruits, coffee, and tea. He *was* surprised to find Georgiana, eating heartily. She was casually attired in a flowing yellow morning dress that wrapped across the front. Her hair was loose. When he entered the room, she covered her mouth with her napkin and gulped. She appeared more embarrassed by her table manners than by being caught in dishabille.

"You are up early!" she said.

"As are you."

"Yes, but I went to bed before supper. Apparently, I missed *everything*. Reg grumbled this morning when I climbed out of bed and tried blocking the light by pulling the covers over his head. I've never seen him that..."

"Green about the gills?"

"Is that what it's called?" She smiled. "At first, I thought he was ill. But he said the war was over. Please tell me it's true."

"It is true."

Georgiana beamed at him. "Please, Benjamin." She gestured to the buffet. "Will you join me?"

He poured himself coffee, took a few biscuits, and sat beside her.

"I am absolutely furious at myself for going to bed." She sipped her tea. "I'm not entirely sure I'm not dreaming."

"I imagine everyone in England is feeling the same."

"I hope Crispin sells his commission and comes home."

"Do you think he will?" Benjamin asked. The army suited him. But the Taverstons would pressure him to return to civilian life now.

"I don't know." Her expression darkened. "What would he do?" Then she changed the topic. "Olivia was quite a success, was she not?"

"So I hear."

"Oh, it was marvelous. Reg had said not to worry, but one couldn't help…well, some people are just awful. And every matron in town had hopes for their daughters with Jasper. His choosing Vanessa put their backs up."

"Was anyone rude to her?"

"Not that I heard." She set down her teacup and put a slice of pear in her mouth. She looked pensive as she chewed and swallowed. "It would be bad ton for someone to be pleasant to her at Olivia's ball but then turn around and cut her at the next event. If they meant to do so, they should have refused our invitation. But some people have no manners. It takes a lot of courage for Vanessa to do what she's doing."

"She is nothing if not brave."

Georgiana smiled again. "I positively adore her."

"Vanessa? I do, too," Olivia announced, entering the morning room, more put together than Georgiana. She wore a pale-blue-striped day dress. Her hair was pulled back in a simple knot. She looked like herself, especially when she scooped two pastries and a boiled egg onto her plate and dropped into a chair. "Have you seen the ballroom? It's a shambles." She grinned crazily. "I am so happy I could burst."

He remembered the feel of her in his arms, just a few short hours ago. His fingertips had skimmed the back of her neck before drifting down her shoulders to pull her close. Close enough to mold her body to his. He felt the smooth thin fabric of her ballgown and the warmth of her beneath. Everything had happened so fast. All at once.

"Wait until you see the parlor," Georgiana said, a mischievous gleam in her eyes.

"The parlor?"

"The florists must have been working round the clock."

"What do you mean?" Olivia asked.

"Go look. Peters has been taking deliveries all morning. Bouquets for Lady Olivia."

Olivia flushed, then waved a hand dismissively. "I suppose I have Boney to thank."

"That is not the reason." Benjamin stood before he said more than he should. "I'd better go look at the ballroom. And then find Peters and see what he wishes to do about it."

FIRST, HE PEERED into the parlor. Good Lord. Young men must have emptied the flower shops. The room smelled like a summer garden. He plucked up the card from one of the more extravagant baskets. Not only young men. The Duke of Lythe. That was who she had been dancing with—the man whose words had given her such pleasure. But the duke was *old*. He stuck back the card. The bouquet beside it, pink tea roses, was much more tasteful. He tilted the vase to see the card. The Marquess of Ebersom. Ah, the man who couldn't come at Twelfth Night. A political colleague of Jasper's.

Two more baskets caught his attention because they were identical, set side-by-side, and contained an eye-pleasing variety of white flowers. Even the leaves were painted white. He went to check those cards as well, to see who the unfortunate suitors were to have had the same thought or bought from the same harried florist. But they were both from Hazard, not a suitor. One for Olivia and one for Alice. Now that he was close, he could see a single pink rose tucked in among the white flowers in Alice's basket.

How extraordinarily kind. Alice had had the misfortune of debuting while Georgiana was still unattached. And now, she would be overshadowed at every ton function by Olivia. Yet

Hazard had made the effort to show Alice he thought she was special.

Well, if it was true she had written his speech for him, she *was*.

Enough. Snooping around Olivia's bouquets was pathetic. In another minute, if he did not leave, he would do something childish like mixing up the cards or pinching the heads off the flowers.

There were better ways to spend the morning after Napoleon's defeat. And once things settled here, in the afternoon perhaps, he would borrow a gig and take Hannah to Kensington Gardens. There would be celebrations to entertain her, he was sure.

CHAPTER TWENTY-FIVE

GEORGIANA HAD NOT exaggerated. There were more bouquets in the parlor than men Olivia had danced with at the ball. Which meant what? That she was a success? Hardly. It meant Jasper was important enough that his marriage to his mistress could be overlooked. All that worry for nothing.

Olivia had always known Jasper was universally well-liked. But now, it would not only be Jasper's friendship that men sought. He was the Earl of Iversley. He was tied through Reg and Georgiana to the Duke of Hovington. Viscount Haslet was his closest friend. And thus, he stood at the intersection of a widespread web of both staunch Tories and influential Whigs. Any young man who managed to snare Olivia would find his consequence multiplied tenfold.

So long as nothing went wrong. So long as Vanessa continued to charm. The ton could be fickle.

She sniffed, picking up a few of the cards, reading them, then discarding them. That one particularly gaudy arrangement? From the Duke of Lythe. He could not be looking for influence. He had enough of his own. It was nice of Papa's friend to send flowers, but she hoped he remembered he'd offered to take her riding. With all the excitement he was likely to forget.

Hazard had sent two baskets. One for Alice. He was the sweetest man. If only he *could* love Alice… The image the two embracing last night rose before her eyes. But that meant nothing. Hazard had embraced her, too. They were all overwhelmed by emotion.

Even Benjamin forgot himself. A shiver ran through her, remembering the way his fingertips had tickled her spine. The heat of his body. She'd thought for a moment he might kiss her.

What would it be like to let him hold her and kiss her and hold her and kiss her?

She surveyed the flowers once more but did not bother looking at the rest of the cards. Then she turned and walked from the parlor. Let Jasper sort out the swains. They were courting his favor, not hers.

THE SEASON DID not pause for a little thing like Napoleon's abdication. That night, they had the Wingsingham ball to attend. It was not the crush that Olivia's had been, but the Earl of Wingsingham had managed to obtain a last-minute license for fireworks in honor of the victory. That would enliven his daughter's ball.

Olivia danced every set but the waltzes. She didn't mind sitting those out. She watched Alice dance with Sir Langston for the first and with Mr. Gamby, the second. Mr. Gamby had courted Alice quite seriously last year but faded from sight in the face of her indifference. It was interesting he decided to make another attempt. Sir Langston, a baron, was not an old man, but he was short and balding. And he was a widower. Really, Alice deserved better.

Georgiana sat with Olivia instead of waltzing with Reg. Olivia had asked her to, not wanting any of the gentlemen who hadn't been able to put their names on her card to swarm her while she was catching her breath. *Dance cards.* That was another source of irritation. Gentlemen did not abide by the rules!

Viscount Howerton wrote his name for the supper dance. He was the lord she'd branded the gambler, and Hazard had not corrected her. She received confirmation when Jasper scanned her dance card, frowned, and said, "I will have to have a word with Howerton." Olivia was amused when Hazard's friend, Lord Chesterfield, appeared at her side for the supper dance instead.

He was a shy fellow, but the liquid refreshment loosened his tongue. She asked him how long he had known Viscount Haslet. She didn't say that she was curious because she'd known Hazard forever and had never heard his name mentioned.

"Ah, we go back a ways," he said, looking down at his fingers as though the question embarrassed him. "Schoolmates, you see. Eton and Oxford."

"How nice. It's lovely you've come to London. Hazard is clearly glad to see you." That was true. He seemed somehow happier these days, though he had never struck her as unhappy before.

"Well, yes, yes." He was quiet a moment. Then he said, "I married very young. My wife did not like London. Neither of us did, I suppose. We rarely left my family estate."

"*Did* not like London?"

"She passed."

"Oh! I'm so sorry."

"Thank you, but it has been three years." He did not sound particularly affected. Was three years enough to mourn a wife? "Listen to me." He grunted a laugh. "This is not conversation for a ball. I am out of practice behaving in company. I should be showering you with compliments. That's what men do."

"La! What men do? Now you will tell me I have lovely eyes and then commence to boast about yourself."

He laughed. Then asked her if she had seen *The Coachman* at the theater. He and Hazard had gone. She hadn't been to the theater yet, but couldn't wait to go. They had a typical, if slightly awkward, supper conversation.

It was just as well to eat supper with Hazard's friend rather than Lord Howerton. But she was not amused when the Duke of Lythe broke the rules again. He had arrived late to the ball and her card was already full. This time, he stole the Marquess of Ebersom's place. The final set. And this time, he did not apologize.

It was the last set, but the ball was not over. It was time for the fireworks. The duke escorted her to the terrace to watch. It was a lovely starry-skied evening. The terrace was chilly but there were enough warm bodies to block the wind. The brickwork flooring was patterned in a series of spirals, and an intricate iron-grillwork balcony encircled the whole. At one end, torches illuminated a viewing point where one had to walk up four brick-faced steps to another tier.

"Here is best to see," he said, steering her away from the torchlights. "The fireworks will be brighter where it is dark."

He held tightly to her elbow. She would rather have stood with the crowd. They were not more than twenty feet from the others, but it was darker in their corner than she anticipated, and His Grace stood too close. *Much* too close. She could smell his wine breath.

To her relief, after the first colorful burst of light and terrace-shaking thunderclap, Reg and Georgiana joined them.

"Here you are!" Georgiana said, looping an arm through hers.

"Lythe," Reg said, reaching out a hand. Lythe had to release Olivia's elbow to take it. "I hear you are responsible for sponsoring the exhibit at Baxter Hall. I'm anxious to see it. Hunt's work, is it not?"

Smiling, Georgiana said, "Mr. Taverston, Lady Olivia and I are not tall enough to see well here. We are going to join Lady Iversley. Good evening, Your Grace."

"Oh? Fine. Go along. I will join you shortly," Reg said, then continued his discussion with the duke.

"That man," Georgiana fumed as they moved out of earshot. "He can bore a corpse to death twice. I'm sure he is lonely, but that's no excuse. He claims to be a little deaf, and that's why he prefers to talk in small groups or one-on-one. But Hazard says he can hear an insult at forty paces."

Lonely. Hard of hearing. Now Olivia felt terrible for what she'd been thinking. Something more along the lines of *lecherous*. She should really be kinder to him. Papa would expect it of her.

"Well, he isn't *that* dull. He has a fascinating stable. But thank you for rescuing me."

Georgiana smiled. "That's what we are here for!"

Was that how the Marriage Mart worked? Throw a lamb in among the wolves and then circle around protecting that lamb? Why put her through this? In another month, Jasper would have the unacceptables winnowed out. Why not simply hand out notices to his top ten choices and let them work it out amongst themselves?

Another burst of fireworks lit the sky. Olivia joined the applause, but not even the elaborate display cheered her. She wasn't sure how much longer she could pretend to enjoy this. To feign excitement. To smile encouragement at men she didn't care for, waiting for Jasper to tell her which one she should.

⇒⇒⇒⟨⟨⟨

OLIVIA THOUGHT SHE'D overslept, and that no one would be at breakfast when she entered the morning room in the midafternoon. But the whole family was gathered. A fire burned in the hearth. Dismantled newspapers littered the table. Reg bounced Arthur gently on his knee, one hand on the baby's belly and one cupped behind his head.

"Oh! Let me," Olivia said.

"Careful," Reg said. "His head wobbles."

"I know, I know. You say that every time." She scooped up Arthur and cuddled him, breathing in his soft, soapy scent.

Mama yawned. "Thank goodness there is no ball tonight. Only the musicale and that will not run late. Olivia, the pink this evening."

Olivia groaned. "Yes, Mama."

"I don't know why you fuss. Pink is a lovely color on you."

Olivia turned, rocking Arthur and humming.

Alice swished into the room, bright eyed and rosy cheeked, stripping off her gloves.

"Were you out?" Mama asked. "Already?"

"I met Miss Frampton. We went for a walk."

"*Hmmm.*" Mama's brow wrinkled. Miss Frampton was one of Lady Rose Posonby's bluestockings. It wouldn't do Alice's prospects any good to start spending too much time with them. It was not Mama's place to say anything, but that hum made it clear what she thought.

Alice said, "Well, I have news. The Belfords' musicale is cancelled tonight. Their soprano cannot make it. Miss Annie DeBelle has an inflammation of the throat."

Reg choked on his coffee. Badly. Coughing until he was red-faced.

"Everything all right there, Reg?" Jasper taunted him.

Reg coughed too hard to scowl, but Mama scowled for him. She turned to Alice.

"Thank you. I assume we'll get a notice from the Belfords, but it is good to know."

Jasper said, "It would have been good to know the performer ahead of time. Eh, Reg?"

"That is quite enough, Jasper," Mama said. Her voice was much too sharp for the offense.

Olivia, Georgiana, Alice, and Vanessa all exchanged confused glances. Reg had stopped coughing but was still red-faced. Jasper popped a biscuit in his mouth and crunched, grinning, but he looked down at the table and didn't say anything else.

Then Georgiana said, "If we have no plans for this evening to prepare for, perhaps we can take Arthur and Hannah to the park to feed the ducks. I'll ask Benjamin if he will come with us or at least lend us his daughter. Arthur finds her fascinating. He stares and stares."

"That sounds lovely," Mama said. "I'm going to rest a while and then Mr. Boring is coming to go over a few things, but you young people should go."

Alice said, "I have to beg off as well. I owe my father a long letter and I have to write it this afternoon or it won't get done."

Olivia kissed Arthur on the top of his sweet head and beamed. A walk in the park with her family and Benjamin. Now *that* was something she would enjoy.

⟫⟫⟪⟪

IT WAS A nice spring day—less of a chill in the breeze, and the sun was at least trying to poke through the clouds.

While servants set up a picnic on the hill, the Taverstons walked to the pond. Leading the way, Georgiana pushed Arthur's pram, and Reg carried a basket of day-old bread. Olivia could swear Reg was walking taller these days.

Vanessa and Jasper lagged, arm in arm, talking. From time to time, they both laughed.

Which left Olivia and Benjamin with Hannah. At first, Benjamin held Hannah's hand tightly, but then Hannah said, "Olly's hand!" So she walked with Olivia. Then she said, "Papa's hand!" So they switched again. Until they realized she wanted to hold both their hands, so they now walked three in a line, enjoying Hannah's excitement.

There were ducks at the pond. Fat, lazy, ducks who waddled closer to investigate the basket, then scattered when Hannah chased them.

"Here," Reg said, handing the basket to Benjamin. "I'm not sure what Georgiana was thinking. Arthur is not yet ready for duck feeding."

Benjamin began breaking up the loaf to distribute. Vanessa and Jasper obliged by tossing a few crumbs, but the day belonged to Hannah, so they left the game to her. She was fearless, marching among the quacking monsters as though she were their queen. Benjamin's eyes grew soft, watching her.

Then Jasper exclaimed, "By God, Livvy-pet, she reminds me so much of you!"

Olivia had no choice but to go dance among the birds with Hannah.

"More bread! More!" Hannah cried. Olivia chanted along. Benjamin put a bit of crust in Hannah's hands.

"That is all. No more, I'm afraid."

"No more bread?" Hannah's eyes widened.

"No more. We have run out." He showed her his empty basket.

Hannah stuffed the crust into her own mouth. Olivia caught back a giggle.

Reg said, *"Now* she reminds me of Olivia."

There was nothing better than laughing with her family until her sides were sore. She couldn't bear for the moment to end. But moments always did. The ducks wandered away. Benjamin hoisted Hannah to his shoulders.

"Are you hungry, Hannah?" Jasper asked. "Because we have a picnic waiting."

They left the pond and climbed the slope. The scent of grass tickled Olivia's nose. Servants had set up tables, chairs, and an impressive array of cold meats, cheeses, bread, pickles, and jellies, as well as tall pitchers of lemonade.

They all began filling their plates, but Olivia saw Benjamin hold back. He had set Hannah down, and now had a hand on her shoulder to keep her from rushing to the table. He had a strange look on his face. Annoyance, perhaps.

"Thank you, Iversley," he said, his voice gritty, as though he had sand in his mouth. "For inviting us."

Jasper started. He looked hurt. Olivia's eyes felt hot. Why must Benjamin be like that?

No one spoke. But then Vanessa touched Jasper's arm and

gestured with her chin.

"Who is that?"

They all looked. A gentleman strode toward them across the hill. A handsome young gentleman. He was dressed in the latest fashion with an excessively high collar, a bright-green-striped waistcoat beneath his brown jacket, and several tassels on his highly shined boots. Even his tall hat had a gloss.

"Oh, the devil." Jasper said. His attention and his venom turned to the newcomer.

"Good afternoon, Iversley," the man said, drawing up to them. His voice was as polished as his boots. He bowed with perfect correctness, yet when he straightened and regarded Jasper, he had a glint in his eye that Olivia did not like at all.

For a moment, she thought Jasper would give him the cut direct. She'd never seen her brother's expression so cold. But then he turned stiffly and indicated Vanessa.

"Lady Iversley, let me introduce Lord Chase."

Vanessa gave him a small curtsy, and Lord Chase once again bowed.

"I believe you know Mr. and Mrs. Taverston," Jasper said.

Appropriate bows and curtsies were made. Reg's expression was wooden. Georgiana did not smile.

"Lord Chase, I present to you my sister." Jasper's voice iced over. "Lady Olivia."

She made her curtsy. Lord Chase took a step toward her before bowing.

"I am charmed," he said. "Congratulations on your coming-out. I only arrived in London this morning and am sorry to have missed your ball. I hear it was unsurpassable."

"Thank you, my lord." From the corner of her eye, she saw Jasper's jaw set so tight she thought he'd crack a tooth. She could tell he would not have invited this man to her ball if he were the only bachelor in the ton.

There was another profound silence. Until Georgiana's good breeding won out. "Will you join us for some refreshment? We had not heard you were coming to London."

"Yes, well, my cousin likes his secrets, does he not?"

Oblivious to the tension, Hannah squirmed out from under Benjamin's hand and said, pointing, "Papa, more bread."

In a very low voice, Benjamin said, "Yes, sweetheart. There is more bread."

Olivia's chest tightened. Benjamin had not been introduced. As though he and Hannah did not even exist.

"And I will not keep you from it, little one," Lord Chase said, bending down to send the words to her. He straightened. "You are very kind, Mrs. Taverston, and this looks delightful. But I'm afraid I have another engagement." He swept a bow. "Good day, to you all."

Everyone said their *good days*. Except Jasper. Who did not speak until Lord Chase disappeared down the rise.

"That man is trouble." He turned to Olivia. "Do your best to stay away from him."

"Can you not keep him away?" Benjamin said.

Jasper turned up his palms. "He is Hazard's cousin. What am I supposed to do?"

CHAPTER TWENTY-SIX

AT LEAST BENJAMIN would not bear the blame for the ruined picnic. That fault lay with Lord Chase. But although Chase cast the pall, Benjamin knew Jasper was not pleased with him either. And now he felt compelled to go to him to apologize and explain. *Apologize and explain.* Two things at which he'd proved himself most inept.

Benjamin paced at the foot of the Taverstons' grand staircase, gathering courage to go up.

Perhaps the mistake had been going on the outing in the first place. He'd gotten caught up in the innocent idyll. Simply being with Olivia and Hannah… He'd been *happy*—an emotion he barely recognized. Until he saw that elaborate picnic spread out for them up on the hill. All the hard work of Jasper's servants and the Taverstons' casual disregard for the effort. Once again, Benjamin felt himself and Hannah suspended between two worlds.

He had to start teaching Hannah now, *now*, that the world would not always be kind. And it would be even more unkind if she did not understand her place in it.

But none of this was Jasper's fault. Benjamin mounted the stairs. The door to the study was ajar. He raised his hand to knock. Reg's voice stopped him. "But has he asked?"

Benjamin paused, dropping his hand. Then raised it again. *No excuses. Just as well to talk to the both of them.*

"No, not yet. Not in so many words. But I fear this is prelude. He will, and then I am stumped what to do."

Has who asked what?

"I don't know, Jasp. I understand your difficulty, but I think you are worrying prematurely. He can't possibly woo her."

Benjamin's gut clenched. *Who? Who were they talking about?*

"He is a duke. He will damn well do as he pleases."

Relief washed over Benjamin. Then he wondered again. Who?

"He is *sixty*, if he is a day!"

"I know that, Reg. But the older Lythe gets, the younger his wives. And he—you saw it—the way he maneuvered Olivia into the dark."

Benjamin clenched his fists. Lythe. *The blackguard.*

"Yes, but it wasn't as though he was assaulting her. Georgiana says he is always like that. Full of his own consequence and not caring that he is monopolizing a lady's company and boring her to tears. She was trapped listening to him at several parties her first Season, but he was not…inappropriate."

"His wife was alive then," Jasper said in a flat tone.

Benjamin knew he should not be listening at the door. Nor should he make his confession now. This was not the time to weigh Jasper down more. But he waited. What would Jasper do?

He heard the slap of a hand against a desk.

"I cannot tell him he is not permitted to call upon Olivia. I would like to, but I cannot afford to offend him and alienate his fellows. They will make it difficult for me to have any say in Parliament. And worse, they will enlist their wives to reject Vanessa, something they are all no doubt eager to do."

"So, then, let him call on Olivia." Reg's reasonable tone struck Benjamin as far too mild. "He will be one of many. He may think she will jump at the opportunity to be a duchess, but he doesn't know Olivia."

"I hate to subject her to him."

"She is stronger than you credit, Jasper."

Benjamin turned on his heel and strode away. Furious. God how he hated the ton. Their posturing and superiority and hypocrisy. Jasper once said if Olivia needed protection, he would provide it. Apparently, he would protect her from a powerless groom at the stables, but not from a powerful duke.

⟫⟫⟫⟪⟪⟪

HE RETREATED ONLY as far as the guest wing. A tangle of angry thoughts whirled in his brain until he stopped, leaned against the wall, and tried to sort them. His life was one wrong decision after another. He should not be here in London. *That,* he could solve.

There had been little enough work he could do in the lead-up to Olivia's ball. They couldn't have laborers tearing the place apart. But he did hire carpenters to fix the steps in the back stairway that were splitting and endangering the maids. And he'd located a mason who could investigate the damp area in the wine cellar. Finley had pointed out a few cracked windows. And the pantry shelves should be shored up or rebuilt. All Benjamin had to do was get estimates for the repairs and hire the workers. Peters could oversee them.

He breathed a little easier. Olivia *could* handle an elderly duke. And she would not want Jasper alienating anyone or to cause trouble for Vanessa. She would be able to gently refuse an unwanted offer. She would be refusing a number of them, he warranted.

And if Hazard's cousin was trouble, Hazard would keep the man away from her.

He pulled himself upright and continued the trek to his rooms. Not room. Rooms. When he was young and came to visit, he'd stayed in this same wing, but in a small guest chamber that had seemed to him luxurious. He had not known what luxury was. Now he had a large bedchamber with a goose-feather mattress, curtains around the bed, a thick carpet, velvet brocade drapes, a wardrobe, a washstand, a writing desk—and that was just the bedchamber. He also had a dressing room, a sitting room, and a water closet. Three doors down, a second suite of rooms comprised a sitting room and two adjoining bedrooms, as well as a nursery.

He hadn't planned to stay in London for more than a few weeks. Just long enough to see to repairs. So, naturally, he hadn't looked for lodgings to lease. He'd done what was easiest. Another wrong choice.

He entered the second suite rather than his own, to spend time with Hannah and melt his irritation away. Miss Jamison looked up from her mending.

"Oh, Mr. Carroll. Good." She stood up and tucked the cloth into a basket at her feet. "Hannah is napping. The picnic tired her. She could not stop chattering about the ducks." She smiled. "And 'Olly.'"

Benjamin forced a smile.

She pulled a card from her pocket. "This came for you. There will be a supper tonight. They want you to come. Hannah and I are to join Millie and Arthur in the nursery."

Benjamin scanned the card and grimaced. At least it was no formal invitation. Just a scribbled line from Van—from Lady Iversley. *Supper at nine. Please come.*

"Is something amiss?" Miss Jamison asked.

"No." He tried again to smile. "Only that I will have to clean my boots." He drew a breath and let it out. "Since Hannah is sleeping, I'll go get ready."

He could use a bath and a clean shirt. And then, tomorrow, he would go to a tailor—someone cheap down by the river—and have another shirt made. Another jacket, too. It was becoming disrespectful not to have a better change of clothes.

With all the bustle of the preceding weeks, he had not had to dine with the Taverstons. They were running in six different directions at once and there were no formal suppers at home.

Even tea was a haphazard affair. Half the time, Reg and Georgiana were at Watershorn, her parents' London house, where her younger brother was down from Oxford to meet his nephew. Benjamin simply asked for trays from the kitchen. But there would likely be more invitations to join the family for supper until he escaped back to Chaumbers.

Unless he managed to have that conversation with Jasper. But already, he sensed his courage slipping away. There was no good time to tell the earl that in choosing an old friend for his steward, he had made a terrible mistake.

THEY CONGREGATED IN the parlor before supper. Benjamin thought he was last to arrive, but Jasper said they were waiting for Hazard and Lord Chesterfield.

"But not Lord Chase, I hope."

Jasper scowled. "Never."

Benjamin went to stand by the fire. Hazard walked in the next moment. He nodded his greetings, but his expression was flat and tired. Not at all like himself.

Jasper asked, "Where is Lord Chesterfield?"

"He has left for the country. He says he hears his hounds calling." Hazard smiled, but there was no humor in it. "But the truth is, he cannot abide London for long."

"That is a shame."

Hazard shrugged. "He has never liked the city."

"Shall we go in?" the dowager asked. "I believe supper is ready."

Jasper and Vanessa led the way. To Benjamin's surprise, the table was elaborately set even though it was just family, and they were generally more casual at home. Jasper sat at the head, Vanessa on one side and the dowager on the other.

Benjamin found himself seated between Georgiana and Alice.

"Now," the dowager said, "there will be no shouting across the table. No reaching. No clinking of spoons on your plates."

Jasper laughed. "Is this to be a lesson in table manners?"

"Yes, indeed. I cannot think of the last time Olivia dined in civilized company."

"At the balls!" Olivia cried.

"That doesn't count. Tomorrow night we are dining with the Edgeworths." She lifted her eyebrows as if to drive home the significance of that. Benjamin didn't understand but the Taverstons did. They all groaned. "Enough of that. I know you will all make me proud."

Dinner was superb. Six courses and an absurd amount of food. There were no deviations from behavior one might see at the queen's own table. Or so Benjamin imagined. He knew enough to only talk with Georgiana and Alice and to alternate his attention between the two. He kept his voice low and said nothing of interest. He picked up the wrong fork once. Alice tapped hers twice to alert him, but Georgiana pretended not to notice, which was probably the more correct response.

It was excruciating. They were all so stiff and formal, it was like watching a play. Until dessert when Olivia picked up her glass of claret, caught it on the rim of her plate with a loud clank, and dropped it. The drink bled all over the tablecloth. Her brothers applauded. Olivia stared at the mess with open-mouthed dismay.

The dowager rose, laughing. "I give up. Go on with you."

They all clambered from the table with alacrity. Except Hazard, who stood slowly, as if rising from slumber. He had been seated beside Olivia. When she'd spilled, Benjamin realized, Hazard had not applauded. He didn't even laugh.

"Brandy in my study, gentlemen," Jasper announced, continuing the parody of a formal dinner party. Benjamin felt a flash of disappointment. He'd prefer Olivia's company to brandy.

The men and women parted outside the dining room. As the men made their way to the study, Benjamin had the strong sense that something was wrong. They filed into the room and Jasper shut the door. He retrieved a bottle and glasses from a cabinet. They each took a glass after he poured.

"We should sit," he said, dropping into his own chair. "We may be a while."

They sat. Benjamin was disturbed by how morose Hazard looked. Jasper regarded him with concern.

"We met your cousin at the park this afternoon."

"Yes, I know. He mentioned it." Hazard's frown looked pained. "I'm sorry. I hope he wasn't too very bothersome."

"No. He behaved perfectly correctly. If anything, I was rude."

Hazard didn't respond to that. Instead, studying his glass, he said, "He appeared on my doorstep this morning. He was supposed to stay in Cumbria. That was the bargain. But he has never in his life kept his word."

No one said anything. They drank, and Jasper got up to pour another round.

"How long does he intend to stay?"

Hazard snorted. "Until he has exhausted his credit. And mine."

The two brothers regarded him with commiseration, but Benjamin didn't understand. He had thought Hazard's fortune to be inexhaustible.

Hazard slammed down his hand. "He marched into my home, *mine*, as if he owned the place already!"

Already?

"Throw him out," Jasper said.

"He will not go. Am I to hire ruffians to toss him out bodily?"

"I would."

Hazard sniffed. Then he turned to Benjamin. "Bertram is my cousin's son, and, to my eternal regret, he is my heir. He has been living on expectations all his life and now he has decided I am not dying fast enough to suit him." He choked and faced toward Jasper again. "He will drive me to my grave."

Jasper made an angry grunting noise.

"The war is over. Maybe I should go to Italy." There was a

quiet desperation in Hazard's tone. His voice dropped to barely audible. "Chester said he would come, too, if I go."

"Haz," Jasper murmured.

The room grew silent enough that Benjamin noticed the faint tick of the wall clock. The walls felt oppressively close.

When Hazard he spoke, it was as though tears were avoided only by anger. "He says he has come for the Season to find a wife. And that someone needs to ensure the family line. The devil of it is, he is right. Damn him." He wrung his hands together. "And damn me for failing to do it. If he goes anywhere near Olivia, Jasper, shoot him." Then he gasped out something that was more a sob than a laugh. "No. Have Reginald do it. You'll miss."

"He will not be permitted to bother Livvy," Jasper said. "Don't concern yourself with that. I will not waste time with Reg. I'll call Crispin home."

Hazard rubbed the back of his hand across his eyes and said, "I am making too much of this. He has done this before. Nothing comes of it."

"This?" Reg asked, echoing the question in Benjamin's head.

"Makes threats." Hazard waved his hand, dismissing whatever threats there might be. But now Benjamin had pieced it together. Why Hazard's heir was this wastrel of a fellow and not a son of his own. Why Hazard would go to Italy. Why Lord Chesterfield would go with him. *Rupe.* So, it was true. This was why no clarification for "threats" was forthcoming. And why no one asked. Hazard was committing a crime punishable by execution.

Hazard drained his glass. Then resorted to his snuff box. When he seemed more in control of himself, he said, "You invited me for supper because you had something to discuss?"

"It isn't important."

"No? Tell me anyway."

Jasper let out a long sigh. "Lythe asked to take Olivia out riding Friday morning."

Hazard scowled. "Tell him 'no.'"

"Yes, well, the problem is that Olivia already said yes."

"Cassieopia?" Hazard said. Incomprehensibly. The men talked in code. Jasper only nodded. "He is fiendish." He drummed his fingers on the arm of his chair. "But he has not asked to call on her? Formally?"

"No. Just the ride. He made it sound like a favor he was granting."

"Bollocks. The man is old enough to be *my* father. Tell him 'no.'"

Reg stood, drawing their attention. "It is not so simple." He spoke quietly but firmly. "Jasper's maiden speech will be in two weeks."

"Eulogy for your father. King and Country. We've defeated Napoleon. Now on with it." Hazard almost sneered. "Not a controversial word."

"Have you read it?" Reg asked.

"No. Not yet. Jasper has not shown it to me. He said he was still working on it."

"Then you will be surprised. It is all that you said, but signals a shift. Father was of his time. Jasper intends to be of his."

Hazard turned to study Jasper, then said, "Good. Let me go over it with you. Don't come too strong. You need to bring your fellows with you before they realize what is happening."

"I thought I would show it to Alice."

Hazard laughed. He sounded more like himself, but not entirely. "That was my intention also." Then he said, "Even so, I don't think you should kowtow to Lythe."

"There is Vanessa to think of," Reg said.

Hazard's eyebrows shot up. Then he frowned. "Yes. Yes, that is difficult. The man could well be vindictive."

Jasper said, "But maybe Cassieopia…bloody hell. Olivia has been…I don't know how to say this. She has been bearing up well. But as Vanessa points out, she shouldn't be 'bearing up.' She should be enjoying herself. Any other girl would be overjoyed. I don't know what is wrong."

Benjamin felt kicked in the gut.

"You think she misses her horses?" Hazard sounded skeptical.

"She misses Chaumbers," Reg said. "The horses, the country…being herself."

Jasper flicked his hand. "She has to grow up—"

"It is not childishness!" Benjamin interrupted, unable to hold back. "It's who she *is*."

"Well, the deuce." Jasper shifted in his chair, but with an expression more perturbed than impatient. "I just don't like to see her long faced when she thinks no one is looking. I thought a ride on a horse like that…but I fear I'm just being selfish."

"Probably a bit of both," Hazard said. "I suppose she would like to go riding—"

"I'll send Alice with them," Jasper said, making up his mind.

"No." Hazard sat up straight. "No, you won't! You must stop treating Alice like some sort of paid companion."

"I don't—"

"Why on earth would you consider her an appropriate chaperone? She is an unmarried, lovely girl in her second Season. She is not a spinster or matron. Would you send Olivia out to chaperone Alice?"

Jasper looked as though he'd swallowed a frog. But Benjamin thought: *Good. Hazard is right.*

Hazard ranted on. "You expect her to be at your beck and call. She has other friends. She has interests of her own."

"Has she complained of this?" Jasper asked, shocked. At least he did not sound indignant.

"Of course not. She is much too devoted to you all. But I have eyes."

Jasper's lips pursed. "You are no better. She spends her time on your political career. She writes your speeches—"

"My dear Iversley, that *is* one of her interests. I dare say, it is her main interest."

Jasper clamped his mouth shut.

"I was about to say," Hazard continued, "that if Olivia would benefit from riding, *you* should take her. Take her out in the early morning and let her have a good run. She doesn't need Cassieopia. She would rather have time with her brothers, before you shove her out of the nest."

"We aren't shoving her out—"

"We are, Jasp. In a way, we are." Reg turned up his hands helplessly.

"I will take her out," Jasper said, scowling. "But if this is how she feels, a few morning rides will not change anything. And there is still Lythe to deal with. I will have to tell him 'no' and deal with the consequences."

"Have your mother do it," Hazard said.

"Mother?" He sounded startled, confused, as if Hazard were changing the subject rather than offering a solution.

"Your mother has power, Jasper. Let her use it."

Jasper's scowl fell away and was replaced by something softer. Gratitude? No. More than that. Benjamin saw layers and layers to their friendship.

Jasper murmured, "Don't go to Italy, Haz."

Hazard shrugged. "No, I don't suppose I will. Leastwise, not until you Taverstons sort yourselves out."

CHAPTER TWENTY-SEVEN

OLIVIA HAD A bad case of the blue-devils that she could not manage to shake. She could not talk herself out of them. It scared her. She was unused to melancholy that would not go away. She'd been bored at the theater. Bored at Isabel's dinner party. Bored at the Hovingtons' musicale. And bored wasn't even the right word.

Jasper took her riding. He allowed her to ride Bolt, a thoroughbred almost as fine as Crispin's Mercury, and even that did not help. They went to an open field in the depths of Green Park in the very early morning so that they could race. And then he spoiled it by letting her win. It was obvious he was doing so because she was trying to let *him* win so as not to embarrass him. Ridiculous. It was the slowest race imaginable.

She knew she had no cause for her sadness. Flowers kept coming. Suitors paid calls. Over the course of two weeks, she was visited by the marquess of this, viscount that, three earls or earls-to-be, a baron, a handful of sirs and one very wealthy mister—the third son of a duke, not a mere cit. She did her best to entertain them, but they had nothing interesting to say, so how was she to respond?

And there was the duke. Mama had declined Lythe's offer to take Olivia riding. She was disappointed and thought it strange and a little mean of Mama to refuse. Nevertheless, she was relieved not to have to spend time with Lythe just to ride his horse. She thought that would be the end of it, but then His Grace came at calling time and spent a polite twenty minutes speaking with her in the receiving room about his stables. Lord Carleton was there at the same time, looking annoyed. And, of course, Mama sat quietly on guard.

There were other reasons for her unhappiness. Alice was often elsewhere. Georgiana was often at her parents' house. Vanessa was busily cutting a swath through the ton—which was a good thing, but it meant she was not home much either. She passed most of her days paying social calls and coming home with orders for boots to be made by her friends in Cartmel. Olivia could not tag along. She was supposed to spend her time being available to be courted.

And Benjamin. Benjamin had informed Jasper that all the necessary repairs were being seen to and he would soon be returning to Chaumbers to see what the tenants required.

He was not going to fight for her. Had she ever thought he might?

This morning, Ebersom was coming to take her for a ride in his carriage. A marquess. Lower than a duke. Higher than an earl.

"The green-and-blue muslin?" Tansy said, moving to the wardrobe.

"Oh, it doesn't matter." When Tansy huffed, Olivia muttered, "Yes, yes. The muslin will do."

She let Tansy dress her and fix her hair. A maid knocked on the door. "My lady? Your caller is here."

She wrapped a shawl around her shoulders and went down the stairs. On her way to the receiving room, she passed Benjamin in the hall.

"You are going out?" he said.

She sighed. "They ask, I go."

He nodded. He looked miserable.

Jasper stepped from the receiving room. "Ah, Olivia. Ebersom is here." He stopped and looked from Olivia to Benjamin and then back again. "Did I interrupt something?"

Benjamin said "no" at the same time Olivia said, "Yes. I was about to ask Mr. Carroll when he would return to Chaumbers. I left my flowered fan there and I thought he could have it sent here by post."

Jasper flicked his hand. "Buy a new one, Livvy. It is a fan."

"But it is my favorite."

He gave her an odd look. Then shook his head. "Benjamin, locate the fan." He walked away.

Benjamin looked down at his feet. Then he nodded to Olivia. "Enjoy your ride."

⟫⟫⟫✕⟪⟪⟪

SHE ALMOST DID enjoy the ride. Ebersom drove a phaeton with a magnificent, matched pair of grays. To her surprise, he was a true whip, handling the ribbons with confidence and ease as he whizzed her through the park. The wind on her face brought out her smile. But not his.

He was not a bad-looking sort, but he might be better looking if he ever crinkled his eyes and showed his teeth. His nose was too small for his face, but she allowed that the imperfection gave it character. His shoulders were narrow, but he had good, strong hands.

His only true flaw was that he lacked conversation. Of course, she hadn't given him much of a chance. He'd only paid one morning call and Lord Galway had been there, too, monopolizing her attention. Yet they *had* danced a few times, and he'd sat beside her at the Edgeworths' dinner party. It was enough to notice that he never initiated talk beyond comments on the weather or bland compliments on her dress. His replies to *her* attempts were adequate, but it was exhausting thinking up things for him to reply to. Worse, he didn't laugh at her jokes and when she'd teased him once, he looked confused.

But flying around the park with the wheels rattling, horses clopping, and wind whistling past her ears, conversation was out of the question anyway. She was disappointed when they returned to the main path. With all the other carriages and the people out strolling, Ebersom was obliged to slow down. He cleared his throat. Coughed. Reddened a little. And said nothing.

Olivia took a breath and dove in. "That was wonderful! Horses are my passion, and yours are splendid. What are their names?"

"Fred and Joe."

Good Lord. She had no trouble smiling; the difficulty was refraining from bursting out with a laugh. No conversation and no imagination.

"It must be grand driving a pair. I've never—well, a wagon about Chaumbers, pulled by Pudge, but not—oh, wait, that isn't true."

His eyes squinted with puzzlement which somehow focused her eyes on his unfortunate nose. "Wh—What isn't true?"

"I *have* driven more than a wagon. I must have been eight years old, and Viscount Haslet let me take the ribbons of his curricle." Now she did laugh. "I crashed it, of course. I fear the front wheels were irreparably damaged."

Ebersom looked aghast. "You might have been killed! What was he thinking!"

"I don't imagine we were going very fast. He wasn't upset that I ruined his carriage, but I tipped him out into the mud." She giggled, remembering. Not Hazard's words, but his demeanor. But that was too hard to convey, and Ebersom did not appear amused by her story, so she changed tack.

"Have you and my brother been friends long?"

"No. Well, s-since Oxford. But we were in d-different colleges. Different…circles."

"I suppose you are in the same circle now."

He lifted his brows, then frowned, as if the thought didn't exactly please him.

She said, "I mean Tories. House of Lords. All that."

"Oh, yes. Yes, of course."

The following quiet stretched between them while she scrambled for another topic that might have more legs. To her astonishment, he broke the silence.

"Along those l-lines…" He paused.

"Yes?" she said, hopefully.

"I am having a…a b-bit of a house party. Next month. At Cherrington. S-small one. Politics, of course." Then in a rush, "But plenty to do for the ladies as well."

She waited while he gathered more words. He stammered, she realized. This was hard for him. Was he simply shy around ladies? Or did it affect his ability to give speeches? Her heart softened. How unfortunate for him.

"I've asked Iversley to bring you," he blurted. Then he pretended his ribbons needed a good deal of attention, even though the horses were calmly trotting along the path.

"I'm fond of house parties." This was true. And it would be an escape from London. But her chest tightened, and her own words failed her. Was she being invited so that he could impress her with Cherrington?

"I should g-get you home," he said, turning the phaeton.

On the path from the park, they exchanged greetings with passersby, but said nothing else to each other. And the streets leading from the park to Grosvenor Square were crowded, so the horses required all Ebersom's attention. They pulled into the drive in front of her home, and he sprang from his perch to help her down. She thanked him for a lovely ride and gave him her smile. He returned only a bow, a "Good day" and a "Give my regards to Iversley and Lady Iversley."

OLIVIA DIDN'T MENTION the invitation to Cherrington. She'd wait for Jasper to bring it up. Tonight, the Taverstons were going to Almack's. Olivia had finally received her voucher. Mr. Boring took care of sending regrets to the Crawfords who had invited her to the theater. This was *Almacks*, after all. And the Duchess of Hovington said Lady Jersey had agreed to grant permission for Olivia to waltz.

Jasper was making a celebration of it. Hazard said he would not miss it, even though he had not patronized Almack's in years. Since the earl's coach would be crowded and the ladies must not wrinkle their dresses, Hazard volunteered to bring the dowager and Alice.

Olivia wore her white ballgown again, but with a gold net overskirt and little golden baubles sewn into her hair. If Tansy ever got the tangles out afterward, it would be a small miracle.

"Ebersom will ask for your first waltz," Jasper told her, escorting her to the coach. He looked pleased.

Oh! She nearly stopped in her tracks. Ebersom was Jasper's choice. *Of course, he was!* All the cards fell into place. He'd been invited to Jasper's wedding months ago—for a quick squint at her, no doubt. And now, she recollected Hazard putting in a good word for him at her ball—Jasper must have told him to.

"Very well," she said, swallowing her indignation as Jasper handed her into the coach. Her whole Season was a farce. It had already been decided. In her head, she may have wished Jasper would just settle it all, but she hadn't meant it!

"What is wrong with Ebersom?" Reg asked, climbing in beside her.

"Nothing is wrong with him. Or Jasper would not have asked him to request my first waltz."

Jasper scowled, ducking inside and sitting down by Vanessa. "I didn't ask him. He asked me, and I said yes. He is a good man, Olivia. Give him a chance."

Georgiana sucked in a breath. Her brow darkened.

"What is wrong?" Jasper said, turning to her.

"You sound like my mother. When we received your invitation to Chaumbers.”

Jasper’s eyes went wide. Then he laughed. “Well, your mother was right. If you hadn’t given me a chance, you would not have met Reg.”

Olivia felt a spark of amusement. “Let us hope Ebersom has a brother.”

Jasper rapped on the roof and the coach began to roll from the drive.

Almack’s was not far. It was also not the palace one might expect. From the outside, it looked more like a warehouse. The ballroom was poorly lit and had a faint scent of must. Upstairs in the supper room, it was said they served only watery lemonade and tiny sandwiches that contained invisible slivers of ham.

Everyone was impeccably dressed. Still, Olivia found it strange that all the men were in knee breeches, a fashion that was falling by the wayside. She saw the marquess across the room. He made a polite bow and nodded to Jasper but did not approach. The orchestra played quietly while guests filled the ballroom. A quarter hour later, Hazard strolled in with Alice on his arm and Mama walking alongside.

Mama approached and put a hand on Olivia’s arm. “Shall we find Lady Jersey?”

Olivia nodded, surprised by how nervous she felt. They proceeded toward a cluster of older matrons, very fussily dressed, near the far wall. One of them broke away and came forward.

“Lady Jersey,” Mama said. “May I present my daughter, Lady Olivia?”

Olivia curtsied deeply and kept her eyes down while the woman studied her through her lorgnette.

“Very lovely,” she pronounced. Then she added, “My dear, I am sorry for your loss. Your father was much admired.”

“Thank you, my lady. He is very much missed.”

Lady Jersey nodded. “Of course, you may waltz. It would give us great pleasure.”

They said their thank yous, wished Lady Jersey a good evening, and crossed the floor again.

"And?" Jasper asked.

"I may waltz." Olivia made herself giggle. "Such a silly per-formance."

Jasper didn't answer. He was nodding over her head. She whirled about to see Ebersom, who was, as usual, flawlessly turned out. His lips were crooked, as though he were struggling to arrange them into the appropriate form.

"Lady Olivia." He bowed before her and spoke to the floor. "Will you honor me with a waltz?"

She held out her dance card and he put his name down. The waltz was the third dance. Hazard took the card next and wrote his name for the first. Ebersom then claimed Alice. Hazard chuckled and took Alice's card and put his name on it for the waltz.

Olivia kept the same smile through it all. The orchestra fin-ished whatever they were playing and then there was a cacophony of tuning instruments and scraping chairs. The master of the evening called the first dance. Hazard took her elbow.

"Come along, dear. You wanted to see Almack's? Here it is."

AFTER THE FIRST set, a small crowd formed around Olivia. Several of her suitors tried nudging each other aside playfully. Her card was full in short order. Lord Carleton claimed the second set. Olivia wished he hadn't. She could smell gin before he even opened his mouth.

Ebersom was waiting beside Jasper when the dance ended. Lord Carleton delivered her to them. Jasper's Chosen One bowed and held out his arm.

He waltzed very well. So did she. He made sure to whirl her past Lady Jersey to receive her approving nod. He held her at the correct distance. His gloves were not sweaty. He wore a scent of bergamot and cloves. She wished she could like him. It would make things easier. She didn't *dislike* him.

The problem was, she felt nothing.

She asked about Fred and Joe. About Cherrington. If he had a sister or brother. He answered with few words. She lapsed into a quiet smile, but her lips felt false. As though she had a bit in her mouth or had someone else's lips glued to her face.

"W-what have you enjoyed most, b-being in London?" he asked, making the effort.

"Feeding the ducks." The words slipped out, but the ridiculousness of her answer didn't seem to register with him.

Over his shoulder, she caught a glimpse of Alice and Hazard. Alice was smiling into Hazard's eyes. The two twirled. Hazard was laughing into hers.

Olivia blinked and looked again, but they had faded into the crowd. She must have imagined it. How *happy* they'd seemed.

⇛⇚

WHEN SHE WALKED into the morning room the next day, the family applauded.

"Another rousing success!" Vanessa said.

"Was it?" Olivia yawned.

Georgiana said, "Are you being run ragged? You needn't say yes to everything—"

"Olivia? Run ragged?" Jasper laughed, a strange laugh that seemed to echo in his throat. "You are thinking of a different Olivia."

Olivia took a piece of toast and a cup of tea. She *was* a different Olivia. This morning, she'd barely dragged herself out of bed. She wished she could go back to it.

Reg stepped to the buffet and nudged her shoulder. "Are you feeling all right?"

"Yes, fine."

She took her food to the table and sat. She sipped her tea, but the toast did not appeal. She wished everyone would stop smiling at her. How was she a rousing success when she was desolate? She'd thought she could do this for Jasper, for the Taverstons, but faced with the reality of a lifetime with Ebersom, she didn't think she could go through with it.

Benjamin stepped into the doorway. Olivia's eyes moistened. He stopped, startled, and turned as if to go.

"Come in, Mr. Carroll," Mama said. "Don't let us chase you away."

"I don't mean to interrupt."

"Nonsense. You have to eat."

He nodded and entered. Olivia watched him pour his coffee. *Cream, no sugar. Two bread rolls, jam, and a sweet bun.* She knew he'd take the sweet bun upstairs for Hannah. She pulled her gaze away. *Two days.* He was leaving in two days.

Peters entered with several cards and a few letters on a silver tray. He handed it to Jasper. He had a sparkle in his eye and although he stepped to the side, he didn't withdraw from the room.

Jasper grabbed the top piece of paper and tore it open.

"Crispin?" Mama asked. Olivia held her breath.

He nodded. He skimmed a few lines and then read aloud.

"Family, I am alive, by the Grace of God. We are going to Paris— better late than never. Rumor is Wellington is to be a duke and to be named the ambassador. I suppose my French will improve. I count on Olivia's having broken at least twelve hearts by now. I would hope she might wait for my return before wedding, but since I do not know when that will be, I will tell her NOT to oblige me. Follow your heart, Livvy- pet. Yours, etc., Major Taverston. Postscript: Arthur? Heartfelt congratulations."

Jasper set the letter down. He looked deflated. Olivia saw the same sorry look on everyone's face that she felt on her own. Even Peters's. Crispin was still in France. He was not coming home.

"He is alive," Vanessa said, looking around the room. "And

he will be back."

Everyone nodded and murmured and tried to look pleased.

Benjamin coughed. "That last. Can you read that again?"

"Arthur," Jasper said. "Smug congratulations."

"No. Before that."

Jasper picked up the letter again. "Follow your heart, Livvy-pet. Yours…" He looked up at Benjamin. Then he laughed. "Major Taverston. *Major*. He has been promoted. Again."

That jollied everyone else, but not Olivia. She didn't care if he was a major. She wanted him home.

And she wanted to *be* home. With Benjamin. But Chaumbers wasn't her home anymore. And Benjamin would never be hers.

CHAPTER TWENTY-EIGHT

AFTER THIS LAST bit of business, Benjamin would be done with his London tasks. He could leave straightaway, except that his new shirt and jacket would not be ready until the next afternoon, and he could not start a lengthy journey so late in the day. Not with Hannah.

He didn't know what he'd been thinking, ordering new clothes.

The longer he stayed in London, the more he watched Olivia draw away from him; the sadder she appeared, the more determined he was to go. If he did not, he risked pulling her into his arms and begging her to elope—and there was nowhere to run away to.

He carried a handful of papers to Jasper's study. The door was open, but this time, Benjamin heard no voices coming from inside. He stood in the doorway and cleared his throat. Jasper looked up from his desk where a few books and pieces of paper lay spread before him.

"I hope I'm not disturbing you, my lord."

Jasper shook his head and waved Benjamin in. His mouth twisted as though he were about to say something sarcastic, but he said only, "What do you need me to sign?"

"Payments." He set the sheets in front of Jasper. "The caterer. Orchestra. And the mason fixing the cellar."

Jasper's eyes narrowed in confusion. "Already? Bills don't usually come—"

"Bills come. They are just ignored. Your books would be a lot tidier if you'd pay people—"

"Yes, yes. Another of your pet peeves. Show me where."

Benjamin pointed and Jasper scrawled his signature without looking at what he signed. The room blurred for a moment and Benjamin had to press his fingers hard against the desk to stave off dizziness.

"Do you know how easy it would be to embezzle from you?" he said, hearing the scratch in his own voice.

Jasper glanced up with an expression of mild annoyance. "I know it would be easier if you would simply sign these drafts with my name."

Benjamin snatched up the papers. This trust was killing him. He turned to go.

"Benjamin, wait." Jasper pulled his hands through his hair, then rested his elbows on the desk. Head in hands. He looked up. The blue of his eyes appeared dulled.

"You have known us a long time. You've known Olivia…" He flushed as if remembering Olivia's obvious youthful infatuation, but pressed on. "How have I gotten this so wrong?"

"What do you mean?"

"I don't know what I mean." He brushed aside the papers he'd been looking at. "Only that I wanted her to have a perfect Season, especially after waiting so long for it. I thought I could do that for her. But I don't understand females and I certainly don't understand Olivia."

"I don't…" *Don't what? Understand Olivia?* He understood her too well.

"I'm sorry. This is not…I'm sorry. I dump everything else on you and now, Olivia."

Benjamin pulled his usual chair over to Jasper's desk and sat down.

"I can't help. But I can listen." And then go drown himself in the Thames.

"Maybe hiring Boring was too much. Maybe it's all too much. Olivia isn't happy. That much is obvious. I don't know what makes *Olivia* happy. I still think of her as our giddy Livvy-pet. She isn't."

"No. She isn't." He hesitated, then asked, "Why do you think something is wrong? I thought she was—what did the countess say—a rousing success?"

Jasper sniffed. "I thought she was. She danced every set. Everyone said she was beautiful. Isn't that the definition of success? But she is moping, and Olivia does not mope. She droops around bored, and Olivia is never bored. And now, have you looked..." He stopped and muttered, "No, of course you haven't. What am I saying? Benjamin, if you were to look in the parlor today you would see two floral arrangements. Two."

Benjamin's heart sank. Every man she danced with, if they were interested in pursuing her, should have sent flowers.

"Do you know what that means?"

Benjamin said, "Only that two admirers sent her flowers."

"*Only* two admirers sent her flowers."

"She has had mountains of flowers."

"Fewer each day. After last night, the room should be full. It was her first waltz at Almack's!" He shook his head. "This must all seem ridiculous to you."

The rules did. But given leave, he would fill her rooms with flowers every day.

"Who sent the bouquets?"

"Ebersom and Lythe."

"Lythe? I thought..."

Jasper raised an eyebrow. "Thought?"

"I thought that your mother might forbid him to call."

Jasper sniffed. "She told him she would not permit Olivia to go riding alone with him in the wee hours and that he should know better than to ask. I think she even rapped his knuckles." He didn't laugh. He glowered. "If he had asked to pay court, I would have said no. But he didn't ask. He just came. I couldn't turn him away at the door."

Benjamin didn't challenge him on that. He merely said, "And Ebersom? He is a marquess?"

"Yes, and he would be perfect. That is, *I* think he would. Olivia seems…"

"Seems?"

"Lukewarm." He stood up abruptly and went to his cabinet. Then he slapped his hand against it and returned to sit back down. "I know I don't need to say it, but this is confidential. I had few words with Carleton last night. I thought he wanted to ask if he stood a chance against Ebersom. But instead, he told me he had to reluctantly withdraw. He said Olivia was a beautiful woman and he liked her very much but—" He stopped and looked at Benjamin with a bewildered expression.

"But?"

"He said he feared she had a melancholy disposition and there was too much of that in his family already. A melancholy disposition! Olivia!"

Gritting his teeth, Benjamin said, "She does not."

"Of course she does not. Carleton's defection means nothing. I would not have wanted her to encourage him anyway. She danced with several better. Not just the marquess, but two earls and a baron. But two flower baskets? Two?"

Names didn't matter? Only titles? Bile rose in Benjamin's throat. He ignored his own anger. That resentment he should not allow himself to feel.

"Iversley, it hasn't been a full month since her ball. Surely, you didn't expect to have her married off in three weeks. She will have more earls and barons at her feet."

"She could. If she were to walk into a ballroom and shine like she can. Olivia is not a melancholy person, but I cannot deny she is acting that way."

Benjamin didn't respond. He knew what was wrong. But he could not tell Jasper. Jasper with his marquesses and his earls.

"I thought you might shed some light," Jasper said.

Benjamin started. "Me? Why?" His voice cracked with guilt.

"The other day, when I saw you two at the foot of the stairs, you both looked…downcast. I thought she might have confided something to you. She certainly wasn't asking you to find her fan."

"She—she didn't say anything." He could not look Jasper in the eye.

"I don't know how to ask this, Benjamin."

Benjamin's pulse pounded in his neck. "What?"

Reg entered, knocking on the door as he did. "Jasper, you need to hear this."

Hazard followed on his heels. He scraped over a chair and sat down. "Were you two discussing Olivia?"

Benjamin did not move a muscle, but Jasper nodded.

"Well, then, this may not come as much of a surprise. I was at Lady Marpleton's breakfast this morning. She asked me if it was true that Lady Olivia was consumptive."

"Consumptive!"

"Apparently, she heard that Olivia was listless last night at Almack's. Lady Marpleton had a cousin die of consumption and she said it started with listlessness." Hazard's nose wrinkled. "I had to hear all the gory details."

"Good God," Jasper groaned. "Listless *and* melancholy?"

"Melancholy?" Reg asked.

"Carleton thinks she is."

Benjamin saw the baffled men look to one another for some sort of answer. Thank God it had not occurred to any of them to simply ask her.

"She is not consumptive," Reg said.

"Of course not." Jasper sounded hoarse.

"But what is the matter with her? Something is. Something real. She is not given to hysterics. Do you think someone might have insulted her? Hurt her feelings?"

"Maybe. But I would expect her to fight back. Enlist us if need be."

Reg pinched his jaw. "Should we take her back to Chaumbers?"

Hazard said, "That is an option. But you should consider it will only fan the rumors. And frankly, a man will be leery of a wife who runs back home whenever she is sad."

"The deuce," Jasper said. "I wish Crispin were here."

Benjamin eased himself out of his chair. "This is family business. Perhaps I should not…"

Jasper reached for his arm. "Actually, I was going to ask you if you would stay."

"I'm sorry?"

"Before Reg and Haz got here, I was about to ask you to stay. I know you need to be at Chaumbers. But I thought maybe Hannah…I'd hoped more time with Hannah might cheer her. Olivia adores her so." He pleaded with his eyes. "Can I persuade you to stay until we figure this out? For Olivia's sake?"

Benjamin let out a long breath. *Heaven and hell.*

"Yes. Yes, of course, I will stay."

JASPER'S SOLUTION WAS Vauxhall Gardens. That very night. Benjamin stood in front of his mirror in a shirt he'd borrowed from Reg, cravat in hand, and attempted a knot he'd seen on others that did not look as difficult to tie as it was.

Jasper had always been a the-more-the-merrier fellow. It never seemed to register with him that not everyone felt the same. At least tonight, the outing was only for family. *Family.* Benjamin was touched that he was included along with Hazard and Alice.

But to speak as though the only people at Vauxhall would be family? The Pleasure Garden was where people went to see and be seen.

He frowned at his knot—*the hell with it*—pulled on his jacket, and went to find the others.

The men were gathered in the receiving hall. For partygoers, they looked a bit grim. He thought it was because of Olivia until he got close and saw that the skin around Hazard's eye was darkened. Benjamin stared.

Hazard screwed up his mouth. "Yes, yes. I had a bit of misfortune."

"Haz," Jasper started.

"Yes, all right. As I was explaining, I arrived home to find my parlor a shambles. Bertram was entertaining—I don't know who. They were not gentlemen. Two were passed out on the floor. The third was playing cards with Bertram. I can only assume the stakes were high and Bertram was losing. I told them to get out."

When he did not continue, Jasper said, "His cousin insulted him. Hazard hit him."

Benjamin swallowed hard. He didn't press for more, but Hazard picked up the tale.

"I did not hit him hard enough. We got into a scuffle. The other fellow picked up a poker."

"Good God!" Benjamin exclaimed.

"Yes, well, fortunately James burst into the room. He'd heard the noise."

Jasper said, "His butler."

"James is a young fellow. Robust you might say." Hazard huffed as though amused. "He knocked the poker from the ruffian's hand." Hazard swung his arm, demonstrating. "Then he laid the fellow out flat with one punch. With my permission, he called in the footmen, and they threw everyone out."

"Everyone?" Jasper pressed.

"Bertram, too. I was angry enough not to question the wisdom of such a move." Then he drew himself up. "And this is not something we will discuss any further."

Perhaps Hazard had heard footsteps, because at that inconvenient moment, the ladies entered the hall all together. If anything could have diverted attention, it was this. They stunned. All so different, they seemed to represent beauty in all its myriad manifestations: Georgiana's red-blonde, Grecian perfection; Vanessa's dark, mature sensuality; Alice's sharp-eyed intelligence and a buxomness that hinted at more. Still, it was Olivia who drew Benjamin's eye. Her evening dress was a pale shade of turquoise. With her hair piled atop her head, her neck looked long and graceful. He had a fierce desire to press his lips against that neck.

The ladies lined up along the wall. At a signal from Vanessa, they lifted their hems a few inches, demonstrating that they were not wearing dainty shoes but boots. Their Christmas boots. Hessians decorated with flowers.

"Very lovely," Hazard said, skepticism thick in his voice. "But can you dance in them?"

"We mean to prove that we can," Vanessa said.

"We've been practicing," Olivia said with a giggle. She hopped foot-to-foot as though stepping in an Irish jig.

Benjamin knew he was not the only man beaming at her, but he was the one she beamed back at.

Jasper laughed. "They will have to open a second factory in Cartmel. Come along. We'll need to take two carriages."

Jasper took Vanessa's arm and gave her a very public kiss before leading her from the room. Reg swept Georgiana after them. He didn't kiss her, but the look in his eyes was every bit as…heated. Hazard glanced at Benjamin, then offered his arm to Olivia. Benjamin escorted Alice.

As they stood in the drive, waiting to sort themselves into carriages, Olivia continued giggling and skipping in her boots.

This was what made Olivia happy. Taking part in a scheme with her sisters-in-law. Not worrying about courting for one night. The promise of an evening with her brothers. Did they not see it?

Then she skipped right up to Benjamin. She put her hand on his neckcloth. To his…shock, she untied it. His knees almost buckled. Then she tied it again, murmuring under her breath, "You are staying. I am so glad. *So* glad." She patted the knot and said aloud, "There."

"Olivia!" A very indignant chorus cried out.

Jasper sputtered, "Livvy, you cannot *do* that."

She shrugged. "It was crooked. I fix Reg's all the time."

"Yes, but…" Jasper cast a helpless look about.

Hazard said, nose in the air, top-lofty voiced, "My dear Lady Olivia, a lady does not touch a gentleman's clothing except a few light fingers on the sleeve when she takes his arm."

Benjamin's face felt hot. And not only his face. He didn't dare try to speak. Or move. He should try to make a joke of it. That was what Taverstons did. But his mind would not function. He could think of nothing but…being undressed by Olivia.

"Oh, bosh," Olivia said. "Well, then, lend me your sleeve, my lord, Viscount Haslet. My carriage awaits."

As Hazard handed her up to the carriage, she spun around and patted his neckcloth. Hazard laughed and shouldered her inside. Benjamin joined in the laughter. Everyone was boisterous. Too pleased to see Olivia being herself to scold her for it.

Only Benjamin saw the obvious. It was not an outing with the Taverstons reviving her joy. It was *him*. He could make her happy. He could make her very happy. And he knew, deep in his heart, she had just challenged him to do so.

CHAPTER TWENTY-NINE

ALTHOUGH OLIVIA HAD been to the Vauxhall Pleasure Gardens before, when she was a child, she had never been at night to see the place in all its glory. Flowers bloomed everywhere. The paths through the gardens were extensive and varied, meandering and straight, wide, and narrow, well-lit, and dark. Something for everyone. Notorious for illicit liaisons.

The Taverstons walked the main wide road to the pavilion where supper was served. Jasper had reserved a box. The ladies settled around a table while the men fetched the food.

The pavilion sat on a hill overlooking a tiled platform for dancing. Softly glowing lamps illuminated the whole, but not well. Vauxhall was equally prized for its shadows. An orchestra played, and music wafted up to them.

"This is grand," Olivia said. She breathed in the perfume of the gardens. "It is the loveliest place I've seen in London."

Georgiana squeezed her arm. "I'm so glad you're pleased."

Olivia smiled. She knew the family was worried about her because her sisters-in-law had told her so while they were putting on their boots. She'd told them she missed Chaumbers, and they sympathized. She told them she found the Marriage Mart overwhelming. She said nothing about Ebersom, but only that she didn't understand how she was supposed to fall in love with one man when they all looked and talked and acted the same.

"Amen," Georgiana said. "Olivia, don't feel you must choose just for the sake of choosing. I think it should be a law that no girl should accept a proposal her first Season."

Alice laughed. "Georgiana refused sixteen."

"Seventeen," Vanessa said. "You mustn't forget Jasper."

Olivia had giggled along with them. She'd thanked them for their advice. And confided nothing more. She hadn't exclaimed joyously, *Everything is all right now. Benjamin is staying in London!*

The men returned with platters of refreshment: slivered ham and paper-thin slices of beef. Something shriveled and green. Stale bread rolls.

Olivia turned up her nose. "What on earth?"

"People do not come for the food," Jasper said. "We must sit here awhile so that people may gawk at us. The commoners love to gawk at peers."

Vanessa said coldly, "Well, I don't."

"Nor do I," Benjamin added.

Jasper had the grace to flush.

They didn't eat, but only talked and enjoyed the fresh air. Finally, Vanessa said, "I think now we may stroll and find some of the entertainments. Acrobats and jugglers and such. Then we come back to dance."

"I only want to dance with Hazard and Benjamin," Olivia reminded them. "I don't want to bother with being polite."

"Good Lord." Hazard shuddered. "I'm filled with dread."

Olivia grinned at him, and then squinted, wondering why he wore his hat tilted at such a strange angle. It cast a dark shadow over his face.

Vanessa said, "Jasper promised you would not have to think of suitors tonight."

"No suitors," Jasper agreed. "Now let us walk."

They left the box and returned to the garden path. At first, they walked in a tight group, in couples. Olivia was thrilled to be paired with Benjamin. Jasper and Vanessa led, pausing to point out statues and unusual flowering shrubs, whatever they came across.

They stopped to join a crowd watching three extraordinary acrobats. Olivia squeezed Benjamin's arm a few times in excitement and then he put his hand over hers, and left it there. She thrilled over the small victory.

When the acrobats stopped for air, a boy passed a hat. Jasper dropped a guinea on top of the pence and shillings. Olivia felt Benjamin tense. She glanced away when he dropped in his coin, but regretted doing that. Benjamin should not be ashamed. She was certain Reg was not throwing away guineas either.

As they walked on, their group spread out. They trailed Vanessa and Jasper down a less popular path. The shrubs here grew close together and were not yet flowering. Before long, Vanessa and Jasper were at least twenty paces ahead, Georgiana and Reg halfway between, and then Olivia with Benjamin. Hazard and Alice kept close on their tail.

They talked about Hannah, whose sentences were getting longer and who was outgrowing her clothes.

"I borrowed a horse from your brother this afternoon," he said, raising a hand to scratch his temple. "The fattest and slowest."

"Turtle."

"We went to Green Park for an hour or so. We rode together first, the way we do, but she kept saying, 'Let me, Papa. Let me.'"

"She wanted to ride by herself?"

He nodded, smiling faintly. "I dismounted and led Turtle. I thought I would have to hold her in the saddle, but I didn't. And then, naturally, she yelled to every bystander, 'I'm riding. See, I'm riding.'"

Olivia laughed. "Will you take me next time? I never see enough of her."

Benjamin was quiet a moment, then said, "She misses you, too. She keeps asking for *her* Olly."

Olivia warmed not only because Hannah said it, but because Benjamin shared it. But then they fell into a silence that was uncomfortable.

She was not surprised when Jasper led Vanessa onto a narrow side track that swallowed them up. There was no sign of them when the rest of the group passed by the spot. Olivia was a good deal more surprised that when another such track appeared in the distance, Reg began nudging Georgiana's shoulder. And when the two of them reached it, he pulled her arm, and she laughed and followed.

Benjamin grunted. "Your brothers are too trusting." He sounded angry.

She tilted her head. "What do you mean?"

He didn't answer.

Hazard and Alice fell behind. Olivia and Benjamin took turns glancing over their shoulders. The path darkened as the lamps became farther apart. Ahead she saw another break in the wall of shrubbery. Another narrow path. She looked back. Hazard and Alice had stopped under the last lamppost. They were quite far behind, but easy to see in the light. Benjamin turned to look at the same time. It seemed as though the two were bickering. Then Alice *put her hand on Hazard's cheek.* Olivia gasped. Hazard caught Alice's hand and thrust it away. The bickering appeared to grow more heated.

"What is it?" Olivia said. "Should we go back?"

"No." Benjamin took her arm and nudged her along. "Hazard's face is bruised. Not very noticeably unless he is in the light, and I imagine Alice just noticed."

"What do you mean? How bruised?"

"He...he slipped getting out of his carriage earlier this afternoon. He said he didn't want to talk about it. Don't bring it up."

"Well, how silly."

"Don't bring it up."

"I won't. But it's silly to get angry at Alice for noticing. It's not like him."

He shrugged but didn't agree or disagree.

"Should we wait for them to catch up?" she asked.

He didn't answer. They walked past the narrow path, staying on the safe one. But they came to a fork, two paths. One appeared to circle back and the other led on. Benjamin steered her toward the longer path. Shortly, they were out of sight of Hazard and Alice. Benjamin's stride lengthened and she walked faster.

"I don't know what kind of trees these are," she said.

"I don't either."

She saw another narrow break off to the left. Overgrown. Dark. She wasn't sure it was even a path. But their footsteps veered left. Olivia looked back and saw no one. Benjamin stopped at the entrance to the path which appeared to merely be a trampled foot track. He looked down at her. Studied her. She nodded. He took her by the hand and led her in.

It was quite overgrown. Benjamin held aside overhanging branches. Leaves and sticks crackled underfoot.

"I'm glad I am wearing my boots," she said to say something.

He gave her a tight smile.

And then the foliage before them became too dense to go farther. A little moonlight filtered in from above and a dim glow from a faraway lamp kept the dark at bay. Benjamin turned to face her. They were hemmed in. Very hemmed in. Alone in their tiny world.

He took hold of her elbows. She listened to her heart beating wildly and waited. Then he let go and settled his hands on her shoulders. When she didn't move, he slowly trailed his fingers back to her elbows, his touch skimming lightly over the fabric of her sleeves, then her arms.

"Like silk," he murmured.

"It is silk." She tried not to giggle. This was not the moment for giggling.

He smiled and repeated the caress. This time, his touch was firmer, lighting her arms on fire. She held very still. His hands went to her waist. Then up to cup her breasts. His breathing sounded ragged. After a several moments, he curled his hands and brushed his knuckles over the front of her bosom. It sent a shock through her. Indescribable. Indescribably wonderful.

"Benjamin," she gasped, looking up into his eyes. "Do that again."

His eyes went very dark. She watched him unbutton the cuff of his right glove, then he stripped it off. He hooked his left index finger into the neckline of her dress and pulled it down just far enough to slip his thumb, his naked thumb, under her chemise. He circled it around, making her shiver.

"Benjamin," she whispered.

His mouth crashed down upon hers. This was what it was like to have him truly kiss her. She didn't understand what he was doing—and then it all made sense as she mimicked him and felt what he must be feeling. There was so much more to kissing than she'd thought.

He gripped her hips and pulled her against him. His hands kneaded her buttocks. It was so very tempting to do the same, but she didn't dare. Instead she dug her fingers into his hair, holding him so that they might never stop kissing.

But he did stop.

"I love you." He groaned the words against her ear. "You know I do. But this has to stop."

"No. It can't. Kiss me, Benjamin."

He let go of her and stepped back.

"I'm not going to take you against a tree. My God, Olivia."

She blinked. And remembered where they were. "No. No, you're right. Of course, you're right." Her head swam. She tried to think, to say the appropriate thing, even though nothing could be appropriate after that. "Not here. But...you will?"

His expression was both angry and pitying. "No. I won't. I can't."

"Stop saying you can't!" Her heart split in two. "Do you want me to have to marry someone else?"

"It isn't what I want. It is what has to be."

"It doesn't! It doesn't! I don't care that you are a steward.

Benjamin, you are—"

"You have no idea who I am! What I am."

"I do! I do know. You are kind and strong and—"

"Olivia…" he sighed and groaned and laughed all in one sound. "I am a man who nearly defiled an innocent in a public garden. I am a liar. A fortune hunter. A criminal."

"Benjamin!" She felt as though he had struck her. Why was he lying like this? "You aren't any of those things."

"Throw in kidnapper for good measure."

"Stop it!" She put her hands over her ears. "You can't make me believe any of that. It's absurd."

"No. Maybe you won't. But Jasper will have to. I can't take advantage of his trust any longer. Look at me." He held up his hands. One gloved. One not. "I am not a gentleman. I'm the worst kind of cad."

He dropped his hands and pulled his glove on. Taking her elbow, he marched her back toward the lighted path. She didn't resist. If he was going to behave like a madman there was no point resisting. As they reached the junction, he held her back and looked beyond to be sure the way was clear, then looked back at her in the better light.

"Bloody hell," he swore, then yanked on her dress to straighten it and flicked a few leaves from her hair.

They had just started down the path and turned the next corner when Hazard and Alice came hurrying toward them.

"We thought we lost you!" Alice exclaimed.

Hazard's eyes shot daggers at them. No, at Benjamin.

"You walked right past us. We were there," Benjamin pointed vaguely, "and you two stormed by, arguing. We've been waiting for you to come back."

Hazard looked skeptical, but lowered his gaze and chewed his lip, giving Benjamin the benefit of the doubt.

Olivia stepped up and tucked her hand into the crook of his elbow. "Come along, Haz. Let's let *Benjamin* bicker with Alice while we go find the others."

"We weren't bickering," he said in a snit.

Olivia made herself laugh. "Oh, now you are bickering with me, too."

⊰⊱

SHE WANTED TO go back to the house, but there was dancing, and she didn't know how to cry off.

She danced a reel with Hazard. He still seemed peeved, but perhaps not with her or Benjamin. He looked as though he had a headache. And in the lamplight, his eye was definitely blackened.

When the music ended, Hazard brought her back to the table. According to the program, a waltz would be next. They would all want to dance unless Alice and Hazard were still at odds.

While the musicians retuned their instruments, Olivia leaned against the table rather than taking a seat, and tried not to look at Benjamin. Would he pretend he didn't remember he was supposed to partner her?

"Good evening, Iversley. I had not known you would be here." The Duke of Lythe strode up.

"Your Grace," Jasper replied. "On such a pleasant evening, we thought we should bring Lady Olivia."

"Indeed." He smiled. "Lady Olivia, I hope you will join me." He gestured to the platform. "We have not yet had an opportunity to waltz."

She shot a frantic glance at Jasper, whose face had gone white.

Vanessa said, "Your Grace, that is very kind of you, but we wanted to give Lady Olivia a reprieve from the whirlwind. Tonight is just for family."

He peered down his nose at her, then at their party which very clearly did not consist entirely of family. He did not deign to speak to Vanessa but turned to Hazard.

"I am sure Viscount Haslet will yield his dance to me. He won't appreciate so pretty a partner."

Even Olivia recognized the implied insult, with its dangerous challenge. No one said anything. So she did. "Your Grace, I have become quite accustomed to you stealing other men's dances."

As she moved to take his arm, she saw gratitude on Jasper's face, relief on Hazard's. The cowards.

The music was beginning, so they hurried onto the dance platform. The duke took her into his arms. He did not dance as well as Ebersom, but he behaved correctly. She didn't know why he worried her. He was pushy, but he was entitled to be so.

After a few minutes of questions about her first visit to Vaux-hall, the duke said, "There was another man in your party. I don't know him."

"That is Mr. Carroll."

"Who is?"

"He is the steward at Chaumbers."

The duke snorted. "Iversley's penchant for the underclasses is getting absurd. Bad enough he felt it necessary to marry his tart, but to—"

"Lady Iversley is my sister-in-law. I will not hear ill spoken of her."

"But you certainly should not speak well of her! Your family confounds me. Your mother thought, rightly I might add, that I should not take you riding in the early hours. But she allows Iversley to bring you to this hedonistic place with his"—he harrumphed—"wife and his *steward*? Your dear father must be spinning in his grave."

Olivia took a purposeful misstep and stomped her boot down on his foot. His leg started to fold.

"Good God! Are you wearing *horseshoes*?"

"I beg your pardon. I didn't see…" She jumped back and swiped her hand across her eyes as if wiping tears. Tears would unsettle him. "But it is unkind of you to use my father's name to insult us." She turned around and began walking briskly away.

He chased her. Limping. He caught her arm, and she shook it off.

"You must let me apologize. My dear, you must."

She stood still, forcing other dancers to swerve to avoid them. She was making a scene. Jasper would not be pleased.

"Dear girl, I am sorry." He rubbed his fingertips nervously against his jacket. "I am something of a relic, I know. In my day we did not...but you are an innocent, and I should not have vented my spleen upon you. Your brother's irregular friendships do not, at least, I do not believe, reflect badly upon you."

"Nor upon him."

"Your loyalty is endearing. But we will have to agree to disagree."

There was no getting rid of this man. She pursed her lips and nodded.

"Now." He gave her a thin smile. "You must let me make it up to you. I will take you riding tomorrow in my carriage. Here is what we will do. We will go to Hyde Park *late* in the morning. Your mother will have no cause to fuss."

Olivia wondered how that was making it up to *her*.

"I will have one of my grooms wait with Cassieopia and my Brutus by the east bridle path and we can escape the carriage and ride horseback. Will that do?"

It would if she could ride the horse without him.

"You needn't bribe me, Your Grace. You have apologized and I accept."

"But wouldn't you like to ride Cassieopia?"

"Well, yes, I would but..."

He sighed. "But not with an old relic like me."

"It is not that! I assure you." She had no excuse to make. None.

"Come, let us get off the platform. We are in everyone's way." He brought her back to the table.

"What happened?" Jasper demanded.

Everyone had been watching.

"I'm afraid I don't waltz as well as I thought." She wouldn't draw attention to the boots.

"It is nothing," the duke said. "A minor misstep. But I am going home now to soak my bunions." He smiled as if he'd made a joke, then bowed to Olivia.

After he was out of earshot, Jasper said, "What really happened?"

"He was rude about Vanessa, so I stomped him." She didn't mention that he was rude about Benjamin too, or remind them he had made incriminating insinuations about Hazard.

"The devil, Olivia." Jasper rubbed his face with his palm. "In that case, you tell me and let me deal with it. You cannot go about stomping dukes."

"I disagree," Alice said. "Perhaps they should be stomped more often."

CHAPTER THIRTY

BENJAMIN SPENT THE morning with Hannah, giving her his undivided attention for an hour before doing what he was determined to do.

The guest nursery was cozy and safe. Warmed by the fire from the sitting room beside it, there was no need for another. The walls were papered white with green vines. There were two big comfortable armchairs and two identical miniature ones.

He sat cross-legged beside Hannah on the carpet while she played. Miss Jamison had located a few toys for her: a box of blocks and a wooden horse. Hannah built fences and lifted the horse back and forth over them. Her hair was coming loose from its braids again. And she had taken off her shoes.

"Horses jump," she explained very solemnly.

"Yes. Some horses do." He wondered where she had seen this. Miss Jamison must have taken her to one of the parks.

"With ladies."

He chuckled. "Yes. Some ladies let their horses jump." He thought of Olivia. Of course, he was always thinking of her. "But not little girls."

"I'm a big girl!"

"You will be a big girl. But for now, you are a little girl." An ache formed in his heart.

"Lady says Hannah big girl."

"Does she? Well, I suppose it is a matter of perspective."

Hannah ignored that. As well she might. She built her fence higher and then crashed her horse into it.

"Oh, no!" She dropped the horse onto its side.

"Good heavens!" Benjamin said. "Is your horse hurt?"

"No." She laughed and picked it up, then crashed it again.

He had no idea what went on in her head sometimes. And that would only get worse.

Miss Jamison entered the room. "Mr. Carroll? The dowager asked if I would bring Hannah by this morning."

"Did she?"

"Yes, well, Mr. and Mrs. Taverston are taking Millie shopping for gifts for her brothers and sisters. The dowager will be watching Arthur, and we thought we'd have a visit."

He could not think of a kinder couple than Reg and Georgiana.

"Splendid." Not splendid at all. His respite was over. He stood up and dusted off his trousers. "I have some business in town." He gave Hannah a pat. "Papa is going to work now, but you are going to play with baby Arthur."

Hannah pushed his hand from her head, unconcerned. He almost rather wished she would throw a tantrum and give him an excuse not to go.

⇶⇷

IT WAS DRIZZLING as Benjamin left the employment agency. The rain stained the building's gray stone front and churned up the stench of the gutters. As his boots clacked on the slick cobbles, he turned up the collar of his jacket against the wet. Utterly dejected.

The agent had suggested two positions he might apply for. The first was a low-level clerk in a bank, the second, as if the Fates were mocking him, inventory clerk in a merchant's warehouse, the same position he'd held with the Hudson's Bay

Company. If he took either, his salary would be reduced to a tenth of what Jasper paid him. He would have to let Miss Jamison go. Who would care for Hannah? Where would they live? What would they eat?

Benjamin took off his hat, shook the water from it, and set it back on his head.

The previous night, when Olivia had untied his neckcloth, that was not just Olivia being silly. It was a dare. And he'd dared. Oh, he'd dared. For the thrill of a few stolen kisses, he'd risked throwing away Hannah's future.

More than a few kisses. He appalled himself. But he could not stop replaying her willing responses in his mind's eye and it stirred him. The true shock was that he'd been able to stop. He'd been *maddened*—maddened by desire and resentment and, yes, love, though it was not at all the way to show it.

How could he ever face her again? Worse, he could not run off to Chaumbers because he'd told Jasper he would stay.

Jasper was blind. They were all blind. Except, perhaps Hazard. That was dangerous. Benjamin knew he had to speak with Jasper before Hazard said something to open his eyes.

It always came back to this. Talking to Jasper. Which he was too cowardly to do.

Benjamin slouched away from the agency. Perhaps he could simply tell Jasper he had to resign because he found himself attracted to Olivia. Jasper might confuse him for someone honorable. He would give him a reference. After all, he was a good steward.

No. It was too late for half a confession. And a whole confession would see him out on the street, with no reference, unemployable, a greater failure than even his father had been.

BENJAMIN WAS DAMP to the bone. At least the paper-wrapped

packet tucked under his arm was relatively dry. His new clothes. If not for the wretched things he would be safely back at Chaumbers and would not have nearly ruined the woman he loved.

He entered 8 Grosvenor Square and greeted Peters.

"Shall I take your hat, Mr. Carroll? There will be tea in the parlor in one hour. His lordship said to tell you if you were home on time."

Home? Ha!

"Yes, thank you. I will go dry off first."

He went to his apartments and stripped off his wet attire. He unwrapped his packet and shook out the shirt and jacket. Wrinkled, but it would have to do. He only had an hour.

There were four Taverstons in the parlor when he walked in: Jasper, Vanessa, Reg, and Georgiana. And a floral spray on the mantel that was practically the size of another person.

"Lythe," Jasper said with distaste, noticing the direction of Benjamin's gaze. "It came this morning. And then the duke arrived in his curricle to take Olivia riding. He didn't announce himself and she slipped out without permission. And she is not back *yet*." He scowled. "I am going to have to speak with him."

Benjamin felt a wash of bitter amusement. He and Jasper had something in common: a cowardly tendency to postpone confrontation.

Where was everyone? The room felt only half full.

"No Hazard?" he asked. Perhaps that was for the better. Although he hoped there were no repercussions to yesterday's scuffle.

"Invited. He said he would try to make it. And Mother is having tea with the Farnsbys."

"Alice?"

Georgiana answered from her perch beside Vanessa on the davenport. "Her father arrived in town this afternoon. She will be having tea and supper with him and my parents."

Right. Alice's father was Georgiana's uncle.

"But you won't?" he asked.

"We will go for breakfast tomorrow," Reg said.

Georgiana laughed. "He wants to meet Arthur, not see us. And Arthur is sleeping."

So everyone was accounted for.

Vanessa said, "I may as well ring for tea. It may only be us."

"No! I'm here!" Olivia said, bursting into the room. Her cheeks looked windburned and her hair…her hair was a shining glorious mess.

"Why are you wearing your riding habit?" Jasper demanded.

Olivia stopped in her tracks. She turned slowly to face Jasper. "It's comfortable?"

"Did he take you riding? After Mother told him—"

"It was not early morning. The park was full of people." She looked away as she pulled off her gloves. "And it was not as though Lythe gave me a choice."

"Oh, Olivia." Jasper's anger melted away. "I'm sorry. This is my fault."

"It wasn't terrible. He's just lonely and likes to talk. He told me all about Angleterre. He says it is grander than Chaumbers, but I told him that was impossible."

Reg and Georgiana laughed. Jasper grinned. "Olivia, you are the only person in the world who finds the charm in Chaumbers."

That was not true, Benjamin thought. He'd always found it magical, and he wagered Hannah did too.

"Well," Reg said, "the important thing is—how was Cassieopia?"

"Splendid! Oh, splendid. So beautiful. And responsive. And I'm sure she would have been fast, but Lythe is a fussy old maid and would hardly let me run."

Jasper looked mollified. Olivia plopped herself into a chair.

"But all in all, I prefer Oatmeal. Cassieopia is a snob."

Benjamin didn't know what constituted snobbery in a horse, but Olivia would.

"I'm certain she got that from Lythe," Reg said, under his

breath. Jasper snickered. Smiling, Vanessa rose and pulled the bell cord for tea.

Benjamin removed to stand by the fire while listening to their chatter. After the maids brought in fragrant, steaming tea and sugary cakes, he took his cup and a plate and went back to the fire. He didn't take part in the conversation. He told himself over and over not to get comfortable because he did not belong.

Reg was saying something about an exhibition at the museum. He and Georgiana had been, but everyone should go. He'd even go again. He was interrupted by Peters in the doorway.

"Viscount Hazlet and Miss Fogbotham have come."

"Together?" Jasper looked startled. "I thought she was at the Hovingtons'. Bring them in."

Hazard walked in with Alice on his arm. Alice looked very prim and pretty, but she had a determined countenance that was a little chilling. And Hazard looked worried. Some sort of powder and paste around his eye may have explained why he looked odd, but Benjamin thought it was more than that.

"Is everything all right with Uncle Charles?" Georgiana asked.

"Yes, wonderful." Alice sounded clipped. "He is looking forward to meeting Arthur."

"Well, come in," Jasper said, waving at them impatiently. "Before the tea gets cold."

They didn't move. No, that wasn't true. Alice pulled on Hazard's arm. Not as though to drag him into the room. It was more of a jostle.

Hazard said, "Yes, well, first." He cleared his throat. "First, I believe congratulations are in order." His voice grew stronger as he spoke. "Congratulate me. Miss Fogbotham has agreed to become my wife."

Georgiana dropped her plate, and it shattered. There was no other sound in the room. Until Olivia squeaked in a tiny, tentative voice, "Congratulations."

"No." Jasper's jaw set, and he rose from his chair. "Hazard, this is despicable. I cannot condone it. You are *using* her!"

Hazard's face collapsed. "I—"

"She deserves a man who can love her. Children."

"I—"

"You—you hush, Jasper Taverston!" Alice exploded. "You have no right—"

"And you have no idea!" Jasper cried.

The whole Taverston clan jumped to their feet. Benjamin thought there might be a brawl. He'd never seen the group of them so riled. Except in joy and this was not that.

"Oh, for God's sake. I have every idea. And Hazard is not using me. If anything, I am using him."

"Alice, please." Georgiana was barely audible and sounded teary. "That isn't true. You've always said you didn't care about a title."

Alice tossed her a sour look. "I don't. Yet if I were to snare some arse of a baron, you would all say I had done well for myself."

Olivia piped up, "Maybe she loves him."

"Then the more fool she," Jasper said. "Hazard, disabuse her of this ridiculous notion."

"I have to agree with Alice," Hazard said, injecting his more typical droll tone. "You really should hush."

Georgiana said, "Alice, Jasper is right. You want—"

"What I want is something only Hazard is willing to give me! I want my words, *mine*, read out loud on the floor of Parliament. I want to see them published in the newspapers. Hear them argued about in the streets and coffee houses. That's what I want!" Her voice broke. "Until women can speak for themselves." She grimaced and cast a look at them all. "Listen to yourselves. You all know what's best for me? Do you? Well, Hazard listened to *me*."

Benjamin had an urge to applaud her. And Olivia regarded her as though she had found a new hero. But everyone else looked poised to argue more.

"What about children?" Georgiana said. "You've always

wanted children."

"And now I feel compelled to remind everyone that I am not a eunuch," Hazard said hotly. "I am perfectly capable of fathering children, one can only assume, and I will find it no hardship to father them on Alice."

"Oh, my God," Jasper said, throwing up his hands. "This is…my God! Olivia is in the room. Olivia, go."

"A little too late, Jasper," Olivia said with a smirk. "My ears are burning."

"It is…" Reg hesitated, then when he had everyone's attention, he finished. "Well, it is a solution."

Vanessa agreed. "They have obviously given this a good deal of consideration."

"Not enough." Jasper huffed.

Benjamin was a little surprised by Jasper's recalcitrance, but the more so by Georgiana's. He would have expected her to be more supportive. She looked despairing. And it was Georgiana who protested again.

"Alice, we all love Hazard, but you aren't *in* love. Don't mistake fondness for love. And he…he can't love you. Not the way you deserve."

Alice's face softened. "Hazard and I are not under any illusions. Believe me. He made sure that I am not. But love like you have with Reg, and that Vanessa and Jasper have, that is exceptionally rare. I am not going to find it and I'm not going to waste my life waiting for it. Haz and I *like* each other. Even that is rare in aristocratic marriages. I expect to be very happy, and I hope to make Hazard happy too."

"But you can't," Jasper said. He turned his focus back to Hazard. He was still glowering, but under that, Benjamin read true concern. "What about Chesterfield?"

Hazard drew in a long, slow breath, then let it out. "I think that is none of your business."

Georgiana looked as though she might cry.

Jasper scowled. "Alice, he is *admitting* he will not be faithful to you."

"Jasper, really. That is enough," Vanessa said.

Alice shrugged. "Faithfulness is also in short supply in our set. And Hazard is correct. It is none of your concern."

Benjamin found the whole business very sensible, awful, wonderful, and very brave.

Hazard said, "Moreover, it is not as though we are asking permission. I spoke with Mr. Fogbotham. He is ready to welcome me into the family. Jasper, this is happening. Georgiana, I am marrying your cousin. If you cannot be happy for us—"

"We are!" Olivia said. "Oh, but we are. I am. I think it is perfectly marvelous. Another wedding!" She raced over and put her arms around Alice and kissed her cheek, then did the same to Hazard.

Jasper pursed his mouth, but then went to offer his hand to Hazard. And then smiled a wry apology and embraced him. And then the whole room did what Taverstons did. They hugged and laughed and vowed their support.

Benjamin remained beside the fire.

CHAPTER THIRTY-ONE

THE FOLLOWING MORNING, Olivia's sadness crept back. She was genuinely happy for Hazard and Alice, but jealous too. Alice looked at a world that was unfair, and rather than crying over it, she bent the world to her will. Olivia was more likely to cry.

If that wasn't enough, half her family had gone to Watershorn so that Arthur could meet his great-uncle. They were probably celebrating Hazard and Alice as well. But Olivia wasn't invited.

Of course, neither were Jasper and Vanessa. This was Reg's other family and Olivia understood that. But she was lonely. Left out.

She wandered the house, feeling blue, and found herself in the billiard room. It was on the third floor at the end of the portrait gallery and felt like the edge of the world. She had memories of her brothers playing here, not always good-naturedly. She remembered Crispin teaching her the rules and how to hold the cue. Now the room seemed filled with nothing but ghosts. They all played billiards at Chaumbers. But in London, there were too many other things to do.

Last night, she had not even dined with her family and didn't know what happened after tea ended. She'd been invited to the theater with Isabel and to a light supper afterward. She'd already accepted so she had to go. By the time she returned home, everyone was in bed. Or maybe they were still out. The house echoed.

She rolled a ball across the billiard table. Then another. Not bothering to pick up a cue. She wasn't practicing.

When she'd learned Benjamin was not going back to Chaumbers, she'd allowed herself to imagine he couldn't bear to part from her. She'd been dizzy with happiness. When he'd kissed her, she thought that it meant he was going to fight for her—the way Jasper had fought for Vanessa. And he hadn't just kissed her. She let him do things that only married people should do. But he had no intention of marrying her. She couldn't change his mind. Not even kissing would change it.

Alice had changed Hazard's. Olivia felt certain that Hazard had made all the same protests against their marrying that Jasper and Georgiana did. And Hazard was in love with Lord Chesterfield. Maybe he had been for a very long time. Hazard waited for him. And yet, Alice convinced him to marry her.

She rolled the balls again. Aimlessly. Hearing the clack. Rolling another.

Then footsteps went by the door. Stopped. Came back. Jasper poked his head into the room.

"Olivia?"

She nodded. And let another ball roll.

He came inside. "Bored?"

"Yes."

"Do you want to play a game?"

"I suppose."

He pulled two cues from the wall and set up the balls. "You start."

She made a pitiful shot, and he winced. He set his cue down.

"Will you talk to me? About what is wrong?"

"Nothing is wrong."

"Livvy." He scolded but gave her the tenderest look she'd ever seen on his face. "Come. Sit down."

She followed him to the chairs by the wall. Awful, narrow wooden ones. No one ever sat on them. He sat, wriggled his buttocks, and scowled. "The blazes. Why do we even have these things?"

She sat. He started over.

"Olivia, since we've come to London, you are like two different people. Sometimes you are Olivia. But more and more, you are some melancholy lady I don't recognize. Explain to me. What is wrong? If there is anything I can do, I will."

She drew a breath. He meant well. She couldn't tell him the truth, but she could come close.

"I went to the theater with Isabel last night. Do you remember her?"

"Yes, of course. Lord Cameron's chit. Married Sir Gavin."

"A very good match?"

"Yes. Yes it was. She couldn't really have hoped to look much higher."

"But I can."

"Of course you can! Ebersom is well on his way to being enamored. Marry him and you will outrank me!"

He smiled and gave her arm a nudge. He really was an idiot.

"I suppose it would be nice if you could no longer scold me."

"I don't scold," he protested.

She continued, "Isabel is not unhappy, but she isn't happy. Sir Gavin was not at the theater with us. We went with her brother and sister-in-law. Her husband had," she paused, "another engagement."

Jasper's eyes shifted away. He swallowed. Then he said, "Oh."

"She said she doesn't care. She likes her position in London. She likes the estate in Wiltshire even though it is small. She says once she has children, things will be better."

"Well, you see why I am concerned for Alice."

"Alice is not Isabel," Olivia said. "She knows what to expect. Besides, she and Hazard are better friends than...than most friends! He'll be good to her."

"As good as he can be."

"Jasper, what I am saying is I don't want to end up like Isabel. With a 'very good match.'"

"You won't!"

"Mama did." Her voice dropped low. It still hurt. "Papa was unfaithful."

Jasper's face shuttered down. He rubbed his hands on his thighs. "Crispin was wrong to tell you."

"No, he wasn't. I hate it when you all know things and I don't. But when Alice said she wasn't going to waste her life waiting for a love match, I thought how wonderful for her to have a choice that gave her equal satisfaction."

"Writing political speeches?" He scoffed. "Alice is odd."

"Then I wish that I was odd, too." Not writing speeches, of course, not being a political assistant, but something equally odd. Like…like being a steward's helpmeet.

He was quiet. Thinking. Then: "Are you saying you don't think you can be happy with Ebersom? He would be faithful, I'm certain."

She shook her head. "I don't know, Jasper. I've never once heard the man laugh." Then she poked his arm and attempted to smile because he was trying so hard. "Although it would be fun to outrank you."

"He does laugh," he said, though he said it doubtfully. He gave her a long look. "Now tell me. Be honest. Is there a particular someone you think you could be happy with?"

She made a heroic effort not to squirm. "No, Jasper, there is not. And if there was, I would not want you twisting his arm."

"It would not take arm twisting." He studied her as if trying, really trying, to see her. "What are your criteria?" His voice changed. Almost teasing. "You must have some. All ladies do." He smiled.

"Criteria?" *Well, then.* "Someone who values me for more than being your sister and the future mother of his son."

Jasper's smile froze. Then wilted. He stood. "You don't have a make a match your first Season. Alice is wrong. Waiting for love is not wasting your life."

She nodded.

"Come," he said. "Let's finish our game. I know Alice has been teaching you tricks. She beat Crispin once, did you know? Show me what you've learned."

⤐⤙

JASPER WON AND Olivia thanked him for not letting her win. Afterward, he left her alone to practice. She opened the window for air and then did practice a while. Until she became aware of yelling coming from the gardens. Hannah's high-pitched yelling and laughter. She went to the window and scanned the garden until she spotted them. Hannah was on Benjamin's shoulders, and he was lolloping in circles.

Olivia raced down two flights of stairs and out the side door. Reaching the garden, she walked more sedately, catching her breath, and pretended to come across them while out for a stroll.

"Olly! Olly! I'm riding!" Hannah cried, smacking her father on the head.

"I can see that." Olivia grinned.

Benjamin held onto Hannah's feet and legs as he ambled up to a stacked pile of bricks.

"Jump, Papa!"

Benjamin stepped carefully over the pile and Hannah squealed with delight. Benjamin laughed too. And Olivia had to laugh with them.

"Again, again," the tyrant demanded.

Benjamin trotted around in a circle.

"Make my horse fall down!"

When Benjamin reached the pile, he nudged it with his foot and then sank to his knees beside it. Hannah shrieked, giggling and patting Benjamin's hair.

"Up, Papa! Up! Fall down again," she said, bouncing on his shoulders.

He got back to his feet, red-faced from laughing.

"Benjamin, *what* are you teaching her?"

"I have no earthly idea."

"Play with us, Olly."

Olivia shrugged and then galloped up alongside and let out a piercing whinny. Benjamin collapsed back to his knees, guffawing, and had to lift Hannah from his shoulders to set her on the ground until he could stop. His laughter and Hannah's giggling warmed her heart.

Olivia took Hannah's hand and they both skipped around the dirt and grass, making horse noises, until they reached the bricks and Olivia swung her over.

Benjamin watched a while, then got back to his feet, and joined them. Olivia could not ever remember being so happy.

Until she came face to face with Jasper.

He had the oddest expression. As if trying not to be angry while unsure that he even should be. He regarded Olivia for a moment and then Benjamin. Benjamin let go of Hannah's hand and quailed.

"Iversley."

"Benjamin. Would you settle Hannah with Miss Jamison and come to my study? We have something we need to discuss."

THEY WERE ONLY playing. It wasn't as though her brother had caught them on the path at Vauxhall Gardens. They weren't doing anything but playing with Hannah.

Nevertheless, after Jasper turned and walked away from them, Benjamin hoisted Hannah and followed, pale as death. They left Olivia to scramble after them.

Inside the house, she watched as Jasper mounted the stairs without looking back. Benjamin continued to lag as he carted Hannah up. They went in separate directions at the top: Jasper to his study and Benjamin to the guest wing.

As soon as Jasper disappeared down the hall, Olivia ran up the stairs, both flights, to the third floor. To the reading room.

CHAPTER THIRTY-TWO

WHEN BENJAMIN ENTERED the study, Jasper was not behind his desk. He stood beside the window, gazing out. An open brandy bottle sat on the desk alongside two glasses: one had a full pour and the other was half-empty. Jasper had started without him. Benjamin didn't touch the liquor. He felt deadened inside. This was not how this friendship was supposed to end.

Jasper did not turn around, but spoke as if to his reflection in the glass. "Explain to me, Benjamin, what it was that I just saw."

"I don't know what you mean. It was a game." The evasion was disgustingly automatic.

Jasper finally turned. His finely chiseled features seemed to lose their definition. His face sagged. "I recall asking you, in this very room, not three days ago, to help me understand Olivia. I asked if you knew what was wrong."

"Jasper—"

"You lied to me."

Benjamin couldn't speak. His tongue felt plastered to the roof of his mouth.

"The devil! It is so clear to me now. I cannot believe I was so blind. Every ball, every engagement with the ton, every carriage ride with a suitor, leaves her morose. The only time she smiles anymore is when she is with you! Benjamin, why didn't you say something?"

"What could I have said?" He ground out the words.

Jasper threw up his hands. "That she was *bothering* you!"

A thud sounded somewhere above them. Jasper's eyes veered ceilingward. He held up a hand, and, for a second, appeared to be listening intently. Then his hand dropped, and his focus returned.

Benjamin said, "She is not bothering—"

"Oh, for God's sake. Stop being so noble." Jasper marched to his desk and took another gulp from his glass. "Have a drink. Or sit down. You look about ready to faint."

Benjamin reached for the glass and saw that his hand shook. He gripped the glass tightly, but didn't drink.

Jasper set his own glass down. "The problem is no other man stands a chance." He laughed roughly. "She is still infatuated. You are still the one who…who will skip around with her pretending to be a horse! Can you picture Ebersom being so ridiculous? Or even Carleton, who is certainly no stranger to playing the fool?" He rubbed his hand against his temple. "I thought she had grown out of this." He stared a moment, eyes glazing over. Then he raised his head. "I am sorry. This is not fair to you. You've always been kind to her—"

"I am not being kind!"

"No, it *isn't* kind. It encourages her." His head bowed and he blinked a few times before looking up. "But damn it. I'm sorry. You wanted to go back to Chaumbers, and I wouldn't let you. You should have been honest with me."

"Jasper, I need to be honest *now*. I can't—"

"We will work this out. I'll speak to her. I should have given her hell when she tore off your cravat. That was beyond the pale." He shook his head. "We can't lose you, Benjamin. You understand, we need you."

Benjamin's jaw dropped. "What the blazes! I've been lying to you! You can't keep me on."

"Your damn honor! This is what I feared would happen! Benjamin, you straightened out the mess that was Chaumbers. My tenants are more content than I've seen them in years. In two weeks, you've seen to at least a year's disrepair in this place. You even got Reg on more secure financial footing without offending him. Which is something I have *never* been able to do." He clenched his fists. "You can't let Olivia's silliness drive you away. Not again."

"Are you finished?"

Jasper started at his tone. "Maybe."

"Sit down. Sit down and listen." He waited until Jasper pulled out his chair and sat. "You might want to pour yourself another."

Jasper glanced at his glass, then back at Benjamin. "I suppose that depends upon what you mean to say."

"You should not have hired me. It is laughable that you talk of my 'honor' when you don't know me from Adam." He stopped Jasper's protest. "You don't. You hired me without references when you hadn't seen me for over four years! That was irresponsible. *Iversley.*"

"I know you. Character does not change."

"You hired me without asking what I'd done in Canada."

"You were working for the Hudson's Bay Company."

"I was *stealing* from the Company."

Jasper's jaw dropped. Then he snapped it shut and scowled. "I very much doubt that."

"I was an inventory clerk. I kept track of what came into the warehouses and what went out. The books I kept never matched the reality." Jasper's only reaction was to keep his gaze steady on Benjamin's face. "Everyone stole from the company. Low-level pilfering occurred daily, but the worst offenders were the officials. Cases of whiskey, blankets, trinkets, guns, and knives—these disappeared all the damn time. No one wanted the corruption uncovered."

"So you didn't report it."

He gritted his teeth. "I was informed by my superior that if any discrepancies were found on my watch, *I* would be held responsible. It would be taken from my pay. These 'discrepancies' went back years, Jasper. Years. I could not begin to sort out the losses. And I certainly couldn't recover them. Instead of making my fortune in Canada, I would end up in debtor's prison. So I learned how to falsify records. How to shortchange trading partners."

"But you never took anything."

"If your servants were stealing your silver and Peters turned a blind eye, would you say, 'but he never took any'?"

Jasper made a bitter face. "A moot point. My household is better run."

Benjamin remembered the footmen sharing a stolen bottle of wine. "You *think* it is."

"Well, what do you want me to do? Shall I hire someone to audit my books?"

"You should after what I've just told you."

"I'm afraid I must continue to be irresponsible. I trust you have not stolen anything. The very idea is ridiculous. You have never been driven by greed."

Now Benjamin laughed. Bitterly. "Jasper, you are so naïve it makes my heart hurt. Do you imagine, as a youth, I could have looked around at what you and your brothers had *handed* to you and *not* have been covetous? My greed almost *killed* me. What do you think I was doing in the backwaters of Canada?"

"I suppose you had better tell me."

Benjamin squeezed his eyes shut to block out the memories that came back to him in a flood. He opened them slowly.

"I signed on with the Company thinking I would work one or two terms. Three years. Six. I didn't expect to get rich. Only to save enough to come back to England with a hope for a better life than my father gave us." He grunted. "And perhaps a *fraction* of the ease I experienced as your perennial guest." He ignored Jasper's embarrassed throat clearing. "But I was misled. We were overworked and underpaid. We had to buy supplies from the Company if we wanted to eat. Or drink. And..." He drew his arms across his chest. "I'm not just whining. The conditions were inhumane. The winter darkness. I swear it seemed always to be winter. You could sleep almost on top of a fire and not get warm. But the worst was the boredom. There was nothing to do but drink. I've always sworn I would not be my father, but Jasper, I stole all day long and drank all night."

"That was your situation. You only drink now when I force it upon you."

"When my three years were up, I did not sign on to stay. I had maybe ten pounds to my name and my passage home. At least the company paid for our fare back to England."

"But you didn't come back."

"No. I was celebrating my release from captivity, that is what we called it, in what passed for a tavern, and I met Simpson."

"Your business partner?"

"Yes. Hannah's father. He was not with the Company. He claimed he'd been trading lumber. He said his father was head of a large lumber firm in Halifax. That was true. It was the only true thing the man ever said."

"Your new business venture was lumber?"

"No." Benjamin needed to pace. The humiliation was still too raw. "No, it was not. I thought it was going to be gold."

"Gold?" Jasper's forehead wrinkled. "Was there another expedition? I thought—"

"You thought those rumors had been thoroughly explored and were found to be false."

Jasper nodded.

"Greed makes rich men cruel and poor men fools. Simpson convinced me that there was gold for the taking deeper in the interior. And he knew where to find it."

Jasper kept silent though it was clear he wanted to say something. Ask something.

"It gets worse," Benjamin said, walking over to the fireplace, staring into it. He couldn't look at Jasper. "He needed a partner to help him purchase supplies and to handle one of the boats. He said our foray would take six months. And that we could barter for food along the way. For that, we needed trade goods. Like those in the Company's warehouse."

"God, Benjamin." Jasper's voice went hoarse. "You didn't."

"I didn't...*take* any crates from the warehouse. But I let him know how it could be done. And I sold my ticket home. Emptied my pockets."

"Benjamin! What made you believe he could find gold when the *Company* could not?"

Then he did turn to face Jasper. "Marie."

"Who?"

"Mrs. Simpson. Simpson took me to the camp outside the fort to meet her. She was...convincing. Not as loose lipped as her husband. She was furious that he had confided in me. I suppose she pretended to be furious. It had to be kept secret, you see. But he said they needed another pair of hands and my savings. When she finally acquiesced, I felt..." He laughed hollowly. "I felt grateful."

"So you handed over your savings. Did they abscond with it all?"

"I wish they had done it that simply. No. We gathered what we needed. What they *said* we needed. And then, I discovered that not only was Marie coming with us, but also, a baby. I balked. Finally, I realized the insanity of what I had signed on for. But they were going whether I went with them or not. With everything I now owned. Moreover, Simpson drank more than you and I and Crispin ever drank combined. Marie asked me to please come. She couldn't handle him by herself."

"They had their claws sunk in deep."

"We went upriver. After the first day, I no longer had any idea where I was. Marie and I paddled the canoes. Simpson drank. Half the time, I took Hannah in my boat to keep her safe from his carelessness. It got colder and colder. Our food ran low."

Jasper's brow furrowed. "But you had stolen goods to trade for food."

Now Benjamin returned to pick up his glass and drain it. Beyond all else, his gullibility was the most difficult to confess.

"Simpson traded for furs."

"Why?"

"Because he knew we were never going to find gold. Fur was the treasure. And by the time I realized the swindle, there was nothing I could do."

"But who was he swindling?"

"Me, Jasper! Me. We'd signed a contract. He was to get sixty percent of the profits, and I was to get forty percent, and I thought that more than fair."

"But?"

"The contract very clearly stated we'd split the profit from the gold."

Jasper stared a moment. Then one side of his mouth lifted. He coughed. Then he laughed.

"For God's sake, Jasper! It isn't humorous!"

"No, it isn't." He bit his lip trying to keep a straight face. "It isn't at all." Benjamin felt bizarrely unburdened to see him so amused. Jasper cleared his throat. "Go on."

"It was not a six-month foray. We were at least five months going upriver. We were paddling through ice and portaging through snow. I told Simpson I was aware we would never find gold and we should turn around. I just wanted an end to the hell."

"But he wouldn't turn back?"

"He did. We did." Benjamin sat back down. He hunched over the edge of Jasper's desk. "I heard them arguing that night. They spoke French when they didn't want me to understand them, but I know a little French. Enough. Simpson thought they should…leave me out there."

"What! To die?"

He nodded. "That had been their original plan, but Marie must have had second thoughts. She reminded him they needed me to paddle one of the canoes. And…" His neck grew hot.

"And what?"

"And she pointed out that I was giving most of my food to Hannah anyway."

"God, Benjamin." He lowered his chin, shaking his head. "That does not surprise me."

"Simpson said…" He swallowed. "They should abandon her too."

"His own daughter?" Jasper's voice thickened with disgust.

Benjamin nodded. "Sometimes, deep in his cups, he would claim she wasn't. But she looks just like him. He was a jackass. If I'd had a clue how to get back to the fort, I swear I would have stolen a canoe that night and Hannah too."

Jasper pushed the brandy bottle closer, but Benjamin shook his head.

"We traveled another few days. Then we were hit with a snowstorm and had to burrow in. Simpson got sick first. Marie nursed him as best she could, but he failed pretty quickly. Then she got sick."

"They both died."

"Yes. I couldn't bury them, Jasper. I couldn't even do that. I put everything I could into one canoe and just kept going down river, praying I would find somebody."

Jasper sat still. He didn't interrupt or prompt. He just waited.

"A band of Cree found us. We were half-frozen and half-starved, but they took us in even though they looked half-starved themselves. I gave them the guns and blankets that were left. The whiskey was already gone." He sniffed. Simpson had polished that off. "We spent a solid month there. Maybe more. And then, I came to myself and told them I would give them all the pelts, too, if they could get us back to the fort. Or close enough to it that I could find my way. I don't know why they agreed. They could have taken the pelts, and I couldn't have stopped them. But they were more honest than…than anyone else I'd met in Canada."

"And so, the adventure came to an end."

"Yes."

"God, Benjamin."

"Well, wait. No. There is Hannah. I said I didn't steal anything, but I stole her. The Cree wanted me to leave her with them. And since I am being honest, I did consider it."

Jasper argued, "That isn't stealing. She's an Englishwoman!"

"Half French."

"Well," he sniffed a laugh, "we won't hold that against her."

"The Cree would have adopted her. I might have left her with them if they were not so ravaged themselves. Disease has hit them hard. The beaver are almost gone. But the main thing was, she had *family*. Simpson's parents."

Jasper made a face. "Who did such a fine job raising *him*."

"A guide took us back to the fort along with the pelts to trade. Your letter was waiting for me there. Jasp, I've said before, it was like a gift from God. I hadn't any money but with that letter I had credit. Credit enough to get to Halifax to look for Hannah's grandparents. I thought it was the right thing to do."

"You once said they wanted nothing to do with her."

"They had already disowned Simpson for taking up with Marie." He didn't reveal that Simpson had met her in a brothel. That was not something anyone ever needed to know. "They didn't believe me when I told them their son was dead. I think they suspected I had come to extort money from them, though I certainly didn't ask for any. I booked passage on the first ship out. But, Jasper, I didn't give them any time to reconsider. I gave them one chance and never went back."

"It doesn't sound as if they deserved a second chance. She was their granddaughter. There shouldn't have been anything to consider."

"But she *is* their granddaughter. And I took her across the ocean. Sometimes I worry that I misled them. Made them think there was a possibility she was my daughter. She was clinging to me so much by then." He shook his head. "And I clung to her."

"You *are* her father. Moreso than that devil who would have abandoned her. You didn't steal her."

"I should have told you all this before I accepted the position. You said once that if you'd thought I would engage in 'no one will know' you would not have hired me."

He snorted. "I say a lot of things. And I should have asked. I was 'irresponsible.'"

"Jasper—"

"You have been talking nonstop. It is my turn. There is nothing in that story to make me regret hiring you. I'm certainly not going to dismiss you because you made a few errors in judgment. You've paid for them. God knows, you've paid."

"Thank you. Thank you for that. But Jasper, you can't trust me. You can't."

"Oh, please." Jasper suddenly grinned at him. "Don't tell me there is more. What else did you do? Turn pirate on the ship home?"

"Jasper—"

There was a knock. Jasper turned to the door. Benjamin grabbed his arm.

"Jasper, we need to talk about Olivia."

"I'm sorry she's been difficult. I'll speak with her. But I'm not going to let you resign because of this."

The knock came again.

"Yes, enter," Jasper said, rolling his shoulders with exasperation.

Finley stepped in. "My lord, the Duke of Lythe is calling. He is in the receiving room. Are you at home?"

"Calling? Oh, good God!" Jasper stood, clenching his jaw. "He is going to ask my consent."

"For Olivia?" Benjamin's blood ran cold. "She can't possibly. Jasper, send him away."

"I'd rather call him out. The man is a dog!"

"Refuse. You are her guardian. Refuse!"

His mouth tightened. "I would like to. But it isn't as though Olivia will say 'yes.' Once she has refused him, I can justifiably tell him to leave her alone." Jasper rounded the desk and went for the door. "Damn it! Lythe isn't half the man you are. None of them are."

"Jasper, this isn't...we aren't finished."

Jasper sighed with annoyance. "Then wait here. This shouldn't take long." He waved a hand behind him as he stepped out. "Just don't pilfer anything while I'm gone."

CHAPTER THIRTY-THREE

IF ALICE COULD do it, so could she. Except that Alice had weeks, perhaps months, to work on Hazard, and Olivia only had minutes to change Benjamin's mind. To bend the world.

She ran to the top of the stairs and shrank behind the banister until she saw Jasper on the first floor, walking toward the receiving room.

If this failed, at least she'd make everyone *else* happy.

She could put up with Lythe's droning on and on, but his toploftiness…his refusal to even speak to Vanessa… Lud. She shuddered. He'd want to *touch* her.

Drawing a sharp breath, she rose from her crouch. Determined to risk it. *It had to be Lythe.* Most probably, within a few years, she would be a widow. She could return to Chaumbers and live in the dower house with Mama. That was a better choice than being trapped in a loveless marriage for the rest of her life with Ebersom, who deserved a wife who could appreciate him.

She ran down to the second floor and straight to the study. She burst in and found Benjamin sitting at the desk, staring morosely into an empty glass.

"Benjamin!"

He whirled around and jumped to his feet. "Olivia!"

She swallowed, taking a step toward him. "I—I am sorry. I've made you so uncomfortable, and you've been so kind."

"What? Olivia, what are you—"

"I heard. I mean, I overheard." She tossed her head. "I think you are heroic, Benjamin. And I've made a fool of myself. I'm so sorry."

He gaped. Aghast. She could see his mind working, trying to think of everything she would have heard him tell Jasper.

"I'll stop bothering you. I promise. But you can't leave Jasper."

"You aren't bothering me. Don't be absurd!"

"Stop!" She blocked her ears. "Stop being so kind to me. I threw myself at you. Again. I'm mortified. Again."

"No. No, that isn't true. I—it isn't kindness. Would I have kissed you at Vauxhall—"

"If you had no intention of asking Jasper for permission to woo me?"

His eyes flared. Olivia couldn't bear the hurt and self-recrimination she read on his face. She shouldn't have used that. But she had to press on.

"I suppose you meant to scare me off," she said, looking down at her hands. "Benjamin, you're a good man. A very nice man. And I've been bothering you for far too long. Jasper's right."

She took a step back, then turned and started for the door. He pushed aside his chair to come after her.

"Olivia, wait. What are you doing? What do you mean?"

"I mean that it is time for me to grow up. I'm a Taverston. I have responsibilities."

She opened the door, stepped out, and pulled it firmly closed. She had not gone three steps before she heard glass shattering against the wall.

Let this work. Let this work, she prayed, dashing down the stairs. She headed for the receiving room just in time to see Jasper come out of it, scowling for all he was worth. He saw her and sighed angrily.

"Olivia. I was coming to find you. To ask you to wait in the parlor to receive Lythe."

"Yes, I heard he was here. I suppose he intends to propose."

"You knew that?"

"He dropped hints." She snorted. "The man is not subtle." She waved Jasper aside. "Does it have to be the parlor? Can I just go to him in there?"

"I should send him to you. But—"

"Oh, bosh. Let me get this over with. I went to find you in your study, but only Benjamin is there. He says he's waiting for you."

"Yes. Yes, I'll go up. And then, Olivia," his voice grew stern, "I must talk with you."

She huffed with exasperation. "I will be so glad when you can't scold me anymore."

He looked confused, and she felt his eyes on her back as she opened the door.

She heard bootsteps careening down the staircase, and Benjamin's voice, shouting, "Jasper! Where are you? Jasper!"

Oh, bosh! He was supposed to chase *her*. He'd better be quick with Jasper. She stepped inside and shut the door.

"Your Grace. How pleasant of you to call."

He stood near the wall, regarding one of the landscapes. Sunlight filtering through the half-open shutters cast stripes across the painting, marring it. The sandalwood scent of Lythe's cologne was overwhelming, as if he had used the entire bottle. He wore old-fashioned breeches and spectacles that he swept quickly from his nose.

"My dear Lady Olivia. Do you know? I brought Cassieopia to make you a present, but your brother said she was an inappropriate gift."

Olivia gasped, then gave a little laugh. "Your Grace, my brother is right."

He came forward and reached for her hand. She didn't see any option but to let him take it. He led her toward the Chesterfield sofa and sat, drawing her down beside him. She tried not to wince when he kissed her knuckles.

"Ah, but it is not inappropriate for my little duchess to have such a horse."

A commotion sounded in the hallway. Pounding feet. Benjamin's voice, rumbling, the words a jumble. Jasper yelling: "What the *hell*? She wouldn't!" Benjamin, a little louder, "She says it's her *responsibility*. To grow up." And Jasper, "The devil! She said I couldn't scold—"

The door flung open.

"Stop! Olivia, don't! What did you say?" Jasper demanded. He looked horribly frightened. Benjamin looked worse, wild-eyed, and panicked.

"He offered me Cassieopia."

"Mercury!" Jasper practically shouted. "You can have Mercury. Crispin will give him to you."

The duke leaped to his feet and puffed himself up. "What is the meaning of this?"

Olivia tried not to laugh at Jasper's discomfiture. Or the duke's. Relief made her giddy. She tapped her chin, pretending to consider. "Mercury *is* less of a snob."

Ashen, Benjamin groaned, "Don't throw your life away. I'll do anything, Olivia. Anything."

"How dare you address her like that!" the duke shouted, glowering at Benjamin. "She is going to be a duchess!"

"No, she is not," Benjamin said, clenching his fists.

Jasper said, "Mr. Carroll is correct. She is not. I rescind my permission. She is underage and cannot give her own pledge."

"You—you wouldn't dare!" Lythe glared. "The Iversley name will mean nothing if I tell men your word cannot be trusted. You are a disgrace. A disgrace! Your father—"

"My father would have your bollocks on a platter, Lythe. No one will fault me for refusing you my sister."

"You are less secure than you think! Playing fast and loose with your position." Lythe flung a hand toward Benjamin. "What will the others say when they hear you allowed her to throw me over for your *steward*?"

"Your Grace," Olivia said, "I did not. I threw you over for my brother's horse."

Lythe sucked in his breath. Jasper gaped, then bit his cheek. And Benjamin let out a long, slow breath. The duke yanked on the lapels of his jacket and marched out of the room, snarling. Jasper closed the door and turned the latch, then slouched against it.

"Good God, Olivia. You gave me a scare. What on earth were you thinking!"

The door rattled. Then shook harder.

"Olivia!" Vanessa called. "Let me in at once!"

Olivia sighed with relief. It was not Lythe returning. Jasper twisted the lock and pulled the door open, to demonstrate Olivia alone on the sofa, and the two men standing sentry at the door.

"What happened? Peters said Lythe had come."

"Olivia dispatched him," Jasper said. "Now we only need worry about Crispin."

Olivia stifled a giggle. Crispin would have a kitten! But she wasn't going to hold them to giving her Mercury.

"Though truly," Jasper went on smugly, "it is his own fault. If he had come home when he should have, he'd have had us sorted out months ago."

Vanessa said, "You are not making sense."

"None of this is." He turned back to Olivia. "Livvy-pet, how could you even consider accepting that old goat?"

Livvy-pet? He was already halfway to dismissing her answer. So she stood and gave him a long look before speaking to be certain he would listen.

"He is the highest-ranking peer to court me. And you've made it clear that titles are all-important."

He frowned. "Olivia—"

"He is an influential Tory, and you need his support. Even more so, I dare say, than you need Ebersom's."

Jasper's head snapped back. His expression turned almost sick. And Vanessa looked appalled. Olivia hated to make her last point, but she did.

"And Lythe is right. You have been playing fast and loose with your position. It is my…my duty to marry well enough to shore up the family's social standing."

Vanessa sank into the nearest chair. "No, Olivia."

Harsh with hurt, Jasper said, "So I have purchased my happiness by selling away yours? Is that what you think? That I believe love is less important for you than for me?"

"Isn't it?"

He stared. Then in a very low, gravelly voice, he said, "No. Olivia, I told you love is worth waiting for. I never asked you to sacrifice your happiness. What made you think…" He halted. "Obviously, *I've* made you think so. But nothing could be farther from the truth."

"So I needn't marry a peer."

"Of course not."

"A second or even third son would be just as acceptable?"

"*Any* gentleman." Then he amended, "So long as he is a good man. And you might love one another."

"But he must needs be a gentleman," she pressed. She heard Benjamin's breath catch, but didn't look at him.

Jasper tensed. His head swiveled to Benjamin and then back again. He let out a pained sigh. "Oh, Livvy. Not this again."

"No! Jasper, stop!" Benjamin threw up his hands. "You are dead wrong. There is no *again*. The truth is that I am in love with your sister. I tried to tell you—"

"What!" His face contorted. "Benjamin—"

"I *tried* to explain! You wouldn't listen! She hasn't been bothering me. If anything, I've been bothering her."

Joy filled her. No more secrets. No more denial. She stretched out her hand, and Benjamin crossed the room to take it, while Jasper stared, open-mouthed. Vanessa rose and went to his side. She touched his wrist and murmured, "Jasper?"

"Give me a moment," he said, then clamped his mouth shut.

"Jasper, I know you must feel I've betrayed you," Benjamin

said, squeezing her hand. She wasn't sure whether he was doing it to reassure her or to stop his own from shaking. "I'm not…not good enough for her."

"No. No, that isn't it." Jasper still sounded befuddled.

Vanessa said, "It isn't confusing. It makes perfect sense. If you would just stop thinking of your sister as a child."

"Well, I *know* she isn't. But"—he rattled his head—"and it isn't that Benjamin is a commoner. Surely, I'm not so great a hypocrite as that."

"Jasper." Benjamin still sounded apologetic. He dropped her hand. "In spite of my earlier confessions, you must believe I'm no fortune hunter. I *love* her. I can't give her the life she deserves, but—"

"Oh, for pity's sake!" Olivia cried. "What I *deserve?* What is that? A dressing room full of the latest fashions? To be first on everyone's invitation list to all the London balls?"

"You deserve to have your children welcome in Society," Benjamin said. "At the very least."

"They will be welcome wherever *our* children are," Vanessa said firmly. "And that includes Hannah, of course. We can't promise universal acceptance, but we can promise the Taverston clout. I never thought they would accept me, yet more have than haven't."

"Let Benjamin finish," Jasper said. "I want to hear what he has to say. Frankly, he's making a better case against than for."

Benjamin screwed a face at Jasper, then turned his back on him. She had his full focus now. He took both her hands in his. "A home. You deserve a home. A household. Servants. A stable for your horses. Comfort. Security. I can't promise very much."

"Enough is as good as a feast."

The room fell silent.

Then Benjamin said, choking, "I can't promise enough."

"That," Jasper said, "should not be a concern. Are you asking for my permission, Benjamin?"

"I—I am." He didn't let go of her hands, but turned to face

Jasper squarely. "Will you grant me the honor of asking for Olivia?" His voice did not falter. "I will do everything in my power to make her happy."

Olivia held her breath until a little smile flickered at the edges of Jasper's mouth.

"This is where Benjamin and I go to my study and discuss details properly—"

"Oh!" Olivia gasped. She barely refrained from jumping up and down.

"Thank goodness," Vanessa murmured.

Jasper continued, "Olivia will go into the parlor and wait." He grunted. "But first, I must apologize. Olivia, I was an idiot to think you were pestering Benjamin. Of course, he fell for you. How could he not?"

Olivia dashed to her brother and threw her arms around his neck.

"Jasper, you are the most wonderful brother who ever lived!"

"I don't know. I have stiff competition." He hugged her back, then put her at arm's length. "There is one other thing." He looked toward the wall and his face knotted up as if agonized. "I hate to ask this, but I've been faulted before for not asking the questions I should."

Olivia gulped and stepped back. "What is it?"

"Do we wait for Crispin's return?" He looked over her head to Benjamin. "Or...do we need to have the banns read *soon*?"

Benjamin made a sharp noise. His face flushed. "Good God, Jasper. We can wait." Then he looked at her. "If that is what Olivia wants."

Of course she wanted all her brothers at her wedding. But... "We have no idea when he'll be back. He said to follow my heart. And I've waited long enough."

WHEN THEY'D ANNOUNCED their engagement to the family, all the well-wishes gratified Olivia. She'd known Reg would be supportive, but her mother's smile surprised her. Papa's infidelity must have wounded her more than she would ever admit.

Georgiana made the only objection. She said it was all very well that they were marrying, but they must not announce their betrothal to anyone else until after Alice's wedding. They could not keep pushing her into their shadows.

She was right. Georgiana always was. Hazard was planning the grandest event of the season at St. George's Church in Mayfair, and the Taverstons would first focus on that. The show was the point. Rumor was that even the prince regent would attend. Jasper said everyone at White's and at Brooks's spoke about it with general relief and a total absence of insinuation. Alice had made it possible for everyone to pretend.

So, Olivia and Benjamin would not have their own banns read until after Alice and Hazard's wedding. The best thing about that was that when Olivia wrote to Crispin and said they would be wed in late June, he said he would be there come hell or high water.

In the meantime, Benjamin needed to see to a few things at Chaumbers, and Olivia came with him. Mama did too, for propriety's sake. Which Olivia thought was silly, given how easy it was to find places to be alone in that "old pile."

Benjamin escorted Olivia to the steward's cottage to show her what had been done. They left Hannah at the house so that Benjamin could ride Goose. Olivia rode Mercury and didn't feel one bit guilty that she didn't have Crispin's permission. They raced across the meadow and Olivia left Benjamin in the dust. Afterward, Mercury trotted up to Goose and Olivia swore he congratulated the lesser horse on a very good run.

They left the animals grazing. Olivia exclaimed over the exterior of the cottage. It looked almost new. Inside, everything was freshly painted. She laughed as she swung open one of the doors. It seemed to be a little crooked, but it wasn't. How fitting for a cottage at Chaumbers!

"Benjamin, it's perfect. We'll be so happy here."

His eyes shone. She could see in his expression that it was more than he had ever dreamed of. Jasper had added it to her dowry along with the surrounding ten acres, saying he regretted that it wasn't more, but it was the only part of the estate that wasn't entailed. Olivia said she didn't need more. A piece of Chaumbers was home enough.

"Come. See the rest," Benjamin said.

Olivia smiled. "You promised to show me…"

"Yes, my love. But come see the rest of the house first."

They walked through the kitchen, the dining room, the morning room, Benjamin's study. They went up the stairs. There were three large bedchambers as well as two empty rooms he wasn't sure yet what to do with. The top floor contained the nursery, a schoolroom, and smaller rooms for Miss Jamison and servants. At least, a cook and a maid or two. They would have to do without a butler. Benjamin scoffed at the idea of a valet, but Olivia would naturally keep Tansy.

Olivia didn't bother with all the details worked out between Jasper and Benjamin. She knew only that, like Reg, Benjamin wanted her dowry invested for their children, and he intended to continue working. Olivia didn't come out and say it, *yet*, but if she were permitted to look to the welfare of the tenants as she'd been doing, Vanessa would be free to spend her time in London and in Cartmel.

From the windows, Olivia could see different views of the property. Their property. Beyond that would be the folly. The lake. The meadow. The house. Jasper's stables. The tenants' cottages. Iversley Village. Everything in the world that she loved.

Benjamin led her back to the second floor. Then into the master bedchamber. Yellow curtains fluttered in a grass-scented breeze. The bed was covered with a blanket and littered with pillows.

He turned her to face him and put his hands on her shoulders.

"Now, remember," he said, his iron-gray eyes growing dark. "We are picking up where we left off at Vauxhall. But leaving some things for our wedding night."

"Yes, Benjamin," she said, suddenly breathless. "You've explained the rules. Show me."

A groan came from deep in his chest. He pulled off his riding gloves.

"Take off yours," he said. She stripped them off. He caressed her fingertips. Then he whispered, "Now untie my cravat and throw it somewhere."

He kicked the door closed.

About the Author

Carol Coventry is a born-and-bred Jersey Girl transplanted to Kentucky. A quarter of a century working in the medical field has taught her that, after any tough day, nothing soothes the spirit like a guaranteed happily-ever-after. Escaping to the Regency Era is like a mini-vacation. After spending so much time there, she felt like a native and began spinning her own tales of historical romance.